FIONNUALA KEARNEY

◆

THE BOOK OF LOVE

Complete and Unabridged

CHARNWOOD
Leicester

First published in Great Britain in 2018 by
HarperCollins*Publishers*
London

First Charnwood Edition
published 2019
by arrangement with
HarperCollins*Publishers*
London

The moral right of the author has been asserted

*A catalogue record for this book is available
from the British Library.*

ISBN 978–1–4448–4123–7

Published by
F. A. Thorpe (Publishing)
Anstey, Leicestershire

Set by Words & Graphics Ltd.
Anstey, Leicestershire
Printed and bound in Great Britain by
T. J. International Ltd., Padstow, Cornwall

This book is printed on acid-free paper

THE BOOK OF LOVE

The book seems to beckon to me . . . I find myself fanning our handwritten pages. The smell of Erin, a vague whiff of her peony scent. I raise them to my face and inhale deeply before opening it on her last entry. From the moment they met, Erin and Dom loved each other too much, too quickly. Everyone said it wouldn't last. But they knew differently. A wedding present, a notebook, brings them together through the good times and the bad. On the blank pages of their love story, they write down everything they can't always say — the secrets, the heartbreak, the highs and lows. It's where they see the best and worst of each other. Falling in love is easy, but staying in love is where the story begins. This is *The Book of Love.*

Books by Fionnuala Kearney
Published by Ulverscroft:

THE DAY I LOST YOU

For Eamonn and Mary and also
Jim and Monica who once
loved like this.

PART ONE

1. Dominic

NOW — 3rd June 2017

From *The Book of Love*:
'I love you because you found me.'

I'm wide awake when I shouldn't be. Completely still, I'm sitting bolt upright on the edge of our bed, ears pricked for any hint of her. There's nothing but familiar sounds from the old building echoing in the silence. A fly buzzes around the bedroom window. Through the oak floorboards, from below in the kitchen, the fridge motor whines. The pipes groan in the walls like a quick, expectant heartbeat. Even the house misses Erin.

Standing, I stretch tall, my hands just about touching the ceiling. Then I start my sweep of 44 Valentine's Way, my early walkabout. The children's bedrooms get a mere glance, nothing new there but another fine layer of dust. I head downstairs, my left hand tracing the original, deco style, curved staircase. At the bottom, just to the right in the study, the desk lamp that sits next to a pile of architectural drawings is switched on. A glance past them, to my paper diary, brings a stabbing memory of Erin, months ago, trying to convince me to digitally diarise everything onto my phone. I resisted, laughed, ignored the jibe about my Jurassic ways and reminded her that it was she who'd dragged me kicking and screaming to the written word in the first place.

Today's date, with a spidery doodle right in the middle of the page also confirms Lydia's birthday party tonight. My sister will have staff, borrowed from the cafés she owns, bearing trays of minuscule canapés and warm prosecco. She'll be floating through our group of friends, and some of hers whom I don't know, with a painted smile firmly in place, pretending everything's fine.

The phone ringing in the hall makes me flinch but I don't move, sensing it will be another hang-up.

'Hi,' Erin says from beyond the doorway. 'We're not home right now. Leave a message.' My voice pitches in, 'If anyone cares, I'm not here either' and she giggles just before the beep and the final click. I walk to the hall — hear her laugh resonate, almost bounce off the walls, and wonder how days without her seem so achingly exhausting. It's always been like that. From that first moment I saw her, and her ridiculous dancing, to the last time we spoke, she has lived in my soul. She just moved in, took up residence. No discussion. No permission. No regrets.

Without realising it, I've approached the mahogany console table, towards the single drawer. The book seems to beckon to me. I imagine flashing lights warning me of the perils ahead, yet the comfort of it in my hand brings familiar relief; the soft nappa leather, like myself, scarred in places. I find myself fanning our

4

handwritten pages. They smell of Erin, a vague whiff of her peony scent. I raise them to my face and inhale deeply before opening it on her last entry. In the hallway of the home we made together, I pace the tiled black and white floor. The first rays of morning light from the glazed dome in the roof above help me read her words aloud:

12th May 2017

Darling Dom,

Back, in August 2004, you took something from here, remember?

Sometimes, usually lying in bed around daybreak, I wonder — no, more than that, I'm quite <u>desperate</u> to know — whether we might have avoided so much heartache if you hadn't.

I mean, what if you'd left that page where it was meant to be? What if those words had been the very words in our book of love that you really needed to say to me back then? Maybe you were honest, reached out, even asked for help. And maybe if I'd read <u>those</u> words of yours at <u>that</u> time, things might have been different? What if I'd been able to see them by holding the next page up to the light and tracing the faint imprint of your pen?

I tried — it only works in the movies.

I know, I know. You call me 'The Queen of What Ifs'. But this is just one of the things that haunts me when I wake too early in those dawn-drenched hours.

You tell me not to be silly, not to dwell on the past. You hold me and tell me everything happens as it's meant to, not exactly 'for a reason', but 'life', you say all the time, 'life unfolds just the way it should'.

So, that missing page stayed very much missing. Absent. Gone. I never knew what it said, and you've never told me. And life unfolded the way it was meant to and there was heartache — but so much love too. God, there was so much love.

There is still love.

That's what I cling to in those restless hours that follow night.

I remind myself that love endures.

Erin x

I sit down on the first stair. The closed front door opposite seems to taunt me. 'What if she walked in here now?' My whisper is just about audible.

My 'Queen of What Ifs . . . ' I'd hold her, touch the soft skin on her face with my fingertips and tell her that she's right, that it's love that brings meaning to life.

2. Erin

THEN — December 1996

'Because without love, you're screwed,' Seamus Fitzpatrick, Fitz, to his friends and audience, announced.

Erin felt Dom squeeze her hand, followed his nervous glance across the table. Seeing her new mother-in-law's pinched lips, she looked away and focused instead on a wet ring mark on the paper tablecloth.

'We've another way of saying that in Ireland, you know, 'screwed', but when in Rome and all that.' Fitz laughed; a soft, uneasy sound.

Oh God, thought Erin. *Please don't swear. Sit down now, Dad. Sit. Please.*

She swallowed hard as his voice filled the small room. It was a private space at the back of the King's Arms located right across the street from the registry office. It wasn't the sort of place she'd imagined her wedding might be. Like almost every small girl, she had, once upon a time, pictured herself in an elegant gown saying her vows in a quaint village chapel. At a grand reception, there would have been a feast followed by a practised first waltz by the bride and groom to 'their song'.

A room in a pub, slightly sticky underfoot, with smoke-scented flock wallpaper, worn velvet seating, loops of stringy tinsel and Christmas lights with missing bulbs had never been part of the dream. And she and Dom hadn't known one another long enough yet to have 'a song'. Erin rubbed her hand over her belly as a familiar anxiety began to gnaw. They'd known each other long enough to create the human being that danced inside her, but not long enough to have a song. It was only Dom's hand on hers that calmed her doubts, reminding her that she had got the most important thing right. Dominic Carter was a prince among men.

'See, without love,' her father continued, 'you're just two people roaming through life, wandering around in a valley of . . . a valley of tears.'

Resisting the urge to pull on his sleeve, instead she prayed to her mother. *Make him sit down, Mam, please.*

'So, it does fill me with joy . . . '

She looked up and her face crumpled as Fitz started to cry.

'It fills me with joy,' he sniffed, 'to see that you two really do love each other, so bear with me while I say,' he peeked at her and Dom over the rim of his oval, steel-rimmed spectacles, 'keep hold of that love and you'll be grand.'

Erin's mouth twitched as she attempted a smile.

'Finally, let's raise a glass to the bride and groom. I wish you both health and happiness and family that will love and anchor you.'

'Thanks, Dad,' she touched his arm, his new, but ill-fitting, suit as he sat down.

'Your mam would have been so proud of you today,' he smiled.

'Thanks, Dad,' Erin repeated and stared at her bump. There had been no way or no gown to hide it and everyone who was there knew anyway.

'Was it alright?' Fitz asked.

She told her father that his speech had been perfect as she, once again, looked across the circular table towards her in-laws. Sophie was scooping imaginary crumbs from the table. Gerard smiled, gave a small nod in her direction.

'Perhaps I shouldn't have — ' Her father leaned into her as he drained his glass. She crooked an arm around his neck and kissed his cheek.

'I told you, Dad, it was really perfect. Thank you.'

Three round tables of ten people squeezed into the room created the background noise that she and Dom needed. 'You wanna get out of here?' her husband whispered.

'You know we can't.' She felt his sigh in her ear and shivered. There was nothing she wanted more than to get back to the flat and curl up in bed with this man and their bump.

'Okay, we'll stay a bit longer,' he agreed. 'But no one really expects us to hang around drinking, love.'

'Let's circulate, give it another half hour,' she said. Pulling herself to a standing position, she dismissed thoughts of the absent music and first dance, reminded herself to be grateful to Dom for putting this together so quickly — on his own, without much help from her or anyone. 'I'm going for a quick pee,' she whispered before heading to the back of the function room towards the corridor and the loos. Just as she was about to turn the corner, a voice she recognised stopped her in her tracks.

'She's shameless.'

Erin's hand automatically protected her stomach. Every nerve ending in her body told her to turn around; that she had no business listening, but her feet had rooted to the tacky carpet.

'You're tired. We'll go soon.'

'Gerard, do not patronise me! I'm not tired. I simply can't stand the girl.'

'That 'girl', as you call her, is carrying our grandchild. Keep your bloody voice down.'

Erin backed herself up against the wall. She tried to edge each vertebra, one by one against it, suddenly caring little for the off-white dress she had carefully chosen in a small vintage shop near Putney. Closing her eyes, she willed herself invisible.

'Is she?' Sophie hissed. 'We don't know that, do we, and he's too besotted to care!'

'Stop!' her husband snapped. 'You want to go, we'll go, but this is not the time or the place for a scene.'

She should walk on up there, Erin told herself. Just walk on up that narrow, dirt-brown corridor, make her way slowly past them, brandishing her bump between them. She should smile sweetly at her mother-in-law, and widen her grateful eyes at Gerard, the man who thankfully seemed to have donated most of Dom's character. Erin knew what she should do but, instead, she pleaded with her bladder and backed into the room to mingle with their friends as best she could.

'You look angelic,' Lydia whispered.

'Divine,' Hannah agreed.

'Well, *I* would,' Nigel, Dom's best man grinned. 'Seriously, there's something very sexy about pregnant women.'

And with one eye on Sophie emerging from the corridor, Erin laughed.

Later, as they were leaving, everyone made a guard of honour to an out of tune 'Here Comes the Bride'. It was only as Dom steered her underneath, past Fitz and her brother Rob, that Erin saw Sophie waiting at the very end. She would be waiting to whisper that he'd always have a home if he changed his mind. Erin stooped low. Dom was not going to change his mind. Dom loved her. He hadn't stopped smiling since she'd told him about the baby. And even though she had never asked it or expected it of him, Dom had asked her to marry him within days of the news. Dom had married her. Because he loved her.

He pulled her through the arch and as she stood, she leaned into Gerard's kiss, matched her mother-in-law's air kiss, and gripped her new husband's hand. At the door, she was pulled into another hug as Dom tried to help her with her coat.

'I'll call you tomorrow,' Lydia squeezed hard. 'Get some sleep.'

Erin nodded. It had been a long day, but she

hugged her sister-in-law back.

'Look after that brother of mine.' Lydia smiled. 'He's the only one I've got.'

Erin nodded, pulled Hannah, her other bridesmaid, into the hug and scanned the room until her eyes rested on Fitz and Rob, who, hating goodbyes, had moved away from the door. When her father placed his fingers on his lips and blew her a kiss, and her only brother winked, Erin nodded and fought back tears.

Nigel handed Dom the car keys and smiled at Erin. 'It's outside and all warmed up for you, love.'

'Thanks, Nigel,' she whispered. Sometimes it was the small acts of kindness from people that made her fill up. She looked at Sophie, who was wringing her hands. And sometimes, she thought, it was cutting words that did it. Against all her better instincts, she turned back to her mother-in-law and whispered. 'I love your son and he will always know that. Always.'

Her response was the tiniest nod, a minute jerk of the woman's disapproving head, a cold but noticeable acknowledgement.

In the car, they both shivered. Dom reached over and rubbed her arms with his hands. 'Who the hell gets married in December?' he asked, laughing. 'Right, let's get you home to bed.'

She closed her eyes briefly, wanting to commit that moment to memory — his desire to keep her warm, to get her back safely. At twenty-seven, Dom's wedding night should have involved honeymoon sex, lots of it. Part of her felt she should apologise — not just for the lack of wedding night love-making but the whole thing. The whole 'meet a girl and within seven months find out she's pregnant and five months later marry her' thing. Whirlwind didn't cover it.

He placed a hand inside her coat and squeezed her knee, bare but for the flesh-coloured tights she'd worn with her short, fitted, lace dress. 'Never more,' he said.

She laughed. 'How did you know what I was going to ask?'

'Because I can read your mind. Plus you ask me every night if I'm happy.'

She stared out the window at the shadows of the icy fir trees that lined the edge of the street. 'Just making sure . . . '

'Erin?'

'Uh-huh?' She leaned forward towards the heated air coming from the front vents.

'Promise me something?'

'Anything.'

'Believe that I'm happy. I wouldn't be here with you, with you both, unless I wanted to be. So, after today, no more making sure, okay?'

'Okay.'

'Promise?'

'I promise not to ask you if you're happy again, unless I'm really unsure for a very good reason.'

Dom shook his head. 'Negotiating already! Christ, what have I done?'

Minutes later he pulled the car to a stop just outside the building they lived in. 'Thank you, parking fairies,' Erin whispered. 27 Hawthorn Avenue had, in Victorian times, been home to single families; gentile people whom Erin often imagined roaming through the rooms. Today, the building was divided into three flats and she and Dom lived in the high-ceilinged rooms of the ground floor, giving them access to their own private garden. Despite having Gerard and Sophie Carter as landlords, Erin loved living there; loved the original ornate cornice and ceiling roses, loved the stone fireplace in the living room, the picture rail in their bedroom, and the groaning wooden floors with years of story in every creak. Having come from a sixties-built, two-up two-down that her parents had mortgaged to buy from the local council, Erin loved the fact that she could *feel* the history in this house.

'Right,' he said, putting an arm around her and locking the car with the remote. 'How are we going to do this?' he asked as they neared the main front door. 'Is this the threshold or is it the door to the flat?'

'Dom, no, it's too awkward, I'm too — '

Before she could finish the sentence, he handed her the keys and scooped her up into his arms, carrying her with one arm under her back and the other under her knees. She opened the door laughing. 'That's enough!' she cried.

'No! We have to do the other one too. Just in case. It might be bad luck!'

After entering the flat, Erin was lowered to the floor. And as Dom feigned an injured back, rolling on the hard, varnished wooden planks, his hand hitting against their three-foot plastic tree with its red and green baubles, her own hand

14

rested on the moving child. Their baby was laughing too.

★ ★ ★

It was, according to things she'd read on the subject, nature's way of preparing her but Erin was tired of being tired, of not being able to sleep at night and having to snatch catch-up naps during the day. She shook the kettle on top of the Aga and moved it to the centre of the heat, careful to stand there as it came to the boil; the thing had a high-pitched whistle and she didn't want to wake Dom.

As she stirred a camomile teabag in a large mug, she walked past the sink, towards the pile of presents sitting on the kitchen table. Her empty teacup from this morning, when she'd been a single woman, sat upside down on the draining board. She took a seat at the head of the table — solid oak, country style with carver legs and a cutlery drawer at one end — it had been a present from the Carter family. They had offered to pay for a wedding; probably somewhere like Erin had dreamed of, but neither she nor Dom had wanted to accept, sensing a disapproval of Erin that was never discussed.

She ran her hand over the array of gifts. There was only one in the tall mound that she was interested in opening, one she knew Dom wouldn't mind her getting the first look at. Fitz had wrapped it in old newspapers, bound it with blue ribbon.

The box was flat, A4 size and inside it,

amongst layers of tissue paper, lay a leather-bound notebook. A bitter chocolate colour, soft nappa leather, with an opening flap like an envelope. From the point of the flap came a single strand of leather to tie around it. Picking it up, it felt lighter in her hand than she'd imagined. Her forefinger traced the embossed words on the front:

What am I?
I am The Book of Love,
The pages of truth with its light and shade.
I am Love,
And if real, I will never fade.

Opening it, a card fell to the table and on the back, her father's handwriting:

Erin and Dom, your mother and I used to do this. I'd swear it rescued us from many sticky times so this is a 'borrowed' idea for your gift. I hope you use it like we did — to talk to one another — to write down whatever it is you can't bring yourselves to say. In years to come, this book will be a place where you'll look back and read about the things you were possibly too young or naïve to understand. Only two rules — First, don't do it too often, it's a route to talking about difficult things, not the only place to mention them. And second, when you write something, start and end it with love, like 'My dearest Erin/Dom' etc. and always, ALWAYS end it with a reminder to each other that you love each other and why e.g. 'I love you because . . . '

Erin appreciated the thought in the gift but still replaced it in its box shaking her head, unable to imagine a time when she and Dom couldn't simply say exactly what they wanted to one another.

The sound of the soft pad of his feet on the tiled floor made her turn around.

'Come to bed, love.' Dom, wearing striped pyjama bottoms but bare chested, rubbed one of his eyes.

'I can't sleep.' From behind, she felt both his arms circle her waist.

'It's three a.m.' he yawned. 'What's in the box?'

'A gift from Dad.'

Dom pulled a chair up beside her, took a sip from her mug and grimaced. 'No wonder you can't sleep. That stuff is powdered shit.' His head jerked towards the gift. 'So, what is it?'

'It doesn't matter — just one of Dad's hare-brained ideas.'

Dom took her hand. 'You remember when we first met, Mrs Carter?'

She laughed. 'It was only a year ago. Of course.'

'Lydia's New Year party. The first time I saw you, you were dancing, all five-foot-ten of you.' He stroked the downy hair on her arm. 'You were doing that weird hippy-sway-thing you do, those long limbs of yours flailing about.'

17

'You called me Tree-Girl and I hated you.'

'You fancied me.'

'Okay, I fancied you a little. I hated the nickname.'

'I knew I'd marry you, right then, that first moment I saw you.'

'You did not.'

'I did so.'

Erin cupped his stubbled chin in her hands, focused on the amber speckles in his tired brown eyes. 'Really?'

'Really,' he nodded. 'Mind you, if I'd known I'd be awake at three a.m. on my sexless wedding night, I'd have left you there, bopping away in the living room.'

'Ouch.'

'I'd have turned right around and never looked back.'

'Liar.'

'You know me so well,' he smiled.

She stared back at the box. 'You reckon we'll always be able to talk to one another. Like this? Just spit out whatever's on our mind?'

'Sure. As long as it's not always at three a.m. It's been a long day, love, come back to bed?'

Erin sighed, stood up with him and slipped into the crook of his arm, knowing he wouldn't sleep again unless she tried to.

Seconds later, when they climbed into bed, she shivered in the cold sheets. She curled her body into a foetal position, slipped gratefully into his spoon, instantly feeling his body warm hers; feeling his quiet mind soothe hers; feeling his love melt from his pores into hers, nourishing

18

her. In the slivers of light angling through the Venetian blind, she caught sight of the third finger on his left hand where, rather than a ring, he'd had 'Erin forever' tattooed. His mother had almost had a coronary when she saw it. Erin had loved it, unable to believe that any man, especially this man; this man who had such passion for everything, had stamped himself as hers.

Her hand squeezed his. With her free hand, she reached back and touched his cheek, the scent of leather still lingering on her fingertips.

'I am Love,' she whispered.

'You too,' he said softly.

She smiled and closed her eyes.

3. Erin

THEN — April 1997

'You're kidding, right?'

Dom was shaking his head, his expression deadpan.

'Yes, you are! You're kidding,' Erin laughed. 'Even you wouldn't suggest strip poker to a woman who's nine months pregnant and who can no longer see her feet.'

She watched him as he held the tray steady in his hands, almost tripping over the small hospital bag she'd packed weeks ago.

'What? So, I get a cup of tea and toast in bed if we play 'because it's the weekend and we can'?'

'Yep,' he said setting the tray down beside her. 'And I'll thrash you. You *will* be naked first.'

Erin took a bite of toast, flicked the crumbs from her flannel pyjamas, remembering the first outing of naked card games. It was only weeks after they met and they hadn't left her room for an entire weekend. 'I have two items of clothing on and I'm not taking them off,' she said, but he was already pulling a deck of cards from his pocket.

'Well, you'd better win then, hadn't you?'

Erin groaned. 'Dom . . . I — ' She felt his eyes on her.

'You're beautiful,' he told her. 'I know you

don't feel it right now but there is nothing sexier than your pregnant body having my baby. And I'm trying to keep your mind off that — the 'having the baby' thing.'

Erin rubbed her tongue over her front teeth. She had morning breath. She had crumbs sticking to the creases at the edge of her lips. She'd been hoping for a lie-in, but here he was with his breakfast tray and his infectious way. She smiled, her hand held aloft for some of the cards he was already shuffling. 'Hang onto your trousers, Dom,' she said.

'Won't need to.' He took a bite of her toast. 'Ugh, sorry. It's a bit cold.'

'When I win, you can go and make some more.'

'When I win, after you've put some clothes back on, I'll take you out for an early lunch.'

'Deal,' she said, curling her hair around her ears, already practising her best poker face.

⋆ ⋆ ⋆

Having spent a perfect, lazy day with Dom, Erin leaned against the back doorway and tried to swallow a sense of unease. Her natural anxiety was, of late, worsened by pregnancy hormones.

'You don't understand,' she whispered, her hand making tiny circles around her navel.

'So, explain it to me.' Dom stopped her hand moving by taking it in his.

Her voice faltered, unsure. 'I suppose I'm afraid.'

'Of what? I mean tell me *exactly* what you're afraid of.'

Erin lowered her eyes. Just outside the door by her stockinged feet lay a cluster of late-blooming crocuses still not quite ready for spring. Maybe the next day, she thought, maybe the next day the purple and golden yellow flowers would open and flash their bright stamens proudly. She watched her bump rise and fall with the pull and push of her lungs. And maybe once her baby was born she would feel ready to become a mother.

Sometimes she couldn't believe that there was another human being alive inside of her. Other times, the ones when the child kicked and complained in the confined space of her stretched womb, she was acutely aware of it. And tonight, as her insides tightened with more Braxton Hicks contractions, 'teasers' that could only have been named such by a man — she wondered if now would be a good time to tell Dom that she wasn't doing this ever again. The thought of having someone else taking over her body again . . .

'Talk to me,' he pressed her.

She closed her eyes, conscious that if she said how she really felt, was truly honest with him, Dom would only worry. She could have confessed she was afraid that becoming parents would change them, that their love might not have space for another person. She might have told him that her hormones seemed to play havoc with old anxieties, fears that had been prodded and poked awake. She might have told him she was afraid she was going to die in

22

childbirth. The sensible part of her brain knew there was nothing logical about the panic that set in when she thought about giving birth, but . . . She batted away the scary thoughts.

'Erin?' Dom said.

Raising his hand to her face, she angled it to cup her cheek, leaning into it. 'I'm just being silly.'

She felt his lips on her forehead — a kiss that confirmed he was right there with her, that he would listen to her 'silly' if she wanted him to. But Erin remained quiet, unable to speak her doubts to her waiting husband who believed he could kiss her fears away.

Four days to go to her due date and the thoughts lined up now, colliding anxiously with one another. What if, she asked him silently in her frightened head, what if I die and leave you alone? What if I live and we have a beautiful child and I can't love it? What if I love it more than you? What if I stay this weight — will you ever fancy me again? What if we've forgotten how to make love? She thought of earlier when he'd beaten her at strip poker and they had lain in the bed naked, just holding each other. She gripped her tightening stomach and breathed through the discomfort.

'You got those false contraction things again?' he asked, and she nodded, thinking he too could probably feel them as he held her. 'Must be the weirdest thing.'

'Yep,' she pulled away from him and doubled over placing her hands on her knees. 'Though these ones haven't gone away,' she said, one

23

hand straight away steadying herself in the doorway.

'Breathe.' Dom rubbed her back. 'Slowly.'

And that's what she was doing, breathing away the uncomfortable 'teasers', feeling Dom's hand massaging her back gently, when she felt a small pop and watched water trickle down her legs onto her socks.

'Shit!' Dom reared upwards. 'Is that . . . ?'

Erin straightened. 'Get the bag, love.'

'Right,' he was staring at her.

'Dom, the bag?' She closed the back door, turning the key in the lock, moving the handle up and down to make sure.

'You alright?'

She nodded. 'The — '

'I know, the bag.' Dom patted his pockets as if the ordered holdall she'd packed six weeks ago could be found in one, and Erin reached for his hand.

'I'm okay,' she said, and in that same moment recognised all her own worries in his darting eyes. Of course. Of course, he was frightened too. 'I'm okay.' She squeezed his hand.

He nodded before moving at speed to their bedroom.

'Get me some clean knickers and leggings,' she called after him.

'Right.'

She heard him in the next room pulling out drawers, muttering to himself, and she began to peel her lower clothes from her body. With the leggings she'd been wearing, she wiped the tiny puddle of water from the floor, ignoring the

24

thought that she'd expected a torrent, a waterfall, and that if that was all the amniotic fluid in her, it could only mean the rest was all baby. 'Shit,' she whispered to no one but herself.

She was stood at the sink, filling the plastic basin with hot water and swishing her soiled clothes with her hands when Dom was suddenly by her side.

'Okay, let's get going,' he laid a gentle arm around her shoulder.

Erin gripped the sink, a wave of pain and nausea overcoming her. 'Knick-ers,' she panted.

'Yes, sorry, I put them in the bag.' Dom unzipped the bag and bent down, sliding the knickers up over Erin's legs. She winced as she felt pinching lace and realised he'd obviously picked a pair from the pre-pregnancy drawer she hoped to return to someday.

'A thong?' she asked as she felt the useless triangle of material sit somewhere on her lower bump and a thin elastic line wedge between her bum cheeks.

'God! Sorry.' He was already pulling her foot through one leg of a pair of black leggings and began to peel it from her again.

Erin tried to smile. 'Leave it — it's fine,' she said gripping hold of his shoulder just as another contraction threatened. 'It'll give the nurses a laugh. Now, hospital,' she said as she pulled the leggings up as far as they would go. 'And step on it.'

★ ★ ★

25

'Noooooooooo!' Erin cried out as Susan, a heavy-set midwife from the west of Ireland, whom they had met nine hours earlier, now mentioned the word 'doctor'. She had read the books, heard other women's stories. A doctor meant a caesarean. She could do this. Her eyes fixed on Dom's — deep brown — set beneath a sweaty, worried brow and above a surgical mask. 'Tell them I can do it.' She gripped his hand. 'Ple-ea-se . . . '

Dom stood, not letting go of her. 'She says she can do it,' he announced to the room in some weird 'I'm in charge' voice that she had never heard before but loved him for.

'Okay, Erin,' Susan looked up at her from between her legs. 'We'll give it one more go. Breathe now . . . then wait for this next one before pushing,' she said, glancing at the screen to her side. Erin had just a few moments to catch her breath before she could feel it rolling inside her; another pain that would gather speed like a determined tide. She tried to control it, watched the monitor strap across her middle stretch and breathed into it just before a torturous tightening racked her body. Without waiting to be told, Erin pushed to the point that she felt as if her head might explode. This was nothing like any book had told her; nothing like the classes she and Dom had practised simple breathing exercises in. And as she screamed into the final thrust that would give birth to her child, she felt sure her body would snap in two.

'Push, love, push,' Dom urged, and she wanted to thump him. She wanted, to yell at him; ask him how exactly he'd shit a melon, but she needed any energy she had and the only sound that left her mouth was a long wail — a piercing cry that lasted the length of time it took for her baby to emerge. And when she finally breathed again, it was to the sound of Dom sobbing. 'You did it, sweetheart. Jesus, you did it.'

Erin waited for a baby's cry. She tried to raise herself up on her elbows. 'Where . . . '

And then she heard it, a tiny mewling yelp, again, nothing like she'd been led to believe it would sound.

'You have a little girl,' Susan smiled at her as she wiped the struggling baby before placing her on Erin's chest. Erin stared, mute, at the frowning bloodied infant, all wrinkles and wriggling limbs. She pulled her into her arms, checked for fingers and toes. Dom's face grazed against hers and together they watched as their newborn opened her eyes. The books were wrong again. Because Erin felt that their daughter could really see already — had spotted them, focused on them both as if to say, 'Hello, Mummy and Daddy. I'm here. Are you the people who've been talking to me for so long?'

She clutched her baby, ignored the commotion south of her waist; paid no attention to words like 'afterbirth' and 'stitches'.

'You were so brave,' Dom whispered. 'Isn't she beautiful?'

Erin wasn't sure. She wasn't sure if their child was yet beautiful but was quite sure that one day she would be. She wasn't sure if she'd been brave or obstinate and wondered if there would be enough dissolvable thread in the ward, in the world, to stitch both halves of her back together again.

She *was* sure of the clear vision she had of Dom as Daddy with his little girl riding her bike without stabilisers for the first time. She *was* sure of his voice acting out the characters during many bedtime stories. She *was* sure of the surge of love she felt for this tiny human being who had claimed her body for so long. It was more powerful than any pain she'd endured, more powerful than any pregnancy magazines had reported. 'Hello, little one,' she said. 'Welcome.'

And Erin Carter was in love for only the second time in her life.

★ ★ ★

When she woke, she woke to every part of her hurting. She woke to a stomach so bulging that she wondered if she'd dreamt the whole thing, or if the medical staff had left another baby behind. Dom was sitting in the chair next to her bed, feeding the child from a tiny bottle. Erin felt a pulling ache in her breasts. She willed herself to sit up, to say no, that she wanted to feel her baby latch onto her nipple, but the words wouldn't form.

Dom reached across to her. 'Sleep, my love, you're exhausted.' He stood, holding their baby daughter in one arm and stroking Erin's forehead with the other hand. She felt the rhythmic swipe of his hand on her brow;

hypnotic. Seized by a sudden panic, she whispered his name. 'Dom . . . '

'You need to rest, love. Your blood pressure's low.'

Erin's breathing only levelled when she reached out and touched their child.

'I've got this,' he said. 'Don't worry.'

Erin didn't tell her eyes to close, but they did and underneath her eyelids, she told herself there would be plenty of time for her to feed her baby. There would be time enough to feel her suckle and to nourish her from her swollen milk ducts. For now, all Erin could feel was a flame like heat surging through the bottom half of her body and for the first time since her waters had broken she thought of herself.

Something was wrong.

You're not going to die.

But something was wrong.

There's nothing wrong. Sleep. And stop thinking bad thoughts. You have someone else to think about now.

'You do.' From nowhere, her own mother's voice punctured her thoughts. 'You're a Mummy now. I'm so sad I can't be with you.'

Something's wrong.

'Nothing's wrong, Erin.'

In her mind, she saw her mother smile, from where she stood just beyond Dom and their baby. She was wearing her favourite dungarees and a colourful scarf rested on her shoulders over a white shirt. Erin's heartbeat quickened. 'Relax, she's fine,' her mum reassured her. 'You are going to be a wonderful mother but for now, you need to rest. Dom's got this.'

Since opening her eyes, Erin had been resisting the slide back into sleep, fearful she'd never wake up.

Relax. Dom's got this.

And as she fought sleep and worry and joy and pain, tears slid from her heavy eyelids because today of all days she really wanted her mother with her.

★   ★   ★

Forty-eight hours later, two days of antibiotics inside her to deal with a postpartum infection, Erin was showered and about to dress when Dom appeared at the end of the bed, his head poking around the curtain. Their daughter slept peacefully, swaddled in a bright lemon woollen blanket.

'Hey, gorgeous.' Dom came in and leant into the clear hospital cot to kiss their child.

'How are you feeling?' he asked, hugging her gently.

'The nurses fed her in the night so I'm not too bad. I managed a feed yesterday evening and first thing today and we did alright. We need to choose a name,' she kept her voice low as she pulled on a T-shirt over her maternity bra. 'And stop ogling my boobs,' she grinned at her husband.

'I can't help myself. They're like one of the wonders of the world.'

'For now, they're Rachel's,' she nodded towards their baby.

'You mean Maisie's,' he replied, both hands on his hips. 'And we should teach her to share from the get-go. Don't you think Maisie suits her face?'

Erin smiled. 'What about Rachel, with Maisie as the middle name?'

'Or just Maisie,' he grinned. 'Look there's something — '

'What?' Erin's hand rooted in the bag for some underwear she'd packed right at the bottom, but her hand landed on the thong from the day she'd arrived.

'I know you're exhausted and I promise it won't be for long.'

She frowned, turned her eyes on her husband, sensing what was coming immediately.

'She's their first grandchild. They haven't wanted to intrude so far and just want a quick peek, so they're going to pop in for ten minutes when we get home.

Erin flopped onto the bed, sighed loudly before placing the thong on her head.

Dom narrowed his eyes and she sensed him watching as she put on a pair of bigger knickers and bent down to pull the leggings back up her body. 'I don't know what I was thinking,' she said grabbing hold of her middle and jiggling it. 'I packed my jeans in the bag. A little optimistic, I now realise.'

'You did hear me saying Mum and Dad are popping in?'

Erin locked eyes with him. 'I heard you. Ten minutes.'

'That's all. You do know you have a thong on

31

your head?' he asked as he sat beside her.

'I do.' She pulled it down around her neck. 'I'll wear it as a necklace until it fits my huge ass again.' She rested her head on his shoulder and together they stared at their baby.

'You think she'll always be this quiet?' he tucked a corner of the blanket that had loosened into its fold.

'In your dreams . . . She just likes to be swaddled.'

Dom smiled, and she stared up at him. 'What?' she asked.

'You know this already,' he said. 'Swaddling stuff. You are going to be brilliant.'

'Flattery . . . I'm still wearing a thong around my neck when your mother calls.'

Dom laughed, stood and pulled her upright. 'She either won't notice, or she won't say a word. Overnight you've been elevated to superstar. No pain relief except gas and air, a healthy eight-and-a-half-pound baby girl. According to Dad, Mum's knitting needles have been clacking all night — all pink wool, of course.'

Erin grimaced. She couldn't imagine Sophie wanting to do anything for her with a knitting needle other than stab her through the heart, but she nodded obligingly, willing to, once again, give her mother-in-law the benefit of the doubt for the sake of her husband.

'I'll just go and check they're ready to let you out of here.' Dom was beyond the curtain before she could tell him she already knew the paperwork had been signed off. They were waiting for her to go. There was likely another

32

woman already screaming in the labour ward who'd need her bed. Erin laid another blanket from her bag on the bed; multi-coloured, made up of small crochet squares — something her own mother had made for her. She had washed it carefully in soft soap, and now halved the square blanket into a triangle.

Gently she lifted the baby from the cot and placed her in the centre, pulling each corner across her tiny body, thinking Dom was right, she did look like a 'Maisie'. The child stirred in her sleep, wrinkled her nose and Erin held her breath for a moment before raising her to her chest. She inhaled the heady scent from her dark brown, downy, hair.

You can do this.

'Everything's good to go.' Dom swished the curtain aside. 'All the paperwork's been done. You alright, got everything?' he asked.

You can do this. Mum's not here but with Dom by your side, you can do this.

'Everything that matters.' Erin breathed deep and kissed Maisie's head.

4. Dominic

NOW — 3rd June 2017

From *The Book of Love*:
'I love you because you put a triangle of
Toblerone in my suit pocket.'

'You know the expression 'a New York minute'?
It's like the shortest measure of time ever but
still so much can change within it? Well, that's
what it was like. Forget Cupid and his arrows
— I was harpooned by Erin Fitzgerald!' My eyes
narrow. 'Are you listening to me?' I'm pointing a
finger at a toy elephant. 'She was dancing,' I
explain, 'a hippy thing where her body just
swayed, and she reminded me of a tree — tall
with long, coppery hair, longer limbs, slender
fingers.'
   It's raining outside, gloomy, relentless rain that
started late morning and would have any June
bride weeping. Our own trees in the back
garden, two majestic oaks, a white blossomed
japonicus, and a scattering of silver birches are
clinging onto their leaves and blooms as the
deluge pounds. I'm killing time before Lydia's
party talking to Maisie's favourite toy, a
threadbare, one-eared grey thing that still sits
regally on one of the armchairs — I've never
really understood why.
   'Anyway, there she was, this autumnal

sycamore rooted firmly in the middle of the old swirly carpet, and all I could think of was what it might be like to feel those fingers rake through my hair or grip my back.'

I stare at the elephant. 'I'm boring you . . . ' My head shakes and I refuse to see this scene as it is. A middle-aged shadow of the man I used to be speaking to a stuffed toy about how he met his wife.

'I called her 'Tree-Girl' . . . ' The elephant is tilting to one side and I straighten him up. 'And she was Lydia's new flatmate, so I suppose it's down to her that we ever met?'

The beat of the rain makes me think of my sister's disappointment today when her birthday barbecue has to shift indoors.

'Erin made me a coffee and we ate chocolate from the fridge.' I'm addressing Elephant again. 'Toblerone. Hers. But my absolute favourite.'

My sigh is long. 'Neither of us ever believed in that love-at-first-sight crap, but . . . ' I glance behind me. The neon clock on the wall says two more hours until I can leave for the party.

'But,' I reach for the elephant and slump into the sofa. 'The thing is, that was then, and this is now.'

The elephant's grey glass eyes look up at me from above his curled trunk and dirty tusks and for a New York minute, I think he understands.

'In between we were happy, really happy. Sure, there were times . . . ' I hesitate, unwilling to confess my part in bad times, even to a soft toy. My eyes land on the leather book sitting on the coffee table in front of me. I never did put it back in the drawer. 'And even through the shit, we loved each other, you know? And our children couldn't have asked for a better mother. Honestly, she . . . '

The grey eyes seem to stretch, and I reply to the imaginary unasked question. 'Me? Yes, I've been a good dad too. I think they'd both say that. They should be there tonight,' I add. 'Yes, I'll probably see them there tonight.'

Two more hours. One hundred and twenty minutes. I seem to spend my time waiting for time to pass. Maybe I should just count to seven thousand two hundred.

'Erin always had this thing,' I'm still addressing the elephant but am mesmerised by the swaying trees outside, 'she had a thing that I thought she'd trapped me.' I laugh out loud. 'Mum thought that for sure, but the idea never crossed my mind. Pregnant or not, all I wanted was to be with her. I think she got it — eventually . . . '

Elephant has fallen over. 'She wasn't always easy, you know. Back then she worried all of the time. God, she could sweat the small stuff, but managed to hide it well. I suppose we all have our disguises.' I place him upright again. 'What I'm trying to say is the good bits far outweighed the bad.'

I lay my head back on the sofa, try to ignore the fact that I've spent the last ten minutes — six hundred seconds — talking to an inanimate object. My eyelids lower.

In my sleep, I dream. I dream about Erin on

our wedding day. I dream of Maisie. And I dream about elephants in the room.

5. Erin

THEN — January 1998

Erin drove . . . She drove faster than the legal speed limit told her she could, the needle on the dashboard sliding past eighty. It was only Maisie's waking cry from her seat in the back that made her take her foot off the gas.

'Sssh, darling.' She reached behind and finding the baby's lower leg, stroked it. 'Nearly there, sweetheart.'

Maisie, the happiest child since the moment she first drew breath, gurgled a giddy response.

Erin angled the rear-view mirror and sang a nursery rhyme from her own childhood, something about Miss Polly having a dolly who was sick. Indicating off the M3, she smiled at the irony. Sick. Poor Dolly. Poor Erin.

In the narrow street outside the home she'd been raised in, Erin parked behind her father's car. Fitz's Toyota, with its thin layer of overnight frost still in place on the windscreen, seemed as old as him and she struggled to remember a time when he'd had another car. A mechanic by trade, at fifty-seven Fitz still worked full time and maintained that car engines were like human hearts. They needed looking after; loving, nurturing and occasional tuning. The front door to the house was open before her hand was off the wheel. Her father was opening the rear door cooing at the baby and removing her from her seat before Erin even had time to say hello.

'You can go now,' Fitz said as he walked off with his grandchild. Erin swung the baby bag over her shoulder, locked the car door and as soon as she saw her father's hand reach back for her, she grabbed it, grateful.

'Joking, of course. It's always great to see my baby girl,' he said. 'Seeing her baby girl too is a bonus. Have you eaten?'

Erin nodded, her eyes cast downwards, sure that if she looked up she'd be caught in her lie. She'd fed Maisie. That was all that mattered. The thought of food today made her want to vomit.

They sat in the small kitchen at the rear of the house. Gone was the shiny pine table she and Rob had sat at for family meals and homework. Whoever had purchased it from the charity shop her father had donated it to would have had to sand away its wounds — some pen or felt-tip messages etched in the wood, her name where she had stabbed it for posterity with the point of her compass, the large dent that the frozen turkey had made one Christmas when her mother had dropped it. In its place was a strange-looking desk-like thing with the longer side placed up against the wall. Two odd chairs, one with stuffing oozing through a small hole, were parked at each end. There's nothing worse, her father had once told her, than eating alone at a big table. Erin took the nearest chair and sat rocking Maisie on her lap.

'Tea,' Fitz announced, filling the kettle.

She breathed in the familiar room with its

wallpaper of patterned tiles, each 'tile' with a different vegetable image. In the corner, a box containing stacks of *What Car?* magazines stood waiting to either be read again or passed on to someone who might want them. Beside it sat a smaller carton spilling with paperchains and tired tinsel. Relieved to be among her father's chaos, she took a deep sigh — she was there — safe and sound.

'You heard from Rob this week?' she asked Fitz.

'He called last night. Everything is going really well.'

It wasn't what Erin wanted to hear. Her only brother leaving to live in New York to work for an American bank had come as a shock the previous Christmas. She still wasn't sure if she'd forgiven him. Maisie, with one fist in her mouth, gnawing at her skin with her cutting teeth, tried to grab at anything in reach on the table with the other hand. Erin's eyes were drawn to the centre, where a well-thumbed notebook sat. Curious, she leaned forward, holding both Maisie's hands to limit her reach.

'Ah-a, don't you touch either,' Fitz called over. 'That's there for explanatory reasons. For my eyes only.'

Erin nodded as if she understood, but she didn't. She wiped her brow, thinking she should be at home tackling the never-ending list of things to do. The washing pile would talk to her if it could. Who knew a baby could create so much laundry? Who knew that looking after one small person could fill her day like it did, exhaust her like it did? Yet there she was, watching Fitz pour two mugs of stewed tea from a pot, exhausted.

'Right,' Fitz sat opposite. 'What's up?'

'My mother-in-law is a lunatic,' she said.

'No. No, she's not.' Fitz laughed.

'You're right but she hates me.'

'Well, that's a different thing altogether. And I thought things had settled with her since Maisie was born?'

'They have, but . . . She adores Maisie, adores Dom but she's still a bit off with me.'

'Having met Sophie, I think she'd be like that with anyone she sees as taking her son away from her. Or maybe it's because she had to wait such a long time for children — how old was she when she had Dom, forty? And she sees you, Miss Fertile, pregnant and married in months.'

Erin flushed, rubbed her neck with her hand. 'I just need to find a way to talk to Dom about stuff. It's one of the reasons I came to see you.'

Her father's forehead creased.

'For example, he's gambling,' she blurted. 'Only small stuff but he doesn't tell me.'

'Gambling?'

Erin thought Fitz looked as if he had a sudden headache brewing. 'Poker games with his mates and bets in bookies, mostly. Stupid arse leaves the stubs in his trousers. It's just a worry.'

'Have you asked him about it?'

'He waffles.' She hesitated. 'I suppose some might call it lies.'

Fitz sighed, sat back in his chair.

'Then again, I don't tell the truth when he asks me if I'm alright, whether I'm coping, when he senses I might not be. I don't tell him when my stomach coils in on itself. Seems that despite the fact we love the bones of one another and laugh together every single day, we both have stuff we . . . we just don't seem willing or able to talk about.'

'Right.'

'Dad?' Erin's eyes filled at the edges. 'We love being together. We're meant to be together. Just sometimes, we're not great at actually talking.' She bounced a restless Maisie on her knee. 'So, like I said when I called — that leather book you gave us when we got married — how does it actually work?'

★ ★ ★

'In only fourteen months since the wedding,' Dom raised a glass to her across the table, 'we're new parents, and I'm newly qualified.' He sipped from his glass. 'You not drinking?' he asked as he began to slice into the roast chicken she'd prepared.

'Tummy's a bit upset,' she said.

'Oh.' He put down his cutlery. 'You alright?'

'Yes, yes, I'm fine, probably Fitz's pâté sandwich.' She made a face and then instantly smiled. 'I didn't tell you — Maisie tried to stand up today! I had her down on the floor and one moment she was there, grabbing my legs and the next she was pulling herself up! Fitz loved it.'

'Sometimes,' Dom's eyes were wistful, 'sometimes, I wish I could stay at home all day and just watch her.'

Erin sliced her meat and nibbled on a piece. 'No, you don't,' she said. 'You'd last a day of shitty nappies and baby talk before you went scrambling back to the office for some peace.'

'I do know what you do for her, you know. I do know that there'll come a day when maybe you want more.'

Erin stared at the vegetables on her plate. She should eat the broccoli. 'Tell me about work,' she said. 'What's going on in the Carter Empire?'

'My father's empire is doing great and his one and only son and heir is being made to work from the bottom up.' He waved a knife. 'I don't mind. It's the right thing but there're moments where . . . ' Dom hesitated. 'Oh, I don't know. It's as if I'm penalised for being his son.'

'By him or others?' Erin asked.

'Gah,' he said. 'It's nothing. At least nothing I shouldn't expect. I am his son and I am only there because of that.'

'You're there because you got a first in Architecture after studying for six years, Dom.'

'Yeah, along with the hundreds of other applicants for entry-level jobs.' His eyes widened. 'I'm there because I'm his son and everyone, including me, knows that.'

Erin stood and came to sit on his lap. 'If anyone can make it work, you can.'

'Mrs Carter, if you're trying to seduce me, could you please wait until I've eaten?'

'I'm on my way to get a soft drink, actually,

need the bubbles . . . ' She traced the line of his five o'clock shadow with her fingertips before grazing his lips with hers. 'And it could be worse,' she said before heading to the fridge.

'Oh yeah?' he asked, cutlery in hand again.

'You could be working for your mother,' she grinned as her eyes scanned the inside shelves and she heard him laugh loudly as she popped open a can of lemonade.

★   ★   ★

Dom's snore, aided by the bottle of red which he'd got from a grateful client and had almost finished, prompted her out of bed. Tying her robe around herself, she slid her feet into slippers and first checked on Maisie.

Running her fingers along the top of the radiator, she made sure it was hot. There was a heavy frost outside, the threat of snow and Maisie hated being cold; she was the only baby that Erin had ever seen shiver. Leaning into the cot, she felt her forehead briefly and Maisie stirred, pursing her bud lips in her sleep. Not for the first time, Erin stayed a minute staring at the child's features. Her pale skin was flawless, velvet to the touch. A hint of strawberry could be seen in her straight golden hair, but only in certain lights. As Erin pressed a few strands between her thumb and fingers, marvelled at its softness, then traced the arch of her daughter's brow with the slightest of touches, she convinced herself that somehow, she and Dom could stay this lucky.

In the living room, she wrapped herself up in a

blanket on the sofa and took the leather book from the changing bag. Remembering what Fitz had said, and without thinking about it too much, Erin began to write.

18th January 1998

My darling Dom,

I can't sleep, so I thought I might as well do this! Fitz says it works; that it helps people focus on exactly what they want to say without any fluff.

I'm not sure what to do, how to do it, other than I start things by being first. And the first thing I need to say is that I love you. All of you, despite the fact that you're snoring away in bed after drinking wine I can't drink and I'm here awake again.

Yep. Sleepless nights, insomnia again. For about another six months.

I bet you're scratching your head now. I can see you; your face is wrinkled, you're trying to work out what the hell I'm saying and how the hell you should respond and whether I expect you to reply. Do I really expect you to write back? Well, yes — I'm going to leave this book on the hall table. I'll stick a big post-it with your name and instructions on the mirror above, so you'll see it first thing in the morning, when you're up with the birds and I'm finally asleep. Read Fitz's card again — it's just on the inside flap and it explains what this is about. And when you write back, please be honest. Be brutal. No, don't be brutal, I'm not sure I could take it. I'll take honest though.

And just because honesty is what this is about. Here it is, the fluff-free version, written down because I'm not sure your poker face is good enough to hide your feelings and I can't bear to see if I'm right:

I'm pregnant again. Over three months, I reckon. It must have happened during that time I was ill in October, probably didn't keep the pill down for a few days. I've only just found out because, since Maisie, it's quite normal for me to miss a period. Or two. But not three . . .

I love you with all the love in my heart but according to Fitz I'm supposed to end anything I write with a reason why, so . . .

I love you because you're a brilliant father and I hope that being a father again won't faze you. And I love you because you iron my jeans, and because you run a bath for me when I'm tired and because I heard you apologise to a snail yesterday when you accidentally stood on it.

Erin x

★   ★   ★

19th January 1998

Beautiful Erin,

This is just the second of our many un-planned plans. You ARE the most beautiful woman in the world. And you're mine and I'm yours and we'll work it out. We will.

Love you mightily,
Dom x

46

6. Erin

THEN — April 1998

'Tea with your mother. Alone. Can't you take the day off?'

Dom laughed.

'I'm serious. You won't be there. Your dad won't be there. The two of you will be huddled by a desk probably both worrying about who's killed who.' Erin stopped folding the laundry. 'What if we have an argument, I mean — '

'Erin, you're overthinking it. Stop. Mum's just asking you and Maisie over for a cup of tea and a slab of Teletubbies cake for Maisie's birthday. That's it.'

'She has a Teletubbies cake?'

'Not only,' Dom stood and took his jacket from the back of his chair, 'has she got one. She *made* the cake.'

Erin closed her eyes, felt his gentle kiss on her lips. 'Shit, I'm going to have to go, aren't I?' she sighed, knowing that there was no way out.

'You are, and who knows, you might enjoy yourself.' He waved a backward wave.

'I'd rather pull my toenails off with pliers!' she called after him. 'I'd rather poke my eyes out with cocktail sticks!' she yelled louder.

'Give her a kiss for me!' he called back and moments after Erin heard the sound of the front door close, she heard the sound of Maisie's voice. She flicked the kettle on to heat her bottle. 'I'd rather have surgery with no anaesthetic,' she said aloud to no one before walking down the hallway and peering around Maisie's door.

'Good morning, birthday girl!'

Maisie stood at the edge of the cot, her arms already in the air, and when Erin picked her up, she balanced her on the edge of her growing bump and danced around the room singing 'Happy Birthday'. She grabbed Maisie's favourite furry toy, an elephant with one ear and, heading back to the kitchen, she cooed the words 'Yes! I'd rather have a real elephant stand on my toe, yes, I would!'

Maisie chuckled, and Erin felt a couple of well-placed kicks just above her bladder. In the kitchen, she placed Maisie's bottle in a jug of boiling water and made a coffee she knew she'd only drink half of.

'What shall we do today?' she whispered into her daughter's tiny ear. 'Shall we go and eat special cake with Nanny?' Maisie began to jump in her arms. 'Okay, okay, I'm outvoted, we'll go and eat cake with Nanny. Mummy would rather eat raw offal but hey, we'll go anyway, eh?'

*   *   *

Erin sipped tea from a china cup and placed it back on a matching saucer on the dining table that Dom would have had so many Sunday dinners at when growing up. She found it easy to picture him there; a boy tall for his age, shy, with hair combed to one side, and short trousers.

48

Looking around the room, at the mass of heavy brocade curtains, the wood store cupboard beside the imposing fireplace, she could see the places that he and Lydia might have played hide and seek as children. It was a grand room, in a grand four-storey Victorian villa, nothing like Fitz's place.

'It's really warm for April, don't you think?'

Erin nodded politely, pushing aside all thoughts of the previous week's relentless rain and the fact she'd worn a woollen sweater this morning. She fixed her eyes on Maisie who crawled around her feet.

Sophie's head shook suddenly. 'Though you must know I didn't ask you here to talk about the weather.'

Erin remained silent.

'I owe you an apology,' Sophie said, her eyes moving from the child to Erin. 'I was most unfair to you when I met you first . . . and . . . for a while afterwards.'

' "She's shameless",' Erin quoted, as she helped herself to a purple slice of Tinky-Winky's hand. It was probably a good idea to eat, probably a good idea to stop herself talking.

'You heard that?' Her mother-in-law's cheeks blushed puce. 'I was out of order and I was wrong. I'm sorry.'

'Sophie — '

'No, Erin, let me say this. I was afraid,' Sophie said, reaching down and plucking Maisie from where she'd crawled under the table. She bounced her gently on her knee. 'I thought I'd lose Dom and that you and he wouldn't last, that you were . . . well . . . it doesn't matter. We sometimes act stupidly when we're afraid, don't you think?'

Erin wasn't sure. She could count the times on one hand where she thought she'd really acted stupidly but couldn't begin to count the far too many times when she'd been afraid. She inhaled deeply. Sophie was apologising, and not just a quick 'I'm sorry'. Sophie was apologising in style, and immediately Erin felt guilty.

'Sophie,' she eyeballed her. 'Don't give it another thought. Please. It feels like it's already a long time ago.'

'I even thought that she wasn't his . . . ' Sophie hugged Maisie and the child grimaced. 'But you only have to look at her . . . ' She was doing exactly that, staring at Maisie who had Dom's walnut brown eyes, his fair hair, rangy limbs and already, his calm nature. 'Do you think you can forgive me?' Sophie handed over Maisie, who was stretching her arms in Erin's direction, cooing an 'M' sound that Erin hoped would grow into 'Mama'.

'Of course, I — ' She had been twenty minutes away from her planned exit when the apology had started. And now, it wasn't that she didn't appreciate her mother-in-law's words, far from it, it meant a huge amount to her, but, it was Maisie's first birthday and she and Dom had bought their own cake, had planned a silly blow-out-the-single-candle ceremony.

'Gerard, he's been telling me for ages I should just come out with it and talk to you and . . . ' Sophie scooped some crumbs from the table into her hand. 'Have you had enough to eat, Erin? What about Maisie?'

Erin watched her scan the table, laden with enough sandwiches to feed a mid-size family for a week. Some part of her was touched at the effort Sophie had gone to. 'We've had plenty, thank you,' she replied.

'Why don't you take some of these and some cake for Dom and you later? Saves you cooking?' Without waiting for a reply, Sophie left the room, calling back that she'd just wrap them up for her. Erin kissed Maisie's cheek and began to do it repeatedly as the child giggled, then she caught Sophie watching from the doorway, a roll of tin foil in her hands. 'She's a total delight you know,' she said. 'A total delight.'

Erin grinned. She was. She placed Maisie on the floor next to her bag, kept one eye on her as she helped Sophie wrap the sandwiches. Whether she liked it or not, she was stuck here for a while with her new best friend and she and Dom were having soggy egg butties and Tinky-Winky's lower body for supper.

★   ★   ★

'Wow,' Dom looked up from his position lying, stomach down, on the floor.

'I know, right?'

'Wow,' he repeated. 'I don't ever remember Mum saying she was sorry.'

'Well, she seemed to mean it, so . . . ' They both looked at Maisie next to them. In the last few weeks, she had been trying to walk and was

51

managing to find her way around the room by clutching the edges of furniture. When she reached Dom, she smiled and sat down on him heavily. The sounds made Erin smile — first the high-pitched chuckle of Maisie followed by a breathless squeal and then Dom's deeper laugh as he took hold of her and tickled her. 'I'm going to GET you!' he crawled on all fours as she scrambled away, giggling. It was contagious, and she was laughing to herself as she went to fetch the cake.

Minutes later, she sang the length of the hallway. 'Happy birthday to you. Happy birthday to you!' She peered, wide-eyed, around the door. 'Happy birthday, our Maisie!' Bending down to where Maisie was sat on Dom's stomach, she held the cake she'd bought in front of her daughter's face. 'Blow, darling, look Daddy will show you. Blow!' Dom obliged by pursing his lips and blowing gently. When Maisie followed suit and tried without success, both of them helped. 'Happy birthday to you!' she sang the final line just as her daughter put her fist in the cake.

'That's right, darling, you tell her,' Dom said as he sat up and looked sideways at Erin. 'Mummy should never sing, should she?'

Erin licked some chocolate icing from a finger. 'What's wrong with Mummy singing?'

Maisie laughed and suddenly realising it was chocolate on her own hand, she began to lick it too.

'Yum, yum,' Dom pretended to chase her. 'Daddy wants some!'

More squeals from them left Erin holding the plate of cake. 'There's nothing wrong with my singing,' she yelled above them both.

★ ★ ★

When bedtime came, Erin listened from the hallway as Dom began to read Maisie's favourite picture book one more time. While he sounded out the phonics for the words and accompanied each farmyard animal with a suitable noise, Erin folded linen into the airing cupboard. Smiling at his braying donkey, she entered the bedroom, lowered herself down beside them on the large beanbag. And amidst the farmyard sounds, Maisie's eyes began to droop.

'She's tired,' Erin whispered. 'She didn't have a nap today.'

'Me neither,' Dom said, his eyes closing.

She grabbed his hand and let it lie on her stomach as she felt one of the babies move and wondered yet again how they'd stack three children into one room. 'You ever get afraid?' she asked Dom suddenly, replaying her conversation with Sophie in her head.

'Afraid?' He said the word as if it weren't in his vocabulary.

'Yes, scared, afraid.' She remembered the same time last year being overcome with worry just before giving birth.

'Not since I was a kid. Didn't like the dark much. Ghoulies and ghosties.'

'You've never felt frightened as an adult, not at all? Not even when the scan showed two babies?'

'Nope,' he confirmed, turning towards her, a sleeping Maisie crooked under his right arm. 'Only when I hear you sing. That scares me.' He shuddered.

She snuggled against him.

Ghoulies and ghosties and things that might possibly bump in the night had never bothered her. Three children. Five of them in a two-bedroom flat. One income. They all sort of scared her.

2nd April 1998

My darling Dom,

   Here's the thing.

   My mother died when I was only eighteen. I can't explain how devastated I was, more at having to watch her die slowly, than the fact that I lost her. When she passed, I felt relief and then huge shame that I felt relieved. And her death changed me.

   And since then I've never been able to take a single thing for granted.

   You and I are so alike in what we both want from life, but so different when it comes to believing we can get it. I'm a worry wart and wanted to say to you earlier, wanted to ask you (again) how we're going to manage with three children on your income with so little space? I said nothing, I couldn't, but I can't shake it from my head, which is how I find myself in here.

   Dom, I love you because of your absolute certainty that nothing can touch us. You believe that love will make everything alright and your faith in that makes me believe it too.

   Erin xx

P.S. And what's wrong with my singing? It sounds perfectly fine in my head.

★   ★   ★

3rd April 1998

Erin, my love,

What's the problem?

Old Mother Hubbard did it, didn't she?!! Wait it wasn't her — was it some 'old woman who lived in a shoe'? Who cares? we'll stack them, top and tail them. We'll be fine.

Is this the part where I have to write down why I love you?

I love you because you want me to write to you when we live together, because when I've finished writing, you want me to put the book away in the hall table where 'it will live' apparently, and then I have to put your name on a post-it, place it on the mirror above, so you know I've written to you.

One day, maybe all, or at least some of that, might make sense.

And I love you because you know you're a crap singer and you do it out loud anyway.

Mightily yours,

Dom xx

PART TWO

7. Dominic

From *The Book of Love*:
'Erin, I love you because even when you're
afraid, you're brave.'

She should have been a photographer.

I'm looking at a spread of her images left on
the kitchen table. They're so good — clean lines,
perfect colours, and a natural knack to frame her
subjects. There's a great one of me flying a
phoenix-shaped kite, and several more of our
gang, all pulling faces, at the pub quiz night. A
few years ago, Erin was never without a camera
— when did that stop?

I find myself studying an old picture of Maisie
that's stuck on the fridge, sharing a magnet with
the menu for the local Chinese take-away. She's
on her feet, chubby legs trembling, and using the
sofa to move herself along. The grin on her face
is pure joy. I remember, despite being out of
shot, being there behind the baby, arms
stretched out waiting to catch her if she fell. I
blow her a kiss before leaving the house.

Outside the front door the rain has stopped.
The temperature has risen and there's a sweaty
haze hovering above wet ground. Lydia's house
is a short walk from Valentine's Way, but I take
the longer route, up Hawthorn Avenue. Outside

number 27, I stop, lean up against one of the stone pillars at the entrance. They're new. And the front garden's different; denser, with loads more scruffy shrubbery that makes me want to get in there with some secateurs. Someone has planted ivy that's grown wild around the front bay window of the ground-floor flat. It looks like shit; messy, unkempt and it saddens me.

Behind that window was once our living room and behind it, in the middle of the flat, was Maisie's bedroom. It was there that Erin first told me how she felt afraid and I told her she, we, had nothing to fear.

I really believed back then that nothing could touch us.

It was there on the 10th May 1998 that I learned she was right and I was so very wrong . . .

★   ★   ★

The air in the flat is tight. I grasp the brass hook handles and pull the sash window in the living room until it raises its standard three inches. There's no fresh burst of outside air but better to leave it open, I think. There won't be any three-inch high burglars getting in tonight.

Erin's asleep, has been for hours. She's exhausted and the doctor has given her something mild to help her sleep. I debate a brandy. Sleep for me feels impossible — eyes will be closed with my mind still pumping, going over and over stuff. Pouring a half glass, I'm already regretting it at the first sip, regretting

60

what I've become. I swallow it in two gulps, look around and check the plugs, like I always do, before looking in on Maisie and going to bed.

Maisie's room, next to the living room, is even more stuffy and still and I open the window, pulling aside the heavy curtain Erin insists on having to try to convince our thirteen-month-old daughter it's night time. She's too clever though, knows she's being duped and we end up listening to her babbling in the room next to us for at least an hour after bedtime every night. Tonight, she's kicked the sheet off and has bundled herself into the furthest corner of the cot, her face rooted into the crumpled cotton and her left arm slung over Elephant.

I move her, turn her over, Erin's maternal words of warning whispering in my ear. 'She shouldn't sleep on her tummy,' something my own mother had always insisted Erin was wrong about. And as my hands touch her, as my fingers grasp my baby, my flesh and blood, I know immediately. She's so cold; my first thought is that there's no coming back from this. As I turn her over, even in the moonlight I can see her face is mottled blue.

One second: she's on the floor and I try to breathe life into her cold lips.

Two seconds: I listen for the sound of her fluttery heartbeat in her silent chest.

Six seconds: She's in my arms and I'm in the living room, the phone in my hand. The voice answering my call for an ambulance is calm and tells me the paramedics are on their way.

Ten seconds: I open the airing cupboard in

the hallway, pull out the first thing I see, a coloured crochet blanket, try to wrap her in it, the phone held in the crook of my shoulder and ear.

'She's so cold,' I say to the woman on the end of the phone, my instinct already telling me her shift will end in tears. My eyes are on the doorway to our bedroom at the end of the corridor, the bedroom where Erin's sleeping.

Fifteen seconds: Inside I'm screaming, 'Erin! Wake up!' But the cries stay put. I'm pacing with Maisie swaddled in my arms. I whisper to her not to worry. I tell her I love her. I ask her not to leave us. Please. Maisie. Please. Don't leave us.

I stop being aware of time when there's a banging on the front door and suddenly three people are all barking orders at one another trying to resuscitate our first child on a blanket on the living room floor. Our bedroom door opens.

Then Erin is howling, a sound I will never forget. She's clutching her stomach, swollen with twins, with one hand, scrambling to grab hold of Maisie with the other. She's on the floor, just repeating, 'No, no, no' on a loop. 'DO something,' she screeches at no one in particular, before folding in half. I get down on the floor, squeeze my eyes shut, grasp her so she can't move, knowing that if I let her go, she will simply break.

* * *

I quicken my pace to Lydia's. It's still bright out, despite a sky laden with lilac, rain-heavy clouds.

Cars, their lights on low, drive by and splash me but I'm oblivious, as I throw my head back and look to the heavens. 'Life,' I tell Maisie, 'is about choices. Some we regret. Some we're proud of, and some will plague us forever.'

8. Erin

THEN — May 1998

Erin couldn't breathe. From somewhere beneath her mouth, beneath her neck, she felt as if she was being kicked. Maybe she was dreaming. Maybe she was dreaming about being mugged.

Her babies were telling her to find air. She opened her mouth, and instead of the gulp she'd expected, she heard herself cry out. *Maisie.*

She began to rock. Forwards. Back. Forwards. Back.

What was she doing on the living room floor? Who *were* all these people? How did she get there?

Dom was holding her. But he was gripping her too tight, so she began to hit him. Hard.

Next to them, there was a man huddled, bending over something. She wanted to pull away from Dom, let her eyes land on the sight she knew she'd already seen; to let herself look at it from further back so she could talk herself through it. Her head moved slowly left to right. No.

No, no, no, no.

One two, buckle my shoe. Three four, knock on the door.

There was someone knocking on the door. And there was a strange woman letting him in. Erin counted. One, two, three, four. There were now four strangers in her living room, all dressed in black trousers and white shirts, all of them bent over something, someone. She began to wail, heard the sounds coming from herself and thought there must be some mistake. Even when she held her mother's hand as she had taken her last breath, Erin had been silent. She wasn't a screamer. Erin wept into Dom's chest and felt afraid, really fearful, that she would now, after this night, always be a screamer.

She could see it unfold. Dom would hand her a cup of tea and she might scream.

He might try to hold her, and she might scream.

Dom would whisper something hopeful, something kind and she might scream.

She forced herself away from him, crawled along the floor towards the huddle and pushed her way through. Maisie was lying on the floor on her blanket, the one Erin's own mother had crocheted so many years ago. A stranger's hand gripped her, tried to stop her getting to her baby. 'You're wrong!' Erin growled, a feral sound. 'Leave her alone!'

Gathering her baby up in her arms, she whispered to her. 'Everything will be alright. Mummy's here. Everything will be alright, won't it, Daddy?' She looked to where she'd left Dom, who sat on his haunches. When her eyes found his, Erin saw something she didn't recognise, as her memory pulled a line she'd written to him once, 'I love your absolute certainty that nothing can touch us.'

She cradled their child, pulled the blanket

tight around her. Maisie loved to be swaddled, and she was so cold. Erin kissed her lips, looked at a woman who was sitting next to her, also crouched down on her knees. The woman wiped her eyes with the back of her gloved hand. 'She gets cold,' Erin told her. 'And she loves to be warm. She gets cold,' she repeated. And as Erin began to rock again, silent, slow tears traced a path down her face. She kissed her baby as she felt another one move inside her. 'Don't worry, darling, Mummy will make it better.' Running a hand over her hair, her fine, beautiful hair, she felt the back of Maisie's neck. Cold. She rubbed the folds of her skin underneath her hairline and moved her up onto her shoulder. 'She likes this,' Erin told the woman as she moved her hand in slow circles on Maisie's back.

'Erin.'

Dom was suddenly in front of her. 'Shall I take her?' he whispered.

Erin's head shook. 'No.'

She needed time. These people had to understand that she and her baby needed time. She felt Dom's hand on hers as she moved both over Maisie. 'We just need to hold her. Everything's going to be okay, sweetheart.' Erin wasn't sure if she was talking to Maisie or to Dom.

They stayed there a few minutes, rubbing their baby's back until she became aware that the strangers in her home had moved. They were no longer huddled. Things that had lain on the floor had been packed into tight bags and slung over their shoulders. Some of them had left. Only two remained; the woman who had been sitting next to her and a man, tall with a tightly cut red beard. 'Look, Maisie,' she whispered in her ear. 'Pirate!'

Erin sat back on the floor, still holding Maisie upright on her shoulder. She felt the front of the sofa support her and she sighed. Turning Maisie over, she cradled her in her arms once again. Erin touched her lips with her fingertip, opened them slightly, waited for that fluttery, quivery breath that Maisie would always do. And then she held her own.

In that moment, Erin figured if she held it for long enough, she too might just stop breathing. It couldn't be that hard, surely. She saw Dom's lips move. He was breathing. Dom. Her Dom. He reached forward and took Maisie in his arms. Peas in a pod. And breath burst from her, against her will. Gasping, she quickly held it again. Maisie was in Dom's arms now.

As he stood and the woman took Maisie from him, Erin closed her eyes. She felt a kick in her stomach. Two kicks. Two babies. Needing their mummy. Again, she blurted the breath she'd held, this time, heard it exit her in a roar. And then, her eyes still closed as she felt Dom take her in his arms, she screamed again and beat his chest with her fists until she had no more fight.

And in her mind, she saw again how life might happen.

Someone, anyone, maybe her friend Lydia, would hand her a cup of tea and she would scream.

Someone, anyone, maybe her friend Hannah,

would try to hold her and she would scream and hit and thump.

Someone, anyone, would just say something kind and the sound would come.

Forever? She wondered as Dom placed both their hands on her stomach.

'Breathe,' he whispered. 'You have to breathe. We need you.'

And Erin did as she was told. In and out, she felt her lungs inflate and deflate.

And when she opened her eyes, Maisie was still there in the stranger's arms. Wrapped up against the cold in her blanket. Dom had stilled next to her. Without him looking at her, she felt his arm tighten around her and she turned her head towards him.

And Erin, who already knew what fear could do, who already knew what loss could do, now feared that alongside Maisie, her husband's blind faith in life being wonderful had also died that night.

★   ★   ★

20th May 1998

Darling Erin,
   Talk to me.
   Write to me.
   I know you're afraid and I know now there's reason to be afraid in life, but together, we can get through it, even if we're on our knees.
   I love you because there's a strength in you still. I see it when you take vitamins for our other babies, when you shush them gently with your

hand through your stomach.

I love you because you will make certain those babies know their sister. I'm sure of it.

I love you because loving you is the only other thing I'm sure of right now.

Dom xx

9. Erin

THEN — February 1999

'You need to look after your wife, Dominic.'

Erin listened behind the door to her kitchen. Her mother-in-law speaking up for her still felt a little odd and her hand rested on her chest.

'We need to look after each other,' was Dom's reply.

Erin placed her forehead on the pine architrave. He was, of course, right but where and how to begin? She moved to push the door in front of her but paused at Sophie's next words.

'She loves you. You love her. You're the one who tells me that it doesn't have to be any more complicated. Look, I'm sorry . . . ' Erin imagined her looking at her watch. 'But I've got to meet your dad at the club for lunch. I'm assuming you don't want to join us?'

Dom laughed. 'Er, no, ta, we're going for a walk down by the river.'

She loves you. You love her. It doesn't have to be any more complicated.

Erin's eyes rested on a black and white image hanging on the wall of the hallway to her left — a picture Hannah had taken of her and Dom on their wedding day — one of those snapped when they weren't looking. Both of them in profile, she was laughing at something Dom had just said.

She could never remember what it was, but the slight tilt of her head backwards said so much more than that she'd just listened to something funny. It said she'd heard something funny from someone she loved. And his eyes, his eyes gazed at her as if he couldn't believe he'd made this woman whom he loved, laugh like that. Wonder, awe in each other . . . She closed her own eyes for one brief moment.

Opening them meant she would either push the kitchen door open or opt to look further left. Left a little, where just beyond the wedding frame hung a small collage of photos of the children. A few pictures Dom had taken of their beautiful twins, Rachel and Jude, now almost eight months old, already making each other laugh. In the centre, just one of Maisie on her first birthday, covered in chocolate cake, only a month before they lost her. Erin had no need to actually look. The grinning images of her three children were burned on her brain. She swallowed hard and entered the kitchen. Crossing the porcelain tiles she'd mopped an hour earlier, she hugged her mother-in-law tight.

'Oh,' Sophie said, obviously puzzled at the embrace. 'What was that for?'

Erin shrugged. 'Just thank you.' Of all the people who had helped when Maisie died, Sophie was the biggest surprise. Overnight her mother-in-law had seemed to realise that losing a child to sudden infant death syndrome while pregnant with twins was too much for any soul.

Erin pulled her padded coat from the back of the kitchen chair. 'I'm ready if you are?' she said

71

to Dom checking the buckles on the twins' pushchair. Despite the sunshine and clear blue sky outside, both babies were cocooned against the cold. She touched Jude's face. He, unlike his sister, was fighting sleep.

'He'll nod off once we start moving.' Dom put his jacket on, wrapped a scarf twice round his neck before ushering his mother towards their front door.

'Bye, Erin!' Sophie called back. 'Give them a kiss from me when they're up!'

'See you!' Erin replied as she angled them through the awkward kitchen doorway, pushing the pushchair along the narrow hallway.

Dom stepped outside and took over. 'Daddy will drive,' he said as she closed the door behind them.

Erin pulled the collar of her coat high, pressed her gloves tight between each of her fingers. It was her favourite sort of day; a crisp, cloudless sky, cold, but cold you could wrap up against. She leaned into the pram one more time and tugged the children's blankets right up to their mouths, before sinking her gloved hands deep into her coat pockets.

Together she and Dom walked the length of Hawkins Avenue, silent, not needing to talk. They turned into Percival Way, a long, wide, tree-lined road, that bypassed the mall and the station, towards the river. They walked, crunching through iced leaves from the aging birch trees, crisp and brittle on the ground. Erin could see Jude was finally asleep.

'You were listening at the door, weren't you?'

Dom, his breath misting, was first to speak.

Erin said nothing.

She loves you. You love her.

'We need to look after each other, apparently,' he continued.

'Actually,' Erin smiled. 'I think what your mother said is that you need to look after me. I think she realises you're already well looked after.'

'Hmmm . . . '

'Do you love me?' she blurted.

'Completely. Mightily.' His ungloved knuckles whitened as he gripped the bars of the pram and she reached across for his hand as he stopped walking.

'And I love you.'

'So, we move on, don't dwell on things,' he said, his head making tiny side to side movements. 'We have each other. We have two more children.'

But no Maisie . . . She nodded.

'While you were in the loo, Mum was suggesting we focus on what it was like before.'

It had been such a short time, just nine months, nothing at all — too soon to imagine laughter, to try and recreate the 'before'.

'So,' he said. 'Is she right? Any idea on how we can inject some fun into our lives?'

Erin began to walk again. He was talking about sex. She did want to talk; she wanted to talk like they used to so very much, but not about sex. 'You mean sex?' Despite herself, she heard herself say it aloud.

'Well, that and any other fun stuff.'

'I had twins, that's two babies one after the other. My nether regions are like the Grand Canyon. If you go anywhere near them all you'll get is a loud echo.'

Dom smiled. 'I doubt that.'

'I know we have to, but I just can't even think about it . . . can we talk about something else?'

Dom following one pace behind, raised his eyebrows. She saw that he didn't even try to hide his disappointment. 'You choose,' he shrugged.

'I think right now we need sleep more than sex,' she said. Neither of them had slept well since Maisie died, and even worse since the twins were born.

'Maybe.' Dom took a small water bottle from the changing bag and drank from it.

'And maybe we need to open up to each other more, Dom.'

He laughed, tightened the cap on the bottle again. 'I'm not too great on the feelings thing, Erin — you know that.'

'So, imagine you're writing something in the book for me,' she said. 'Imagine you have to write how you're feeling today, what would you say?'

He raised his hands up and blocked his ears. 'Argh!'

Gently, she moved his hands down. 'Tell you what, I'll ask you questions and you reply.'

'Is that the time?' he nudged his head in the direction they'd just come from and grinned. 'Shouldn't we head back?'

'Indulge me.'

'Two questions,' he kept walking towards the river.

Erin tried to match his new pace. 'Right. What are you finding hard to tell me right now?' She noticed a deep frown settle as he seemed to wrestle with the question.

'I'm not sure,' he hesitated.

'Try harder,' she pressed. 'Pretend I'm not here — I'm never going to hear your answer.'

He thought about it a moment. 'In that case, I'm feeling frustrated.'

Erin said nothing. *Sex again* . . .

'I miss sex. I miss feeling that close to you. I feel tense and I know I'm an irritable bastard,' he continued.

Erin didn't disagree.

'Sometimes,' he said. 'I'm completely confused by how much I love you and the kids, yet I still feel . . . I feel almost trapped.'

Erin almost waved a white flag there and then. That word 'trapped'. Stuck. Caught. Imprisoned. Ensnared. It played to every insecurity she had ever felt since first peeing on a stick years ago — since they both realised they'd unwittingly hitched their wagons to one another.

'You did ask,' he said.

She glanced in the pram. Both children were asleep, though not for long. Jude didn't seem to nap at all during the day and when he woke, he always woke Rachel who would probably, given the chance, sleep for hours.

'Erin?' From his expression, she could tell Dom was already regretting speaking. 'This is why I hate talking about shit,' he confirmed. 'I want *you*.' He stopped walking and reached for her gloved hand. 'You. You're the one. Maybe I'm wrong but I think the good life we both want for us and the kids — it'll follow. It will still come.'

'There was a young woman called Er-in,' Erin's eyes locked on his.

'Limericks? Now with the Limericks?' He laughed quietly.

She made a face, rolling her eyes inwards. Her ability to make up silly rhymes on the hop had always made him smile.

'Who was struck on the head by a bin.'

His head was shaking.

'The rubbish tipped out, it was flying about,'

She hesitated. 'And a nappy got stuck to her chin!'

'Nope, not one of your best ones.'

'There was a young man called Dom,' Erin was walking ahead of him.

Who so wished he'd been christened Tom,

'Because Toms have more fun, from problems they run,

'And Toms go through life with aplomb . . . '

'Oh, that's good,' he nodded. 'That one's really good.'

She turned around, linked her arm with his and, with the river almost in touching distance, planted one foot firmly in front of the other and matched his pace.

There was a young couple called Carter,

Who were madly in love as a starter,

But tragedy struck, and their life, it seemed stuck,

Split into before and then after . . .

76

Sitting on a cold bench at the river, Erin realised when her son stretched an arm out and laughed out loud at a passing family of swans, that the world could still make her smile. She realised when she caught her husband looking at her — with the same look in his eyes that had been captured in the wedding photo in the hall — that his love carried on regardless of loss.

'Please,' Dom said. 'Don't think too much about what I said. It's what happens when you push me to talk. I talk complete crap.'

Erin leaned across Jude and kissed Dom gently on the lips.

When Jude almost leapt out of her arms at the sound of a boat, she allowed herself to really believe he *would* grow up, and that he might have a love of sailing. When someone nearby played a radio and a piece of music she and Dom both recognised had them humming aloud, Erin allowed herself to lock eyes with her husband; to really see him, as if for the first time, again. And when Rachel giggled as Dom made silly noises at her, Erin gripped Jude tight, closed her eyes and immersed herself in the sounds of love and life.

★   ★   ★

4th February 1999

Dearest Dom / Tom,

Today was so lovely, not so much like it used to be as like it can and will be.

Please be patient with me. I know we both

need sex but right now I can't. Not because I don't want to but because I'm afraid it won't be like before and <u>I'm scared shitless of getting pregnant again</u>.

You don't have to write here if you don't want to, but Fitz is right about these pages, for me anyway . . . I find it easier to say stuff here, things that I hold back from saying when I'm with you. Sometimes, when we're face to face, I'm so afraid of letting you down and other times, I'm just not brave enough to say things out loud. If things are said aloud, they're so much real, aren't they? Like what you said today . . .

For now, I'm just trying to hang on to what matters. You and the twins. Fitz family. But I feel as if I'm on top of a mountain trying to breathe. My lungs are tight, I can't call out. I suppose it's my own version of feeling 'trapped'.

Be patient? I'm trying.

I love you because I know when you've read this that you'll hear me.

Erin xx

★ ★ ★

5th February 1999

My love,

I will wait as long as I have to. I will do whatever it takes. But please don't ask me to write shit down. I'm shit at writing shit down.

And I hurt too.

That's all I can say here. I hurt too.

I love you mightily,

Dom xx

78

6th February 1999

Darling Dom,
You're not that shit at writing things down.
Those few lines say a lot.
All my love,
Erin xx

★   ★   ★

7th February 1999

To my super-talented wife,
Unlike you, this took me HOURS!
'There was a young woman called Erin
When I met her the room had no air-in
She danced like a tree, I knew we would be,
Together through thick and through thin.'
I think from now on for Limerick purposes you
should be called Pam and I should be called
Steve?? Rhyming would be so much easier!
I love you.
Because you're funny and you make me laugh.
Because you look sexy in heels and because you
always get the spiders out of the bath.
I love you because you put a triangle of
Toblerone in my suit pocket yesterday.
Forever yours,
Dom xx

10. Dominic

NOW — 3rd June 2017

From *The Book of Love*:
'Fuck-it, who cares why, Erin? I love you
just because I do.'

It's Lydia's party and I'm standing with a man
and woman I don't know who are having an
animated discussion about Brexit. He's ignoring
me and nodding sagely as she speaks. She's
paying no attention to me either, only interested
in jabbing the air with her forefinger to make her
point. I look around the room — a large
front-to-back ground floor of a Victorian villa,
it's packed with people, all deciding they'd rather
not risk rain outside.

The Brexit duo and I are in the exact spot
Lydia and Nigel have their pine tree in December. Except for last year. Last Christmas Lydia
understandably went all Grinch-like and trees
and baubles and sparkles and tinsel and laughing
were banned. My eyes search her out in the
crowd. She must be in the kitchen directing
operations, so I head that way, only stopping
when I hear familiar voices in the hallway. Nigel's
booming laugh followed by a quieter, higher-
pitched, tone. She sounds just like Erin — their
voices have the same timbre, but the tell-tale
hair-style confirms it's Rachel, our daughter.

I scramble past strange faces but as soon as I near, I see that she's brought Paul and I turn back on myself. Though I've heard about him, I've not met this older live-in lover of hers. Holding back, I watch from my vantage point. And while he doesn't exactly have liver spots on his hands, it's there. The age gap is, to me anyway, this big gaping thing standing tall, almost proud, between them. He's a chino-wearing forty-year-old; shirt nicely ironed, fair hair a little too coiffured for my liking — screams 'father figure' — which makes me feel a little sick. Her two-tone, blue-bottomed, dreads are tied back in a ponytail; her silver nose ring glints under the light from the ceiling spotlights as she rests her head on Nigel's shoulder. He's hugging her tight and I want to do that so badly.

'Jude here?' she asks Nigel about her brother.

'Jude's taken a few days off,' I hear his reply.

Jude is interning at the school where Nigel is head teacher and term-time breaks are not encouraged. I wonder if he's already decided teacher training isn't his thing — he's never been great at sticking to things. I keep moving, disappointed I won't see my son, acutely aware that I've always had many more flaws than him and that *I* spent the afternoon talking to a stuffed elephant.

'Oh,' Rachel replies, her neat eyebrows arching, 'he never said. C'mon,' she grabs Paul by the hand and says. 'I'm famished, let's find the birthday girl.'

I follow, feeling like the guy in that movie, *Father of the Bride*, chasing his daughter, not quite able to reach her, too many people in the way. Through the kitchen door, I can just about spot Lydia's head, when some idiot bumps into me, spilling his drink on me, carries on walking. Christ, something's telling me I should have just stayed away. I swear quietly. All I want to do is hug my daughter, hug my sister, and let them feel my arms around them.

I ask myself what Erin would say to me right now.

'*Get over yourself and get your ass in there. It's a party! Go party! And maybe see what you make of Paul?*'

Or something like that.

So, without her on my arm, that's what I try to do.

It takes very little time for me to conclude that he's a boring asshole not worthy of Rachel. If Erin were here, she'd have an elbow firmly wedged in my ribs, primed for an urgent poke. If Erin were here, she'd have hissed. 'This is *her* choice, not yours.'

But Erin is not here, so after another hour, I slip away unnoticed and take the shorter route home.

11. Erin

THEN — March 2000

'I'm not going.'

'You *are* going.'

'I can't.' Erin rubbed her palms on her jeans as she peered in the door at the cots. 'I won't be able to relax.'

'Erin, you're going.'

She watched as her friend Hannah hobbled across the living room towards where she stood in the doorway, felt her take her hand in hers.

'Lydia will be here soon. There's two of us, that's one child each — just for one night. We'll manage.'

Erin looked down, both eyebrows high, at Hannah's cast on her ankle, a souvenir from her falling from a pavement after too many cocktails.

'What?' Hannah said. 'Lydia can do any of the actual running after them.' She wagged a finger. 'You're going. Now get in there, have a shower and pack — Dom will be home in forty minutes.'

Erin hugged herself tight before moving towards her bedroom.

'He's put a lot of effort into this,' Hannah called after her. 'Just wants to whisk you away from thankless motherhood. Erin, he wants to see you happy!'

In her bedroom, Erin rubbed her neck with both hands. She hated surprises. She held her breath and exhaled slowly. She couldn't leave them . . . What if something happened? What if the *same* thing happened? *You're being ridiculous. Rachel and Jude will be two in a few months* . . . Robotically, she stripped off her clothes, dropping them in a line on the way to the shower. 'Rachel and Jude will be fine.' She repeated the sentence over and over again, gently tapping her head on the tiles as she felt the comfort of the hot water on her neck. She placed her hands by her side, repeated the words again, 'Rachel and Jude will be fine.'

In the car an hour later, Dom was like a child on Christmas Eve. He patted her thigh often during the ninety-minute journey to a small hotel on the edge of the New Forest.

'We here?' she asked as he drove up a snaking driveway.

Dom nodded. 'Just in time for a quick change before dinner.'

They held hands as they entered the building, Dom carrying their one overnight bag. In the bedroom, he bounced on the edge of the four-poster bed and she laughed, opening the window. Leaning on the windowsill she said, 'Hear that?'

'What?' he didn't move.

'Baa-aa. Baa-aa. Lambs, lots of them.'

'We're next door to a farm, it's lambing season.'

'It's spring,' she laughed. 'I love that sound and the birdsong in the morning.'

'Whereas me, I just love the sound of your laugh,' he replied.

Erin sat beside him, leaned her head on his shoulder, and laced her fingers through his. 'You should probably go and have a shower before dinner,' she said. 'I'm already done.'

'You could join me. Look . . . ' He smudged her cheek with his thumb as if removing some dirt. 'You missed a bit.'

She laughed. 'Race you?' She leapt up, tore off the two layers of clothes she wore on top. Braless, she grinned, pulled her jeans and knickers down and stepped free from them. 'I win,' she said, and turned to run.

Dom grabbed her hand. 'Don't.' His voice was no more than a whisper. 'Let me look at you.'

Instinctively, Erin crossed her arms over the breasts that had fed the twins for three exhausting months when they were newborns. Her eyes glanced down at the fleshy part around her middle and she fought the urge to cower, to hide. She knew what should happen. She *wanted* it to happen. In the last year, she could count the few times they'd made love. No, she corrected herself, they'd had sex, where their bodies met while both of them had an ear open for the kids. She longed to make love again, to be touched slowly by him again. It was time.

Dom stood and, still fully clothed, pulled her to him. She felt him stiffen against her as a memory flashed — a time just after they'd first met when they'd played strip poker. She'd won but took off her clothes for him anyway — slowly, teasing, burlesque-like. 'Not fair,' she whispered now. 'Get naked or get lost.'

She watched him peel his clothes from his

body. His sweater, he reached with one hand on the back of his neck and pulled it over his head. His jeans, and boxers, he lowered slowly.

Erin met his gaze as he rolled his socks off with his feet. 'We'll be late for dinner.' She raised her eyebrows in an arch as she took his offered hand.

'We will,' he nodded.

And together they moved, naked, slow dancing through the room, as if glued to one another at their hips. Each of them held a hand in the air at shoulder height, laced their fingers together. Their free hands curled around one another's necks. Erin stroked the skin just beneath his hairline. They circled slowly, totally in time, as if a slow ballad filled the air.

'We never did find a song.' Her lips grazed Dom's ear.

He stopped moving. 'Let's agree. We'll turn the radio on now, and whatever's playing is meant to be. It's our song.'

Erin panicked. 'What if it's that Chumbawamba thing? Or the Britney one about something one more time? Or — '

'Have faith.' Dom leaned across, keeping hold of her and switched the radio on.

Immediately, Erin smiled. ' 'At Last',' she said. 'Etta James. How perfect is that?'

'It is,' Dom agreed, pulling her back to him.

'You've never heard of it, have you?' she laughed.

'Nope, but you're right. It's perfect.'

★　★　★

86

The next morning the car needed two minutes to warm up and Erin glanced at her wrist.

'Four times,' Dom told her. 'That's every thirty seconds you've looked at your watch.'

She made a face. 'Sorry. It's just I'm anxious to get back now.'

Dom groaned. 'Can't we revel in the early morning love-making for just a little longer?'

She bit her tongue as he put the car into gear. All she wanted to do was get home, see the children, put her pyjamas on and cuddle up, all of them huddled on the sofa. She switched the radio on, kept the volume low. 'You know, I normally hate surprises, really I do, but that was a lovely thing you did. The hotel, the late dinner . . . ' They both laughed. 'Thank you, Dom,' she added, 'Just in case you didn't hear me last night, thank you.'

Her husband pursed his lips and blew her a kiss. 'But surprises are a no-no . . . ?'

She nodded.

'Have I changed your mind?'

'Maybe. Yes, I mean. Agh, no, sorry. I still hate surprises. Think it's about being in control.'

'No shit, really?' His look told her he already knew that much.

'No . . . surprises are not cool . . . like, when I found a wad of bookie receipts stuffed into your suit pocket.' Erin angled herself in the seat to look right at him. A tell-tale flush, just pink enough creeping up his neck. 'Dom?'

He stared ahead. 'That was months ago.'

'Yes, I know, but . . . ' she chose her words carefully, unsure about the timing of this conversation. She didn't want to spoil things but had promised herself to talk to him about it. 'I just want to be sure you're not risking money we can't afford to lose, especially when you go to that club of your dad's.'

She watched him slowly scratch the stubble on the end of his chin. 'I know he calls it a gentlemen's club,' she said, 'and I've already checked with your mother that there are no strippers — '

Dom laughed, turning to glance at her. 'You 'checked with my mother that there are no strippers'. How did that go down?'

'She laughed at me. Explained that it was just a posh members-only place with poker games and roulette tables.'

'That's about it. But you know all this, Erin.'

'I suppose I do. I think I just want you to tell me you never gamble there, that bookies are your limit. Betting there seems like something we definitely can't afford.'

Dom chewed his bottom lip while Erin regretted saying a word.

'You've nothing to worry about.' He patted her knee and she sighed aloud. 'Honestly.'

'Good, because money's going to be tight with the new mortgage.' Erin swallowed her concerns enough to allow a smile at the fact that from the following Tuesday they would own their own home. The flat at Hawthorn Avenue, the place she so loved living, would be theirs. Sure, it was small, the twins had to share a room, but as Dom had pointed out when the idea was first muted — stay there a few years, by which time he'd be earning more, and then they'd move to somewhere bigger. It was a hugely generous thing his parents had done — selling them the flat at the price they had paid for it five years earlier, handing them the equity already gained.

She was thinking of her generous parents-in-law when Dom spoke again.

'Do you *really* hate surprises?'

Erin laughed.

'It's just I didn't know that about you.'

'I suppose there's a lot we still don't know about one another.'

'So, say if I won the lottery and only told you when we got the cheque?'

She frowned. 'That wouldn't work. I'd want to know sooner.'

'Why?'

'The control thing. The fact that it would be something we'd both have to decide how to handle. I mean would we remain anonymous, for example? All of that would have to be decided *before* we got the cheque.'

'You wouldn't trust me to make the right decision for us?' He glanced again, eyes wide and Erin hesitated for just a fraction too long. 'Really?' Dom shook his head laughing. 'To hell with that. If we ever win the lottery, I'm going to surprise you with it.'

'If we ever win the lottery, you'd better tell me and don't try and double the amount either in a bookies or your dad's club before you get home.'

'Ooo-hhh.' He winced. 'Noted. And I've learned you definitely don't like surprises.'

Erin flushed. 'Last night was a lovely surprise, I — '

'You're just an ungrateful wench,' he teased.

'Stop, Dom, I loved it. I . . . '

'Relax, love. I'm messing with you.'

Erin dropped her head back on the headrest.

'Why don't you try and sleep for half an hour. When we're home with the twins crawling all over us, you'll wish you had.'

She closed her eyes. 'Thank you.' Reaching across she found his hand on the gear stick. 'For everything.'

★　★　★

'Surprise!'

Erin leapt backwards in the doorway almost knocking Dom over. In the same moment, she caught sight of a sea of faces lining the hallway. She spotted Fitz, at the back, as always. In front of him were her in-laws and above the picture rail running the whole length of the room was a sign: 'Congratulations on your new home!'

He whispered in her ear. 'Sorry.'

Erin forced a smile as Hannah limped forwards and handed a crying Jude to her and Dom headed to Lydia to take a silent Rachel's hand. 'I tried to tell him,' Hannah murmured. 'Tried to say you wouldn't like it.' Erin cuddled Jude, bounced him on her hip, fought a strong urge to turn around and run. Fast. Back to the forest in Hampshire. She shook her head at the glass offered by Nigel.

'Just a toast, love,' he urged, so she took it.

Lydia was by his side. 'Good time?' she asked.

'Lovely,' Erin smiled. 'Thanks for being here. Were they okay for you?'

'Good as gold until an hour ago. Jude's tired. He needs a nap.'

'I'll put him down now, then we'll catch up.'

In the twin's bedroom, she paced the floor holding Jude, whose head was crooked into her neck. With her right hand, Erin stroked the little boy's sandy hair with the barest of feather-light fingertip touches they both loved. Within minutes, he slept, a soft snore fluttering through his little mouth. 'Jude and Rachel will be fine', she whispered to the darkened room as she lay him down on his back. She blew him a kiss, put her hand on the cold brass door handle and took a very deep breath. On the other side of the door, she closed it softly, trying not to wake him and headed towards the noise of the living room to find Rachel and Dom.

Across the span of people, she spotted Fitz and smiled. It was so good to see him. Her father had a way of refilling her well, making her see the positive in everything. As she made her way to him, she watched as he stood aside and with a dramatic sweep of his hands revealed her brother, Rob, whom she hadn't seen since he visited briefly two years ago. Erin's hand went to her mouth. Next to Rob, Dom with Rachel balanced on his hip, raised a glass in her direction. 'Surprise,' he mouthed, and she burst into tears.

★ ★ ★

Darling Dom,

You do so much for me. (Thank you for the wonderful night away, and for Rob!) Thank you, thank you, Dom. You get me, and I love you.

Remember when we were lying in bed in the hotel talking and you promised then to try harder at this; try harder at coming to these pages. I think you heard me when I said I find it easier, safer.

Today, because we're feeling close right now, I'm able to open up to you about how I'm feeling, how I'm actually struggling. And also, because tomorrow, though there's no actual moving involved, we will own the flat, it feels like a new chapter. So, here goes:

If I'm honest I think you already know. I think you've probably tried to talk to me about it and I've shut you down before. I'm sorry.

I suffer with the most awful, consuming, frightening anxiety. When I feel it coming, it's terrifying because there's nothing I can do to stop it except pass through it as best I can, knowing it won't last, knowing I'll get to the other side. When you've tried to talk to me and you've used the words, 'postnatal depression' I get pissed off because this is nothing to do with having been pregnant. The fact is, my stomach's been twisting around itself for years. I've been dealing with anxiety of some sort since the day Fitz told me my mother was dying. I was sixteen.

I don't want labels or pills. I want to be able to talk to you, the man I love. But, I can't. I mean I'm doing it here, but something stops me being frank with you in person. I think it's because I can't bear the thought of disappointing you, or maybe I'm afraid you'll judge me and think I should just pull myself the hell together.

I'm not looking at you now so I'm just going to do this, tell you ALL of the stuff that's getting me down and probably contributing:

1. *Money. I know it's tight. I want to help and feel terrible that I can't add to the household pot.*
2. *Your 'dabbling' as you call it. It's not dabbling, Dom, it's gambling, and we can't afford it.*
3. *I need more, not more from you, but more than dirty nappies and I feel so guilty for feeling this. I think I want to get back into work. (Maybe re-train?)*
4. *I hate being fat. I hate my body after pregnancy. I know you try and make me feel good, that you tell me I'm still gorgeous, but I don't believe you.*
5. *I feel like I'm losing my friends because I'm such a misery and I smell of baby wipes. Lydia and Hannah went out to a wine bar last week and I only heard about it afterwards.*
6. *Sex. Hopefully we're getting back on track because I miss it too. I really do. I miss touching you. I miss you touching me.*
7. *Have you realised that it used to be me asking you if you were happy? And nowadays not a day goes by without you asking me instead, and I smile a reply 'Of course I'm happy . . . '*

When did that happen?
All my love, Erin xx

*   *   *

7th March 2000

My darling Erin,

Tomorrow, we're going to the doctors together. Don't make me bring this book to show him how you really feel. You can talk to me any time — here or in person — but you need to talk to him too, Erin, please?

Love you mightily,
Dom xx

*   *   *

8th March 2000

Darling Dom,

There was a young man called 'Steve'
Whose wife, 'Pam', in him did believe
They went to the docs, she got pills in a box
And he taught her just how to breathe . . .

I love you for a million reasons but mostly, because you're you.

Erin xx

12. Erin

She was in her last day of her second week of a three-month intensive business-skills course, when Erin cut class before lunchtime. A pin-prick of guilt niggled as she walked down the steps of the entrance to the local university. The fast-track diploma had taken every penny they had, and it took effort from both Fitz and Sophie to collect the children from playgroup and look after them while she was in tutorials. Though she was grateful to everyone for the help with her desire to get back to work, today she was restless, fretful. She'd woken up that way, reached across for Dom in the dark to find him already gone, and the twitchy feeling had stayed with her through the morning.

The day was warm and sticky, weather reports promising an Indian summer to last well into October. Erin fanned her T-shirt over the stomach she kept flat with fifty sit-ups each morning, filled her lungs with still air and looked at her watch. She could do the right thing and head back to Sophie, telling her she didn't need her that afternoon, or she could do the other right thing. The thing that had been on her mind since her lecturer had mentioned the balancing of cash books and excel spreadsheets and she'd realised she needed to see Dom. If she saw him,

95

just plugged herself into him for a few minutes, last night could be forgiven and forgotten. She'd be recharged and her impatience with the day would pass.

She turned, headed through town to the riverside office of her father-in-law's practice, stopping at a shop for supplies. As she approached the glass-fronted structure, she scanned the small car park, saw the car and headed through the revolving door.

'Hi, Paula,' she spoke to the receptionist who had been with Gerard since setting up the firm decades ago.

'Erin, how lovely to see you, is Dom expecting you?'

'No, I thought I'd see if he was free for lunch.'

'He's up in his office, is in now for the afternoon. You guys are so sweet,' Paula said.

Erin thought about the comment as she stood in the lift and pressed the button for Dom's floor. Was that how people saw them? 'Sweet.' The row they'd had the night before had been the furthest thing from sweet that she could imagine. It had been a rare screaming match — about money, again. He earned the money, she spent some of the money, yet every month *all* of the money seemed to be swallowed up. His cold reaction to the familiar argument had been why she'd stormed off to bed and why remorse had made her reach for him first thing. It was why she hadn't settled in class, why she'd needed to see him. Life was too short to argue, when they were both just doing their best.

'Aren't you meant to be in class?' He asked as soon as he saw her, before adding, 'You are so playing hooky.' He shook his head, wagged a finger in her direction and tried to hide his smile as he kissed her cheek.

'Come join me,' she suggested.

'What? I can't.'

'Of course you can. It's an emergency.'

'Can't do that. You ever hear of the boy who cried wolf? Let's not tempt fate.' He had taken a seat, gazed at her over steepled hands.

'But this *is* an emergency.'

'Erin . . . '

'Dom, do you trust me?'

Fifteen minutes later, they were sat in a darkened cinema, empty, but for them.

Though Erin hadn't paid for VIP seats, they sat in them anyway. 'Sue me,' she'd said aloud as she pulled Dom along the row.

He shuffled in his seat, tried to straighten his suit trouser crease, kept glancing around.

'Take your jacket off, relax, and turn your phone off,' she said.

'Look — '

'No, you look. We're doing this. You'll love the film. It's called *Rock Star* and it's all about this guy who plays in a tribute band for his favourite rock group and then something happens to the guy who sings, you know the lead vocal guy, and then they look to recruit a new singer and . . . ' She caught her breath. 'Pure escapism, you'll love it.'

'Erin, it's twelve thirty on a Monday, the start

of a very busy week.'

'Life is full of busy weeks. We need this. The kids are with Sophie. You can relax and enjoy it or fight me.'

She heard his loud sigh just as the opening credits rolled.

'You hungry?' her voice had dropped to a whisper.

He shook his head.

From inside her shoulder bag, she opened a plastic bag and several noisy rustlings later, she placed what looked like a sandwich on his lap.

'What is that?' he asked.

'Lunch,' Erin smiled. 'Eat.'

Dom picked it up and peered at it. 'Is this really a Toblerone sandwich?'

'It really is two triangles of Toblerone in between two slices of bread, yes.'

'Yum.'

'Don't knock it 'til you try it.'

'Not knocking it. I mean it. Yum . . . We really doing this?'

She placed a hand over his. 'When was the last time we did something silly?'

'I can't remember.'

She raised his hand, grazed it with her lips. 'We used to, way back when we met. We'd just take off to the river, the beach or maybe a National Trust house for the day. We'd pack smelly egg sandwiches and warm beer in your rucksack. We'd do karaoke nights in the King's Arms when you didn't dare tell me I can't sing.'

In the dark, she could feel his eyes on her. 'This is about last night,' he said.

'It's about last night and it's about today, now shush, it's starting.' She retrieved her hand, sat back in the wide leather seat, and dropped her head to his shoulder.

Ninety minutes later, they exited the cinema hand-in-hand.

'I should get back to work.' Dom stretched out his back.

'Why?'

'I just think I should.'

'No. You should take that infernal phone out of your pocket, the one your father insists on you having with you all the time. And you should call him and tell him that you need time with your wife.' She shrugged. 'He'll hardly sack you.'

'You should go back to class.'

'I should but I'm going home to the kids and I really want you to come too. I want us all to watch CBBC together, then after feeding them crispy pancakes and chips, put them to bed early while you and I have a more grown-up meal — together. Maybe by then we could talk about money without shouting.'

Dom looked towards the river, towards the route he would take back to work. 'You're a bad influence, Erin Carter,' he said, taking his phone from his jacket pocket and leaving a message with Paula that he wouldn't be back.

★ ★ ★

He was cooking a chilli while she read to the children. Afterwards, in the hallway, with both

Jude and Rachel tucked in for the night, she tweaked her hair in the mirror, smacked her lips together. From the kitchen she heard him speak, his voice low. He was on the goddamned mobile phone again. She hated that thing — hated the way it interrupted family life.

'Dad,' Dom was almost whispering. 'I said we'll talk about it. I'm not ignoring it. And today was unavoidable. Erin and I needed some time together.'

She smiled. *Atta boy.*

'No. I haven't told her.'

Her hand already on the door, she lowered it, poked it into her trouser pocket.

'I'm aware of that. Yes, I do know that — '

She listened to a large sigh.

'Dad, can we do this tomorrow? I've told you I'm not ignoring it. I appreciate what you've — '

Erin shoved the door open and stared at him.

'Gotta go, Dad. See you in the morning.'

Her husband hung up the phone and smiled widely at her. 'Just ready to dish up, think I might have gone a little overboard on the chilli.'

'What was that about?'

'What?' he asked spooning rice and beef chilli into large bowls. 'Can you get some water?'

Erin turned the cold tap on, filled two glasses and sat at the table. 'What were you talking to Gerard about?'

'Just some work stuff.'

'What did you mean when you said you hadn't told me. What haven't you told me?'

Dom frowned, two vertical creases deepening between his eyes. 'No, that wasn't about telling

100

you something. It was Louise in work. Client's not happy with her latest drawings and I've got to find a way to tell her. Eat, don't let it get cold.'

She could smell it immediately — the clear scent of bullshit. She heard it in the waver in his voice. She could see it in his clear avoidance of her eyes. As she reached for his hand when he handed her a bowl, she could feel it — that reassuring tap-tap of his on the back of her palm, a touch that didn't comfort. And she tasted it in the food, as if whatever lie he'd just told her had been laced in chilli flakes.

* * *

10th September 2001

Darling Dom,
You lied to me tonight. I don't know why but I know you lied. Now I want to know why. And don't give me some crap about Louise's drawings in work.
Here's the place to spit whatever it is out.
Come on. I can't shout or scream. At least not until I read your reply.
Whatever it is, tell me, because the thought that you've lied already has my stomach churning. Whatever it is can't be as bad as what I've imagined.
Dom, I love you because I know there are depths to you that I don't always see but I believe in you. I trust you. So, be honest with me.
All my love
Erin xx

101

* * *

11th September 2001

To my beautiful wife, Erin Carter,

The woman of my dreams and the only woman I have ever loved. I didn't lie last night and us arguing over whether I did or didn't seems so puerile right now, so let's not.

Because all those people died in those towers today and you and I are still here.

I can't get my head around it. The horrific images have been stockpiling in my head since it happened this morning. You and I know more than most; we know how one bloody awful moment can be a turning point in two people's lives. But thousands of people, in so few moments, so many dead, and so many other lives completely destroyed . . . It's hard to believe that New York Minute is even real.

What sort of a world do we live in? What sort of a world are we raising children in?

I want to understand yet I never want to understand.

Dom xx

* * *

12th September 2001

Dom,

Love is far more powerful than hate.
Love is far more powerful than loss.
That's what we will teach our children.
I love you because you feel.
Erin xx

13. Dominic

From *The Book of Love:*
'You have faith in the human spirit.
And God. Your God, Erin, not mine,
but I still love you for it.'

The day after the birthday party I wander downstairs to an angry answerphone message from Lydia telling me off for leaving without saying goodbye.

Shit.

Outside, the blue-grey light of the early morning backdrops the silhouettes of the trees. Without checking the time, I can tell it's about seven. Already the air in the house is warm and I go out to the rear garden, glad of the cooler breeze. The garden, full of begonia, freesia and gladioli, erupting from bulbs I planted months ago, is awash with colour. I take a walk, the earth still damp underfoot from yesterday's downpour. I touch leaves, smell the flowers, and am back standing in the doorway, asking myself what might be next, reminding myself of my own words to Erin 'Life unfolds just the way it should', when I hear the sound I've been waiting for.

My eyes dart to the other end of the hallway. The click of the key turning twice in the lock echoes in the space and there she is. She pushes a suitcase in the door ahead of her and the relief I feel when I see her face is total. She's home. She's wearing those bug eye sunglasses that I hate, probably because she won't have slept much on the flight — never does. Her slim ankles poke out the end of skinny jeans and, on top, her white T-shirt has a small dribble of something at boob-level, coffee probably.

'Hey you,' I say. 'Surprise!'

Front door still open, she removes the glasses, then grins widely.

It's as if the house suddenly fills with the sound of her laughter, as if an empty vacuum crams with needy air. If I were outside, looking in, the house would be smiling too.

'You're home.' I state the obvious.

She runs to me, grabs hold of me. 'Dom . . . '

My hand strokes her straightened hair, and I inhale her. I don't move until she does. 'You alright?' I whisper.

'I'm okay. It's so good to see you. You look . . . tired.' She runs a hand slowly down the side of my face.

'Lydia's birthday.' I say, deciding it was the reason sleep evaded me last night.

She grimaces. 'I'm sure I wasn't missed.'

'*I've* missed you,' I hear myself say.

She kisses me softly on the lips.

'You have a good time?' I ask as she pulls away.

'Tiring. I'm exhausted too.'

'And Rob okay?' I ask about her brother and Mel, his wife, and their two kids and am greeted with monosyllabic answers so I leave her there staring out the kitchen window, looking at the view of blooms that had captivated me ten minutes earlier. Sixteen days in New York. And now she's home. She's back in Valentine's. With me.

'I'd better call him, Rob, he'll know I landed hours ago.' She heads back into the hallway towards the stairs. 'I'll use the phone in the bedroom.' She stops a moment, looks back at me. A familiar anxious look criss-crosses her forehead. 'And we're okay?' she asks.

I give her a reassuring nod.

'I'm glad,' she says and with that, she's gone, and I stare at the space she took up as if she's left damp footprints on the tiled floor.

Shortly after, I find her, face planted in a pillow, fully clothed. Letting her sleep, I lie beside her on our bed and study the fine lines and contours of her still beautiful face.

★ ★ ★

Having slept for too long, she's wired and still on New York time. I stay up with her, chatting. Her legs tucked under her, she's next to me on the sofa sipping a large glass of white wine.

'That won't help you sleep,' I warn her.

She frowns, then eyeballs me. 'Tell me about the party. Was it a bit weird for you? And how was Lydia?'

'I didn't stay long. She was on autopilot at first and then quite pissed. She was leaning on Hannah by the time I left.'

105

Erin nods as if she's not surprised.

'Of course, you could go and see her, see for yourself.' I risk the words because I need to do everything I can to help make things right between them. It's vital I get them talking again.

'Not going to happen.' She shakes her head. 'Were the kids there? I haven't been able to reach them on the phone.'

'Rachel's working tonight, she did say that, and Jude — who knows — apparently he took Friday off from school and is away for a few days.'

Erin's frown deepens. 'Weird that he's not answering his phone.'

'He's a grown-up, Erin.' I grin. 'Or he likes to think so. As grown up as a boy can be at nineteen.'

'Exactly . . . ' Erin peers over her glass at me. 'And Paul? What did you think about him?'

I hesitate. 'From what I could tell, I thought he was a very pleasant young man.'

She snorts. 'No, you didn't,' she says, 'you thought he was a very pleasant *old* man.'

'Okay,' I concede. 'I thought he was boring as fuck and far too old for her.'

Erin laughs. 'He *is* thirty-eight. Exactly twice her age.'

'Shit.'

'Yup.'

Since I saw Paul for the first time last night, I've been trying to dispel all the stereotypical notions of sugar-daddies that I have, because Rachel is happy and Paul, he seems happy too.

I'm running through it in my head when Erin speaks again.

'Maybe they're in love . . . '

My head moves left to right slowly. 'What can they possibly have in common, Erin?'

'What did we ever have in common?' she asks. 'Seriously,' she adds. 'You come from money and have always been blasé about it. You have a university education and became an architect, then set up your own specialist firm. Squash with Nigel three times a week, love sport and fancy cars. And you've always cared what people think. Me? My family had nothing, I worked in a boutique after leaving school and, admittedly, went on to help run a business. I count pence and pounds — believe in saving. I hate sport of any kind and the only exercise I get is walking. I drive a ten-year-old Mini and, even during my most anxious moments, don't give a shit what people think of me.'

She doesn't stop to draw breath and I'm mulling what she's said when she pokes me. 'Dom?'

'That's a list of stuff that doesn't matter,' I reply. 'It's got nothing to do with what we *do* have in common.' She's quiet as I speak.

'We've been together for most of our adult life. That's what we have in common. We share the children, our home, and our friends. You should read some of our Book of Love and remember just how much we both share.'

Erin bites her lower lip.

'Our determination to survive, our ability to work hard at our marriage, the way we both believe in love. That rare forever love . . . ' I'm on a roll.

'Okay, okay.' She smiles, holds up a hand.

'He's nearly twenty years older than Rachel. My concern would always have been, and is, whether they can ever want the same things at the same time if they tried to share a life together.'

'Okay,' she repeats. 'But Rachel really knows herself better than most nineteen-year-olds. She's comfortable in her skin — much more so than Jude. She knows her own mind and is pretty good at expressing it.'

I smile. 'That she is. And as Fitz would say, 'she didn't lick that off a stamp . . . ' '

'You remember,' Erin adds, 'remember way back when you couldn't express any feelings at all? I dragged you kicking and screaming to writing things down.'

'Yeah, and do you remember when you were an irritating over-sharer?'

We both laugh. Without realising it, she has picked up Elephant and is stroking his only ear as her head leans on my shoulder.

'I'm so glad you're here,' she whispers.

'Where else would I be,' I reply, ignoring the pounding, drumbeat thought in my head:

This can't last.

14. Erin

The last month of spring was always the toughest of the year. Erin could almost taste the flavour of fear in her mouth come the first of May. April thirtieth, everything would be fine: her anxiety would be under control, life would be ordered, routines in place, and then the new month and the countdown to the anniversary would begin. It did, as people promised, seem a little easier each year, but, she thought as she lay in bed, it could still derail her if she let herself think about it. And earlier today, in her new working environment, she had allowed herself to think about it, and the thoughts had lined up and rammed into one another until she couldn't breathe.

Lydia had brought her home from work, put her to bed and looked after the children until Dom came in.

She could hear them now; talking at the front door, their voices hushed. Erin blinked slowly in the darkened room. Grateful for the flow of air from the open window, she tried to focus on the sounds coming from the television in the next room. She could tell it was the children's favourite DVD; Maisy, the tales of a tiny white mouse and her mates. Her children happily watching Maisy Mouse.

109

When the door opened, she closed her eyes as she felt him sit on the edge of their bed and take her hand.

'Not the best day, eh?' he whispered.

Erin said nothing.

'Do you want to talk about it?'

No, she didn't. She didn't want to talk about how she'd been standing in the middle of the control room when it happened. She didn't want to tell him how she'd felt adrenalin pulse through her body in shockwaves, how her lungs had emptied of air, how her whole body had felt paralysed with fear. It was the worst anxiety attack she'd ever experienced.

'Erin?'

No. She didn't want to tell him how Isaac, her boss of only four months, had known exactly what to do, how a room full of health professionals had helped her breathe her way through it. No. She didn't want to tell him, and he didn't need to know.

She had thought she could do it.

Erin pulled her hand away and curled up in the bed. 'You'll just tell me you were right. You'll be nice about it, but whatever you say, you'll really mean 'I told you so'.'

'That's not fair.' Dom murmured. 'Yes, I thought working right in the hub of the ambulance service might be asking too much. I know, I know,' he held a hand up. 'I know it's a 'part-time PA role' but you're still there, immersed in 999 shit — hearing whatever — '

'I thought I could help in my own way.'

'I know. Now move over, Grumpy.'

Erin shifted as Dom climbed in beside her, sighed deeply when he wrapped his arms around her. 'You should have called me.' He stroked her hair.

'I didn't want you to know.'

'Why not? For God's sake, Erin, why not?'

That's why not, Erin thought, that slight hint of exasperation. Dom was someone who was so in control of everything in his life. How could she begin to explain today's episode when she couldn't yet rationalise it herself? All she could tell him was one moment she was walking across the control room, a tray with two coffees on it in one hand, one for Isaac and one for her, and the next minute she was bent in two, drinks askew, unable to breathe.

'Have you been taking your pills?'

'Yes.' He didn't need to know that either. She didn't want to hear him talking calmly about how the pills kept her steady. And he didn't want to hear that the truth was that she'd stopped taking them because she'd been feeling so well.

'The money is helpful,' was the start of her defence. 'It goes straight into the moving-house-pot.'

'Being there. In that place,' he replied. 'I still think it's too much for you.'

'The money helps us,' she repeated, 'and I have to work. I *want* to work.'

'I realise that, but we have to find something where you're not surrounded by other people's disasters!'

There. There it was again. That slight irritation. She chomped her bottom lip — maybe she was being unfair to him. 'I wanted to be somewhere I could make a little bit of a difference.'

He kissed her head. 'Wherever you are, Erin, you make a difference.'

She began to cry. Soft fat tears dripped onto his shirt sleeve and he never moved.

'Something else will come up,' he whispered. 'And you'll love it, and everything will be okay.'

She nodded.

'But you need to take your meds.'

She nodded again, swallowed another needless denial and stopped short of asking for the bottle there and then, so she could take a few together, so that they might help chase away the crippling, invasive dread lodged in her chest since midday.

There would never be a better time, she thought, to try and tell him, to try and explain what it was like. Yet, she held her words, unsure if they would spill later in writing, and unsure if she would even try. How do you explain a blindsiding paralysing irrational panic to some-one who is in complete control? Even if you do love him. Even if he does love you?

'Once,' Dom lay on the flat of his back and pulled her up onto his chest. 'Once I drove into a bollard in the supermarket car park and never told you. The twins were babies and they were in their car seats in the back. It was just a bump, they were fine — I got the scratch fixed and never said a word.'

'What?'

'I'm just letting you know we all tell white lies. Take your pills, Mrs Carter.'

She tapped his chest twice. 'Once, I lost my purse and it had a whole week's shopping money in it. I got the purse back, no money, but we had a week of beans on toast and I never told you either.'

Dom laughed, and she inhaled the sound of him. 'I hate it when I'm trouble,' she whispered, 'when I'm less than perfect in your eyes.' She sat up in the bed, grateful for the dusky light, imagined his brown eyes boring holes in her own.

He reached up and stroked her face and she covered his hand with hers. 'When will you learn that even when you're trouble — you're perfect,' he said.

'Now *that*'s just not true but keep talking.' She hugged him. 'I'm sorry. I'll take the pills.'

★   ★   ★

'So, what's he like? Your boss, the guy I met the other day?' Lydia asked the question the following Friday night when they met Hannah for a drink.

'He's quite cool.' Erin's reply was instinctive. Isaac *was* cool. She'd found it hard to age him but had guessed at late thirties. He was single, a little bit flirty, but not in a heavy-handed way, and he liked to laugh.

'You're smiling,' Hannah frowned. 'And your boss is 'cool'. Hmmm . . . '

'He *is* cool. He wears a uniform with flip-flops.'

'You fancy him!'

113

'I really don't.' Erin batted the comment away and sipped from her soft drink, respecting the fact that alcohol and her pills didn't mix. 'Besides, he won't be my boss after next week. I've resigned.'

'Oh, Erin.' Lydia's hands went to her face. 'I'm sorry.'

'Dom was right. You were all right. It wasn't the best place for me.'

Erin was smiling at the tumbleweed silence when Lydia grabbed her arm.

'Come work for me! Sorry, *with* me. You can manage the Bean Pod while I look for premises for the next one.'

Though Erin admired all that Lydia had achieved in opening the first of her gourmet-coffee-pod-cafés right opposite the university, she hoped her face didn't reveal exactly how much she didn't want to pour coffee for a living. She winced as Lydia dug her in the ribs.

'And you won't be pouring coffee,' Lydia read her mind. 'This is just the first premises in my five-year plan. By the time we reach 2007, we could be ready to franchise the idea.'

Erin rubbed her diaphragm, arched her eyebrows.

'I'm being serious,' Lydia said. 'I've just advertised for a manager. Now the first Bean Pod is up and running, I need someone who can do the books for the company; someone whom I trust and who's business savvy. You'd be brilliant, and coffee, trust me, it's the way forward.'

'Yeah,' Hannah's expression was dubious. 'A few major American firms think so too.

'We're different.' Lydia smiled. 'Small premises, a narrow bar at the window with six stools maximum. Our idea is get them through the door for their takeaway coffee — always cheaper than the Americans', by the way — give them a free mini-muffin, yes free, but what keeps them coming back is we sell the best coffee. We really do.'

Despite herself, Erin found herself thinking about it.

'Come on, Erin, it would be fun. Join the world of the flat white, espresso, cappuccino, mocha latte, you know you want to. Do it for three months and if you hate it, no hard feelings. You could be part-time, work mornings, some days from home. I know you want to be around for the kids after school.'

And in that moment, Erin decided to do something she rarely did. She agreed. She agreed to go and work for Lydia for the next three months at least without thinking about it, without analysing it, without measuring up the pros and cons. She just breathed deep and nodded.

Minutes later, she was nursing the one glass of celebratory champagne she'd allowed herself when Hannah blurted, 'There's something I need to tell you guys.'

Erin noticed an immediate twitch on her friend's scarlet-painted mouth.

'Now seems like a good moment,' Hannah took a deep breath.

'What?' Lydia stared.

'I've met someone, no one you guys know.

115

We've been seeing each other a short while.'

'Someone at work?' Erin asked. Hannah worked as a croupier in a five-star London hotel casino.

'Someone *through* work,' she said.

'Name, date of birth, physical details please,' Erin counted out on her hand.

'Girls, I haven't known him very long.'

'He must have a name,' she said.

'Walter, Walt,' Hannah replied, rubbing a spot on her arm.

Lydia giggled. 'Walter? That's it, he's seventy-five, isn't he, that's why you've said nothing?'

Erin could sense Hannah's discomfort. 'She's only teasing,' she said. 'How old *is* Walt?'

'He's thirty-six.'

'A bit older than you then.'

Hannah nodded.

'Do we get to meet him?' Lydia asked. 'I'm not sure I've ever known you to be quite so coy about someone.'

'He lives in Brighton.'

'Nice,' Erin nodded. 'I'd love to live by the sea. Does he work in London?'

'Yes.'

'Okay, this isn't right.' Lydia grabbed Hannah's hand. 'Why haven't you told me, told us, about him before?'

'I just don't want to jinx it, Jesus!'

Erin's instincts immediately fired up as her friend's discomfort increased and snippets of recent conversations she'd half had with Hannah came back to her. 'He's married, isn't he?' she whispered.

Hannah whipped her head around to them, was just about to deny it when her face crumpled. 'Please, it's not what you think.'

'Does he have children?' Lydia asked quietly.

'No. No children . . . '

'Jesus, Hannah. A wife . . . ' Erin watched Lydia's hand cover Hannah's and Hannah toss it off as if she'd been scalded.

'Don't judge me,' she snapped. 'I love him. I've tried not to, but I love him.'

All the other sounds in the busy wine bar — the buzz of people talking, the clatter of plates from behind the open pass at the restaurant end, the distant ring of a telephone — everything quietened but for the sound of Erin's own voice.

'No judgement, Hannah,' she said, but inside she thought she was. She found herself wondering if his wife knew, whether this was some awful arrangement they'd agreed to live with or worse, if she knew nothing about it at all. But, in the years she'd known Hannah, a time when she'd seen lovers, and two relationships, come and go, Erin had never heard her friend use the word 'love'. She looked at her glass, almost empty and though she knew she shouldn't, she filled it one more time.

'Definitely no children?' Lydia asked again.

Hannah shook her head. 'Definitely not.'

'You say you love him. How does he feel about you?' Lydia asked. 'You said you haven't been with him very long — '

'It's been six months. He feels the same.' Hannah said the words very slowly and swallowed visibly.

'Six months?' Lydia folded her arms, unimpressed.

'We love each other,' Hannah repeated.

'What's love anyway?' Lydia's tone was curt, and Hannah replied instantly.

'It might not be the same for you and me.' She sought Erin's eyes. 'I find myself thinking of him all of the time when I'm not with him. And all the time we're not together I wish we were. He makes me smile as soon as I see him, I mean just catching sight of him makes me smile and then when we're together we laugh a lot.'

Erin looked away.

'I miss him when he's gone,' Hannah continued. 'Sex with him is just . . . ' She began to cry, tears that Erin could see needed to be cried, shared, with them, her friends. 'I realise now I just shagged other men and they shagged me. With Walt, I'm making love to the man I want to be with, it's like being home.'

Hannah grabbed both Lydia's and Erin's hand. 'Please, I need you guys to understand.'

Despite herself, despite struggling with a hundred 'buts', Erin found herself thinking, *sounds like love to me*.

* * *

9th May 2002

Dear Dom,

It doesn't seem like four years since she died; since she was bouncing on my knee, yet today when I closed my eyes and thought of Maisie, I felt that the picture I have of her in my head is fading.

118

I had to focus hard to remember the arch of freckles around her nose, her tiny pursed lips . . . I know our focus is on our blessings, you and me and the twins but I don't ever want to forget her, Dom.

We don't ever really talk about her, do we? And we've absolutely never talked about that night, have we? The twins being born so soon after made sure we had to get on with things. But, that night, it was you who found her and I don't think I've ever told you how grateful I am that I was at least spared that. And you dealt with everything afterwards while I fell in a pregnant heap. I've never thanked you for taking care of everything back then — thank you, Dom. I mean it.

Will you tell me that you're alright? Sometimes, I wonder . . .

You're the one so in control while I'm the blubbering fool buoyed up by pills, but are you? Are you in control or are you just bloody good at pretending you are?

For example, earlier, you and I were just chatting, avoiding all talk of the anniversary tomorrow (where I'll go to church with the twins like I always do and you'll . . . what will you do, Dom? What is it that you do on 10th May to remember her?) so we were talking about Hannah when suddenly you were tying your trainers and gone — off on another 10K run. I was left drowning in the conversation that we almost had!

I love Hannah. And I'm not judging her. I really don't think I am. I do believe she's in love with this guy, but it doesn't make what she's doing right. I suppose I'm just not sure how it'll all end for her (meaning I know marriage and kids were always

119

what she talked about wanting) and in the meantime how's it going to affect the friendship group? Anyone Hannah loves, we have to welcome, right?

I'm confused. Genuinely. And I'd really like to talk to you about it without you changing into running gear while I'm trying.

I'd ask you what you're running away from if I thought you'd answer me. I think you're afraid. What are you afraid of, Dom?

This has turned into a bit of a rant. I didn't mean it to be. I just wanted to reach out to you. Let me know you're alright. Let me know we're alright?

And Dom, I love you, because when you come home from your run, all sweaty and just wanting a shower, you'll look at the mirror in the hall and sigh loudly. You'll grab the neon post-it with your name on it and scrunch it up. You'll want to toss it on the floor and swear at me under your breath, but you won't. You'll reach in the drawer, and then you'll write something in here too.

I know you will.

Erin xx

⋆ ⋆ ⋆

10th May 2002

Darling Erin,

I'm not like you, my love. It's because of this we work. You're the yin to my yang and all that bollocks. I know you like these pages, but, to be honest, I just find it silly. But I'll try my best, for you.

I really am alright. Of course, I miss and grieve for our beautiful little girl but as I said, we're different.

The only thing I'm afraid of right now is your need to forensically delve into things. And see, I come from the school that says if you go looking for something, you'll find it!

So, my fear is more that if we try and take things apart too much to see how they work, that maybe they won't fit back together again.

Love you mightily.

Dom xx

P.S. Hannah and this bloke she's seeing. Why are you even thinking about it? It's her business and it will never last, so we need never worry about whether he'll fit in with us or not.

P.P.S. And so you know, I'm just running to keep fit!

P.P.P.S. Every year on Maisie's anniversary, I make a phone call. I never have any idea, until the day, who I'll be talking to, or if I'll be talking to anyone. It's something I do since you and I were first in contact with the local SIDS group about doing some fundraising. I try and find out if there's someone who recently lost a child to SIDS and whether they're happy to talk. And I talk to them. If they want. That's what I do when you go to church.

★   ★   ★

11th May 2002

Dear Dom,
I love you because you talk to a stranger about

121

their pain and probably really help them through a dark time. I hate that you can never really share yours with me.

I get it. I just hate it.

Erin xx

15. Erin

THEN — December 2003

'Boy, am I glad to see you.' Erin held onto her father at her front door.

'Hey! I love it!' Fitz touched her shorter hair. 'What made you do that?'

Closing the door, she took his coat, never getting the chance to reply.

'Hello, mate.' Fitz bent down and lifted Jude into his arms. 'You'll be too big for me to do this soon!'

'Rachel's just getting her pyjamas on,' Erin said. 'Do you mind reading their bedtime story while I get ready?'

'Sure.' Fitz lowered the boy. 'Sorry I'm a bit late, the traffic was crazy — got stuck near the big M&S. Thousands of people buying last-minute presents and sprouts . . . ' He shuddered and laughed aloud. 'Nasty little green things!'

'Grandad!' Rachel peered her head around their bedroom door. 'Do you know it's only one more sleep until Father Christmas comes?'

'I do! Have you been the best girl?' Fitz dropped himself to her level, to her enthusiastic nodding.

'Jude was horrible to Mummy though.'

'What?' he said. 'I don't believe that.'

Erin sighed as her father's eyes landed back on Jude. 'He doesn't like my haircut,' she explained.

'She looks like a boy,' Jude said.

'Never!' Fitz laughed. 'Your mummy is far too pretty to look like any boy I know. That gorgeous smile and see those lovely green eyes.' He offered a hand to Jude. 'Come on, let's get you two into bed and I'll tell you the story of Oz and the Emerald City that's just the same colour as Mummy's eyes. She needs to go and get ready now.'

'Thank you,' she mouthed the words to her father and went into the bathroom where her clothes hung on a hanger on the back of the door. She turned both taps on the bath, knowing there was little time for a soak but needing one to ease the tension in her body. After pouring some salts in the water, she sank into it, conscious of the low laughter coming from the children's bedroom. Fitz would have them immersed in the land of Oz while she immersed herself in her watery real life for a few precious minutes.

Erin kept her head above the waterline and practised some deep breathing techniques she'd learned in a book. She had done everything. The 'to-do-before-Christmas list' at the Bean Pod office had been completed; every invoice had been tallied, every order for the new year made, and the papers for Lydia's next business premises had been lodged with the solicitors. All the presents were wrapped and stored safely away from any risk of the children finding them. All she had to do was put them under the tree when she and Dom got back that night. Christmas day dinner tomorrow was at Sophie and Gerard's, so she had nothing to worry about there. And tonight, Fitz was here to look after the kids while she and Dom joined their friends for the monthly pub quiz at the Coach and Horses.

She flinched at a knock on the door.

Dom's voice. 'It's me, I'm home. Just changing — you okay?'

'Yep, I'll be out in a minute.' She could have stayed there another hour, but she opened her eyes and looked at her outfit. Black jeans and a black sparkly top that Hannah had given her last Christmas. A night out was just what she needed — glad rags, makeup on, a few drinks, not too many that she'd forget Father Christmas, but just enough to unwind and have a laugh. With the doctor's help over the last few months, she'd managed to cut her medication to such low levels that they were both hopeful the new year would mean she could consider cutting it out altogether.

Standing, she shivered and wrapped herself in the towel she'd placed on the heated rail. As she dried herself, she caught sight of her reflection in the full-length mirror. Definitely not a boy. She tilted her head, raised her breasts a fraction with both hands. Not bad. Not as pert as they had once been, but not bad. Turning to the side she patted her flat stomach. No six pack but not bad either. She slipped into the only matching black underwear she owned, hesitated a moment and then put her ankle boots on before mussing her hair, tweaking it into the shape it had been hours earlier when leaving the salon.

Erin smiled, gathered her clothes and left the bathroom.

'Wow!' Dom stared at her as she walked into their bedroom and shut the door. 'Shit, your hair. Wow!'

She stood there, all six-foot of her in heels, her hands on her hips, and watched each emotion cross his face. A wide-eyed lust for a gamine stranger, then shock that the stranger was her. 'You look . . . '

'I look good,' she interrupted. 'I feel totally knackered, but I look good.'

From the other side of their bed he seemed to appraise her head to toe. 'You look hot.'

'You like it?' She touched her head.

Dom came around to her and put his hands on her waist, stared at her face. 'I love it. Makes your eyes brighter.' He kissed her gently. 'Now, get dressed before I throw you on the bed and shag you senseless.'

She rolled her eyes. 'Jude hates it, told me I look like a boy,' she said as she pulled up her jeans. 'He's been making weird faces at me all afternoon.'

'He'll forget about it tomorrow morning.' Dom began to sing softly about Santa Claus comin' to town.

'Go and rescue Dad while I throw on some makeup, will you?' she nudged him as he brushed his lips against her neck.

'Easy access to your beautiful neck, Mrs Carter. Love it.'

Minutes later, Erin joined him and the children. 'Be good for Grandad,' she told them.

'Or Father Christmas won't come,' Rachel said gravely.

'Yes, he will.' Jude said.

Erin's eyebrows arched. 'Nope,' she said. 'Not to naughty children.'

'He always comes,' Jude replied. 'And I'm a good boy.'

She smiled and leaned in to him in the bottom bunk. 'You're the best boy in the world.' Erin felt her son's arms wrap tightly around her neck. 'I miss your hair, Mummy,' he whispered as she inhaled the soft scent of baby shampoo from his.

'I'm still your mummy, just with shorter hair,' she kissed his cheek.

'Maybe tomorrow I'll like it,' her son offered, and she could feel Dom's smile behind her back.

'Night, darling,' she said before standing and grabbing hold of her daughter in the bed above.

'I like it today,' Rachel whispered into her ear.

'I'm glad,' she tucked Rachel in. 'And you're the best girl in the world.'

'I am,' she agreed, and Erin smiled at her small, serious face. Behind her, Dom had left the room.

'You both need to go to sleep really soon,' she said backing out towards the door.

'Mummy, how long will you and Daddy be?' Jude had turned towards her.

'Not long. We'll be back very soon.'

'Are you going out with Aunty Lydia and Uncle Nigel?'

'Yes. And Hannah too.' Hannah, Erin knew,

127

would be alone — with Walt, the man she still claimed to be in love with, at home with his wife over Christmas.

'To the pub?'

Erin grinned. 'Yes.'

'But you'll be back before Father Christmas comes?'

'Of course.' Her hand was on the door handle.

'You're not allowed see him, else he won't leave presents.'

'We'll be home way before then.'

'Okay. But what if Rudolph doesn't eat the carrot? Will he . . . '

'Jude, go to sleep,' Rachel called down from the top bunk.

Erin felt Dom appear at her shoulder.

'Sleep, now, both of you,' he said. 'Night, night.'

She closed the door gently.

'Come on,' he said. 'Or we'll be here all night.' She took the coat, gloves and scarf he handed her, glanced back at the bedroom door. There was always a moment, just before she would leave the children, a moment where she felt she should stay; a split-second where Maisie's death would wrap itself around her like a shroud, a feeling that time had taught her to consciously shed.

'Dad, call us if they don't settle,' she said, kissing his cheek.

'Go, go out and have some fun,' Fitz told them as he ushered them out of the flat.

Outside, Erin shivered. 'It's bloody Baltic,' she

whispered. Almost running to keep pace with Dom, she looked back and told herself everything would be fine at Hawthorn Avenue without her. 'So, what do you really think of our son sulking over my haircut?'

'I really think he won't even notice tomorrow.'

She heard Dom thump his hands together to warm them. 'He's so determined though,' she continued. 'I'm not so sure, when he makes his mind up about something, he's so stubborn and — '

'Erin, he even said so earlier! 'Maybe tomorrow I'll like it.' He's five years old. Tomorrow he'll be playing with his toy cars on his toy road and will love you just the way you are.' He paused before speaking again. 'There once was a girl with a mane.'

Erin laughed.

'Who thought her long hair was a pain.'

She linked arms with him as he struggled to continue.

'So, she had it all cut,' she interrupted, the air frosting around her words. 'Her son thought she was nuts. But come morning he'd love her again.'

★   ★   ★

Four hours later, after pub food and wine and laughing out loud with their friends, Erin was back in the kitchen staring blankly at Dom as he scratched his head.

'That's not funny,' she said.

'I'm not kidding, Erin, I can't find it.'

She watched as he rooted through the 'tat drawer' in the kitchen, her stomach doing somersaults.

'I know I put it in here.' Dom emptied the contents onto the kitchen table and sifted through them.

'You have to find it.' She was careful not to shriek, not to panic.

'It's not here.' Dom's hands steepled over his nose. 'Let me think.'

She followed him to the living room to where he searched another drawer, to where Fitz remained sitting on the open sofa bed, the television muted.

'We simply have to get it open,' she whispered staring through the window to where Dom's car was parked under the streetlamp just outside the house. The top box, which they'd bought the previous year, when they'd holidayed in Cornwall, had seemed the ideal place to hide the wrapped Christmas presents, space being a problem in the small flat. At the time, they'd both thought it was genius. Until now, midnight on Christmas Eve, and the key to their state-of-the-art impregnably strong, top box was nowhere to be found.

'I'm sorry, Dad,' Erin apologised. 'You probably just want to get to bed.' She chewed her lips, wondered if they could tell the children the next morning that they'd counted the sleeps wrong. No — somehow, they had to get into the box.

Together they changed their clothes and armed themselves with knives and forks and a hammer and a drill with only a minimal battery charge.

Outside a low-lying fog gathered around them as Erin knelt on the empty side of the roof rack and tugged while Dom tried the drill in the lock.

When the whirring noise stopped, and the lock still hadn't budged, she began to cry.

'Don't,' Dom said. 'We'll get this thing open if it's the last thing I do.'

She stood up, balanced herself, rubbed her arms and watched from above as Dom played with the lock with the narrowest of drill pieces.

Neither was aware of a car pulling up opposite them.

'Anything we can help you folks with?'

They both turned at the same moment to see two uniformed police officers approaching.

'Well, good to see the neighbourhood watch scheme works,' Dom looked at Erin.

'We can explain,' Erin said almost losing her balance. 'It's our car, our top box and it's full of the kids' Christmas presents.'

'Name, please,' the taller man said, and Erin had an instant vision of both her and Dom being flung into cells overnight.

'Dominic Carter,' Dom almost growled, 'we live in there, 27a Hawthorn Terrace, and you'll find that this vehicle is in my name.' He reached inside his pocket, pulled out a wallet and handed them his photocard driving licence. 'Now I appreciate you've got to go over there to your nice warm car and huddle to check what I've just told you is right but after that, could you please just help?'

Erin stared at him, never prouder. 'What he said,' she said, smiling.

Moments later, the officer approached again while the smaller man searched in their boot for something. 'Pretty indestructible, these things.' He shook his head. 'Still, Christmas Eve, you gotta try . . . John, there, is getting the tools we have.' He jerked his head towards his colleague.

'I'll bring the drill in and put it back on charge,' Erin said. 'Hot drink anyone?'

'Oh, yes please, ma'am,' the man named John replied. 'I could murder a sugared black coffee.'

Within minutes Erin had taken orders, had enough cups lined up on the counter and the kettle boiled. Fitz stood watching her as he plugged the drill battery in, Dom's dressing gown hanging open over his clothes. 'Sorry,' he said, looking down at himself. 'The heating's gone off and it's all I could find quickly.'

Erin hugged him. 'Jeez, for just a second I thought we'd be taken away in cuffs.' She laughed, a slightly hollow, nervous sound. 'We will get it open, won't we?'

'We will and if we don't we'll go through their toys and root out things they haven't seen or played with in ages and wrap them in newspaper. They're five years old.'

She stirred instant coffee into the boiling water, added milk to one, sugar to two. 'You remember giving me our leather book wrapped in newspaper?'

'I do. An idea borrowed wrapped in something old,' he shrugged.

'The best wedding present we got.' She took

two cups and smiled as she passed.

'Good. I'm glad.'

'But by Christ at Christmas, we're getting that boot open. Santa Claus *is* coming to town tonight if I have to spend all night dancing on that box.'

Fitz followed her with the last cup.

'No better girl,' he said.

★   ★   ★

It was three forty-six when, after they'd placed all the gifts in stockings and under the tree, their heads hit their pillows. 'We have three hours if we're lucky,' Erin yawned.

'Our little family will have the most brilliant Christmas,' Dom replied before the sound of immediate deep breathing. God, how she envied that of her husband — he could sleep standing up if tired enough. Her head pulsed with the day's events. And she didn't know it, but because the cheering policemen breaking into the box with the recharged drill was the last conscious thought she had, she went to sleep smiling.

16. Dominic

NOW — 9th June 2017

From *The Book of Love*:
'I love you because you and me — we made a
brood of new Carters.'

Family. Love . . .

It's all that matters. Erin is setting the table
and I'm in the back garden, concentrating for
just a moment on the background buzz of nearby
bees collecting pollen. They're busy, like bees
should be; probably about to head back to their
honey empire and the queen they love. We have a
lot in common — me and the bees. I shade my
eyes and look at the back of our gorgeous home;
white render, black-framed windows, some
curved, each with four vertical panes of glass.
Today, both the glass dome and the chrome
balustrade surrounding the flat roof glint and
shimmer in the strong summer sun.

The ring of the doorbell makes me walk the
length of the garden quickly. Our children are
here and Erin's already at the door letting them
in. Though nineteen, they're still firmly attached
by umbilical cords, Jude's one is twisted and
knotty and as long as forever, and Rachel's is
straight and elastic. She's Erin's boomerang.
Even when she makes her leave, Rachel always
springs back.

* ★ ★

'So, you're *all* here!' Erin's smile is tight as, somehow, she divides the medium chicken with her special herb and onion stuffing into more portions than she'd intended. Freya, Jude's girlfriend, sits on his right, his arm stretched protectively along the back of her dining chair. Paul, Rachel's boyfriend, is on Jude's left, nodding. I'm tetchy; wondering why he and Freya are here. This was meant to be family only.

'Smells great, Mum.' Jude wafts the scent of the food towards him with his hand.

'Dig in,' I say as I pass Erin's chair. She smiles at me, touches my hand before she sits down.

'Lovely flowers,' Rachel says. I look at the gorgeous blooms that I had to stop Erin from throwing away when they arrived earlier.

'Lydia,' Erin looks over at the full vase as she picks at a roast potato.

'You and her alright now?' Rachel asks, and I smile because she doesn't miss a thing, our girl. Even though the upset between Lydia and Erin all happens off camera, nothing escapes her.

So, it's Lydia's flowers and Rachel's all-seeing and all-knowing nature I'm thinking of when Jude clatters his cutlery down dramatically. 'I'm glad you're all here,' he says. 'Freya and I have something we want to say.'

Erin immediately finds my eyes and instantly I read her mind. *'Don't let her be pregnant,'* her eyes plead. *'We were lucky. It won't work for them.'*

'I know you really meant for it just to be

135

Rachel and me tonight but, the thing is Freya is family too.'

I can't help my face. It does an exaggerated, 'oh, no she isn't' pantomime frown.

'The thing is we got married last week,' he blurts it out as if he's speaking directly to the vegetable selection in the centre of the table.

My throat closes a little. Erin is completely muted, her face frozen in disbelief but she manages a weak 'How . . . ?' My head repeats conversations she and I have had about our children's weddings one day — how we hoped they would be a very different affair to our own.

'The how was easy; we just did it.'

'Gretna Green,' Rachel fills in the gaps and I glare at her.

'What the absolute fuck?' I stare at my only son, who can't look me in the eye.

'I wasn't there,' Rachel adds quickly. 'I knew nothing until we all shared a cab on the way here. Honestly. He just called me and told me to bring Paul along too.'

Paul is shifting in the narrow dining chair. He probably thinks he's wandered onto a set of *The Simpsons*.

'Wh-yyyy?' Erin stretches the one-syllable word mercilessly.

'Because we love each other, and we didn't see any point in waiting. Nor did we want any fuss.' Jude's tucking his long hair behind his ear and I notice he's not wearing a wedding band.

'Perhaps I should say something else at this point,' Freya says.

'Are you pregnant?' Erin spits.

'No!' Jude answers for her. 'Nowadays we use contraception! And before you go off on one, Mum, you were only a few years older than me when you got married.'

'Five years older and your father and I got married with our loved ones around us. No fuss either but . . . friends and *family.*'

I swallow hard, unable to speak, knowing she's totally gutted.

Paul is the only one eating. It's as if he decided not to waste the food — we're all going to do whatever it is we're doing anyway. I'd rather he left, that he had the good sense to opt out of this particular Carter moment.

'We work long hours,' Freya says about the fact she's already a teacher. 'The little time we have together, we want it to count. I told Jude I didn't need a big wedding that we could wait or not — he's the one who chose Gretna.'

Go on, throw him under the bus, why don't you. He's only your new husband.

'It would have been nice to be consulted,' I tell Freya, wishing I'd marked her cards earlier, like when I met her a year ago.

She looks to each face for reassurance, this girl who's older than our son by a few years. 'Jude assured me that no one would mind us cutting out all the frills.'

'Jude was wrong,' I say, though my words seem to fall on deaf ears.

My eyes seek Erin's as hers are desperately seeking Jude's who won't look at his mother. Instead, Jude is tapping his new wife's hand,

137

reassuring her that it's fine. Her new family are just chewing the cud.

Erin's chair makes a scraping noise on the floor as she stands. 'I'm not feeling great,' she says.

'No, Mum!' Jude leaps up, thumps the table and we all jump. 'This is one of the reasons we did it. I can't take your control freakery!'

I catch Rachel wince from the corner of my eye just as Paul slaps his neck with his hand. The back door is open on our little family scene and now the summertime mosquitos have sent their death squads in.

Jude is finally looking at his mother. 'I'm sorry,' he says before plonking himself back on the dining chair. 'That came out wrong.'

'Leave it,' Erin sighs and sits again. 'It's done.'

There are probably a hundred things that could be said but instead there's a swollen silence that lasts until Rachel raises her glass. 'Congratulations, Jude and Freya,' she says. 'I hope you'll be really happy together.'

Jude nods at her, looks across in my direction, his eyes finally filling. He's such a brave coward, my son. 'Yes, congratulations.' My toast is stiff, insincere.

'Where will you live?' Erin asks, quietly.

'Nothing changes, Mum. We're staying in the flat we have — it's close to the school and the rent's cheap.'

'Everything changes when you get married, Jude.' Erin looks across at me as she tears up. 'Otherwise, why do it?'

I wish I could reach across the length of the

table and grab her hand. Instead, I decide that since our children are so bloody self-sufficient, now is probably really the ideal time for Erin and me to fuck off into the sunset together.

★ ★ ★

She's on the deck outside and, having sprayed herself in insect repellent, she's nursing another glass of wine. She's sitting, just moving slightly, in the swing chair, a circular sixties-looking thing held on a metal chain to a single hook.

Everyone has gone. The kitchen looks like a bomb site and I take one of the garden chairs next to my wife.

'Let's you and me just take off, Erin.'

'They'll never last,' she looks up as she speaks.

'Maybe not but look at how many people said that about us.'

'It'll just never last,' she sighs.

'Did you hear me?'

'I heard you. You know we can't. We need to be close to home.' Her head tosses back on the chair. 'Jesus Christ. One of them married too young, the other living with someone old enough to be her father.'

'I blame the parents.'

She sticks her tongue out at me.

'Too soon?' I smile.

'Far too bloody soon,' she fights the urge to laugh, leans back, sways on the chair and stares at the sky.

While I, in the meantime, feel dizzy watching her. And completely useless. And nothing I say will work because I can't undo our stupid prick of a know-it-all son eloping at nineteen.

17. Erin

THEN — August 2004

Darling Erin,

You were saying the other day how it's been ages since you wrote in The Book of Love. How you didn't really feel the need, maybe because you feel less anxious and feel safer than you used to actually talking to me. I was rarely here anyway — usually more in response to you than volunteering myself in here.

Yet here I am.

You don't know this but there's not a day in our beautiful life together where I don't live in fear. Ironic, I know, when you're the one on the pills.

My biggest worry? Losing you.

I can hear your instant response to that. One of your disbelieving giggles. How could I ever think that you might not want to be with me. You love me, right?

It's because you love me, I'm afraid. I'm afraid when you realise what a lying shit I really am, you'll be able to stop, because I'll no longer be worthy of that love.

You're away overnight tonight, looking at premises in Portsmouth with Lydia for a potential new Bean Pod café next year. You're loving the job. You're brilliant at it. And because we can both save from salary, we're going to be able to

141

move to a house next year.

If I speak, that won't happen. If I speak, I know your feelings will change. I know you better than you know yourself. You love me, sure, but if you heard the truth, you'd find the 'off' button for that love and move forward without me. You would. You're stronger than you think.

But I have to take that risk, hope I'm wrong, hope that love will win out and hope that forgiveness will prevail.

Because there are things I need to tell you. Things I can't write down.

I need to look into your beautiful face and tell you I've lied. I need to tell you when and why. I need to explain the underlying tension between Dad and me.

Or maybe I need to shut the fuck up, keep my indulgent guilt to myself and keep living the life we've made together.

I love you so very much, Erin. Mightily, in fact. Dom xx

★　★　★

It was the third Friday of the month. Quiz night followed by chicken basket supper at the Coach and Horses, a ritual for the last few years. Their team, 'The Fabulous Five', friends for more than ten years, was missing Hannah. The remaining four had moved outside, moaning about having come second last, moaning about the crap food, wondering why they insisted on their habitual return, for their habitual thrashing when Erin raised the subject.

142

'Hang on.' Lydia frowned. 'Let me get this right. You *write* to one another? In a book . . . ?'

Erin nodded at her sister-in-law, her boss. 'It's a large leather notebook. Dad gave it to us as a wedding present and *he*,' she pointed her finger at Dom, 'he wrote something in it and then tore it out. That's against the rules.'

'There are no rules.' Dom was reaching across Lydia pouring from a bottle of Merlot.

'Yes, there are, and that was against the spirit of the whole thing.' Erin raised her palms skyward and looked at Nigel for confirmation 'It's where we write the things that are sometimes difficult to say and tearing it out afterwards, that's just not on.'

Nigel shook his head. 'Don't look at me. I'm still getting over the fact that you write to one another in a leather book.'

'Yes, well,' Dom's eyes seemed to narrow in her direction. 'It's something that until now, we'd kept between us.'

Erin sighed. 'Give me the page.'

'No.'

'And pass me the wine.' She frowned. 'Don't top up everyone else's glass and not mine. Do not decide how much I should or shouldn't drink. I manage my medication and alcohol intake perfectly without your passive control, thanks very much.'

'Christ,' Lydia said quietly. She was flattening the crease marks in her white linen trousers with her palms. 'Give her the goddamned page, Dom.'

'I was pissed when I wrote it. She's not having

the page so let's talk about something else,' Dom smiled.

'Nah, we're quite happy listening to your shit, aren't we, Lyd?' Nigel seemed to be enjoying himself.

Erin watched him down half a glass of wine in one go before speaking.

'We should have a book, Lyd,' Nigel said. 'Imagine all the angst we could have saved if we wrote stuff down instead of rowing about it.'

Erin laughed. 'Oh, no that's wrong! We often row about it. Though to be fair, it usually leads to a face to face discussion. Like now. That's sort of the point of it.' She ate some crisps from a bowl, licked her fingers. 'Give me the page, Dom.'

He laughed. 'You are *not* getting the page.'

'We'd have filled a few books by now, Lyd.' Nigel filled his own glass again. 'Book one — all about Nigel's 'snoozing sperm',' he lowered his voice. 'Book two, we'd fill with Lydia's 'lazy ovaries'. Book three we'd talk about the universe fucking with us by making us fall in love when we both want children and definitely can't have them together.'

'Nigel — ' Erin tried to interrupt.

'Book four would be all about the decision to give up IVF as a bad investment and instead concentrate on our careers. My eventual head teacher role will be my baby — when I have responsibility for two thousand other people's babies.'

'We haven't given up,' Lydia whispered. 'Not yet.'

'And Lydia's businesses,' Nigel added, 'they're her babies. She has two already and is now expecting her third.'

Erin looked to Dom for help but he was staring at the scorched grass by his feet. 'I'm sorry,' she told her friends. 'I've suspected but . . . ' She took Lydia's hand. 'Why have you never told us?'

Lydia's teary face looked straight at her. 'Tell my friend who's lost a child how desperate I am to have one. Tell my friend who has beautiful twins how IVF has failed for us and make her feel as if she has to apologise for them. I don't think so.'

Erin felt Dom's eyes on her too. 'I'd like to have known. I'd like to have been there for you.'

'You are here for me. Without knowing it, you've helped with the workload and general support when I've needed it.'

'So,' Erin leaned on an elbow, spoke through her fingers. 'You weren't really on several mini-breaks in Wales this year.'

Lydia attempted a smile. 'No. I either had my legs in stirrups having eggs harvested or my legs in stirrups having a few embryos put in — embryos which ultimately didn't like the taste of my womb.'

She had miscarried too . . .

Erin had so many questions but found herself realising something as she noticed Dom's absence from the conversation. 'You *knew* all of this?'

He nodded.

145

'Nigel told him,' Lydia added quickly. 'And not with my approval — I didn't want *anyone* knowing. I only ever intended telling people when I got pregnant. And Dad and Mum know nothing at all. I don't want to give them anything else to worry about.'

Erin closed her eyes. Sophie . . . Sophie had recently undergone memory tests and everyone, especially Dom, was still reeling from the diagnosis of Alzheimer's. Since the news he'd become expert at dodging any discussion about it.

'You want another drink, ladies?' He waved at a barman walking by, ordered himself a neat whisky. Erin and Lydia shook their heads in unison. Nigel jerked his head. 'I'll have one of those too,' he said.

'Is it why you've never married?' Erin braved her next question and Nigel snorted.

'I ask her to marry me once a week. She's the one who sees no need.'

'*She's* right here,' Lydia sighed.

'Guys, guys . . . we all have something,' Dom said. 'Everyone has something we have to deal with. Us, you guys, even Hannah.'

Erin shook her head in annoyance. 'Hannah's not here. We're talking about Lydia and Nigel.'

'I know, I'm merely adding that Hannah has a thing too.'

'I'm not even sure what you mean.' Erin stopped short of tutting aloud.

Dom looked surprised. 'She's fallen in love with a man she can never have.'

Erin took his wine glass and drained it, stood

146

and walked around the other side of the table to where Lydia sat and wrapped her arms around her from behind. 'I'm sorry. And if you felt you couldn't tell me before, I'm glad I know now. I'll try to be someone you can talk to.'

'What about him?' Dom asked, obviously still thinking that a change of subject was what was needed. 'Walt. Do you think he's in love with Hannah?'

Erin felt a light kiss on her hand just before Lydia pulled away, nodding slowly. 'He seems to be.'

And Erin's stomach sank deep. Fear for all of her friends suddenly flooded her system. Love; something she'd been raised to believe was the strongest force in the world, something she'd been lucky enough to give and receive, was the thing she now considered. *Was love enough for Nigel and Lydia to survive or would a child's love become more important? Would whatever love Hannah and Walt have for one another last?*

She looked at Dom, who had known all about this, casually stretching his long arms. She chomped on peanuts — chewed on her anger. It could wait.

Does any love last forever?

'Book five,' Lydia raised her glass, 'where we try IVF one more time, have a child and get married and live happily ever after.'

Everyone raised a silent glass.

'And Dom, give your wife the missing page.'

★   ★   ★

147

They were lying in bed, the small portable television on, both watching the latest episode of *24*. A fan working at full throttle rattled in the corner blasting much needed cold air on the sticky night. When the credits rolled, Dom switched the television and the bedroom light off.

'I have no idea what's going on in that programme anymore,' he mumbled.

'Me neither,' Erin said, resting her head on his chest as her eyes adjusted to the dark. She wasn't tired. 'How do you think your mum was when you saw her earlier?'

With his left hand, he played with her long hair, twirling the end of it between his fingers. 'The same, a bit worse. She's not going to get better; all we can hope is that we can slow progression.'

'You think she knows what's happening?'

'Christ, I hope not.' His tone closed the subject down.

They lay silent a while before she spoke again. 'I was thinking we should try and get to the coast this weekend. We could take your parents with us?'

'Good plan.'

His hand had stilled, his breathing had quietened.

'I thought we'd pack a picnic, bring the kids' bikes, head down to Brighton.'

'Great idea.'

'Though Gerard would have to drive too . . . '

'Erin?' he sighed. 'Is this going to be a late-nighter? You going to want to stay awake talking about what to pack in the picnic, what the weather might be like, or can I go to sleep?'

'I'm leading up to what I really want to say.'

Dom groaned. 'I'm exhausted.'

'Why did you never tell me about Lydia and Nigel?'

'This again?

'I only asked you once when we got home last night. Once. And despite me being really upset, you waffled. That *bothers* me.'

'Right.' Dom pulled himself upright in the dark. 'Do we need the light on for this?'

'Preferably not, no.' She wasn't sure she wanted to see his face.

'Nigel swore me to secrecy.'

'And I'm your wife, we have no secrets.'

Dom sighed. 'So, if Lydia had told *you* and asked you *not* to tell me, you'd have told me.'

'Yes. Yes, I think I would. Because I see *us* as different to any other relationship I have. If Lydia had told me something and asked me not to tell Hannah or your parents, of course, I'd have respected that. But you — I tell you everything.'

'Well, we're going to have to agree to disagree. I think if I'm sworn to secrecy then that's what it should mean. I can't believe you're upset by my being loyal.'

'Right.' She lay down. 'I think you're wrong. I think you should have told me something so important going on in our friends' lives if you knew.'

'Come here . . . Come on.' He pulled her back to him as he lowered himself on the bed and she lay on his chest, flattened his chest hair under her face.

'You should have trusted me,' she whispered.

'Erin, Nigel trusted *me*.'

She tugged the cotton sheet, turned on her side. 'Go to sleep, Dom.'

'Don't be like that.'

Wide awake, blinking slowly, she felt the soft touch of his lips on the nape of her neck.

'Night,' he said.

Erin bit her own lip.

'Night?' he poked her gently in the side.

Erin got out of bed and slipped a T-shirt over her head.

'Don't do that, please, don't leave.'

'I'm not tired.'

'I have to be on site at six tomorrow, can we not do this?'

She slipped her feet into her slippers. 'I'm going to go and make some herbal tea. I'm going to read for a bit. Go to sleep, Dom, I'm just not tired.'

Erin flinched as he thumped his pillow.

'Goodnight,' she said as she left the bedroom.

In the hallway, she opened the console table drawer and removed the book. In the kitchen she made some tea. In the living room, she sat, sipping it, staring down at the leather cover, wearing away at the edges. It was where she should write it all down, like she always had. It was where the toughest conversations between them usually began. It was where she should try to explain how she felt let down by the fact that he hadn't told her about Lydia and Nigel — that they should share everything. It was where he'd been the last to write something and then for some reason changed his mind. She stared back at the bedroom door and stood up, the Book of Love slipping from her lap onto the sofa.

In the bedroom, she switched the light on. 'Dom, I'm sorry, love,' she said, 'sorry you have to be up early, but we need to talk and brace yourself. This *could* be a long one.'

18. Erin

'Have you used all the eggs?' Erin yawned and scratched her head as she searched every shelf of the fridge.

'Yup, sorry,' Dom said. 'Thought I'd double up, keep some of the mix for tomorrow morning. That way we get a Sunday lie-in for an extra ten minutes. Jude! Rachel! Pancakes!'

Erin pinched one from a stack and got rapped on the back of the hand by a wooden spatula. 'Wait! And sit and eat at the table with us!'

'Too much to do.' She lowered her voice in his direction. 'Half term has me so behind. Are you sure you don't mind having them all day? I promise when I get finished with work I'll do some packing.' Her head nodded towards a two-foot-high pile of flat-packed boxes.

'Why don't you just take some time out? Go out with the girls. Have a bath? You and I can start on the packing tonight. We have at least another fortnight before exchange.'

'Nope, I'm looking forward to the time on my own! And a bath is already in the plan.' She kissed his cheek. 'So, you two — what have you got happening with your dad?'

Jude rolled his eyes. 'We have to go and see Granny and Grandad.'

152

'Well, that's a nice thing to do for them. You know how Grandad and especially Granny loves to see you.' Erin watched Dom study the ingredients on a bottle of maple syrup.

'After that we're going to McDonald's for lunch,' Rachel added.

'And then the cinema to see, what's it called again?' Dom asked.

'*Nanny McPhee*,' Rachel said with a mouthful of pancake. 'And tomorrow's trick or treat!'

'No, that's Monday.' Erin corrected. She needed at least another two days to think about creating witch and Superman costumes from scraps.

'I told them I'll carve the pumpkin tomorrow.'

Erin nodded. That was tomorrow. Today she had at least three hours of paperwork to catch up on. After that, she was, she decided, going to start the packing in their bedroom — the kitchen was too daunting to begin alone. She would pack away summer clothes, take the opportunity to recycle old stuff and make a pile for the charity shop. She would go through that jewellery drawer of hers, most of which was cheap crap. She would run a bath with bubbles and soak in it without Rachel begging to come in too. She would put on her fluffy robe and slippers and watch that DVD of the second *Bridget Jones* movie.

Two hours later she was dressed, sat at the same kitchen table with a pile of work and the flat was quiet but for the constant tapping of her fingertips on the laptop. Her Nokia pinged a text from Dom:

You've done enough work. Go have that bath! X

She smiled, looked at the time and closed the manila file she was working on. The rest could wait. There were packing boxes to be made.

★ ★ ★

She had filled three with summer clothes. Trying to eat a sandwich and assemble another cardboard crate, she sang along to the Sugababes's 'Push the Button' on the radio as she opened the drawer of her dressing table. Green beads. Red beads. Cheap beads. Some expensive pearls of her mother's. She pulled them all onto her lap and began to unravel them. As she did, she allowed herself to think of their house, the house, all being well, that they'd move into in another six weeks. Two streets away, it was a modest semi, built in the sixties — totally charmless — but it had space and potential and they needed space and potential more than period features. It was another stepping stone to what Dom called their final home, whenever and wherever that might be.

She rummaged through the back of the drawer and pulled out an old purse of hers, and an ancient wallet of Dom's. Her fingers poked inside to see if the tiny passport photos of them both, that he'd kept in there, had been left behind. She tugged on some paper — frayed and pink, almost falling apart. She flattened it, smoothed the torn creases as best she could, rested it on top of the dressing table.

Two passport photos remained, one of Dom and her and one of the two of them and Maisie. She picked up the one of the three of them, all smiling, all happy, all oblivious. With her fingernail she followed the tiniest trace of the baby's mouth. Though she thought of her child often, she realised that the passing of time had meant the days that she didn't now passed without guilt or recrimination. She looked around the room at the boxes of their lives. Leaving the flat meant leaving the place where Maisie had lived and died. Erin placed a hand on the dresser in front of her, steadied herself. She was leaving a place but taking the memories, most of them good. Her fingers touched the pink paper and she glanced at the eight rectangles made by the folds. Tilting her head, she read handwriting she didn't recognise, before picking it up to check.

The entry was dated. It was timed. A date and time branded on her brain.

It couldn't be.

Churning nausea sent her hand to her mouth.

It was.

She stood. As her heartbeat quickened, coloured beads fell to the floor in slow motion. From somewhere, her mother's voice nudged her as she watched the pearls land on the carpet. *Pearls can mean tears.* For a second Erin wondered where the silly myth had come from before she put her hand to her chest and tapped her heart. White spots appeared before her eyes as she tried her best to hold down the horror that threatened to block her throat.

He had lied.

Later, when any of their friends would ask, she would say it was that moment. Up until then, until that split second, as possibilities of mistakes whirled around her head, she'd not been sure. Then — certainty — under her open eyes, the second top row rectangle, just there, in her direct eyeline.

Erin willed it to be gone, then bending over at the waist, cried like a wounded animal.

★ ★ ★

In the kitchen the next morning, she opened the fridge, heard him approach from behind. She removed the jug of pancake batter, placed it on the countertop between the hob and the sink next to the uncarved pumpkin.

His eyes, she could see with the quickest of glances, were heavy and bloated — his clothes wrinkled from a night on the sofa.

'I want you gone before the children wake.'

'Erin — '

She placed the jug in the sink and lifted the washing up liquid bottle, squeezed it over his batter. 'Do you hear me? Leave.' She refused to cry anymore. '*Don't* make me ask you again.'

★ ★ ★

30th October 2005

To my most beautiful wife, Erin,

I am completely ashamed of myself. That's the first thing you need to know, and this is the place for honesty, isn't it? I did try to tell you once before, but then ripped that page of honesty out, decided I preferred living with you and my lies rather than without you. I knew. I knew what this would do.

After last night, I have no option but to be honest so here, in true 'pages' fashion, is the whole, uncensored truth:

Once, I lost money, an accumulation of bad gambles in Dad's club. It was a lot of money and the only way I could fix it was to try and win it back. So, I did — I went back late one night, and I tried to win it back only I didn't — I made it worse. I called Dad, begged him to help me, to loan me the money, begged him not to tell you. He's never been happy with that part, well with either part, but please don't blame him. He has tried over the years to get me to tell you about the loan, and about my habit, but I knew if I did, I would have to tell you everything. And I'd have to tell him everything — because he never knew that that phone call I made to him wasn't made from home . . .

That night, I drove home to my pregnant wife and child. Relieved. And because I just wanted to get back quickly, I was caught on camera speeding. Yes, that hand-written endorsement for a fine and three points that you saw on my old paper driving license was for the night of 10th May 1998.

No, I wasn't home, where I was meant to be, on the night Maisie died.

And I've had to live with the question of whether she might never have died it I'd been where I should have been.

157

I wasn't there, Erin.

You will hate me. Knowing this, I'm still begging you to forgive me. I promise, I mean promise like the word has never been used before, that I will never enter a bookies or place any form of bet for as long as I breathe.

I promise I will never let you down again.

Forgive me.

Because I loved her.

And I still love you and Jude and Rachel mightily,

Dom xxx

★ ★ ★

30th October 2005

Dominic,

Your things are packed. I want you to leave. I don't want you here and I never want our children to witness us screaming at one another like we did last night again, when one more time you tried to lie your way out of something.

You made your choices. Choices have consequences.

You're a coward. How have I ever not known that about you? I'm aching with the reality that my love had been completely blind.

You were gambling and lying to me about it for a long time. (I don't blame your father.) I already know we'll do anything for our children. Ten thousand pounds . . . God knows we had so many arguments about money back then. And you were out doing that same thing again the night Maisie died.

Not home.

I was exhausted, only sleeping with a doctor's help and you knew that. You were meant to be there. You weren't and that's just unforgivable.

And you've been running from it ever since and I've tried. I've tried to get through to you, make it possible for you to tell me anything. I've tried to reach you and I don't want to anymore.

Right now, I hate you. I hate you because everything is different, and you've made me question everything we've had. You've made me question if any of it was real.

Maisie was real . . . And you should be ashamed of yourself.

You and I have other children together and I will never stop you seeing them.

But I choose not to see you.

I want you gone.

Erin

PART THREE

19. Erin

NOW — 11th June 2017

From *The Book of Love*:
'When I thought I couldn't breathe, I found I could. And when I thought our life was over, it was really just beginning.'

I watch Dom leave from our bedroom window. He looks the same as he did the very first night he came into my life over twenty years ago, and just as he did when I watched him leave my life on a dark morning in 2005. Yes, there's less hair, a few of them grey, some ageing lines around the eyes and a slight roundness in the stomach, though I'd never tell *him* that. He stops and waves, has that same sloping stance he had when he gave me that silly nickname.

Tree Girl . . .

I loved him instantly. And now, as he disappears around the corner, my heart pitches in my chest because it's still love I feel. I try not to dwell on the years in between when I hated the sight of him, and I head downstairs. In amongst the mail I pick up from the floor, there's a pizza menu addressed to Jude. My son — the married man. I shake my head. He's barely a man — how can he be a married one?

From deep in my pocket, I retrieve my phone and dial his number. Jude's voicemail kicks in. I listen, convinced his voice has only just broken; convinced my boy can't possibly know what he's doing, what he's done, when Dom's hour-old comment pokes me. '*He has to be allowed to be an adult, even if you're not ready.*' Despite Dom's calming me down over the whole debacle during the last few days, I'll probably never be ready.

My laptop's open on the dining table and touching the mouse, I can immediately see that there's a tonne of emails. *I should be at work in the Bean Pod.* I've had months sick leave and I should have gone back to work when I returned from the States.

Lydia has phoned. Lydia has called around and I've pretended to be out. Lydia wants a conversation with me, and Dom tells me she deserves one. His words. Her indignation — they make my insides boil, my face flush from within. I owe Lydia nothing. Not a hint of a thing. Nada. Sod all.

When I try telling him this, he tries a different tack. There's always a deep sigh followed by a 'You'll have to forgive her sometime, you know.'

I don't. I don't know this and though I've tried explaining, he just looks at me with sad eyes and nods as though he knows something I don't. Lydia has, in my eyes, done something totally unforgivable. 'It's not like you,' he tells me. And I want to remind him that in fact, it is, that forgiveness is a life skill that doesn't come naturally to me, something I've had to work very hard at. He, of all people, should know that.

★　★　★

Darling Dom,

While you were looking in on your dad, I re-read the last entry I wrote here before I left for New York, 'The Queen of What Ifs' one.

A month has passed since then, and I think I've heard you use that expression rather a lot yourself. In fact, you've always been the King of What Ifs. We just use it differently. I tend to look forward and say, 'What if we were to' etc. etc., whereas your use of it has always been around the past, around regret.

Dom, I think we have yet another chance at happiness here despite every fibre of me saying we shouldn't. So, what if I just ignore logic? What if I throw caution to the wind and just accept things the way they are, without worrying or trying to make sense of them. I'm ready to be. In this moment. Just be. With you.

As for Lydia, we'll have to agree to disagree for now. She knows I really can't get past what happened.

I love you, am so glad we're still together.

Erin xx

P. S. Do you know you've actually written more in here than I have? I've just worked it out! Most of it while we were apart but still . . .

20. Dominic

THEN — December 2005

3rd December 2005

My darling Erin,

Did you know? I think you did. I think you knew that you'd packed this book with my things. I think you know just what a statement that would make, the best way to let me know you're done talking. You're done writing. You're done, and we're finished.

I don't accept that, Erin. I won't accept it.

I've just had to hand our children back to you. Watch them walk up the path to the flat we were planning to move out of. You're serious about this, aren't you? That's what I don't believe. I thought you'd calm down, that I'd spend a very long time making it up to you and life would carry on with some new normal that I'd somehow eventually fix.

And you were right. If I'd known what would happen, I'd never have told you. I'd have lied my way out of that speeding fine. A handwritten wrong date — whatever . . .

I'm writing this from the budget hotel room I've been living in for weeks.

Please know that I haven't been within sniffing distance of any form of gambling joint since October. I accept I had/have a problem.

I miss you. I miss the children. I miss our lives

together. I wish you'd just talk to me. Please talk to me.

I love you because you're you and because I genuinely can't imagine not.

Dom xx

★   ★   ★

He arrived early and kept a seat for her, not wanting their sitting apart to be an option. Silently, she took his wave cue, sat next to him, placed her handbag on the ground, her coat on the back of the chair.

'You alright?' Dom asked, aware the air around him was suddenly scented by her. L'eau d'Erin.

'I'm good.' She patted her windswept hair into place then hugged her arms, glancing all around the school hall.

'You can look at me, you know, neither of us will spontaneously combust.'

She arched her eyebrows, stared back, wordlessly admitting she thought him bursting into flames wasn't that bad an idea.

'Thank you for this,' he said.

'The children want you here,' she replied, again those unspoken words seeming louder.

I don't. I don't want you here at all.

'About Christmas . . . ' Erin seemed to be searching the group of children gathering on the stage for the twins.

'They won't be on until later,' Dom said. 'Donkeys. Manger. Later.'

'Right.' She turned to him. 'Christmas Day.

We're at Lydia's from the night before. Fitz is coming too, so on the day — '

'I don't want to cause any problems. I'll go to Mum and Dad's. Can I see them for presents for an hour in the morning?'

She hesitated a moment, scratched her lower arm. 'Yes, that's fine. An hour,' she said.

'And I'll send you over some extra money for the gifts. They should still be from us. And Father Christmas, as well, you know?'

Erin waved at someone over the opposite row of chairs.

'They should still be from us?' he repeated.

'Yes,' she said wearily, 'yes.'

'I know you didn't choose this. I know this was never in the plan.'

Erin turned her head away.

'Just promise me you won't punish Dom the father for Dom the man,' he whispered.

'I wouldn't do that to *them*,' she said, watching the stage, leaving him under no illusion that had she had a choice, she'd have cut him from her life completely.

'Have you found a flat yet?' she changed the subject.

Dom shook his head.

'Dominic, I'm not letting them stay overnight in your shitty little hotel room. If you want them the weekend after Christmas, you'll need somewhere to live.'

Dom chewed his lower lip. Without realising why, his eyes had closed, as if it allowed him to concentrate more — to ask himself if that hard edge in her voice was temporary or there for

168

good. He'd put it there — he knew that much — but surely it would dissipate over time? And what was with the 'Dominic'?

'I'll make sure I have a place by then.' He heard her sigh.

'If you do, there's no reason they can't stay over. If not, just take them out for the afternoon.'

Images collided in his head. Faceless people; men mostly, that he'd seen over the years, at the park or in McDonald's, eating alone with their children, one eye always on the clock.

He only opened his eyes to the first sounds of 'O Little Town of Bethlehem'. Through the nativity she clapped loudly and sang along with every carol. Dom was lost. She was the one who had a faith. She was the one who'd wanted to send the children to a Catholic school and he'd gone along with it. He looked at the tiny stage. All he knew was that his children made the most perfect donkeys and his wife still couldn't sing.

As the lights went back on Erin turned to him.

'When they come down, they're going to want us all to go out together, will probably suggest a pizza. That's not happening. I'd be grateful if you'd see them and then say you have to go — make some excuse — don't make me the baddie by saying no. They already think I'm the baddie.'

And when the moment came, the words had gathered in his gullet. 'No sorry, kids, not tonight,' had almost choked him. 'I've got to go back to the office.' Their faces. The glances from him to her and back to him again. 'You were both so wonderful!' he hugged them. 'We'll celebrate another night, yes?'

Rachel had looked back over her shoulder and blown him a kiss.

And then he'd watched the three of them walk away.

★   ★   ★

'I'll take it,' Dom told the agent. 'Just get whatever checks you need to do done urgently. I need to be in by the weekend.'

She was young and pretty and — from the way her eyes lit up at Dom wanting to take what was a small, low-rent flat — new to the job. He felt a bit sorry for her, tried to flash a smile as he gave her his bank and accountant details to take up references, but by the time she'd completed the form he was feeling even sorrier for himself. Nowadays, if he stopped to think about his situation at all, Dom felt as if he'd stumbled into another man's life.

It was Tuesday 27th December and the next two hours were spent furnishing his new home with stock from Ikea. Everything would be delivered and in place by Friday and for the first time in months, he felt a lightness in his chest as he drove to his parent's house.

His mother made him coffee that tasted like tea and they sat together in the familiar drawing room. Dom squinted at the green and brown swirls of the twenty-year-old carpet, put his drink down on a coaster with Oscar Wilde's face on it, one of a set he'd bought her for Mother's Day one year.

'You look so thin,' she told him, wringing her hands together. 'Not like yourself at all.'

He raised an eyebrow. Living in a 'shitty little hotel room' will do that to a man.

'How are the babies?' His mother always called the twins 'the babies' even though they were seven. 'And Erin, how is she?'

'Rachel and Jude are great,' he said and hoped his mum would forget asking about his wife, as she did many things nowadays.

'I told you a long time ago you needed to look after your wife,' Sophie shook her head.

Dom sighed as quietly as he could, saw his father fill the doorway behind the sofa that his mother sat on. Today was obviously a good day for her. Not every day was, and the fact that she could focus and remember details, that was a good thing. Not so good for him, but something to be grateful for.

'What are you doing about it?' she asked him, her eyes narrowed.

'What I can,' he said. 'I'm giving her the time she needs and hoping she'll listen to me and change her mind.'

His mother shook her head.

Dom raised the now almost cold coffee to his lips. He looked at her; her back resting against a floral cushion that his father had placed behind her when she'd first sat down. That was what he'd wanted, what he'd expected and believed he'd always have in his marriage. He and Erin, growing old together, possibly irritating the hell out of each other, but together whatever happened.

And what had happened? Despite himself, he found the whole thing flying around his head yet again. He'd lied. He'd lied about his gambling. Tick. He'd left Maisie with Erin, while Erin was in a deep sleep. Tick. Anything could have happened. Tick. And it had. Tick.

'She has a right to be disappointed in me, Mum.'

'She has.' His mother agreed. 'But your family, your lovely family . . . ' Sophie began to cry, and Dom took the seat next to her, took her hand in his.

'I'm trying to make it right.'

'Well, make sure you do, Dominic.'

He could hear his father's breathing behind him.

'Are you still going to meetings?' Gerard asked.

Dom looked at the family photos on the piano, the latest frames holding images of his children. 'Once a fortnight.' He laughed, a low-pitched, sorry sound, rubbed the hair on the back of his head, created a static arc. 'I can't say Gamblers Anonymous are helping with the situation with Erin, I — '

His father interrupted. 'Have you told her you're going?'

'Dad, she's not interested.'

'So, where's this flat you've taken on?' Gerard moved from the doorway, made a clipped change of subject and took the seat Dom had been sitting in.

'A few minutes from Hawthorn Avenue. It's small, tiny in fact, but it does have two bedrooms and I can just about get bunks in the second one.'

'How's Erin, darling?' His mother turned her head towards him, a new, almost glazed expression on her face. At least, Dom thought, at least the look of disappointment had disappeared. 'Do give her my love when you get home. Turned out to be such a lovely girl . . . '

★   ★   ★

The following Friday evening, Lydia stood up from her haunches to open the window. Though Dom had already taken the door to the bedroom off the hinges and it now lay on its side in the narrow landing, the space to put the bunks together was still tight.

'Sorry,' he said to her, 'It's not easy but we're nearly there.'

'Will you leave the door off?' she asked.

'No, it'll be okay.'

Lydia sighed, pushed hair from her face and fixed her brown eyes on him. 'None of this is okay, Dom.'

He remained silent, tightening screws with the screwdriver in his hand.

'It's not just you and her, you know,' Lydia continued. 'It's her and me, and we work together. And as for all of our friends ever eating dinner together again . . . '

'I'm sorry, okay?' Dom was growing weary of apologising.

'I'm trying to explain to you that it's not just — '

'Don't you fucking think I know this already?' Dom threw the screwdriver on the floor and it bounced and hit Lydia in the leg.

'There is no need to shout.' She rubbed her leg dramatically.

'There's every need to shout. I know! I know! I know I fucked up my marriage and your relationship with my wife. My children are probably ruined by one bad decision I made. I know, okay? I know.'

'Three bad decisions, actually. Gambling. Gambling the night Maisie died, and then lying about all of it for far too long. Oh four, you never told your wife you'd borrowed money from Dad. And stop swearing.'

Dom turned, left the room and headed to the small galley kitchen. He opened a cupboard, took down a half litre bottle of gin and took a deep slug from it, before wiping his mouth with the back of his hand. Lydia stood in the landing watching. 'What? You're now going to add drinking to your list of woes?'

Dom took another gulp.

'Don't you see, Dom? What you did made all of her worst fears real. She's Fitz's daughter. She was weaned on love being the answer to everything. She met you and you made her believe in that even more and then suddenly — it wasn't, it's not. This isn't her getting back at you. This is her *destroyed* . . . '

Dom felt his insides gnarl as he screwed the cap back on the bottle. 'Good people can do bad things if they're in a bind. She has to find a way to forgive me, so we can move on.'

'Jesus, Dom.' Lydia was shaking her head as if he was a complete idiot. 'You should hear yourself. This,' she waved her hands around his bijou space. 'This *is* her moving on.'

'Oh, just fuck off, Lydia.'

He couldn't look at her face; didn't want to see any more heavy disappointment.

'Fine.' His sister bent down, grabbed her handbag from the floor and slammed the door on her way out.

Dom went back to the bedroom, picked up the screwdriver. He had a job to do. He had to get this place looking as if it could be a home and he had less than twelve hours before his children came to stay the weekend. He would pick them up the next day and they'd stay until he dropped them back on Sunday — New Year's Day. His free hand circled his stomach. Christmas had been a sad affair and now the eve of another year loomed — a year he simply couldn't contemplate spending without Erin; without Rachel and Jude.

Tightening the screws on the wooden frame, though he told himself that he had more important things to deal with than Lydia, he reached for his phone and dialled her number.

'I'm sorry,' he said to her voicemail. 'This week is our ninth wedding anniversary . . . but I'll snap out of this feeling sorry for myself lark. You're only trying to help and I'm a jerk.'

⋆ ⋆ ⋆

At midnight, he sat on the bed in his own bedroom. The linen he had bought didn't fit.

175

The mattress was way harder than it had felt in the shop. The space, though small, seemed to echo with his every movement – as if to amplify his loneliness. He reached into a plastic crate and removed the book. Earlier, the internet had told him that willow was no longer the traditional gift for a ninth anniversary — that leather was the more modern alternative. He wondered if he should just give it back to her but thought she'd toss it in some cupboard.

Whereas he — he still needed it.

He read some of the first entry he'd written just after he and Erin had split:

You're serious about this, aren't you? That's what I don't believe. I thought you'd calm down that I'd spend a very long time making it up to you and life would carry on with some new normal that I'd eventually fix.

Erin had never been more serious in her life.

And Lydia was right — this was her, this was his, new normal.

He clicked the Travelodge pen that had sat on top of his new Ikea bedside table on and off, listened to the rhythmic sound before he began to write. He sat up, his legs straightened ahead of him on the bare mattress, and with his back against the wall, he wrote with the absolute certainty that Erin would read his words. Someday, not today, but someday, Erin *would* read his words.

★ ★ ★

30th December 2005

Darling baby Maisie,

Where does it say in this non-existent rulebook that I always have to write to Erin in here? I mean I know that's the point of it, but the point of it is sort of lost at the moment anyway. And I say, 'at the moment', because I still believe your mum and I will get back together. Sometime. Soon, I hope.

She believes you're an angel or that robin that used to scutter about in the low-level plants in the garden. I used to hear her talking aloud to you when she thought she was alone. Maybe she's right. I hope she is. I hope that spirit exists. I hope you live on in some way because it lessens the pain of you being gone for the last seven years. You'd have been eight years old.

Sometimes, days pass and I realise that I haven't thought of you and I feel guilty — even more than I feel normally anyway. I should have been there. Logic tells me that even if I had, more than likely you'd have died anyway, that I wouldn't have been able to do anything but there are so many 'maybes' and 'what ifs'.

What if we'd bought one of those baby monitors we said we didn't need because you were only ever in the next room?

What if I hadn't gone out and decided to sit and watch you quietly as I sometimes did on my own, just listening to your breathing. I'd surely have noticed it stopping, your last inhalation and I'd have jumped up, picked you up and breathed life into you, Maisie. What if . . . ?

What if I'd been home and you'd died anyway?

177

Some part of me realises that I'd have been there more for Erin. I think I'd have been a better support for her, noticed how bad she was with anxiety when you died, and the twins were born. I think I'd have been able to see through the grey and reach her, grab hold of her, had I not been consumed by guilt and grief myself.

Yes, grief. I didn't howl or bang walls or make any noise. But in those early days I saw you everywhere, Maisie. I saw your face in the sky. I heard your giggle in the office. I tasted the loss of you, the missed opportunity of your life for what I know you would have become — I chewed it in a piece of toast. What if . . . ?

It faded, that level of grief, of course it did, but the guilt never went.

And now, every day, rather than be consumed with the 'what ifs' around what would have happened had you lived, I'm buried in 'what ifs' around truth.

Don't tell anyone, Maisie, because this is not standard parental advice, but truth? It's so bloody overrated.

Because if I hadn't told her, I'd still be with her. We'd have moved to a new house; your mum, your brother, Jude, and sister, Rachel and me. Next May, on your anniversary, we'd have talked about you, about what sort of young girl you might have been then. I'd have held Erin as she cried, and we'd have laughed too, remembering your funny ways. She'd have brought the twins to mass. I might even have gone. I might have watched Erin, head down, praying like she used to as a child, praying for your heavenly soul while

I chatted to you in my own way and bribed the twins to stay quiet.

Instead, I'm chatting to you here.

What if you'd lived, Maisie, and none of this had ever happened? What could you have done? Who would you have been? I imagine you'd have been the child in school who stops all the bullies. You'd have corralled all the 'bad kids' and escorted them to the head teacher. You might have been a teacher, like Jude already says he wants to be. Imagine, you could have gone through uni together, introducing him: 'This is my little brother' and he'd be towering over you. And you and your sister — you'd have been close, like twins your- selves. And your mum and I would hover, watching . . . We'd be together and the three of you would look at us and say, 'See that? That's what I want. I want to be like Mum and Dad.'

As it is, I'm never going to be able to inspire you, Maisie. You're never going to give me one of those hugs that tells me I'm loved. I'm never going to walk you down the aisle and hand you over to someone I hope is worthy of you. I'm never going to see you grow up except in my mind, where, admittedly, you grow up a pensive, thoughtful child and I'm sure with each year, you'll grow up to be a beautiful girl and woman, and probably discover the cure for cancer.

Tomorrow is another day.

Another day to move forward and still miss you.

I love you, Maisie-Daisy-do,
Always have and always will,
Dad xx

21. Dominic

THEN — May 2006

Dom sat in his car outside 27a Hawthorn Avenue munching on an apple. He blew into his hands, hoped the weather for the few days he had with the children would feel more like May and less like January.

When it was time, Dom tossed the core into one of the bins lined up by the entrance and noticed that the tree line creeping over the side return of the ground-floor flat was far too high. He heard Rachel's squeals as he rang the bell, quelled the feeling in his stomach that he always had on his own doorstep.

'Hey,' he said when Erin appeared. 'You want me to lop those Leylandii when you're away?'

'What? Yeah, okay. Hi, come in, it's cold.'

Dom did as he was told, stepped over the threshold for one of only a few times since he'd crossed it going the opposite direction last October. 'You all set? Excited about the trip?'

'Yes. It'll be great to see Rob again. The kids are ready. I've packed everything they'll need in one suitcase.'

Dom looked to his left where a case that was almost bigger than the twin's room in his flat sat up against the wall.

'They're just brushing their teeth,' Erin added, looking at her wrist anxiously.

He held his breath. He had two things to do. One, pick up the kids and the other to give her the envelope.

'This is for you,' he pushed it into her hand.

'What is it?' Her eyes met his.

'It's a CD,' he attempted a smile. It was an old joke between them — from a time they'd given each other CDs one Christmas and spent an hour playing a silly game making up crazy guesses at what was in the obvious package.

'Stop messing about. What is it?'

'Dollars, okay? Look, I just want you to have a good time.'

'I don't need your money. I have that sorted.' She tried handing it back to him, but he stood back.

'Will you let me do something for you? No agenda. The business is doing well, probably because I'm there twenty-four seven nowadays, but I want to be able to share that with you.'

She shook her head. 'Dominic, I'm glad your decision to go out on your own is working but I really don't want this.'

'Consider it a birthday present.'

'My birthday's not until October.'

He lowered his voice. 'You got nothing except some awful truths last October. Go shopping in New York. Have some fun.'

There was a tiny flutter in her throat as he watched indecision cloud her lovely face.

'Erin, we are, at least, two people co-parenting two children whom we both love. We're, at best, two friends who used to be a lot more to each other. Please, take the money. Have some child-free fun in America.'

She folded the envelope, put it in her rear jeans pocket. 'Thank you,' she said, doing that thing with her hair that she did when she was nervous, where she used both hands at the same time to curl it around her ears. Usually, it was followed by a tiny smack of her lips. She'd grown her hair long again and all he wanted to do was to reach out and stroke it with the back of his hand.

He coughed.

She smacked her lips together before speaking. 'Dominic, the Leylandii . . . '

'When was it that you stopped calling me Dom?'

Erin looked back at Rachel, who had run from the bathroom to the kitchen yelling that she was just getting her rucksack. She leaned back against the wall and placed a hand on her stomach. 'I wasn't aware I had.'

Dom put his arms out to Rachel, who had stopped dragging the bag she had and was now running towards him. He bent down and raised her high in his arms.

'Where's Daddy's favourite girl?'

'Here!' She laughed as he tickled her before putting her down.

'Where's your brother? Go on, get him, Mummy needs to get going.' Rachel ran off yelling Jude's name. 'You're meeting Fitz at the airport?' he asked Erin.

Erin nodded, rubbing her left arm with her right hand. 'It's cold,' she reiterated.

'Well, you might even get some sun over

182

there,' he said, wondering how two people who had fallen in love the moment they met; whose limbs had clung to one another in an ecstasy he would never feel with anyone else; who had conceived three children in love — how they had ended up in the doorway discussing cold fronts on two different continents.

'You definitely got a lift there? I don't mind driving you.' Their eyes met. Hers, once grass-green and liquid-soft, now granite, impenetrable, moved to the suitcase and she walked towards it.

'I've got a lift, thanks,' she said.

'Okay . . . Hey, buddy,' he said to Jude.

'Hi, Dad,' their son replied.

'Right, you two,' Erin bent down and pulled the two children tight to her chest.

Dom swallowed. However hard he'd made her, Erin was a wonderful mother and would miss the children. He'd had to beg her to let him have them for the week when he'd heard it was planned they'd go to Lydia's. That was the first row he and Erin had had since he'd left. The first airing of her anger, her fear, her reluctance to trust him for longer than twenty-four hours with their children.

'I'll miss you,' she said into their hair. 'Be good for your dad. And I'll call you, yeah?'

Dom reminded himself that she had never left the children to go abroad before.

'I'll look after them, Erin,' he said. 'I promise.'

She sighed and since they were already out the door blew them kisses. 'You'd better,' she replied.

'Looks like your lift is here,' Dom jerked his head to the street outside. 'Stop, guys!' he called to the children. 'Wait for me!'

Erin's face flushed. 'I'll call you tomorrow to say goodnight to them,' she said.

'Have a good time,' he said. 'Stay safe.'

'You too.'

He reached for her, held her for a brief moment and kissed her head. 'Say hi to Fitz and Rob for me.'

She didn't pull away, at least not immediately, and as he walked the children past and loaded them into the car as slowly as possible, he tried to glance at the tall male driver in the parked car. He couldn't see him clearly, but whoever he was would have seen that hug. And whoever he was, he was simply a blip in Erin's landscape — a friend to spend time with rather than be lonely. Not someone to love. No, he'd felt it in the moment they'd touched. Despite inclement weather conditions there had been a definite thaw in Erin. There were no sparks or electrics — just a longing. No need for words in that tiny moment.

★   ★   ★

Dom was exhausted. The three days and four nights with the twins, though amazing, were tiring and he had a whole new respect for Erin. Cooking for them had been a challenge in the tiny kitchen and the morning before he drove them home, he saw similarities in the twins he'd never noticed before.

184

'Mummy puts the eggs in a cup to mix them first,' Jude explained, his questioning face a mirror of his sister's.

'Daddy, that's not the way you make scrambled eggs,' Rachel agreed.

Dom scratched his head. 'I make pancakes for you, that's what I always make for you.'

'But we want scrambled eggs,' Jude said, and Rachel nodded.

'Right.' He looked down at the pan, knowing that the eggs would indeed have been scrambled by the fork he was about to use on them.

'They won't taste the same,' Jude warned.

'Right.' Dom repeated as he opened the bin and tossed them. Seven months had passed and still life without her felt like he moved through living and breathing as a half and not a whole. 'Right,' he eyeballed his children. 'Tell me exactly how Mummy does it — what do I do?'

★   ★   ★

'It's tough alone,' he reiterated to Nigel as they both held cold pints of lager shandy at the bar in the Coach and Horses. They'd just played a squash match at the school gym and Nigel had thrashed him.

'Don't use a few days with your kids as a reason for your playing shit tonight,' he grinned, nodded his head at a man who passed by whom Dom didn't recognise.

'All I'm saying is, I'm ready for my bed, even if it's still like sleeping on a board.'

'You need to date again.'

185

'Have you been listening to me at all?'

Nigel stretched his eyebrows as if daring him to tell him one more time that he was going to get his wife back.

'She texted me earlier, asked me for my email address. What do you think that's about?'

Nigel's expression told him he didn't care, that he might be just a little bored of the Dom and Erin saga.

'I set up a new one and sent it to her, smartdomnot@hmail.com.'

Nigel laughed.

'Erin thought it was funny too. See, I'm breaking her down . . . This time next year, my man, the plan will be complete and normal services will resume.'

'Do I need to worry about you, mate?'

'Nope.'

'You do remember there's another man sniffing around?'

Inside, Dom's stomach liquefied. Outside, he waved the suggestion away as if he was swatting a fly. He felt Nigel's hand touch his, three soft taps. 'I'm trying to let you know that you may be deluded.'

'And I'm explaining that she and I are bigger than any other possible her and him.'

'Right.'

'Right.'

Nigel sighed. 'And you know this how? I mean you don't know if it's a thing yet or ever will be. Have you met him, seen them together?'

'Have you?' Dom glared.

'No.'

'Exactly,' he replied.

'Right.'

'I am.' Dom smiled and clinked his glass against his friend's. 'You'll see.'

⋆ ⋆ ⋆

As soon as he got in, Dom switched on the desktop that sat on top of the chest of drawers next to his bed. He logged onto the internet and there sitting in the new inbox was an email from Erin:

— Original Message —
From: Erinthebrave101@btinternet.com
Sent: 20 May 2006 16:55
To: smartdomnot@hmail.com
Attachment: Numbers re 27a
Subject: 27a Hawthorn Avenue

Hi D,

That email address still makes me smile. Do you like mine? Fitz's suggestion . . .

While I was in the States, I had planning consent through for that extension that you drew years ago which will give the children that third bedroom we need. The twins are getting older. We need more space — I can't afford to move and this is the best way. Your dad has agreed to loan me the money — he's insisted on it in fact and he's trying very hard to *give* me the money, but I really want to do this on my own and will be able to if you agree to increasing our mortgage a bit? I'll pay the extra monthly portion it will cost? I've attached some figures here, so you can have a look.

I'm hoping you can see the sense in this — we need the space here, we really do, and the flat is ultimately an investment for both of us.

We'd go out the back into the garden and create an open-plan living room off the kitchen and a third bedroom in the existing living room at the front — remember the drawings?

What do you think?

If you want to, if it will help you decide, come around and have a look again this evening or tomorrow evening.

Let me know,
Erin.

Dom typed an immediate reply.

— Original Message —
From: smartdomnot@hmail.com
Sent: 20 May 2006 18:37
To: Erinthebrave101@btinternet.com
Re: 27a Hawthorn Avenue

Hi
I'm busy tonight but could come tomorrow evening.
Can I see the kids beforehand?
    D

— Original Message —
From: Erinthebrave101@btinternet.com
Sent: 20 May 2006 19:01
To: smartdomnot@hmail.com

Re: 27a Hawthorn Avenue

Would you mind coming over after they've settled? I don't want to confuse them, and they would be if they saw you here. If you come for 9pm?
    Erin

From: smartdomnot@hmail.com
Sent: 20 May 2006 19:22 PM
To: Erinthebrave101@btinternet.com
Re: 27a Hawthorn Avenue

Erin, I'll be there at 9 tomorrow evening. D

                    ⋆   ⋆   ⋆

                                    20th May 2006
Gorgeous Erin,
    So, I've just had the kids for a few days while you were in the States and kudos to you.
    I'm not sure how you do it alone.
    I took them to Center Parcs and the weather was wet, and I was a neurotic idiot in case they ran off or slipped on damp leaves or something and I'd have to give one of them to you with plaster of Paris on some body part. So, we swam a lot in the heated pool where they were in my eyeline all the time. They loved it. I loved it. But, Christ, was I exhausted! Bed asleep by ten every night.
    Rachel really does not stop talking at all, does she?! If she came with an on/off switch I'd have turned her off for at least an hour a day, just to

catch my breath. But, God, is she fun to be around. Soaks up everything. I can't imagine her taking any shit when she's older. Remind you of anyone?

'Daddy why are these trees so tall? Daddy. why are they so green? (Thought she was a bit young for photosynthesis, so that was one of the times I replied, 'because they just are').

'Daddy, do you prefer white or brown bread? why? Mummy says brown bread is better for us but I like white bread when it's toasted.' Agree. Totally.

'Daddy what's snot made of?' Honestly!

'Daddy, why can't 'fumans' breathe under water?'

'Daddy, you have a fat belly.' Yes. Less toast with runny butter for me when I get home.

And Jude . . . Our quiet little boy who lets his sister do all the talking for him and seems happy enough with that status quo. Jude, the little boy who draws with his left hand and writes some of his letters back to front. I'm a leftie too and used to do the same. Just in case you were worried — he'll grow out of that. Hopefully, he'll grow into taking part a bit more too? Have you noticed how much he's a watcher?

Yes, I know. I can near you echo, 'Remind you of anyone?'

It was fun. I loved having them. We missed you. They missed you; often wondered what you were doing and couldn't really get the whole time difference thing when you called.

I'll sign off for now, leave you with something Rachel said in the car on the way back:

R: Daddy, do you love Mummy?

Me: Yes, darling, I do.

R: Does Mummy love you?

Me: I'm really not sure . . .

R: I think she does love you.

Me: no response.

R: I think if two 'fumans' love each other they should live in the same place like we used to.

Me: But you love coming to Daddy's too, don't you?

R: I loved it more when you were home with me and Jude and Mummy.

It's sad. I can't tell you in person what she said, and I can't tell her that she'll get her happy-ever-after ending. BUT! I live to fight another day. Softly, softly, slowly, slowly.

If I get my way. Rachel will get her wish someday.

Love you mightily,

Dom xx

★   ★   ★

21st May 2006

To the one and only, beautiful Erin the Brave,

A hug. I got a hug. From YOU, that's you to me, not me to you. And Jesus, I tried to make it last just a fraction longer than I should have. But it was contact! Only terribly brief but I remember my lips touching your cheek and it was all I could do not to lock you in the hall cupboard and yell to the kids, 'I'M HOME!'

I talked to myself in the car on the way over. Seriously, actually addressed myself in the rear-view mirror, warning me to play it cool. I'd already told you I was busy the previous evening (white lie) so cool and collected when I got there was important. And I hugged you for that tiny extra nanosecond and I felt you pull away. Bad move, Dominic. Not cool at all, Dominic.

Anyway, we had a glass of wine together as we went over the plans for the flat.

Let me just get that out of the way immediately. I've always known and been worried about the flat being too small, have known that at some point the family would have to move. As far as I'm concerned, your solution is the best, until that day when maybe we all move back in together.

A glass of red. The simplest of things. Sitting with you (although you sat on the armchair and me on the sofa) and listening to you explaining the build. I'd have agreed to anything, Erin. Hearing your voice.

In the car on the way back, that's what hit me. I just haven't heard enough of your voice (forget the phone — I'm talking in real life) in such a long time.

Tonight, I wanted to explain, at least to try and explain that I'm finally realising what I did to you. It has taken months of listening to other people's voices and stories, months of hearing what I did played back to me, months of being away from you, to help me realise I should have trusted you. I'm so sorry for not trusting you enough with my truth. I know now that if I had, things would have been very different.

So, we, a married couple, who don't live together, are applying to extend our mortgage.

You and the children will live there. You and the children will live with Lydia and Nigel for the six messy weeks it will take but afterwards it will look lovely and our (your) space problem will be fixed.

And all I want you to think about is that I, Dominic, Dom, helped sort it, have agreed to pay for it (which according to you will help you save some money every month) and I am an imperfect but essentially good bloke.

Any chance you might think of me differently? Anything I could do to make you see me like you used to? I'd climb a mountain, cross a deep blue sea.

Won't even mention the fact that I sneaked a look in the bathroom cabinet when I went for a pee. You're still taking those antidepressants — I'm sorry. I know you hate taking them.

And birth control, but we won't mention that.

Love you mightily. I love you because your face is the first thing I think of when I open my eyes every morning.

Dom XX

★　★　★

21st May 2006

To the fabulous Dominic!

Darling, darling Dom! (Not really. This is Dom writing this. I'm Dom. No, I'm Spartacus. No, I'm a little pissed because I'm pretending to be Erin.)

'There once was a man in a flat,
A flat just the size of a hat,

193

He so missed his wife and his previous life,'
And I have no idea what to write now.
Dom, you are one sad idiot who needs to seriously get a grip.

22. Erin

NOW — 11th June 2017

From *The Book of Love*:
'I love you because we laugh together,
you and me.'

I'm washing my ancient Mini when he gets back, have just thrown a bucket of sudsy water over it.

'I'll never understand why you do that,' Dom says. 'Bring it down the road and let the garage do it for you.'

'Therapy. It's good for core breathing. 'Wax on, wax off'.' I smile.

'*The Karate Kid*,' he grins. 'Brilliant movie. I was fifteen when Lydia and I went to see it.'

I move a huge sponge over the windscreen. 'How was your dad?'

'The same. Lydia was there actually.'

I fire him a warning glance.

'What else have you been up to?' he says, catching the look.

'Reminiscing.' I hold a damp palm against my forehead to shield the sun and watch him sit on the front step. 'I was reading The Book of Love. I wrote in it. Hey, you want a laugh?'

'Laughs are always good.'

'You've written more than me in there.'

He makes a face. 'See, I'm not so sure that's even funny.'

'It is,' I nod. 'It really is.'

'Funny was when I turned up at Hawthorn Avenue drunk and tried singing 'At Last' through the letterbox.'

I giggle, switch the hose on to rinse down the car. 'That *was* funny. I never quite got the part where you thought it would win me over but, yeah, it was funny.'

'Funny was when I messed with your car battery and just happened to be coming out of the same supermarket at the same time your car wouldn't start. Me on my white steed . . . '

'Nah, that was a freezing cold day. The kids were whining in the back and I saw right through that one.'

'Funny was you dancing on the top box that Christmas we couldn't get into it; or your attempting *Riverdance* with Rachel and Jude one birthday where you sang imaginary words to it. Or your dancing like a tree the night I met you.'

'My dancing has given you much pleasure.'

He reaches for me as if to take my hand and waltz around the garden together, but I raise the hose, laughing.

'You wouldn't dare.'

'It would be funny.' But before I can even aim for him, he's scarpered and is on the other side of the living room window, making faces at me. Knowing he's watching my every move, I rinse the car, and as the soapy water slides down the narrow driveway into the drain, I feel uplifted, excited — ready to talk about the future.

23. Dominic

THEN — June 2007

The sound of the front door opening and closing made him straighten up on the sofa.

'All good?' she asked throwing her keys in her oversized bag.

Dom yawned, as she came and sat on the arm of the chair. 'Yep, what time is it?'

'Just after ten.'

He patted his cheeks repeatedly. 'I've had a long week. How was yoga?'

'Great, I love it,' she said as she placed her rolled-up mat against the wall and headed over to the other side of the room to put the kettle on. 'A coffee before you go?'

'Please.' He crossed the new extension at the back of the flat. 'Still can't get used to this space,' he said before taking a stool at the breakfast bar.

'Just as well you don't have to, isn't it?' She raised one eyebrow and he laughed.

'How come such a long week?' she asked.

Dom didn't want to talk about how his brain hurt he was so busy. It might have come out as a complaint and all he felt was bloody lucky that since his father had retired, he had taken over most of his clients and his business was thriving. 'Just long days and not enough sleep.'

'Well, you need to get proper sleep. Maybe *you*

should take up yoga? Honestly, it's been a lifesaver for me. Breathing techniques for anxiety, breathing techniques to help me sleep.'

He looked at her spooning coffee into a mug for him and wondered if there was a breathing technique that could make him not love her. 'No time,' he said.

'You still going to GA meetings?' She had turned and asked the question, eyeballing him.

'No,' he couldn't lie, felt her bristle from the other side of the room. 'Erin, it wasn't for me. I went for ages but in the end — '

'In the end, what?' She slid a coaster across the worktop and handed him a mug of black coffee.

'In the end, I don't believe in God.' He shrugged. 'It's wrong for me to be there with a lot of very good people who all have similar struggles, but they really believe that God and prayer will help them change. I believe I'm the only one who can do that.'

Erin's head was shaking. 'So, what you're saying is you can only stick to the 'Twelve Steps according to Dom'.'

'I suppose so, yes. I find the meetings, the sharing, really helpful. Believe it or not, I've done it often, but I just . . . I just recoil when it comes to the whole faith thing and it's founded on having a faith. It's not right that I doubt God's existence when I'm there, especially when others believe so strongly that He's responsible for their recovery.' He looked over at her, leaning on the worktop, rolled up his sleeve and held his arm out for her to see. 'You were the one who always believed in God and angels and heaven et cetera, but *this* is my faith.' He tugged at something on his wrist. 'It works for me.'

Erin came around his side of the island, looked closer at the silver rectangular tag attached to a leather band. 'What does it say?' She peered at it. 'I don't have my glasses.' She sat next to him, reached across for her own cup of herbal tea. 'Is it 'AAH . . . ?' '

'It is.' He laughed at the face she scrunched. ''A' for Admit. 'A' for Atone and 'H' for Hope.' Admit I was powerless to gamble in the past and admit I hurt myself and others doing so. Atone,' he cleared his throat. 'Make amends to those you've hurt, and Hope, well, hope for forgiveness as well as hope being something we all cling to, whatever's going on.'

She was sipping her drink slowly, staring at him over the rim of her cup.

'Say something,' he said.

'The steps according to Dom . . . Why am I not surprised?'

'I was going to have it tattooed on the back of my wrist but decided on this dog tag idea. I'm happy with just the one tattoo.'

'Those atonements,' she said, ignoring the reference to 'Erin forever' on his wedding ring finger. 'Are you done with them?'

Dom tugged on his open shirt collar. 'I'm not sure I ever will be.'

'You and your dad good?'

Dom nodded.

'You and I *are* good. Finally,' she said. 'What about you and Maisie?'

He flinched. 'I suppose she's where the whole God thing gets a little confusing. I don't believe in Him, yet I 'pray' to her, talk to her in my head often. But we're good, I think we're good.'

'You and Jude and Rachel?'

Dom thought for a moment. 'Erin, all of this is an ongoing thing. That's why I wear this — to constantly remind me. I'm not saying everything's perfect. The kids really hate the fact that we're not together. I'm forever trying to make that up to them.'

'But we're good, you and me.' Her eyes widened, and he realised it was her needing confirmation from him, and not the other way around.

'We are.' *If I forget you're seeing another man. If I forget we're no longer lovers. If I tell myself it doesn't matter that you don't love me like you used to — there's love there, that's enough to build on.* 'I should get home. I've an early start tomorrow.'

'You're working Saturday?'

'Just the morning.'

'Well, be here by three, won't you? Oh, and by the way, your parents have brought the same thing as us for their birthday, so I'll tell the twins after they've opened their grandparents' present what's happened and that we'll get them something else soon. I just don't want to disappoint Gerard and Sophie.'

Dom frowned. 'Right.'

'Three o'clock, Dom. *Don't* be late.'

'I won't.' He kissed her cheek and headed towards the hallway.

'Dom?'

He looked over his shoulder.

'You left her . . .'

His stomach flipped.

'Every time I tell myself how hard you've worked, and I'm an inch away from forgiving you,' she held her hand up, thumb and forefinger poised in a circle almost meeting, 'then I remember — you left her.'

'I know.'

'I was asleep, and she was *alone*.'

'And I'll have to live with that for the rest of my life.'

'*We* have to live with that for the rest of our lives.'

He scratched above the dog tag. 'And I'll never forgive myself. For her, for losing you and the kids. I still love you, Erin.'

From the corner of his eye he watched her shake her head, lower her eyes to the floor, place her hands on her hips. 'Dom, life is different now. We're moving on, both of us.' She looked up and as he eyeballed her, he felt the closeness of five minutes earlier disappear into the permanent chasm he'd put between them.

★   ★   ★

At three o'clock the next day, Isaac greeted him at the door. 'Dominic, welcome,' he said, and Dom smiled one of those broad smiles he normally reserved for prospective clients. He wanted to reach out and grab the man by his thick neck and squeeze really hard — but killing his wife's lover at his children's birthday party wasn't a good idea.

'Would you like a beer? I've got some in the fridge.'

Dom followed Isaac to the large American-style fridge that he had bought. The man who had briefly been Erin's boss in the paramedic service, stood amiably by his side. Two men, sipping cheap beer. To anyone looking, it would seem like they were friends. Two friends, possibly both fathers of some of the attending children. None of Erin and Dom's friends were there. He wondered if any of them had met Isaac — if they had — they were keeping quiet about it. He heard Rachel before he saw her, felt her run at him, as she always did, straight into his arms. And he held onto her, tried not to adjust his smile on seeing her into a smug expression for Isaac. One that would mean: *You might be fucking my wife but this girl, she's my daughter.* 'Happy birthday, Pipsqueak, where's your brother,' he asked.

'He's outside playing.'

'I'll come with you.' He jerked his head back to Isaac. 'Thanks for the beer.'

Tosser, he thought, knowing Isaac was staring at his back, possibly wondering confidently what Erin had ever seen in him. *You don't know, mate. You don't know what we had, what we still have.* He caught sight of her from the corner of his eye. She was deep in conversation with his mother which, in itself, was hilarious. Ten years ago, Sophie Carter had told her only son that he was marrying the wrong woman.

Then years later, she had told him that he had upset the wrong woman and to do whatever he had to do to get her back. He waved at them both, mouthed that he was just going to find Jude.

He found him in the garden with his father. Jude was with a group of other children playing marbles. 'Hi, Dad,' his son said without even looking up or moving. His eyes were concentrating on a large glass ball with red stripes.

'Hi, Jude,' he laughed and hugged his own father. 'Marbles?'

'I found them at home,' he said, 'yours, I think. I sanded some down and re-polished them. And we got them one of those new-fangled Nintendo DS things each.'

'Dad, you shouldn't have spent so much money,' Dom said, meaning it.

'Leave me alone, Dominic, my man. They're our only grandchildren and may always be our only grandchildren.'

He nodded, didn't allow himself to be pulled into a discussion about Lydia and Nigel.

'So, the marbles?' he asked his father.

'Found them in the loft. Thought they'd like them.' He raised a finger in the air as if making a point. 'I made sure to give them to them both but as you can see, somehow in the world of marbles, boys reign . . . '

'You got a drink?' Dom asked.

'No, there's kids' fizz and squash. Where'd you find that?' He pointed to the beer.

'Oh, the man of the house gave it to me from the fridge I paid for.' He couldn't help himself.

'Dom,' his father's quiet voice had a warning tinge to it.

'I'll go get you a beer,' Dom said and went inside the kitchen where the noise levels seemed to have risen. He looked across the room to where Erin had been standing earlier with his mother. Sophie had been replaced with Isaac whose arm lay around Erin's shoulder — casual but possessive. Dom wondered whether if he stared at the arm for long enough, he might have been granted a superpower — Superman's laser eyes — that would mean Isaac's severed arm would just fall on the floor. He shook his head. His children's birthday party was definitely not the place.

'Son.' His mother greeted him with air kisses as only Sophie could. 'Have you seen your father?'

'He's outside with Jude and some of the boys playing marbles. I'm just getting him a drink.' Dom reached into the fridge and took a second beer. 'Can I get you something, Mum?'

'No, thank you, dear. I had a lovely cup of tea.'

He noticed his mother's glance darting from one end of the room to the other, as if she was looking for someone, or something.

'And a lovely slice of cake,' she added, wringing her left hand with her right one.

'Have you seen your father?' she turned to him and faced him square on, her agitated eyes suddenly filling with unspilt tears.

'Come with me, Mum.' He looped one of her twisting hands through his arm.

'No, I should wait here. Your nice lady, she's waiting for me.'

Dom glanced at Erin, met her eyes and before he could form a thought, she had crossed the room and was standing beside them.

'Sophie,' she said, 'there you are! I've been looking for you!'

'There you are, dear. Dominic, look, it's Erin.'

Dom patted Sophie's hand. 'Yes, Mum,' he said. 'Shall we go out to the garden and find Dad?'

'No, no, dear. We used to own this place you know.' His mother had wiped her own tears away with the edge of a twisted SpongeBob napkin she'd had in her hand.

'Yes, you sold it to Dom and me.' Erin looked at him and he felt their life, the life they'd lived together here in this flat, flash between them.

He blinked slowly. It was the small things that still got to him, like his wife calling him Dom lately rather than the Dominic she'd insisted on the last couple of years.

'Who's that man?' Sophie asked, pointing across the room to Isaac. Dom pulled her hand back gently. It was confusing and painful for *him* to have to see Isaac in this place. He couldn't even begin to imagine what it must be like for Sophie.

'That's my friend, Isaac,' Erin said.

'Yes, dear, but who *is* he?' Sophie insisted, and Dom fought the urge to laugh. *Who indeed, Mum.*

'You should introduce me, dear. He's quite good-looking, isn't he? Is he married?'

'Come on, Sophie, I'll introduce you.'

I've got her, Erin mouthed to him and Dom watched as she took over with his ailing mother. And in that moment, he was consumed with the woman Erin had become. She had already become the best person she could be, and she'd done it without him. She had already proved she could hold down a full-time job and be a mother too. And she was bloody good at both.

'Dad, look what Granny and Grandad gave us!' Rachel's excited voice filled the room as she waved something at him. 'It does this and look it's got the pony game that I love.' He felt his daughter huddle into him, stroked her hair. 'Let me see? Oh, wow,' he said, 'show me how it works?'

Erin's head poked around the bookshelves that divided the large room. 'Isn't she a lucky girl?'

'She is,' he looked up as she beckoned him to join her.

'Just a minute love, show Grandad how it works and maybe we can play a game when I'm back.'

'What's up?' he said to Erin, who gestured to him to follow her down the hallway to Rachel's bedroom.

He scratched his ear, stood in the doorway as she turned to face him.

'I just wondered if you had any idea what else to get them? I'll take the Nintendos that we bought back on Monday, is that okay?'

'Yes, fine, okay.'

'You alright? You look pale.'

He swallowed hard. It was, despite the pretty

wallpaper, despite the different carpet, the new sash window to replace the falling-apart-older one, it was still Maisie's bedroom in his head.

Erin rubbed her neck, then hugged herself, as if she could suddenly read his mind and had decided she didn't want to. 'Right, well that was it,' he heard her say.

As she went to pass him, he reached for her arm. 'Erin?'

She stopped moving. 'Huh?'

'Yesterday, I told you that I still love you . . . '

Her arm moved from his grip as she turned to face him under the lintel and he could almost feel her breath on his face. 'I just wanted to say — '

'There you are!' Isaac bounded down the hallway like a Labrador puppy. 'People will be going soon. Should we do the cake?'

And it was that exact moment — the second that Isaac had used the word 'we' in a sentence about his wife and his children — that was the moment he formed a hard fist and hit him square in his perfectly dimpled chin.

★   ★   ★

20th June 2007

Darling Erin,

I'm sorry I'm not sorry.

That man brings out my primitive side. I want to thump my chest and show him who the silverback around here is. Then, I want to beat the shit out of him.

Okay. Maybe not. I'm not a violent man; have

207

never hit someone before this and the son-of-a-bitch made me spend a night in a cell after being charged with assault, so I'm not feeling remotely generous towards him right now. I wouldn't really want to beat him, not properly. Maybe just injure him a little, rough his pretty face up a bit.

Okay, okay, I'll stop. I'll never touch him again, but I know what's coming. You're going to tell me I have to apologise and I'm saying sorry to him when I'm not.

Not. Going. To. Happen. I loathe the man.

But as I was trying to tell you. I still love you, always will. And today I found some little foil triangles of Toblerone in my car. Tucked away in the glove compartment, melted to mush. I love you because once upon a time you put them there for me.

Dom xx

24. Dominic

THEN — July 2007

Dom was multi-tasking. With one hand, he cleaned the worktop in his narrow kitchen and with the other he swept the twelve square feet of linoleum with a half-bald brush. He'd already changed the linen on the bunks; Rachel had a new set bearing cuddly Care Bears while Jude's was covered in dinosaurs just like those from the story of *The Land Before Time*. But something niggled him as he passed the room and he stopped walking. Erin hadn't been happy the last time they'd been here, when he'd watched that video with them — Rachel had cried every night the following week because Littlefoot's mummy had died.

Shit. He'd bought it for him ages ago, before the sleepless week and when he'd put it on just now he'd been on autopilot. He looked at his watch. They were late. Quickly, he pulled the duvet from the top bunk and stripped the cover from it, rooted in the airing cupboard for another, before putting it back on the bed uncovered. Everything was in the washing basket and Jude would kick it off him anyway in the tiny, sweaty room. Dom opened the window and looked at his watch again. *Where was she? Where were they?*

An hour later, she was waving her hands in a

209

wordy apology. 'I'm so sorry,' she said, as he met her at the car where both children had fallen asleep. 'I know this is eating into your time with them, but Fitz was playing with them in the garden for ages. He had a paddling pool filled and we left late and then the traffic . . . Sorry. Did you get my text?'

'No, it's okay.' His phone pinged in his pocket. 'That'll probably be it. The signal in the flat is awful. Can you manage Rachel and I'll take Jude?'

She nodded and together they carried their children from her car to his flat.

He lifted Jude onto the top bunk as she slid Rachel into the bottom.

'We'll have to leave them dressed?' he whispered, standing to watch them for a moment.

She nodded, turned around, seemed to notice there was no door on the children's bedroom.

'Head in there,' he pointed to the opposite side of the landing. 'I know,' he said looking back, before closing the living room door. 'Their bedroom is a glorified cupboard.'

She wiped her hands on her jeans and looked around the space. 'It's weird I've not been in here before. It's . . . nice,' she said and he laughed.

'It's not weird and it's not that nice either. I've never wanted you to see how small it is. It serves a purpose. I just sleep here.'

'And work here.' Her head moved towards a pile of architectural drawings on the small dining table. She walked towards it.

'I was worried,' Dom said, wringing his hands. 'When I hadn't heard from you . . . I was imagining all sorts of things.'

'Well, we're here,' she said without looking at him.

'I thought you'd wrapped the car around a tree,' he said the words aloud that he'd thought he'd keep to himself.

'I thought I was the anxious one of us,' Erin replied, eyes still down on the papers on the table. 'Dom catastrophising . . . not sure I like that idea.' She picked up a set of estate agent's details. 'Valentine's Way, gosh, I love those houses.'

'I remember.'

'A refurb for a client?'

'Glass of wine? I have some open.'

She hesitated, looked at her watch and then said, 'Okay, why not,' before sitting on one side of the two-seater sofa, still reading the property details. 'God, Dom, it's gorgeous. Look at those windows. Are they original?'

Dom didn't reply, not wanting to call out from the kitchenette and wake the children. He brought two glasses of wine in, shut the door, opened a window and took the seat beside her. 'Cheers,' he said clinking her glass.

'Four bedrooms and two bathrooms,' he said, going into agent-speak. 'Yes, the windows are original, and it has so many authentic deco features including a small but stunning glass dome in the flat roof.' Dom had been careful not to answer her question about a client. Lying to Erin Carter wasn't something he ever planned

211

on doing again. 44 Valentine's Way, one of a row of ten thirties-built art deco style houses on a tree-lined street, two and a half miles from Kingston station — it had gone on the market last week and he'd just agreed to a second mortgage that made his eyes water.

'Would you like to help me choose the kitchen and bathrooms?' He could almost hear her mind working; watched her eyes narrow in thought, those dark green eyes flanked by thick, black, blinking lashes.

'What about Cora?' she asked after Dom's PA who did everything from his typing to his colour schemes.

'Maternity leave from next Friday. I've got a replacement for her, but for this, I don't know, I think you might be better?'

Erin frowned, shifted a bit and sat back in the chair, seemed to mull it over.

As she did, Dom concentrated on the sounds outside his first-floor window. Though it was after nine, it was still bright outside. Some traffic. A late lawnmower. Birds in the oak's branches just outside. *Tree Girl.*

'Can I have a think about it?' she said.

Tree Girl was sitting beside him.

'Of course. Take your time.' Dom was chewing a hangnail, watching her eyes roam his tiny home. 'You could be involved as little or as much as you'd like to be. All I want is your good taste.'

'You know you really shouldn't have hit him,' Erin changed the subject.

'Yes, I really should,' Dom's reply was instant. 'He's a tosser.' It was three weeks after the event, after his arrest for bodily harm which, only thanks to Erin, Isaac Chalmers wasn't pursuing any further.

Erin sighed.

He sipped his wine. 'I'm sorry I disappointed you. That said, I'm not sorry I thumped that idiot.'

She was playing with a tiny spot on her chin, rubbing her forefinger over it again and again. 'Oh, Dom . . . '

'You know you call me Dom again now.' He grinned. 'I knew I'd break you.' He regretted the comment immediately as her back stiffened and straightened, her nostrils flaring a little. 'Look,' he tried to pull it back, anxious not to lose what had taken him months to build in a few foolish seconds. He rested his head on the back of the sofa, acutely aware of the nearness of her. 'Do you remember once you asked me to talk to you as if I was writing in the Book of Love and you were never going to read it?'

Erin seemed to stare at the ceiling. 'That was a whole lifetime ago.'

'Maybe, but if you'll listen, I'd really like to do that again.'

She didn't flinch, which Dom took as permission.

'I love you,' he began.

She closed her eyes.

'I've always loved you. I'll die loving you and if that stuff you believe about angels is true, I'll still love you even then. I particularly love this new 'Zen' you.'

A tiny flicker of a smile appeared on her lips.

'I'm not going anywhere. I'm just here in the background watching you play with Isaac.'

Her eyes flashed open and narrowed.

'I'm waiting for a chance, for the right time, whenever that might be, to tell you that I can't love anyone else. If you don't ever give me another chance I'm doomed to that life — loving you, wanting to be with you and having to watch you with someone else.'

'Dom, you're hardly a monk.'

Actually, he was, but he didn't tell Erin that. 'If I were that, not a monk I mean, it would only be sex.' Dom could hear her breathing. 'Not love. Tell me you love him, and I'll stop talking. Or tell me you really don't love me, you have no feelings for me whatsoever, and that you'll never love me again, and I'll stop talking . . . '

Her lips twitched before she spoke. 'I have no feelings for you whatsoever and I'll never love you again.'

For a second his heart splintered and then he smiled. 'I don't believe you.'

She laughed softly. 'Not sure if that's confident or arrogant.'

'I'm laying my heart between us for you to stomp all over or pick up and hand it to me.'

He watched as her throat moved slowly with her swallow.

'Dom,' she shook her head. 'Too much has happened.'

They both turned as the door creaked open.

'I've got a tummy ache, Mummy.' Rachel stood framed by the door and Dom raised his arms.

'Come here, Pipsqueak.' He circled them around his daughter and pulled her up onto his lap.

'You really have a bad stomach?' Erin asked Rachel, doubt obvious in her eyes. 'Or did you just hear us talking?'

Dom tightened his grip, whispered in her ear. 'Tell the truth.'

'I just heard you,' she said.

'Bed, come on,' her mother replied. 'Daddy's taking you to ballet in the morning.'

'Are you staying here, Mummy?' Rachel asked. 'On the sofa,' she added quickly, and a little piece of Dom died inside.

'No love, no one can sleep on this sofa! See, it's too small, even for Mummy,' he told her neck.

Erin clapped her hands together once. 'Bed-ee-byes, young lady. Your dad will tuck you in.'

Dom led Rachel by the hand to her bedroom and helped undress her to her knickers and vest. Rachel lay down in bed and Dom pulled the duvet up to her chin.

'I'm too hot,' she complained, kicking it off.

He kneeled by the bed, wiped her brow and kissed her forehead. He leaned across to a shelf and pulled her favourite doll down. 'Here,' he said, 'Ruby will keep you company.'

'I don't play with dolls anymore, Daddy,' she announced.

'No, no.' He placed Ruby back on the shelf. 'Of course you don't.'

'Will you lie beside me until I go to sleep?'

'Sure, I will, budge over.' Dom lay the length of the bottom bunk, hovering on the edge, one arm thrown over her.

When Erin came to find him, he placed a finger across his lips and she stood on the landing watching them both for a few seconds, before heading back to the living room. Minutes later, with the sound of Rachel's deep breathing, slowly he eased himself off the bed. He kissed his fingers and rested them on her cheek and did the same to Jude.

In the living room, Erin was sitting forward on the sofa, elbows resting on her thighs, her head in her hands. He picked up his glass, stayed standing.

'They're both asleep. Where were we?' He grinned, searched his repertoire for the smile she loved most.

'Somewhere between you being arrogant or confident and me possibly stomping on your heart.'

'Do you remember the scene in *Titanic* where Celine Dion does her thing?'

The change of subject made her play with her chin again. 'What about it?'

'That bit where they're on top of the bow and Leonardo DiCaprio tells Rose to trust him.'

'*Jack* tells Rose to trust him,' she corrected.

'That bit — where Rose tells herself that she really should head back to the first-class cabin where whatshisface of the big jewellery is waiting.'

'Cal,' Erin smiled. 'Where Cal is waiting.'

'But every nerve-ending in her body is telling

216

her to trust Jack, that life with him could be truly amazing.'

Dom stared over the rim of the glass. 'We could have amazing, Erin. We had amazing once and we could have it again. Imagine that, another lifetime of amazing.' He drained the glass, out of words, spent.

'What if . . . ' Erin's voice was no more than a whisper. 'What if I *could* trust you again . . . ?'

'You can.' Dom placed the glass on the table and got down on his knees and, without touching her, said. 'I swear I would never let you down or hurt you again.'

She hesitated, blinked her eyes shut, to avoid looking at him. 'I can't,' she whispered.

He reached out, placed a hand on her face and rested it there. 'You can.'

'I have no feelings whatsoever for you and I'll never love you again.' Her eyes remained shut as she repeated the words rote.

His hand stayed. 'I still don't believe you.'

Tears slid from the edge of her eyelids. 'Your hand smells of bleach.' She smiled, a closed-lip smile.

And Dom took the biggest risk he had since the night he'd left his child and she'd died — he kissed away Erin's tears. Slowly, one by one.

'I'm not saying that I — ' she said.

Dom shushed her. 'Please. Please, don't say anything at all.' He stood up and pulled her into a standing hug. 'Just let me hold you.'

Overwhelmed, he felt his whole body react to her. He willed his cock not to scare her away. He willed her not to end the embrace, not to suddenly decide that stomping on his heart might be a better option. He held his breath and allowed himself to believe she'd heard him, that she believed him.

'I should go,' she spoke to his chest.

He held her face to his shirt, willing *her* to miss his scent as soon as she moved.

Inside, he cried, as she pushed him gently away and they stood, inches from one another.

'I'm not sure I can ever go back.' Her head moved side to side.

'Not sure is good. I'll take that, and we'd be going forward not back.' He paused. 'I don't know what to do, whether to let you walk out of here or beg you to stay. Do you love me, Erin?' He heard his own voice break like that of a thirteen-year-old choirboy.

'I love you. I hate that I do. I've tried very hard not to and even succeeded for a while.'

She loved him.

'And I love you mightily.'

Erin burst into tears and still he didn't move until she took a step towards him and arms stubbornly by her side, she leaned her face on his chest again. Then he wrapped his own arms around her and inhaled her, raised her spotted chin and kissed her gently on the mouth.

Slowly, he told himself. *Do not screw this up.*

He raised one hand and together, fingers laced, with no music but the sounds of the evening birdsong through the window, they slow danced in the tiny room like they had done many years ago in a New Forest hotel. Very quietly, he hummed the music to 'At Last'.

After a few minutes, she looked up and said, 'What about Isaac?'

'Isaac's the guy in the first-class cabin,' Dom replied. 'He'll be fine.'

★   ★   ★

13th July 2007

Erin,

Tonight, I touched your face, felt the tingle of your skin on my fingers.

Tonight, I kissed you, just gently, felt your lips on mine again, so strange, yet so familiar.

Tonight, you left to go back to what was our home, and I stayed in a place that will never be home.

I know I have to earn your trust, and not mess with the fact that you say you love me. I know I have more to do.

But I will wait for you forever, my Erin,
Dom xx

25. Erin

NOW — 12th June 2017

From *The Book of Love*:
'Dom, I love you because you're my friend
before anything.'

'You need your roots doing.'

Hannah is as charming as ever. 'Thanks for that,' I tell her.

'That's what friends are for,' she says. I don't reply, because I want to quote all the times I kept my mouth shut with her over the years, like the fact that I never told her how I honestly felt about her and Walt.

She links her arm through mine as we walk down the High Street. 'You look tired,' she adds.

'I love you too.'

'Sorry, but you do. You not sleeping?'

'Not brilliantly.'

'Maybe see the doctor?'

I glare at her. 'I think I've seen enough doctors for a while, don't you?'

She looks as if she's about to respond, in a 'that-doesn't-matter-you-need-to-see-another-one' manner and then thinks better of it. 'So, what sort of a wedding present do you want to get them?' she asks instead, as we enter the department store, both of us immediately spritzed by some girl spraying perfume which makes me sneeze.

'I don't know.' I rub my nose with the back of my hand. And I don't know. My nineteen-year-old, too-young-to-be-married son lives in a small studio with his girlfriend, scrap that, wife. The place has little room for anything other than themselves.

'I called him,' Hannah says.

'Did he answer?'

'Yes.'

'And?'

'I offered them both my congratulations, asked all about it. Of course, he's completely unrepentant.'

I laugh, walk around someone who's just stopped moving in front of me. 'When have you ever known my son to be anything else?'

'I fear 'tis the genes.'

'Mine or Dom's?'

'All of them. Poor chap's doomed.'

Up the escalator, turn right, past the crockery and I'm soon handling a set of very expensive bed linen, show it to her and she shakes her head.

'Wasted,' she says, no doubt remembering the state of Jude's bedroom when he lived at home.

'You're right, this is useless, maybe we could send them away to a nice hotel for a few days?' I drop the linen, drop the idea of a physical present, convinced that a hotel break is the best idea — a sort of mini honeymoon. 'Let's just go for lunch.' I turn and head downstairs again. 'But I have to pick up some dry-cleaning first.'

My phone sings 'Zip-a-Dee-Doo-Dah' from inside my bag.

'Hi, darling, how are you?' I say to my other child. Hearing Rachel's voice grounds me. We chat about her day and eventually she asks how I am about Monday night's revelation. I tell her in my live-in-the-moment-recently-acquired tone that there's nothing I can do to change the facts.

Hannah, who can just about hear both sides of the conversation, rolls her eyes, probably because she's not fooled.

After I've hung up, we walk together towards the dry-cleaners and Hannah waits outside. There's a queue. I stand directly under the air conditioning unit and raise my face to the cooling air. When it's my turn, the young girl behind the counter hands me the cellophane-wrapped items while looking at me oddly.

'You Mrs Carter?' she asks without waiting for a reply. 'I've got something for you,' she says searching under the counter.

'Oh?'

She hands me a small envelope. 'It was in Mr Carter's jacket, I think.'

'Oh . . . ' I look down at the cleaning. All mine but for one linen jacket of Dom's.

'Thank you,' I say and am rewarded with a lovely, braced smile.

Moving aside for the woman standing behind me, I nod again, wave the envelope, and mutter another thank you before leaving. The clothes are heavy, so I'm forced to sit on a bench in the pedestrianised area off the high street. I push them onto Hannah's lap and rip open the envelope. Two tickets for an Etta James tribute concert, for a date while I was in the States. I burst into tears as I remember Dom when we were going to Cornwall last year talking about a surprise he'd planned.

Can't tell you. It's a thing, not a place.

Hannah roots in her bag for a tissue. 'You're alright, Erin.' Her calm voice assures me.

'We missed it. I was in America and — '

I've never been good with surprises.

'You're upset about Jude too and you know what? He's going to be fine,' Hannah offers.

I feel her squeeze my hand, tight enough to make me wince.

'Maybe now's not the time but I'm going to take a chance.' She hesitates before catching my eye, focusing hard. 'You should see Lydia. It's time to let go of — '

My jaw tightens, and I interrupt her. 'I'm never going back to work for her.'

'Okay, but — '

'Dom and I have been figuring out what happens next.'

'Erin, look, this is crazy, you can't be — '

'No, you look, Hannah, what you need to realise, hell, what you and Dom both need to realise is that I've let go already.'

Hannah knots what's left of the tissues and shakes her head gently.

I end the conversation with, 'You say 'Lydia' and I say 'Lydia who?' Okay?'

* * *

At home, Dom and I are listening to a playlist of our favourite music from my phone; everything from Etta James to American rock, followed by Ed Sheeran. I'm curled into his frame on the sofa. 'You never told me you bought tickets for an Etta James tribute concert.'

'Ahh,' he says without flinching. 'How — '

'The tickets were in your jacket, and I picked up the dry-cleaning today.'

'It was meant to be a surprise.'

I make a tiny grunt-like sound. 'You should have said something.'

'You wanted to go to the States. Those tickets wouldn't have stopped you.'

I link my hand with his, careful to touch each finger one by one, slowly. 'I would love to have gone to that concert with you.'

He puts his finger on my lips and shushes me, 'Listen.'

Ed is reaching the end of his serenade and just as he pleads to his lover to take him in her loving arms, Dom squeezes me, kisses my hair.

'Just wasn't meant to be, my love,' he whispers.

26. Dominic

'Remind me again how you did this?'

'Did what?' Dom asked Nigel.

'You know what I mean.' Nigel wiped the sweat from his brow with his shirtsleeve. 'You're all back together and moving in here? May I remind you that only eight months ago, you spent a night in the cells for decking her lover?'

Dom leaned both his hands on the top of the sideboard they were moving and stared at his friend. 'Hitting the guy was the best thing I ever did and the worst thing I ever did. I hate violence of any sort.' He shrugged. 'But when I heard Erin tell him he'd goaded me, I knew, I knew all wasn't well in the land of Isaac and Erin. After that, I waited and on the thirteenth of July, I kissed my wife again for the first time in almost two years.'

'Yeah and then you gave her a house for Christmas, that'll do it every time. Smooth bastard.'

Their laughter was interrupted by the sounds of the children arriving up the path.

Dom looked out the window. They were here. He stopped and stared, determined to commit the moment to memory. Jude, already four inches taller than his sister, was dragging a suitcase. She ran behind him, shouting 'Whoever gets there first, gets the bigger room!' Jude dropped the case and ran ahead of her and took the stairs two at a time.

'Dadd-yyy,' Rachel screamed. 'He pushed me and now he's going to get it!'

By the time Dom followed, Rachel was already in tears. 'Hey, come on.' He pulled her towards him, rubbed her glossy hair with the back of his hand. 'Rachel, I told you before, we'll toss a coin for the bigger room. That's the fairest way.'

Dom watched as his son stuck his tongue out at his sister. 'Cry baby,' Jude sneered.

'Jude . . . ' Dom warned him. Downstairs he heard Erin and Lydia in the kitchen. She'd obviously decided to let him sort this one out.

'Right.' he put his hands in his pocket and pulled out a pound coin. 'You both agree that this is the fairest way to do it?'

Both heads nodded.

'So, call, heads or tails.'

'Heads,' Jude said.

'Tails,' Rachel called.

Dom flipped the coin in the air and watched it land, the Queen's image obvious from a height.

He smiled at Rachel as she sighed and headed down the landing to what would be her smaller room. 'Don't be smug about it, Jude,' he told his son as he went to follow her. 'You won, but don't be smug.'

In the rear bedroom that sat next to his and Erin's room, Rachel was sitting on the floor, her back to the radiator.

'It's cold,' she grumbled. Dom bent down and twisted the controls. 'It'll warm up soon,' he said, taking a seat on the ground beside her.

'You know sometimes what we think we don't want is exactly what we do.'

Rachel tilted her head and raised her eyebrows as if to say, don't bother trying to make me feel better.

'This bedroom has the biggest window in the house and the best view of the garden.' He leaned towards her, lowering his voice. 'It's also much quieter than the one at the front. You get all the street noise at the front.'

He kissed her cheek and saw the beginnings of her lips curving. 'Not to mention this has a built-in cupboard for a certain little person's clothes and shoes.'

'Okay,' she smiled.

'See, what you thought you wanted . . . '

'Can we get a dog?' she asked, 'Mum would never let us have one in the flat.'

He laughed. 'That's not something we're doing now, Rachel Carter.'

'Please?' she asked. 'Just say you'll think about it.'

'I'll think about it, but Mummy needs to think about it too.'

'Okay. Is that your bedroom next to mine? Yours and Mummy's?'

Dom pulled her to him, felt the heat begin to flow through the radiator behind their backs and leaned into it. Knowing how confusing the last few months had been for both of the children, he spoke softly, 'I know it's all a bit strange, love but — '

'I don't care what bedroom I have, Daddy. I

just don't want you to go again.' Rachel squeezed her eyelids shut to stop herself crying.

'That room next door is mine and Mummy's bedroom and I'm not going anywhere,' he said. 'I promise.'

'I like being closer to Mummy at night.'

'I know, darling. Now you can be closer to both of us.'

Dom sensed, rather than saw, Jude hovering behind the door, imagined him, one hand in one pocket, leaning on the door surround. Unsure if Jude could see him or not, he winked at the gap where the door was open. And as he heard him move away, he spoke to Maisie in his head, asked her to help him to be up to the job that Erin had managed mostly alone for the last few years.

★   ★   ★

At nine o'clock he unloaded the last box from the van he'd hired. It had been tiring — thirteen loads back and forth from the flat to the house but he and Nigel had done most of the heavy lifting while Erin, Lydia and Hannah had unpacked the boxes as soon as they landed in the hallway. Everyone else had finally left, sensing the family needed to be alone and surprisingly the house already had some order to it. Dom shivered as he carried the last box up the path, placed it on the frosted ground in front of him so his frozen fingers could get a better grip. As he bent down to pick it up again, his mobile buzzed in his pocket. Fitz. He saw his father-in-law's name and hit the answer button.

228

'Fitz,' he said. 'How are you?'

'You all in yet?'

Dom looked at the crate by his feet. 'Almost, just about to bring the last box in.'

'You alone?'

Dom's brow creased. 'Yes. What's up?'

'Hurt her again, Dom, and I swear . . .'

Dom swallowed. This was a conversation he'd known was coming, one he had to admit he'd been afraid to begin many times. 'Fitz, I — '

'This isn't a chat, Dom. I don't want to hear you speaking, I just want you to listen. That's my little girl in that fancy new house. They're my grandchildren. If you hurt her or them again, I will make it my life's work to make you pay.'

Dom looked through the window to the living room to where his wife and two children were eating pizza.

'You understand that?' Fitz added.

'Completely.'

'Good.'

When the line went dead, he approached the glass and immediately Erin beckoned him in to eat. Shaking his head, he stood and just looked, for a moment, unable to move. Erin walked to the window and placed her palm against it. The heat from her hand against the cold single pane created a cloud around her fingers and he placed his own palm against hers. With his free hand, he counted out the fingers, watched her face as he did so.

'One, you. Two, me. Three, Maisie. Four, Jude and five Rachel.' He spoke the words aloud and breathed out, the icy air frosting his long breath.

Erin nodded, blew him a kiss and when he removed his hand, saw the smudged print it had left, he wished it could have stayed there forever. Dom hoisted the crate up from the ground and entered the house.

An hour later, when the kids were asleep, he and Erin were in the bedroom hanging and folding clothes into the cupboards.

'I'm sorry I have to go to work tomorrow,' Dom said over a pile of sweaters.

'Can't be helped. Don't worry. The kids are in school. I'm off so I'll sort the kitchen when they're out of the house and we may even eat home-cooked food tomorrow night!'

Dom looked at his wife, at the tracksuit she wore, the bleach marks on it from where she had scrubbed the loos today. She would disagree, tell him he was insane, if he told her out loud at that moment how beautiful she looked but she did. She was here, and she was here with him and the children and she was as beautiful to him as the first time he'd ever seen her.

'Do you remember the first night?'

'Which first night?' she grinned. 'The night we met, the night we first made love, the night we were first apart from one another?'

He grimaced.

'This,' she said. 'In a few years, this will be our first night in what's going to be our happy place.'

'I mean the night we first met at Lydia's party, New Year's Eve 1995.'

'I do.'

'Do you remember what I told you?'

'I do.'

'I told you that I thought I'd love you forever.'

'Yeah, you did.' She came across to him, pushed him back onto the bed and straddled him before removing her top and bra. 'Wanna prove it?'

'Happy Valentine's Day, Mrs Carter,' he said, reaching up for her and lacing his fingers behind her neck.

'Happy Valentine's Way, Mr Carter,' she replied.

Dom closed his eyes as she kissed him, as certain as he could be that she was right. This would be a happy place for them.

★   ★   ★

15th February 2008

Darling Dom,

It's good to be back. It's good to have the book in the same hall table that was in the flat, sitting under the same mirror in the hall, even if it's a different home. It feels very odd, being here, knowing the last time I wrote to you in here was October 2005 — that awful time.

I'm another person now and I think you are too. For me, all I can say is I feel stronger — to the point that I'm not even sure I need this route to talk in the way I used to. I feel we might be okay without it. But let's see, maybe you still feel the need — let's watch this space . . .

I haven't read what you wrote in here during the time we were apart. Someday I will just not now. I think maybe I want to pretend none of it happened but at the same time, I realise it had to and I'm glad it did.

In years to come if someone asked us where it all went wrong — would we point to the day Maisie died? Or to the time before when maybe we still didn't know how each of us really worked? Maybe to when you first lied about gambling and felt you couldn't show me that side of you?

I kept the card that Fitz gave us with this book and reunited it today! And I've pasted it in the back page because I think the sentiment behind it really matters:

In years to come, this book will be a place where you'll look back and read about the things you were possibly too young or naïve to understand.

Should I not have asked you to leave, and forgiven you? Possibly. But if things hadn't unfolded the way they did, you would never have gotten help. You wouldn't wear that dog tag; you wouldn't live your life by Admit, Atone and Hope.

And I would never have learned that love, real love, endures.

I'm so looking forward to being with you again, so looking forward to our family being together again.

I love you, Dom, because you waited.
Erin xx

27. Dominic

THEN — September 2008

Dom listened to the distant hum from the motorway, opened his eyes and stopped himself reaching for Erin's outline. It was cold. The tip of his nose was freezing; he was cold and though he craved the warmth he knew her body would give, holding her would wake her.

In three hours, she'd get up, get the children ready for school, get herself ready for work. In the kitchen, she'd take something out of the freezer for dinner tonight, let it defrost in the sink. If he was still around when she left on the school run, she'd kiss him goodbye, a slice of slightly burnt toast in one hand, her car keys in the other. He'd yell at the children to make their beds before they go. And after they'd all left, he'd look around their happy place and pinch himself as their voices echoed in the space.

He breathed deep, held it, then exhaled slowly. This was how she used to feel when anxiety owned her, he thought as dread pulsed in his veins. There had been a mere seven months of pure bliss together. Not long enough, he thought. Not long enough.

Then again, who knew what might happen when he looked her in the eye and told her. There would be, he'd promised himself, no hiding in the written word. This was one where he'd fix on the edges of her green irises and speak.

But not yet. He slipped from their bed, put the same clothes on he'd removed only hours earlier and quietly left the house.

★ ★ ★

Every morning, very early, Dom's father tended to his mother in their bedroom and the first thing he did was kiss her before turning the key in her music box. On the rare times that Dominic witnessed it, he never failed to be moved. It was a tune his mother had loved, something she and his father had once learned to waltz to. Gerard would graze Sophie's Vaselined lips with his own and then brush her hair, just a tender caress with the soft bristles and every time — every time, Dom had to look away.

'You're here early,' his father said to him. 'And you look absolutely awful. She might not know who you are, but you could at least have had a shave, smarten up a bit.'

'Dad — '

'Dominic, don't tell me you're forty-eight years old and a grown-up. That much I know. It's just about respect for your mother.'

'Dad — '

'What is it?' His father's irritated impatience, which Dom understood, given what he had to deal with every day while his mother disappeared slowly, vanished the instant he turned around to look at him. It was as if Dom's face finally revealed that he hadn't come for a social call.

'Dom?' Gerard's voice softened. 'What's happened? Is everything alright?'

'No, Dad. No.'

'Erin, the kids?' His father's hand moved to his heart as he took the seat next to his and Sophie's bed.

'No.' Dom shook his head. 'They're fine.' He ran a hand through the head of hair he would swear had thinned in the last ten days. 'Dad,' he began to cry, something he had not done in front of his father since he was nine years old; not even the time he'd had to borrow money to pay a gambling debt, nor the last time he'd turned to his parents, when Erin had asked him to leave. 'I'm in trouble, Dad. Serious trouble.'

As his father stood and approached him, pulled him into an embrace, all Dom could see was his mother's face, the tiniest bit of drool sliding from the corner of her mouth.

'Son, nothing's this bad, eh?'

But it was. It was that bad and he had no idea how he was going tell Erin. Everything had turned to shit. He looked through the window behind his mother. The silver birch twenty feet from the building had already shed most of its leaves, the grass covered in an array of rust and golden leaves; all beautiful but dead, as dead as the life he had yesterday. According to the books he and his accountant had worked on through the night they were going to lose everything. All the savings, stocks, shares he'd worked so hard to build up, the cash she'd squirrelled away over the years, all now in one pot. And the worst thing, the thing he couldn't face Erin with, the house.

It had been more than a black Monday yesterday. Now international global banks had collapsed, it was a black month. A fucking ebony hole which threatened to swallow him and his family. Dom sobbed into his father's shoulder, hating the fact that he had to turn to him again. He caught a vague scent of stale cologne and closed his eyes to avoid seeing his mother. But there, behind his eyes was Erin's face instead, and in that instant, just for the briefest of moments, Dominic Carter thought of throwing himself under a train or off a bridge. Because he'd sworn off risk in October 2005, never, ever, touched a card or a craps table since. But as his accountant had innocently pointed out at midnight last night. 'These stocks and shares — it's all a gamble isn't it, all a game of chance.' And Dom had lost one more time.

★   ★   ★

'It's not your fault.'

He would, he thought, take Erin's white expression to the grave with him. He studied her face, looking for something that might reveal she meant those words.

'I'm sure we both signed whatever it was.'

He could see her straining to remember if she had. She had; all things financial were always signed by them both, but it didn't matter — he was the one who should have asked more questions.

Slowly, her features, as always with Erin,

exposed each feeling. At first, disbelief, a slight thought crossing her mind that this might be some sick joke on his part and then almost immediately, the realisation that no, he wouldn't do that to her. He was more likely to really lose everything they possessed rather than joke about it. And then shock — her fingers spreading over parted lips. Next, disappointment. It creased her features — her eyes as they focused directly on him narrowing and filling at the same time. And finally fear, what would they do? Something he needed to talk to her about because, very soon, the vultures would be coming to pick.

Erin stood from the kitchen chair she'd been sitting on, tapped his shoulder as she passed him. 'I have to get the kids up for school, get them off. After that, we'll figure something out. I'm phoning in sick — I need to understand this, we'll go to the accountant together when I get back. Okay?'

He nodded.

'Go get cleaned up. Don't let them see you like this, Dom.'

Dom was staring at their dream kitchen.

'Dom. Shower. Now. I can hear them moving around upstairs.'

★ ★ ★

Spreadsheets. He hated them with every fibre of his being. And the accountant going over and over the same facts waving the sheets of paper with columns and red figures and agreements that they'd been party to made him hate them even more. He and Erin went to the pub afterwards and as he placed two glasses of Pinot on the table between them, he felt the same icy fear he'd felt years ago when they'd separated.

'We can't afford them,' she said, her arms folded. 'You should have asked for two glasses of tap water.'

'I've ordered a plate of chips too. Just one plate, we can share.' He tried to raise a smile.

'We have to have one row about this, Dom, and I don't want it to be around the kids. And I don't want it to be a screaming match. That's why we're here. How the *hell* has this happened?'

'The investment portfolio, it's, it *was* in stock and bond markets. Everything's gone to shit, the markets, the banks, the world, I — '

Erin turned her lips in on themselves as if she was stopping herself speaking.

'By signing what we did, we agreed with the broker — he could lever the portfolio — it meant bigger returns.'

'Obviously not.' She found her voice. 'Did you ever actually speak to him? Surely you knew what this could have meant?'

'The markets have gone up every bloody year for the last God knows how long. He invested in derivatives. Yes, we, I, if you like, *I* gave him permission, *I* didn't fully understand what the risk was. It's my fault.'

'Dom, I get what goes up also goes down, but this?'

She had walked out of the accountant's office before the end of the meeting and he had followed her here.

'How much?' she asked now as she ran her hands through her hair, leaving them there.

'Everything.' He looked directly into her eyes because he knew he had to. 'Plus, the equity in the house.'

'Jesus,' she said, and gulped some wine.

Dom thanked the woman who brought the chips that Erin only stared at. 'What nobody saw was the financial world imploding like it just has. There was obviously always a gamble — '

'No shit. And this from the man who *swore* he would never gamble again.'

Dom shook his head vigorously. 'This is not the same thing at all,' he tried.

Erin banged a fist on the table before realising where she was and sitting back. 'It's exactly the same thing,' she seethed. 'We took something and played with it when we couldn't afford to lose it. It doesn't matter whether it's with money or stocks and shares or your marriage.' She leaned forward and almost hissed. 'Do not fuck with it if you care about it. And *never* let someone else decide what to do with it.'

Dom could feel a tendon pulsing in his neck. He looked at the table next to them. Two women were sat opposite one another using sign language. He had no idea what they were saying but was glad that they smiled and seemed completely unaware of what he and Erin were.

'They can't hear me,' Erin said. 'I've been watching them, and them not hearing allowed me to tell you how I really feel.'

'You'd have said exactly what you just did, how you just did, even if they could hear you.'

Dominic tore the edges off a damp beer mat.

'You're right. I just feel a little better that they can't.'

He heard her take a deep sigh before speaking again.

'What do we do? What's next?' she said.

'There is something,' he put up a placating hand, tried to grab one of hers which she snatched out of reach. 'I've spoken to Dad.'

'No.' Erin spat the word. 'Your father has helped enough in the past and he has a lot on his mind.'

'It was his idea. Erin, either we and our family are fucked,' he let his words sink in before finishing, 'or we let Dad help.'

'No. He has enough stress and someday he's going to have to pay for your mother's care.'

'Dad has money, real money, and unlike us, kept it in cash the last few years. He's escaped this mess and wants to help. If we don't take his help, we lose everything, declare bankruptcy.' Dom let the words sit between them before speaking again. 'Clients would get wind of it, work would be affected. We'd never be able to borrow again.'

Erin sucked air. 'What does he suggest?' She had lowered her eyes to the floor and was hugging herself.

'He'd buy our house, market value, a proper investment — the equity we get pays the last of the debts. We then rent it from him. That way we get to stay there. The kids get to stay in their school. Dad is nearly eighty, Mum is . . . ' Dom caught a catch in his throat. 'He'll amend his will

240

that Lydia gets the family home and we inherit Valentine's when both he and Mum are gone . . .'

Erin picked up a chip, smelled it and threw it back on the plate. 'Your dad — can he really afford Valentine's?'

'He says he can.'

'What about your mother, when she has to go into a nursing home?'

Dom shook his head. 'He says he's never going to allow that to happen, that he'll continue to care for her at home with help like he's already doing.'

Erin breathed out slowly through her hands.

Dom sat on his, desperate to reach out and touch her. 'I'm sorry.'

She gave an ironic laugh. 'I saw a movie once, a beautiful love story where it claimed that love meant never having to say sorry.'

Instinct made him reach out again and she didn't pull away as he stood and pulled her into his arms.

'But that's rubbish.' Erin began to cry, her mascara staining his shirt. 'I'm sorry that I was naïve enough to trust you to deal with money stuff. And I need to hear you're sorry and to forgive you — because, without that, it'll be 2005 all over again.'

As he held her tight, Dom realised that though the ladies next to him couldn't hear a word, they were obviously pretty adept at lip-reading. One of them looked over and offered a sympathetic smile. The other shook her head tightly and stirred her tea.

'I'm sorry,' he stroked his wife's hair, then lowered his mouth to it, kissed her head and whispered. 'We will not lose our home. I promise.'

★ ★ ★

29th September 2008

Dear Dom,

Of course I don't want to lose Valentine's but even though we've both worked so hard, here we are. We were stupid (I'm being nice here) and the world conspired against us and now we have diddly squat again.

I want to keep our beautiful home if possible but more importantly I want to keep us.

It does feel as if our life together is two steps forward and ten back but this time, we're together.

I choose to believe in us. I choose to believe in you and though this might take a long time to repay, to sort out, we'll do it. Somehow. And I'm just so enormously grateful to your father that I can't find the words. But I will.

Erin xx

28. Erin

NOW — 14th June 2017

From *The Book of Love*:
'I love you because you get me, and you
still persist in sticking around.'

Christ, it's quiet.

Dom's in the study and because I'm not at work, I've already unloaded and reloaded the dishwasher, put the washing on, done the ironing. I've mopped the bathroom floors. I've called and spoken with both the kids and I'm wondering what's next, when the sound of the home phone makes me leap.

I grab it just before the answerphone kicks in and I hear Fitz's voice.

'Dad, hi.' I'm a little out of breath but he doesn't seem to notice.

'Hello, love, just calling to catch up. How's things?'

Fitz, I've come to realise doesn't want to catch up on these bi-weekly calls. Not really. He's my father. I love him but since he's rediscovered sex in his late sixties, his finger's not on the Erin pulse anymore.

'I'm great,' I say.

'You back at work?'

'Yes, yes, it's busy. Usual stuff. Busy, busy.' I feel my cheeks colour.

'And the family?'

'All well.'

'You're full of news then.'

'Well, Dad, not a lot has happened since I got back, really. How's Penny?' I ask after his girlfriend, the woman I still blame for his move away.

I sit on the last step of the stairs, know he'll talk about what they're up to, which motor-rally they're off to this weekend, by which time, I should be able to politely escape.

'Are you sure you're alright, Erin?' he asks me after I've made appropriate noises.

'Of course.'

'You'd tell me, if — '

'Of course,' I say again.

He talks, and I listen for another few minutes and after I understand the real reason for his call, I stand up and ring the doorbell. 'Dad, sorry, I've got to go. That's a delivery I have to sign for. Talk soon? Love you!'

As soon as I hang up and am staring at the phone, I can't believe I haven't told my father that his only grandson just got married. I can't believe I haven't told him that I've not gone back to work at all.

But all I heard in the whole conversation was that Dad is selling the house; the house I grew up in, the house my mother died in.

⋆   ⋆   ⋆

Later, I catch Dom peering at some shots I took of New York that hang framed in his study. His

244

eyes are inches from the frames, and he holds a hand out to me. 'Fish scales,' he says, and I have no idea what he means. 'Do you remember,' he continues, 'when I blew up this shot of yours, the top of the Chrysler Building flashing in the sun?'

I remember. It's one of my favourite photos taken with a camera Dom bought me years ago.

'I wanted to emulate the idea of a roof with oval, fish-scale tiles. This photo was what inspired that house, remember the big one with the sea view down in Portsmouth? We had some small pointed, triangular windows in the loft space too.'

I nod as he continues.

'Sounds weird,' he's musing to himself now, stroking his chin with a thumb and forefinger. 'But it worked,' he says, then sits on his office chair, the one with swivel wheels. He pulls me onto his lap and we spin across the room.

My grip on him loosens. 'Dizzy,' I whisper, standing up and steadying myself on the desk. All I can think of is Fitz asking me to meet an agent at his and Mum's house. I need to get a copy of his key made and hand it over.

'Erin, what's up?'

'Huh?'

'You're doing that thing with your hair, twirling it around your ears. You only ever do that when you're nervous. Or lying,' he adds, a hint of a smile forming.

'What do you mean?'

'I mean you look just like you did, oh, back during the time when the financial world got fucked up the ass and our world went tits up again.'

I'm muted, keep my hands still, know exactly what he's talking about. 'I never lied then.'

'A lie of omission, my dear wife, but let's pretend that you just *forgot* to tell me you were ill.'

'There was too much other shit happening. I didn't want to worry you and I told you when I had to.'

'Yeah, so you've always said.'

Out-loud words. More frightening to me than tiny handwritten ones in our book. And the health scares that I've had, have always, always, been discussed with him in whispers on my part. Those tiny treacherous skin cells that I had removed a few times. Subconsciously, I run my forefinger over the last one — a small, moon-shaped scar on my shoulder.

'So, if you're not lying now,' Dom grins. 'Why would you be nervous?'

I am nervous. And I suppose I'm lying to *myself* because I haven't been taking my anxiety meds. Usual reason. Everything seems fine, I don't feel tense or anxious, so I think I don't need them. I keep my fingers away from my ears and smile back.

The man knows me so well.

29. Dominic

THEN — July 2009

She had done this.

Erin, his wife, who no matter what life threw at her picked herself up and ploughed straight ahead. She was the one who'd made all this happen; started the ball rolling after Maisie's ninth anniversary in 2007, telling him it was about time they did something to raise funds for Sudden Infant Death Syndrome. And last year, just before their life imploded, she had organised this event and they had swum their first sponsored 10K relay. She had somehow found purpose in Maisie's death and had helped others to too.

This year, though all their training had happened at the pool in Nigel's school, Dom was grateful the event itself was outdoors in a nearby lido.

The day was bright, the sun high in a cloudless sky. Nerves jangled as Nigel play-punched him in the arm, teased him with typical 'Let me know what it's like coming in behind me' remarks. He tried to focus, looked across at Hannah and Erin sitting calmly on striped deckchairs, their goggles around their necks. Hannah's face was angled back to the sun, Erin was stretching her arms gently as she sat under a wide umbrella in the shade.

'Try not to think about the number of lengths.' Lydia handed him a small piece from a banana. 'You guys have this sorted — five ten-length relays each. A doddle.'

'Says the non-swimmer.'

'Hey, I'm helping with the barbecue later! And I'm over there, all set up with the Bean Pod stall. My lovely staff, and your lovely kids, are handing out teas and coffees. I'm doing my bit. If God had meant us to swim he'd have given us gills.' She winked and headed to the girls with her bananas.

Dom raised his right leg behind him, pulling from the ankle, feeling the stretch on his thigh and repeated the same on the other side. Recognising Rachel's laugh, his eyes were drawn to the Bean Pod stand, where she stood behind the table with Jude and some kid from school that they'd brought with them. He strained to hear but he could see — he could see her with her hand in her hair and the sound of that giggle. His eleven-year-old daughter was *flirting* with her brother's friend. Heading to Erin, his hand was pointing at the scene when she started to laugh.

'Don't point! Leave her.'

'She's flicking her hair and giggling!'

Hannah laughed out loud as she passed them both on her way to the blocks.

'Yep.' Erin nodded. 'And your first ten is after Hannah, so keep stretching.'

Dom frowned. 'I know what I'm doing. Do we know what she's doing?' His head jerked towards their daughter.

'Relax, Dom. It's all harmless stuff. You'd be better off worrying about Jude. He looks more than a little pissed off.'

Dom looked — she was right. Jude sat at the edge of the table, his arms folded, staring into the distance. 'Shit.'

The sound of the gong and a loud splash meant Hannah was in the water already.

'Go and cheer her on,' Erin said. 'I'll make sure Jude's alright.'

As Dom and Nigel rooted for Hannah at each turn, he had one eye on Erin. Noticing she stood a few feet from Jude as she spoke, he thought, good, that's good. Jude did not like public displays of affection either *from* one of his parents or *between* his parents. Whatever she'd said she'd managed to persuade him to follow her, handing him something on the way. As they neared he could see it was the stopwatch. She'd asked him to take the splits — the timing of each lap. Nigel had some way of telling who 'won' from the lap timings, which for some reason was important to him even in a charity swimathon that was all about finishing and not about winning.

As Hannah touched the wall after ten laps he dived in — not coming up for almost half the length of the pool and immediately drawing air from his angled mouth. Dom had discovered in training for this event that he loved to swim. It was odd. Erin had been right, years ago, when she'd touched on his 'mini obsessions' — his need for a high. He'd never found one like the inside of a bookies gave, despite trying, but with

249

swimming something different happened. He relaxed in water, without ever feeling the need for speed or a win. He found himself not caring for competition like Nigel urged him to do, just loving that slow slide through the pool, with nothing but his thoughts and his own heartbeat for company.

And the water was, he'd found, a place where his thoughts lined up automatically in order of importance. It was as if that with every few strokes, with each breath he'd take, first left-hand side and then right, he found his worries lessen as the rhythmic breathing became the only thing he 'needed' to do. Everything else seemed to matter less.

As he swam, he thought of his mother, Sophie, as a young woman and her likeness to Rachel. Work followed; the latest building, the newest contractor, a jovial guy called Tim Chimes, who made the job feel fun and easy. And Erin . . . As he felt his arms stretch into the turn underwater, Erin's body flashed in his mind. Still images from his memory bank; her lying on her side the first time they'd made love in her tiny room in Lydia's flat, her long hair spilling over her; her wandering through their own flat naked in the early days. Her wandering through Valentine's this morning naked, oblivious to those tiny tell-tale scars where basal cells had been removed. One tiny carcinoma on her left shoulder and another, even smaller, on her right thigh. Gone. She hadn't even told him about that first one last year, claiming the tiny mark left by the scalpel was a rogue horsefly bite. None of that mattered now. Clear scans had confirmed it was gone. Now you think you see it, now you think you don't . . . Gone, gone, gone. And Maisie — Maisie was allowed in his stream of consciousness today. When all was said and done, this fundraiser was about her. And breathe . . . By the time he'd swam his first ten lengths and Erin had already dived in just above him, he caught sight of Jude bending over with the stopwatch and didn't even glance across at his teasing daughter.

★ ★ ★

Valentine's garden had become the natural hosting ground for the post-swim barbecue with guests bringing a variety of salads and Dom and Erin barbecuing burgers and sausages until late. After he'd showered and changed, Dom was rushing downstairs to help when he found Hannah sitting at the top of the stairs, rubbing her hair with a hand towel.

'I wanted to thank you,' she looked up.

'You don't need to. Are you alright?' Hannah had pulled out of the last ten laps, meaning each of the others had to do a couple more with Dom swimming the last six.

Hannah rubbed her stomach. 'Just a twinge, I didn't feel I should keep going, sorry.'

Dom edged by her so that he was a few steps lower on his way down. 'You sure you're alright?'

She looked over the curled staircase as if checking for other people. 'No,' she replied.

He sat on the step beneath her. 'What's up?'

'I'm forty next week,' she whispered.

He laughed. 'I was forty last week.'

'Walt and I are finished.'

'Aah . . . ' Dom said, and, without realising it, tugged on his leather band. 'I did wonder why he wasn't around this morning.' Walt had only ever been a part-time member of their gang, there by invite of Hannah, and not every time they met. Everyone knew — no one really 'got' it, but everyone knew what it was. In Dom's eyes, it had had the scent of doom attached to it from the very beginning. 'I'm sorry,' he said, because he was. He was sorry for Hannah. He stood and tried to squeeze in beside her on the top step.

'You need a hug.' He put an arm around her and she laid her head on his chest.

'It's sad. I'm sad, he's sad.'

'Why is it over? Why now?' Dom asked.

'Because I'm having a baby.'

'Jesus.'

'No, it's Walt's.' Hannah gave a weak smile. 'I've been trying to convince him for the last two years. I told him I wanted a child — he told me he didn't.'

'Please tell me you didn't do this deliberately without him knowing.' Dom moved to a standing position, leaned against the wall.

Hannah's hand went to her throat. 'I can't tell you that because I did. And before you yell at me, I truly, truly believed that he'd come around if it was real.'

'Oh, Hannah.' Dom looked straight at her.

'And now it's real and not only has he not come around, but he hates me. Dom, this is my only chance at having a child. And though I'm not proud of doing things this way, I tried so hard to leave Walt for the last few years because I knew,' she rubbed her stomach, 'I knew this was something I wanted, and he was the one who would never let me go.'

'Does anyone else know?'

Hannah shook her head. 'I wanted to tell you and Erin today.'

'Do you need to see a doctor? You pulled out today.'

'It was just a twinge, I'm fine now — just did it to be safe.'

Dom wondered what Erin would say if she were here and found himself speaking the words she might have.

'Is he really not going to want to be involved?'

'I've had to accept that, because I've been number two since we met, he has,' Hannah paused, 'responsibilities. He's made it clear he wants nothing to do with this, with us.'

'I'm sorry,' Dom repeated. 'How many weeks are you?'

'Thirteen. I've just had my first scan.'

'Alone?'

'Yes, but he and I are going to be alone, aren't we?'

'You know it's a boy already?' Dom asked.

'It's too soon to tell for sure but I think it is. Look, just so we're clear. I'm doing this alone. I'm financially able to do it alone. I've told Walt he can be involved or not in the child's life. He's decided 'not' so I have to respect that. And I do. I really do.'

The sudden sound of bottles clinking and Lydia's laughter coming from the kitchen made Hannah jolt and both of their eyes meet. Dom sighed and bit on his lower lip. After years of trying for a much-wanted child, this would devastate his sister and her husband.

'I know,' Hannah shook her head and lowered it to her hands. 'Christ, I know . . . '

★   ★   ★

The next day Dom was in the back garden scrubbing the barbecue clean when Nigel poked his head around the kitchen door. 'Oh,' Dom said. 'When did you get here?'

'I'm supposed to get you to the park in the next ten minutes.'

'For what?'

'So, leave that, move, come on.'

Dom dropped what he was doing, wiped his hands on a sheet from a roll of paper towels and allowed himself to be led through the house, out the front door, and into Nigel's car.

'Where is everyone?' He looked back at the house that fifteen minutes earlier had his wife and children in it.

'At the park.'

Dom nodded slowly, taking in Nigel's mood.

'Lydia?' he asked.

'Not at the park,' Nigel said.

Dom felt his stomach sink. When he had suggested to Hannah the night before, not to let time pass and just to tell Nigel and Lydia outright, he hadn't meant for her to do it quite so quickly.

'You speak to Hannah?'

'She's not at the park either.'

'Right.' Dom rubbed the fingers on his left hand. 'Nigel . . . '

'Don't speak. Don't look at me. Let me just get you to where Erin and the kids have a present for you. She ordered it to arrive at our house for your birthday last week but it only came yesterday. Look, mate, I'll stand there and clap my hands like I should do and then we'll all go about our business for the rest of the day.'

'Can I say something?'

'No.'

For the rest of the five-minute journey, Dom remained silent. When Nigel stopped the car, Dom noticed his white knuckles still gripped the steering wheel.

'We said all the right things to her; 'delighted for you, blah, blah, blah'. But please, Dom, just for today, let Lydia and I be alone with this? Let us be that couple who, though we're pleased for a friend, we have to grieve all over again.'

Dom nodded, suddenly aware that his next words were on a loop in his mouth. 'I'm sorry.'

'I know, now move or Erin will kill me for you being late.'

Dom could see his family in the distance. 'Why don't you go home? Whatever is happening here now, Erin will understand. Neither of us need you to bloody stand and clap. Please. Go home to your wife, Nige. Please, and remember we love you both.'

Dom shut the door, saluted him through the window and walked off, the sound of Nigel's car driving away behind him.

Jude and Rachel ran towards him.

'Daddy!' Jude yelled. 'Wait until you see!' They grabbed his hands and ran towards Erin where she stood beside something large and colourful on the ground.

'It's an eagle, Daddy!'

For a second, he was confused as he looked at the six-foot-wide something that was obviously upside down and then he saw the string and paddle in Erin's hand.

'Happy birthday! What do you get the man who already has everything?' She handed him the kite controls.

'Make it fly, Daddy!'

They were at the highest point in the park. Dom widened his eyes. 'I've never flown a kite before!'

Erin was looking over his shoulder. 'No Nigel? I thought it might take two of you to get it to fly.'

'No Nigel.' Dom shook his head. 'Now,' he leaned across and kissed his wife, 'who's going to help me? I suppose I just run and let it go?'

'It's an eagle, Daddy,' Rachel repeated.

Erin shrugged. 'Try it — the running and letting go — and I prefer to think of it as a phoenix, by the way.'

Whatever it was, Dom loved it. And as he ran, tossing a six-foot balsa wood frame of a flaming bird into the air, hoping the wind would make it rise and soar, he pushed all thoughts of Nigel and Lydia from his head and immersed himself in the moment. He held the reins with Jude and Rachel, somehow, naturally, teaching them to make it soar and swoop. He would recall the swishing sound of that first kite flight many years later, not just whenever he looked at the framed photograph Erin took of the three of them, but anytime he needed to feel hope overcoming sadness, he would close his eyes, and hear the flapping of that bird's ascent.

★   ★   ★

14th July 2009

Dearest Erin,

I'm braving the Book of Love to say something that I want to say but don't feel able to say out loud and I'm not sure I want you to either. I'm not even sure I want you to respond.

I'm worried about Lydia.

I worry about Lydia.

Nigel, though he's hurt, can withstand a tsunami of pain. Lydia has her limits and I think she's close to them.

There is nothing we can do, I know, except to be there and hope she's okay.

Why am I writing any of this down for Christ's sake?

I'm crossing this out, NOT tearing it out, just wish I hadn't started it.

Love you,

Dom XX

30. Dominic

Showers through the night had made the earth soft, malleable, easy to dig. When the tree had been delivered that morning, it was already in blossom and as he'd moved it, he did so gingerly, wanting to preserve as many as he could of the bell-shaped white flowers that clung to its skinny branches. 'Styrax Japonicus', the label said, and Jude had translated it earlier from the internet as 'Japanese Snowbell'. Dom looked at the hole by his feet. Not deep enough for the root ball yet. He poised the spade one more time, wiping his brow with the back of his arm.

Just as he was wondering what the temperature might be in the humid heat, Jude approached with a glass of water. 'Mum said to give you this and wants to know if you're ready yet.'

'Almost,' Dom replied, downing the water in one go. 'Thanks, Son.'

'Okay.' Jude turned to leave.

'Jude?'

'What?'

Dom ignored the ever-present impatience that edged every word that came from his pre-pubescent son's mouth. 'I just wanted to say thank you. This was a great idea.'

'Okay.' The two syllables were grunted just before Jude walked back up the garden.

258

'Would you like to help? I could do with a hand getting it in?' Dom didn't need a hand lifting the six-foot-high specimen into the hole and Jude probably knew that. 'I just don't want to lose the blossom.'

Jude first folded his arms across his chest before letting them loose by his side. 'Okay,' he said, and Dom smiled. Together, they lowered the young tree into place. 'Why have you put it in this part of the garden?' Jude finally spoke a full sentence as he used the spade to fill the earth in around the root ball.

'Because this one will grow tall, it loves sunlight. It'll be slow but should get to twenty or thirty feet. Here looks like the best place, what do you think?'

Jude seemed to look around then nodded.

Dom held the tree straight. 'Pack it in tight,' he told his son. 'All around and pat it down with the back of the spade. Then, we'll have to water it.'

'Mum says it's going to rain.'

'Doesn't matter, we have to give it lots of water, bed it in. I'll go get the hose. Do you want to start on the other hole?' He watched his son as he studied the surrounding earth.

'Where, how close to the tree?' Jude asked.

'Not too close, we want to allow the roots room to spread. But, we also want to know exactly where it'll be.' Dom watched Jude work it out, moving in a straight line about four feet from where they had just planted.

'Here?' he asked, tapping a space with the shovel.

'Perfect. I'll be back.'

As Dom unreeled the long hose that sat on the rear patio, Erin opened the kitchen window. 'Ready yet?' she asked, then looked at the sky. 'Those rain showers won't be long.'

'Almost, the tree's in, Jude is digging the other hole. Give us five minutes.'

As Dom soaked the roots, he watched his son with his typical almost-a-teenager gait. His drainpipe jeans were slung low over his slender hips. His hair, straight and the same sandy colour as his own, was long and tucked around his ears. Above his top lip, a line of dark fuzz had prompted Dom to show him how to shave recently. Jude, being Jude, had opted to keep his furry lip and could be seen chomping on it regularly as if to convince himself that it was still there. Dark green eyes, the same shade, but somehow much more serious than his mother's, looked across at him. 'That deep enough?' Jude asked.

Dom nodded, to the sound of the girls walking down the garden. Under her arm, Rachel held the large glass coffee jar, now sterilised and containing folded sheets of paper. He kissed her head as soon as she was stood opposite him.

'Dad, you going to say something?' Rachel asked.

Dom looked at Erin. They hadn't actually discussed how this might unfold, just agreed with the children when Jude had suggested the idea as a good way to honour Sophie. He wasn't sure he wanted to talk; not because he was overwhelmed with grief since her passing three

260

weeks earlier, but the opposite, because the major feeling he'd felt since losing his mother had been relief — the disease had already robbed him of his vibrant mother a long time ago. Whatever grief he felt had been spent a long time.

'I'll say something,' Erin stepped in and he winked at her. 'Has everyone put what they want in the jar?'

Dom licked his lips and ran his fingers along the edge of his mouth. 'No,' he said, reaching into his rear jeans pocket, and pulling a small manila envelope from it.

Erin unscrewed the cap and held it in front of him.

'Just a letter, like the rest of you,' he said quietly.

'Okay,' she cleared her throat. 'We're planting this lovely tree today in honour of Sophie, whom we all loved. And we've all written something for her to remind her of that. I think she'll have fun, reading them somewhere . . . ' She looked skyward and frowned. 'That's it,' she said, 'rain's coming.'

Dom held a hand out feeling the drops. 'Great, now let's get this thing in.'

He put both arms around Erin and Rachel and watched as Jude lowered the jar into the second hole. Each of them kicked some soil on top and Jude finished the job with the back of the spade just before the heavens opened.

As they ran up the garden he considered what he'd just done. It was only one of those white lies. There *had* been a short note to his mother,

261

but the sealed envelope also contained that 'missing page' that had been burning a hole in various pockets and drawers over the years. He'd never been able to get rid of it, saw it as a permanent reminder of his failure to do the right thing at the right time. And now it was time to let it go.

★ ★ ★

Later that day, in between the predicted showers, he'd been walking to see his father and took a detour onto the high street. His steps automatic, the route instinctive, it was as if he was testing himself without it, without that page to constantly remind him.

At the place he'd known all along he was going to, he stood back at the heavy glass door as two men exited. Once inside, his high was instant — all of his nerve endings fired up — he felt an actual tangible feeling of both pleasure and pain. Pleasure because the feeling of a win was something his body and brain remembered greedily. Pain because right there beside the high was the anguish he'd caused, the suffering he'd cause if he ever gambled again.

He perched himself on the edge of a stool near the door, inhaled deeply, played with his bracelet — rolling the dog tag over and over on his wrist. Years of historic cigarette smoke that lay embedded in the walls made him want to gag. He closed his eyes, listened to the pulsing commentary of the two thirty at Doncaster and when the favourite passed the post first, some innate part of him wished he'd had thirty quid to win on him. Dom focused, remembered a man called Peter whom he'd met at Gamblers Anonymous. Peter had gambled everything but the air he breathed away and would have gambled with that too if it allowed him another fix. Dom concentrated on recalling his features; eyes that had probably once been bright and ambitious, dulled by disappointment, his face scrawny and skin mottled from lack of proper nutrition. Peter had been the most extreme case in his group, and because of that he was the one he talked to, prayer-like, during these moments. Dom prayed to Peter, wherever he was, because he, Dom, was godless, motherless and now pageless. He asked for the strength to leave the place because he had so much to walk away for.

When Dom stood, he didn't look back and once safely outside the door, his breathing levelled. The thank you to Peter, a whisper, disappeared into the soft summer breeze. He began to walk towards the old family home, what was now just his father's house. He pulled his phone from his jeans pocket, pushed a button for the last number dialled.

'What's up?' she asked.

'I wanted to hear you.'

Erin laughed. 'You only left fifteen minutes ago!'

Dom didn't hesitate. 'I just spent seven of them sitting in the bookies.'

Silence crackled between them until she said 'And?'

'And I walked away. I smelled the air, remembered the high, swallowed the fact I thought it might be what I want today, and left.'

'Good,' she said. 'I'm glad.'

'So, I wanted to hear you, to remind me why I try to be a better man.'

'Oh, Dom.'

He sensed she might be about to cry. 'Because even after all these years, everything I do, I do to impress you. I still want to make that Tree Girl fall in love with me.'

'She did. Twice.'

'I still want to make her proud of me.'

'She is. Always. Especially today.'

'See you later.'

'You will. Kiss your dad for me.'

'Yeah, I will.'

★ ★ ★

Gerard was, Dom could see, doing remarkably well. He'd found him cleaning the oven after baking mini-muffins from a recipe Lydia had given him. Though he hadn't dared to raise the subject, Dom suspected his father too felt some relief at Sophie's passing. As if he'd read Dom's mind, Gerard looked at him over the rim of his mug of tea and whispered. 'I miss her, but I'm glad she's at peace.'

Dom took a bite of the cake his father had insisted he have.

'She's up there looking after your little one now.'

He sucked the crumbling mixture in his

mouth, swallowed it. 'That's a nice idea, Dad,' he said.

Gerard smiled. 'I know you don't believe in it, Dom, but that's just because you think with your brain instead of feeling with your heart.' His father sipped some tea from his mug. 'It's different when it's someone we've loved. The only way we can keep going is to believe that somewhere on some other plane, they do too.' He raised his mug as if in toast. 'For all of my previous cynical beliefs as a younger man, now, I choose to feel with my heart.'

Dom shifted in the chair.

'Heck, Dominic, you must believe what you believe.' His father looked all around him, waved his hands around and said. 'But I can feel her all around me still.'

'I'm sure she is, Dad,' he told his father what he wanted to hear.

'Did you hear Lydia's offered me a job?'

'What?' Dom's look was one of surprise.

Gerard continued, 'I can't rattle around this house on my own. I'm going to become a barista!'

Dom smiled at his father's smile as Gerard shrugged. 'How hard can it be? I'm going to serve coffee in the Bean Pod three mornings a week.'

'It's a good idea, Dad.'

'Maybe make some muffins for them?'

It had been a long time since Dom had seen his eighty-one-year-old father smile and he nodded repeatedly.

'How are *you*?' his father asked and Dom for

a split second debated telling him of his detour to the bookies.

'I'm okay,' he replied. 'We planted a tree in the back garden for Mum, Jude's idea, and buried some letters for her.'

'She'd have loved that,' Gerard said. 'She *will* love that,' he added, looking out the window next to him.

'She'd have loved the idea of you serving coffee,' Dom poked his dad with his elbow and Gerard laughed.

'You're right, she'll probably hate that, but she'll want me happy,' he shrugged.

'That's all I care about too, Dad.' He looked around the old, dated kitchen, at the scarred oak worktops that his mother had once lavished with linseed oil. 'Is there anything you need or want?'

Dom looked down as his father's liver-spotted hand covered his own. 'I want you and Lydia to carry on leading your own lives and not worry about me. No fussing.' Gerard shook his head. 'No feeling you need to pop in and check on me. I'm good to go,' he tapped his watch and smiled at him, 'for another few years at least.'

* * *

19th June 2010

Darling Dom,

I'm proud of you. I've already told you this face to face tonight so why tell you again in our Book of Love? How can I tell you I'm proud of you differently in here?

266

I can say it without you shushing me, or blushing, or being generally uncomfortable when I praise you to your face. I can say: I'm proud of you, Dom — for putting us first, for handling your demons, for walking away today, for being a good son today and always. And your mum knew that about you too.

I also wanted to share my last memory of her with you in here — that way you can read it as often as you like. The week before she died, I went over to help your dad on Wednesday morning like I always do. Sophie was quiet, and I urged your dad to go for a walk, to see a friend, just to get a break. He left me with her for an hour and we talked. Well, I talked, and Sophie listened, but I was chatting about the time we'd all gone camping together in Cornwall and the tent collapsed, remember? Well she did, because she smiled, Dom. I'd swear it — she smiled — a big wide grin. She smiled, and it was such a lovely moment and made all the more special because I think she knew who I was, and I think she knew that I was special to her and that she was special to me.

A lesson to our children that relationships can change and do change and that we should never judge. A lesson to me that she could still hear, that she was still in there somewhere.

Today we planted that tree together. The kids are well. We're healthy. All the things that matter are in place — as Sophie herself once said — 'The rest is noise.'

If you need me, I'm here. Right beside you.
All my love,
Erin xx

Erin the Brave,

I've been wondering what exactly I need to convince me that Mum lives on, watches over us. You believe that; Dad believes it and I'd really like to, but it's never been part of the way I'm wired.

Memories are what live on — the happy images and feelings we can recall with our loved ones and I have many of them with Maisie and Mum. But do I believe in some heavenly place we all go to live happily ever after? It's a bit too sweet (and convenient) a notion for me. Do I believe, like you, that spirit lives on? No. I don't. We are our loved one's legacy. Their spirit and energy live on in us.

Mum's not with us anymore, but that steely part of her? That part of her that lived for family — I like to think she and I share that, and that maybe that part of her energy stayed behind to strengthen it in me for the rest of my life. It was certainly with me the time I sat in that bookies the other day.

Family. It meant everything to me before she left us and if it's possible it means even more now.

Mightily,
Dom XX

PART FOUR

31. Erin

From *The Book of Love*:
'You told me once, after you'd lied, after the shit had hit the fan; after you'd left, after you came back, you told me the only truth that mattered was me and you.'

17th June 2017

Darling Dom,

You weren't here this morning when I opened my eyes and I woke really wanting your arms around me. That squeeze of yours that always lasts just a couple of seconds that tells me you're here and I'm here and everything else, as Sophie would have put it, 'is noise'. I was lying there in our bed, thinking of the night we know Maisie was conceived and I was right back there . . . 1996 in my bedroom in the flat I shared with Lydia; my tiny room with a double bed edged up against the wall and just enough floor space to walk around it.

That night, we'd been out to see a movie and afterwards we went straight to the bedroom. We were just standing there, and you ran your fingers slowly the length of my arms, shoulder to wrist and I remember feeling that that was the most erotic thing I'd ever felt.

And this morning, before getting up, before that long stretch I do every morning, my eyes closed,

271

thinking about that time, I remembered the zip on my dress, opening as if I was back there again with you. A slow movement, the sound of each metal tooth catching, just enough to slide it off my shoulders, lower it down my body. I could almost feel your kisses, again, barely touching my skin. Before we made love that night, there wasn't a square inch of my body you hadn't kissed. There wasn't a part of my spirit your eyes hadn't reached. And I knew — I knew you were the one I'd be reckless for.

And Maisie being conceived that night was possibly careless, but you've always said that life unfolds the way it should, and I like to think that was the first time I believed that, believed you. Friends, parents, said we were hasty, irresponsible even; but we were Dom and Erin and we were so ready to take a chance on love.

Right now, instead of writing this to you, I wish you were here, that we were together upstairs. I wish I could just plug myself in to you again. I wish we'd just made love and were lying down, limbs knotted, my hair sprawled across your chest. I wish your hands were twisting through it and I could just listen to your heartbeat.

Da-dum, da-dum, da-dum.
Love you always,
Erin xx

Change is coming.

I can feel it in my bones as surely as I can feel the gentle waft of warm summer air whisper past my bare legs, as sure as the white blossoms on Sophie's tree shiver next to me. Dom is sitting on the stump of an old oak that we had to have cut down last year. He's leaning forward, one elbow on his thigh and his head resting on his hand, just like Rodin's *The Thinker*. I'm sitting on a low deckchair in the shade of the tall Japonicus watching him think.

Summer . . . my favourite season.

By October, autumn, the killing season, Sophie's scented buds will wither on the wet ground and the foliage from the two oaks that still surround me will cover the lawn in a shrivelled rusty carpet.

Dom shifts, his arm reaching out, his hand catching mine in his.

'Everything is going to be okay,' he speaks with his usual confidence.

A football bounces onto our patio from the two children playing next door. Dogs bark from the house on the other side.

Then silence descends and almost all is well in Valentine's Way.

I smile, lock eyes with him and I believe him over again.

32. Dominic

He could see her at the entrance to the tube just as he exited the solicitor's office. Despite being shrouded in a full-length green padded coat, some rust-coloured strands of the hair she'd been growing again for the last year escaped the fur-lined hood.

'How'd it go?' she asked as he kissed her cheek.

'All done.' Dom put an arm around her shoulder and began to walk. 'Now, how about a quiet hour together before returning to the teenagers who like to hurl food and insults at one another.'

'Dom, people are arriving at seven.'

'We have time for one celebratory drink.'

Minutes later as they sat in a bar off Soho Square, Dom ordered champagne. Sensing she was antsy, he reached for her gloved hand. 'Erin, we both know this is the right thing for now.'

'Putting our savings into you and Tim going into business together *is* the right thing to do. We can wait to own Valentine's again.'

Dom listened to her practised mantra, let go of her hand and leaned back in his chair. He watched as she handed her coat, which had lain on her lap, to one of the staff, as her eyes roamed the bar. It was as if she were looking for confirmation of what she'd just told him in the floral wallpaper, or the bartender's shoes — anywhere but his eyes.

'Erin?'

'Uh, huh.'

He sat forward, turned her face to his. 'I can go back. I can go back to that office and instruct the solicitor to tear up the papers. I can do that because we *both* need to be on board.'

'I am, I am,' she said, covering his hand with one of hers as they were served two glasses of bubbles.

She was first to raise her glass. 'To you and Tim and the new partnership, Carter & Chimes. And to us.'

He clinked her glass, relieved that her smile seemed genuine. 'To all of that,' he said.

★　★　★

It was seven minutes to seven that night when Dom had to agree with his daughter's message. Laughing was infectious. Both he and Erin were stood in the living room watching Rachel and her group of friends.

'It's like this,' Rachel kept the straightest face possible and on the count of three, she and the others all waved their hands in the air and laughed. Ha! Ha! Ha! Ha! Ha! He couldn't help it and began to join them as Erin laughed aloud too.

'See?' Rachel giggled. 'You have to laugh when you hear a certain sort of laughter.'

'We should send them out to the Middle East

as envoys,' Erin whispered.

Dom glanced at the face of the grandfather clock in the corner. 'I'm just going to pop outside and check everything's in place. Jude?' He called his son's name as he walked to the rear of the house through the kitchen. Jude was stood by the French doors swigging from the top of an open beer bottle. Dom looked at the line of bottles he and Erin had opened for the visiting adults.

'I can see that, you know. You should probably at least *attempt* to hide it.'

'It's one beer, Dad.'

'You're thirteen years old. Put the beer down and come and help me outside.'

'It's freezing, I — '

'Jude,' Dom was already in the garden handing him a large torch. 'We'll be two minutes. Come on, just hold this and point,' he said.

In the garden, Jude pointed the beam of light skyward. 'A clear night,' he said.

'All the better for fireworks,' Dom replied as they neared the rear of the garden. 'Aim that light over here.'

At the end, by the back wall, Dom had lined up the boxes.

'Okay, looks good.' He clapped his son on the back as they both shivered heading back to the house. 'Nine o'clock kick-off. Who have you got coming?'

'Just a couple of mates from school.'

'Do these mates have names?'

Jude hesitated and handed Dom the torch. 'Tigger and Tosh.'

'You have friends called Tigger and Tosh?' Dom was greeted with a rare smile.

'Yep. Tigger because he can't sit still and Tosh because he talks shit all the time.'

Dom laughed as he rubbed his arms warm. 'I see. What do they call you?'

'Lanks'.

'I don't get it.'

'I'm tall and skinny — lanky.'

'Ahh,' Dom replied. At six foot, he was tall for his age, already taller than Erin and just two inches short of him. And his shoulders seemed to have widened of late. Dom was looking at a young man and absently patted his own hairline where it had begun to thin recently. 'Let's go in, Lanks, get our coats lined up for later.'

Erin was in the kitchen. 'We're missing a beer,' she said glaring at Jude's back as he left the room. 'Chilli's ready, rice is done, people will start arriving any moment.' Erin pointed at things as she spoke before walking over to Dom, resting her head on his shoulder.

'I've just this minute accepted I'm losing my hair,' he whispered. 'And did you know our son's nickname is Lanks because he's tall and skinny.'

Erin laughed, a soft comforting sound, next to his ear.

'And he hangs out with two lads called Tigger and Tosh.'

She laughed louder, moved away, towards the ringing doorbell.

'And our daughter is running laughing classes,' he murmured to himself, shaking his head.

★ ★ ★

'Need a hand out there?' Fitz was already putting his coat on.

Dom nodded. 'Jude is supposed to help but . . . '

'You got some water nearby, just in case of — '

Dom interrupted, 'Hose nearby, they're all lined up. All I need is you to hold the torch while I light the match and then run like hell. That's both of us, Fitz.' He put an arm around his father-in-law's shoulders. 'You *can* still run, can't you?'

'Cheeky fucker,' Fitz laughed.

'Okay, folks,' Dom called out. 'Anyone who wants to see the fireworks, they're a minute away so come to the back doors, or out on the patio, now.'

He slid his arms into his overcoat, looked back at the house to see a crowd gather inside and out and shook the box of matches in his pocket. At 9.03 p.m. Dom Carter lit the fuse on the first rocket of the night, but the real explosion came the following morning.

★ ★ ★

After eating breakfast alone, Dom closed the door to his study behind him and sat at his desk, his legs crossed and stretched out in front of him. He had caught up with emails and was filing the signed contracts from yesterday in a new file, with the tab 'Carter & Chimes', when he heard shouts coming from the kitchen.

Instant adrenalin kicked in and he ran towards the voices.

Erin was sat at the head of the table, with Fitz seated on her right staring at his twisting hands in his lap.

'Erin?'

'Dad's got some news,' she said as she stirred her tea into a beige whirlpool.

Outside, a car backfired and Erin flinched.

'Well, someone speak!' Dom poured himself a coffee from the cafetiere on the table.

'I'm going to the States.' Fitz raised his head.

'Why the commotion?' Dom blew the steam from his mug and took a seat opposite Erin. 'Why don't you join him — it's been ages since you visited Rob.'

'You misunderstand,' she murmured.

'I'm going there to live,' Fitz announced, 'at least to see if I can. The plan is to stay for at least a year. Rob has an annexe, well you know that, that Rob has an annexe . . . '

Dom looked at Erin. His father-in-law had been born just outside New York but had lived in Ireland since the age of two until moving to London at twenty. Dual nationality made it possible for him to mess with Erin's head now. Shit. She was devoted to Fitz and vice versa.

'It will be a chance to see some of his kids growing up too,' Fitz added.

'Dad's met a woman.'

'What?' Dom frowned. 'Fitz?'

'I'm not moving there because of her. Erin, you know that.'

'Dad met a woman when he was at Rob's last

Christmas. Remember I told you?'

Dom didn't remember her telling him, and Fitz meeting a woman at sixty-eight was something he thought he would remember, but now was not the time to argue so he nodded.

'Well,' Erin said, standing up, 'Dad met Penny at Christmas and now he's moving to the States, yet one has nothing to do with the other.'

'Erin,' Fitz said.

'Yes, Dad.'

'I know you're upset, but — '

'You have to do what you have to do, Dad.'

'Don't be like that, please. This is hard for me too.'

Erin shook her head and walked out of the room.

'You could have given her some warning.' Dom stared after her. 'Shit, you could have warned *me* last night.'

'Look, there's always been an open invite from Rob and . . . ' He looked down the empty hallway after Erin. 'I know there's not much point in going after her.'

'You know fuck all.' Dom thought of everything Erin had been through, the things that she had kept back from their children and her father. He stood and walked over to Fitz's chair. 'You get your ageing ass up those stairs and reassure her nothing will change between you two even though we all know it will.' He pulled the back of the chair as Fitz stood. 'And who's this Penny anyway?'

'I'm not moving for Penny. I'm doing it because if I don't do something different now, I

280

never will. As you so sweetly put it, my ass and the rest of me are ageing.'

Dom listened to him thud up the stairs and heard their raised voices again. Fitz was moving. That was bad news on any level. Erin would miss him. The kids would miss him. Hell, even he would miss him. And a woman.

Despite himself, he smiled; *there was life in the old dog yet.*

⋆ ⋆ ⋆

4th November 2011

Darling Erin,

How do you tell your father, when you've kept your health scares a secret, that you're on constant skin change watch? You decided not to tell anyone — that's your choice — but I saw today that you'd wished you had. You wished you'd already said something to Fitz during the last few years, because you won't now. It would look like you're telling him to make him stay and you'd never do that.

I'm sorry. I'm sorry he's going to live in New York and I hope he'll hate it.

You've gone dark. Quiet. And I can't reach you, but I want you to know I'm trying.

Love you always,
Dom xx

⋆ ⋆ ⋆

5th November 2011

Dearest Dom,

I never really told you how my mother died, did I? You know she died of cancer, but I've never talked about how long she was sick for, except in very 'general' ways. I was fourteen when she was first diagnosed with melanoma and eighteen when I held her hand as she died from secondary cancer. None of it was pretty and all of it is responsible for creating the fearful me.

And Dad, he helped me through that time. He has always been there when I needed him and now it feels like he won't.

Childish. Silly, I know, but I'm going to miss him and the thought of him not being there makes me stupidly scared all over again, worrying about the what ifs of these basal skin things. They may be a good type to have had and I know there's nothing there now, but strip that away and they're still cancerous.

Love you,
Erin xx

★   ★   ★

6th November 2011

Erin, baby,

My scared baby . . .

Now listen here. You and I have had more than enough to deal with to date and the truth is we're both going to die in our beds from old age. Okay, you'll go first, but not until we're old and decrepit and losing our marbles and bladders. And not the way your mum or my mum went. Neither of those things are going to happen, okay?

No, we wait until your eighty-second birthday

282

and then I'll let you stop breathing, just a few minutes before I do the same. By then (I calculate 2054), I imagine all this will all be in our control. What do you think? I think you'll love the idea, and I love the idea because I don't want to be without you for longer than those few minutes. I'll do them; I'll wait them and make sure you've gone, but that's all. No longer,

There you have it. They're your orders, Erin. There's no room for skin cancer to interfere. Don't let me down.

Love you mightily,
Dom XX

*   *   *

12th November 2011

Darling Erin,
Come away with me.
I have the tickets booked.
You and me on a far-off beach for a week under a large brolly to keep you shaded from the sun. I've raided what's left of the House Fund. Valentine's will be ours again someday but today — we need this. Tim will keep the coal fires burning at work and Fitz is organised to come and live in with the kids. I've spoken to Lydia and booked your time off. We leave on Thursday next.

Let's make crazy love, outside, inside. And just so there are no surprises, I've arranged a thing at the hotel. It's a sort of a thing that you'll need a new dress for. Maybe a white one, maybe not — buy whatever you want. All I ask is that you feel special in it.

283

Let's renew our vows . . . just you and me and the palm trees.
Love you mightily,
Dom xx

★   ★   ★

16th November 2011

Darling Dom,
I'll be the one on the beach in a gorgeous scarlet silk dress. And a very wide-brimmed hat.
Love Erin xx

33. Erin

NOW — 18th June 2017

From *The Book of Love*:
'You're good at that, Dom. You know how to stop me fearing the worst. You know when not to talk about tomorrow — when to just help me breathe on this side of midnight.'

'I realise you need me to resolve things with Lydia.' I've a bag of split-peas and grains in my hand and am tossing some into the swans gathered at the edge of the river bank. Dom is walking ahead of me, facing backwards. 'If you fall in, I'm not going in after you,' I tell him.

He laughs out loud. 'You so would.' Then he tilts his head and whispers it again, those brown eyes of his narrowed sadly. 'You *so* would . . . '

My head shakes and as I empty the contents of the bag, the six swans watching my every move go crazy.

Dom stops walking, just says, 'You were saying. Lydia?'

'Well, firstly, I'm resigning — going to send her an email today.'

Beside me, he looks out across the river, pauses a moment before turning towards me. His hands cup my face. 'So, you won't work together anymore. But what about the twenty-two years of friendship?'

'Twenty-one,' I correct him. 'I've hated her since October.'

'You don't hate anyone. Not even me when you said you did all those years ago, and what was it you were saying yesterday in the garden about life being short?'

Suddenly, I feel the cold as if the river's whipped up a breeze and goose bumps scatter over my arms. 'I know,' I tell him.

'Come on, Erin, what do you want from life, now, what do you want?'

My jaw trembles. 'Family. You. Us.'

For a moment, he's quiet. 'Lydia is family too,' he then adds cautiously. 'And you know, you *know* you need Lydia now more than ever.'

'I'll do it,' I tell him, listening to the pulsing sound of a siren nearby. 'Don't say any more. I'll talk to her.'

— Original Message —
From: Erinthebrave101@btinternet.com
Sent: 18 June 2017 15: 04
To: Lydia@TheBeanPod.co.uk
Subject: Everything

Lydia,
Having been on extended sick leave for a long time now, please take this mail as my official resignation, with immediate effect. I know you've sent a hundred emails and messages — I've read none of them but if you want to meet, I'll see you tomorrow at the Bean Pod at 11 a.m.
Erin.

I press 'send' on the hundredth version before I can think of some other nuanced way to say, 'I'll see you, but I'm not sure I want to.' Thankfully, Dom has stopped looking over my shoulder at earlier attempts and is now busying himself somewhere else.

Twenty seconds after sending the email and two mouthfuls into a much-needed coffee, my mobile rings.

'Dad,' I say when I answer.

'At last!' he says. 'Your phone is on and you actually picked up!'

I ignore the jibe. 'You're up early.'

'I am.'

The doorbell rings and before I can say a word, he interrupts saying, 'How come every time we're talking, your doorbell rings. Anyone would think you don't want to talk to me.'

'Dad, just hold on a second. Stay on the line. Let me just get rid of whoever's there.'

I walk quickly to the front door and pull it open.

'Surprise!' My exhausted-looking father is standing on the doorstep with a holdall slung over one shoulder.

'Dad.' I look at my phone and hang up. 'What — '

'I felt like you needed me,' he shrugs. 'You going to invite me in?'

I needed you six months ago. Where were you then? I'm tempted to leave him on the doorstep but open the door and wave him through.

Shit. Dom will not be happy. Just as I try to get Lydia sorted, Dad turns up . . .

And when will the people in this world who love me get the fact that I *hate* surprises?

34. Dominic

THEN — September 2012

'Who knew it would be me telling you to be brave!'

Dom stared through the windscreen at the worsening weather as he listened to Erin's voice through the hands-free. The rain had turned to a light sleet. Switching the wipers to max, the car was suddenly silent except for their rhythmic swish.

'Dom?'

'I'm listening,' he said, but he wondered if he was. The Cairns View project that his partner Tim was proposing had had Erin and him talking into the early hours last night. A site, forty miles from home; a hundred acres with three stately homes needing complete renovation and outline planning permission on a corner of the site for the building of one hundred new homes. It all sounded wonderful — almost too good to be true — and in Dom's experience, if something seemed too good to be true, it often was.

'You should do it. I know you've banned the word from your vocabulary, but this sounds like it's worth a gamble.'

He winced. 'Things are good. I don't want to be greedy and I couldn't face you if things went wrong again. There wouldn't be a hole big enough for me to crawl into.' He indicated left and stared at the line of red lights ahead of him. 'Look, we'll talk about it when I'm home. I'm just a few miles away but the traffic's a bitch.'

'So, think about it for the next few slow miles. We're not talking about this again tonight.'

Dom laughed. 'We're not?'

'No.'

'Why not?'

'Because when you get home to your loving family, your first instinct will be to run from the house, call Tim and find some project really far away that will mean leaving home until both the children do.'

'Okay,' he sighed. 'What's happened?'

'I'll see you soon,' Erin said, adding, 'drive safe,' before hanging up.

★   ★   ★

'What in Christ's name have you done?' Dom spoke through his right hand, stared at his daughter then looked across the room to where Erin was sitting on the sofa, her long legs tucked up under her. Before waiting for a reply from Rachel, he sat next to Erin. 'Did you know about this?'

'All I knew is that she was having a sleepover at Claire's and she arrived back this morning like that.'

'Don't you like them?' Rachel asked.

It was a moment before he could speak. 'Not really, no.' He thought of his daughter's luscious and shiny hair now packed into a head of matt dreadlocks.

Rachel shrugged her shoulders. 'No, Mum doesn't either. Still, it's my hair.'

'How the fuck did — '

'Language,' his daughter tutted. 'I did it with Claire's help, a lot of patience and YouTube.'

Dom rubbed an itch under his eye, looked to Erin for guidance. He wanted to grab hold of Rachel, pull her upstairs to the bathroom and tell her to sort her hair out — now.

'It's a phase,' Erin lifted her book. 'I'm going to go with the hope that it's a phase.'

'I'm still here, Mum.'

'I'm aware you're still here and you're right; it's your hair.'

Dom grabbed hold of Erin and pulled her away instead. In his study, she rubbed her arm dramatically. 'What the hell, Erin?' he groaned.

'What do you want me to say? Or do? It's done now. If we don't make a fuss, I'm hoping she'll see sense and — '

'And if she doesn't?' Dom was staring back into the hallway, towards the line of pots he'd planted up only days earlier that Erin must have brought in to avoid the night's predicted late frost.

'We have a beautiful daughter with dread-locked hair.'

Dom slumped into his chair, the swivel wheels taking him halfway across the floor. 'Fuck's sake — sometimes I hate the way you're so bloody reasonable.'

'You handle it then,' Erin's hand was already on the door. 'I'll not say a word. Off you go.'

Before he knew it, she'd gone. Back to her book, back to being reasonable. He stood and followed her, a trace of her perfume still in the air ahead of him.

'Rachel,' he said from the door of the living room.

She turned her head and a mouthful of expensive braced teeth smiled. 'Dad?'

Erin reached for the television remote and muted the programme Rachel had been watching, arched her expectant eyebrows.

'I really don't like your hair,' he said, eyeballing his daughter.

'I'm sorry,' she replied. 'You'll get used to it.'

'I don't like it either,' Jude responded only when the television was no longer a distraction. 'Looks rank. Remember that time Mum cut hers and looked like a boy, well you look like a weirdo.'

Dom had no idea what 'rank' meant but he nodded and pointed at his son. 'See?' he said. 'Why, Rachel? You had beautiful hair . . . '

'I still have beautiful hair.'

Dom shook his head.

'Well, see *I* think they're beautiful.'

'Don't they give you a headache?' Jude asked.

'You give me a headache,' she replied. 'You were supposed to be on my side.'

'I hate them,' he replied.

'Tough,' she muttered. 'Thanks a bunch.' She stood, and with a toss of a hundred dreads left the room.

'You knew she was doing this?' Erin asked Jude.

'Yep.'

'You should have said something.'

Jude stood and took the pile of books by his side with him. 'I may not like them but I'm not a grass,' he told his parents before following his twin up the stairs.

'You two should be doing schoolwork anyway!' Dom yelled after them. 'They should be studying or something,' he repeated, pointing a finger at Erin.

'We ate earlier by the way,' she said without looking up. 'You're an hour and a half later than you said you'd be. Your dinner's in the microwave.'

★　★　★

Erin joined him when he was halfway through the chicken curry.

'Thanks, this is really good.' He held up his thumb and forefinger together in a circle and repeated, 'Thanks.'

She sat opposite him, silent at first before clearing her throat. 'You do probably need to go up and give the kids a nudge,' she began. 'I had a call from Nigel today — an official call. Neither of them get that they have to start studying now. These are important GCSE years and Rachel's already told him that they're a total waste of her time, that she doesn't want to be there and that she's absolutely not staying on for sixth-form college afterwards.'

'She what?' Dom placed his cutlery on top of his plate.

'So dreadlocked hair is probably the least of our worries.'

Dom stood, the sound of the chair scraping on the floor making Erin wince. 'Rachel!' he yelled from the kitchen door and Erin rolled her eyes.

'Not exactly how I'd planned on doing it, Dom.'

Rachel thumped down the stairs to the kitchen. 'What now?'

'Your mother has just told me that Mr Maitland called her today.' It felt strange for Dom to call his brother-in-law and friend by the name he deserved as head teacher.

'Yes, she said that.'

'What's this about you not wanting to be in school?'

'I don't.'

'For God's sake, Rachel, what's gotten into you?'

'I know I have to be there but it's not right. I know what I want to do, and I just want to get on and do it.'

'You're fourteen years old!'

'And I've found the course to do it . . . Two years chef-training.'

'If you want to do that after your GCSEs, we can talk about it then,' Erin interrupted. 'You don't *have to* go to sixth-form college.'

Dom glared at Erin. 'Well, I'd prefer if you didn't decide now,' he said, feeling the dream of Rachel possibly following his and his father's footsteps into architecture slip through his fingers.

'Already decided, Dad.' Rachel's head was shaking.

'Whatever happens you'll need your GCSE grades. You need to knuckle down and study. So start now.' Dom watched his daughter as she sighed and looked to the heavens. 'And don't you roll your eyes at me, young lady.'

'You do know Mum left school at sixteen. She didn't go to college and she's fine.'

Erin put her face in steepled hands.

'If she's leaving after GCSEs, then I am too,' Jude appeared in the doorway.

'See, that's just silly,' Rachel waved a hand in his direction. 'I have a career plan. I have it all worked out. He's just a lazy bollocks.'

Erin closed her eyes and slumped back into her chair.

'That's right. Pick on Jude,' he yelled. 'Why does she get to leave and not me?'

Dom watched his son's sulky pout form; the son who'd been saying he wanted to be a teacher since he'd first had one.

'She says she has a plan,' Erin said.

'I have a plan!' Jude slammed the door, still yelling. 'I'm going to leave school, leave this house and doss for a whole year before even thinking about a plan!'

'Told you,' Rachel stared in his wake. 'Look, Dad, Mum — I have all the information. It's a great college. I have a folder upstairs with everything in it, ready for you to read.'

'Rachel, this is all a long time down the line

yet.' Dom softened his tone. 'There's work to be done beforehand.'

'They even have residential internships over school holidays for people who might want to apply for the course later.'

'Where is this place?' Erin asked.

'Pembrokeshire. The college say they help set people up in local houses together for the duration. Look, I want to be a chef, and this is much better for me than A levels.'

Dom's mind fast-forwarded to the time when his dreadlocked daughter would probably be missing from their home and had a strange vision of him laughing hysterically as she left, just like she'd taught him.

'Go get your file, Rachel. Your mother and I will read it tonight.'

★ ★ ★

Erin's head lay on Dom's lap as he paraphrased the contents of the glossy college brochure for her.

'It sounds great,' she said quietly.

Dom stroked her hair. 'She's gutsy, knows what she wants. I suppose we have to encourage that.'

'Don't you think she'll still be a bit young to go off and live somewhere else?'

'She'll be home most weekends.'

'I'm not ready to even think about losing her.'

'We won't be losing her. She's just on loan somewhere else.'

'It all just happens too quickly. One moment,

they're tiny and the next . . . Besides, there's you talking about her knowing what she wants. If I know you, Dom, I know you *want* to do the Cairn's View project. You're scared shitless but you want to do it. And for the record, I think you should take a chance. It could be the making of you, of us,' Erin said.

Dom said nothing but when his mobile rang beside him, he checked the time. Almost midnight.

'Nigel,' he said when he answered, almost immediately straightening up, pulling Erin to a sitting position beside him as he listened.

'Where?' he asked. 'I'll be there in ten minutes,' he added before hanging up.

'What is it?' Erin asked.

'Lydia.' He was already pulling clothes on. 'It's Lydia.'

$$\star \quad \star \quad \star$$

29th September 2012

Darling Dom,

Here I am in our pages, our Book of Love, where Dad told us 'to write down whatever it is you can't bring yourselves to say. In years to come, this book will be a place where you'll look back and read about the things you were possibly too young or naïve to understand.'

Never before have those words meant more. Even during the worst times, I think in here, we've always been able to write some nugget that could lead to us talking. But I'm not sure you'll ever look back on these last few weeks and understand why Lydia did what she did. At least, that's what you've told me. Nothing else — that's all you're telling me.

So, for what it's worth, here's today's nugget.

Do you have to understand? Does anyone have to understand, except maybe Lydia, so that she never does that to herself or the people who love her again? She's already regretful. She's already getting the help she should probably have got years ago. And both she and Nigel are finally going to be able to talk about their pain. Funnily enough, her counsellor recommended she write things down, so though they laughed at us over the years with this book, maybe one could really work for them too? I hope so.

They have a lot to fight for. She has a lot to live for. He loves her for his own million reasons and she loves him back for a million more. So, she, they, will be alright. I really believe that.

Dominic Carter, I love you because in your desperation to do right thing, to help her, you'll eventually realise that all you have to do is love her.

All of mine to you,
Erin xx

★ ★ ★

30th September 2012

Darling Erin,

She took enough paracetamol for it to work. I had to lie to our elderly father and tell him she was in hospital for a 'procedure' which thankfully he assumed was 'woman's stuff.'

Why do I want to understand? Because somewhere, I've lost who Lydia is as a sister. I suppose that's the one thing I want to change.

I just want to find her again.

In the meantime, and always, I love you because, because, because . . .

Dom xx

★ ★ ★

31st September 2012

Dearest Dom,

Did you hear our daughter teaching Lydia how to laugh again today? Neither you nor I told Rachel what really happened. I think Lydia might have, so wasn't that the most wonderful sound in the world?

Erin xx

35. Erin

NOW — 19th June 2017

From *The Book of Love*:
'You're a pain in the ass. You're a pain in my ass. You're my pain in my ass.'

Dad was up half the night with jetlag and looks older than I ever remember him looking when he comes into the kitchen. His hair has silvered this last year, just a few streaks of his original raven-black left. His eyes look swollen and tired; the whites sore and red with a double layer of dark bags parked beneath. I push a peppermint tea towards him.

'Bins are out,' he says, washing and drying his hands at the sink.

'Thanks. I hate hauling those things up and down the path.'

'The fact that your recycling bin is full of cardboard cartons says a lot. What shite are you eating? Processed, quickie, microwave shite, that's what.'

My eyebrows arch. 'I'm almost forty-five-years-old, Dad,' I say, leaving out the words that I think I'm both old enough to and capable of choosing how I eat.

He sits down opposite me, avoids my glare.

'Jude emailed me,' he shifts the mood.

'Dad, about Jude . . . '

300

'Told me he got married.'

'Yep, what can I say? Gretna Green.' My fingers drum the table next to me. 'She's a nice girl . . . '

'Hopefully I'll get to meet her this trip. Rachel emailed me too.'

'She did?' I look at my watch.

'You have somewhere to be?'

'I'm meeting Lydia.'

'Oh,' he grins. 'That's good. Please tell me you're going back to work so I don't have to talk about Rachel's email.'

My sigh is long and loud. 'Well, you're going to have to now.'

'She's worried about you. You've been off work a long time apparently.'

I nod.

'What you told me when you came over a few weeks ago. Your skin problem . . . I wish you'd told me when you first went through it. I wish Dom had told me. I wish someone had told me back then.'

Dom has made himself scarce, which is probably just as well. 'Don't blame him,' I say. 'I didn't want anyone to know. And the reason I've been off work has nothing to do with that . . . '

'I need to know, Erin. Are you okay now?'

I fight the urge to laugh but just respond to the particular health-issue question. 'I'm good, Dad, really. All clear.'

'Well, you should be taking care of your body better. Eating properly.'

'I should.' I nod in agreement.

'Let me cook something before I go down to the house.'

I place a hand over my father's left one, notice it too has aged. His veins are raised; a purple labyrinth of worms. His skin is papery and thin to the touch. On his third finger, he still has the Claddagh ring my mother gave him on their wedding day. 'You still wear this,' I whisper.

Instinctively, he moves my hand and touches it. 'I'll always be married to her. The hands that clasp the heart mean friendship. The heart, love, and the crown, loyalty. They all still stand.'

My smile is wide as I think of Dom tattooed evermore with 'Erin forever' on his finger but I focus on Dad. 'What does Penny think of that?'

'I've never asked her,' his reply is simple. 'So,' he looks straight at me. 'Shall I cook, or shall I head off?'

He means well but the thought of some kale and lentil stew invading the house isn't what I need today, so I encourage him to leave — back to meet the agent, back to empty the family home into piles to keep and piles for charity.

Away from Dom and me.

36. Dominic

THEN — January 2013

He couldn't sleep. Hair loss aside, it was the thing he hated most about getting older — that need to lie awake in the middle of the night when everyone in their thirties lay fast asleep. And Erin. Whatever decade Erin was in, she always managed to sleep through his moving quietly from the room.

Yawning widely, he made his way onto the landing, automatically checking that Jude was in. From his bedroom door, Dom's eyes scanned in the dark for the outline of his son's shape. He saw one foot stick out the end of the bed and walked over, through what he regularly told his son was his 'own personal landfill site', and pulled the duvet to cover it. And on the floor, next to where one of Jude's arms hung over the side, next to a GCSE Biology textbook, he saw his and Erin's Book of Love, lying open.

Dom picked it up, closed over the door and skim-read the open page, something he'd written to Maisie when he and Erin were apart. He went downstairs, fought the urge to stomp back up them and tear his nosy son from his teenage-scented cocoon. Instead, he poured a glass of red wine from an open bottle and sat in the living room, waiting to watch the sunrise through the double doors. By the time the naked silver birches looked like pen-and-ink sketches on an orange sky, he wasn't sure if it mattered. Maybe his son had learnt something about his parents. And he and Erin had left the book in that same place over the years, somehow certain it had remained private. Quietly, he climbed the stairs and stood outside his son's bedroom. Tell-tale heavy breathing let him open the door one more time and place the book back where he'd found it.

In the kitchen again, he made a pot of coffee. Erin would be up soon. He cut himself a slab of marzipan-covered fruitcake, not the ideal breakfast, but the hour felt more like late lunch by the time he heard movement upstairs. He opened the cupboard under the stairs, removed several empty boxes and placed them beside the tree in the living room. The cream carpet was laden with needles from the 'non-shedding' tree. Next to the fireplace the poinsettias were about to lose the last of their scarlet leaves. Outside, the day had dawned — a light dusting of icing sugar frost had settled on the front lawn and though he would have left Christmas in the house for another month at least, it was Sunday the sixth of January, Epiphany, the twelfth night and he knew Erin would wake saying it would all have to come down and be packed away by the end of the day.

In fact, she woke complaining of a rare headache and he told her to stay in bed, brought her a cup of tea. 'Take these,' he instructed, handing her two Paracetamol. 'Hangover, or are you coming down with something?'

304

'Hangover,' she muttered. 'I heard you mooching about. Have you been up all night?'

Dom dropped his dressing gown, lifted the duvet and got in beside her. 'Most of it.'

'Christ! You're freezing.'

'Heat's just come on.' He pulled her towards him, snuggled into her. 'I need warming up.'

Though he willed it not to, he felt his cock grow as they spooned.

'Dom . . . '

He laughed. 'I can't help it.'

'I really do have a headache!'

'Stop talking. Pretend it's not there.'

'I have a cock lying in the crack of my ass.'

'You're imagining things. Go to sleep.'

'I'm trying. You should get some sleep. It's Sunday.'

'Yep . . . ' He kissed her left ear.

'Dom . . . '

'Sssh, I'm waiting for your headache to clear.'

She groaned out loud, pulled away from him.

'Spoilsport,' he murmured but felt his eyelids lower.

When he woke, he moved to her empty side of the bed, able to tell immediately how long it had been since she left. Less than an hour, he reckoned. Feeling dog-tired still, he yawned, inhaled the floral scent of her from her pillow. His phone pinged a text and an image flashed on the screen. Light snow in the front garden where Rachel was on a sleep over with friends.

'Afternoon, sleepyhead.' Erin walked into the room and pulled the curtains open.

'What time is it?'

'Quarter to one.'

'You're fucking kidding me.' He sat upright as if he had somewhere to be.

She laughed. 'I am, it's ten thirty. Jude's made pancakes, you want some?'

'Jude's made pancakes?' He eyed her suspiciously.

'I know,' she whispered. 'Get up quick before we realise we're dreaming.'

Dom stood, wrapped himself in his dressing gown and followed his wife downstairs. Lingering behind her, he quietly opened the drawer in the console table where their pages once again sat comfortably in their home.

'Pancakes!' he called out as he entered the kitchen and his son came into view. 'What made you decide to make pancakes?'

Jude looked across at him, shrugged. 'Haven't had them in ages.'

'Coffee,' Erin handed him a steaming mug and took a seat beside him.

Dom picked up a newspaper from the pile that had been delivered, searched his pocket for glasses and coming up empty crossed the room to a drawer where he kept a spare pair. His son was now taller than him. He nudged him. 'How do you even know how to make pancakes?'

'I watched you often enough, and the internet. Duh.'

'Savoury or sweet?' Dom asked.

'What would you like?'

'Nothing beats lemon and sugar.'

'Sweet it is, then.'

* * *

'These bastard things get everywhere,' Dom complained, pulling pine needles from his sweater. He looked across to Erin, who was staring at the digital screen on the camera he'd given her for Christmas. 'What can you possibly be taking a photo of?' He looked around at the twenty-fifth of December all packed away, walked across to her and looked at the small screen over her shoulder. 'A box,' he confirmed.

'I can never decide whether it's happy or sad.'

'The box?'

'No. Is this a happy moment because everything's stored and in the same place and its sort of hopeful or is it sad because everything's stored and in the same place and Christmas is over?'

'You need to get out more,' he told her. 'And by the way, speaking of keeping things in the same place, Mister-Pancake-Jude has been reading our book.'

She lowered the camera. 'What?'

'You heard.'

'The little snoop.'

'Hell, they've both probably read it over the years.'

'I bloody hope not.' Erin had crossed the room and was already opening the drawer in the hall. She came back clutching it. 'This is ours. We should never have assumed it was safe.'

'Hey,' he held her, 'we'll move it.'

'Yes, we bloody will, though we don't use it so much anymore. I've just checked and we haven't written in it for ages. Must mean we can finally talk to one another.'

'You reckon?'

'How do you know he read it?' she asked his chest.

'I checked in on him when I got up last night. It was lying open on the floor. The 'me to Maisie' entry,' he told her, knowing she would want to know.

'He made pancakes before he went out.'

Dom nodded.

'Something poked the memory.'

'Probably. Or maybe he just woke up wanting pancakes.'

'Will you come to midday mass with me?' She looked at her watch suddenly.

Dom made a face. 'Really?'

She had already left the room, taken her coat from a pile on the end of the stairs. 'I feel the need to be quiet and to think.'

The last time Dom had been in church, he didn't remember it being a place of solace, just somewhere he had no clue why people were standing or sitting, and somewhere he never felt comfortable.

'I've got to put all this stuff back under the stairs,' he said.

And when she looked at him, slight disappointment in the edges of her eyes, he knew, knew where he'd be for the next hour.

'This being quiet and thinking thing — how does that work when I know you'll sing hymns at the top of your bloody awful voice.'

'In between I think.'

'I'll spend the hour thinking how much longer . . . You know how I feel about God and the God squad — I'm a complete fraud even breathing the same air,' he said, getting his coat.

'You don't have to come, and you'll be glad to know I couldn't drag either of the kids to church nowadays, so they take after you. They didn't even come on Christmas Day.'

'I'll come.'

'You know like you say lane swimming gives you space and time to sort out your thoughts?' She shrugged. 'Church can do that for me. Not always. Sometimes it feels like nothing more than an inherited habit, but sometimes . . . Anyway, I feel the need.'

Dom closed the front door behind them, pulled a beanie hat from his pocket and put it on. 'Why now, Jude's pancakes, packing up Christmas, his reading our private words, what's up, what prompted the need?'

'Nothing's up. It's Sunday and sometimes it's more the need to say thanks, to be grateful.' She looped a hand through his arm as they walked.

'You are a strange woman, Mrs Carter.'

'Nothing strange about me, weirdo with the hat.'

For the rest of the way, they walked in silence, the wintry ground crackling beneath their footsteps. Standing to let people pass through the huge oak door, Erin leaned in to him, kissed his cheek and whispered, 'I'll sing quietly. Promise.'

★ ★ ★

309

Darling Erin (Read Jude),
There once was a boy who was nosy,
who lived in a landfill so cosy,
But one day he read something private that said,
Not all things all the time are all rosy.
His parents they hoped he would see,
For them it was just meant to be,
Their Book of Love were a means to an end,
They'd write, they'd talk — they'd heal.
Love you mightily,
Dom XX (Read Dad)

37. Erin

NOW — 19th June 2017

From *The Book of Love*:
'You killed my trust but earned it back.
And in between I had to learn to forgive you.'

I drive. I stop at red lights. I sing along to the radio badly. I go at green lights.

There's a free parking space near the café and I reverse park into it — slowly, carefully, just like a learner. From my vantage point, I can see she's not sitting on the window row of stools. From there she'd have been able to see me arrive, so she's probably back in the tiny office behind the coffee bar. It used to be my office — there's one chair, a desk that's no wider than a washing machine with a filing cabinet underneath and a cork board above, covered in Post-its and photos. At least, it used to be covered, it's possibly not now.

The dashboard tells me I'm three minutes late but when I try to move, I can't. My legs won't work. The command to move them leaves my brain but that's it. My hands, white-knuckled, stay gripping the steering wheel. The engine, stays running. I talk to her in my head, tell her I'm here but I can't move and then I see her blonde head appear at the window. She looks left and right and then at her wrist and takes a seat

311

on one of the chrome stools. Her head is down. She's texting. She's on Twitter or Facebook updating the Bean Pod's accounts.

Dom designed this first coffee-bean-pod-café and it became the template for the three others. I remember it as if it were yesterday, the five of us, Lydia, Nigel, Hannah, Dom and me all huddled in the kitchen in Hawthorn Avenue, Dom scribbling on A4 sheets of paper constantly saying, 'What about this?' while we ate homemade nachos and drank cheap red wine. Lydia eventually shouted back, 'That's it! That's exactly what I had in mind!' And the Bean Pod empire was born. And I loved, loved being a part of it.

My nose is running, and I search in the glove compartment for a packet of tissues, find one, plus a wrinkled old Toblerone that I'd obviously once had Dom-shaped plans for. I bang it shut. I'm now four minutes late. Lydia raises the phone to her ear and I half expect mine to ring but it doesn't. She chats to someone else and I still can't move.

Eventually, I wait to see her give up, have a chat with myself, telling myself if she passes the car, I'll wave. Surely, I can move my hand in the air and move it left to right. Except she doesn't leave, and Hannah arrives. Of course, Hannah will have known about the meeting. And of course, it was Hannah she called. Those two have become thick as thieves. Something unexpected, something like jealousy, pierces my heart and my hands do move. They flick the indicator, turn the wheel, and I head for home.

★ ★ ★

In the living room, I pull up a chair beside my favourite curved window in the house. It has a window seat that was the twins' best hiding place as small children. At that moment, Dom passes by outside and immediately, I feel my shoulders loosen.

'I'm in here,' I call out.

'Hiya,' he pokes his head around the door.

'Where were you?' I don't mean it to sound accusing but I hear it — my tone is all wrong.

'I went to see Dad again.'

'Oh,' I pat the chair next to me. 'How is he?'

'Seems the same. From what I can tell he's totally fed up and trying to pretend he's not.'

Dom's devastated by his father's health decline this year. Old age and recurrent kidney infections now have him bed bound and assisted with his basic needs.

'And Lydia?' he asks. 'How was it?' He comes inside and sits down. 'You two okay?'

I shake my head, unable to lie, certain he'd see through it if I tried.

Dom runs a thumb and forefinger around the edges of his mouth.

'I'm sorry,' is all I can muster.

He's just about to risk his considered reply when we both see Lydia through the window storming up the garden path.

'What the hell?' I stare at him as she pounds on the front door with her fists.

'Erin!' She is screaming at the top of her voice. 'You let me in!'

'Shit,' he whispers.

My mind whirrs, running through what must have happened. She called Hannah and since I didn't turn up to the *entente cordiale*, Hannah spilled the beans. Hannah must have told Lydia everything I shared with her when she and I met in town last week — everything I confided in her about Dom and me. And now Lydia's here yelling through the letter box.

'You let me in Erin, or I swear I'll break one of your precious deco windows.'

I pull my knees up to my face and hug them, try to block her out. She finally runs out of steam and sits down on the step with her back up against the front door. 'Let me in. I need to talk to you. Or him . . . please?'

I look up and Dom's moved into the hall and my heart breaks for him, for myself and even for her.

38. Dominic

THEN — July 2014

'A pot-luck supper does mean we have to bring something,' he told Erin on the phone.

'I forgot, but it's all sorted now.'

Lydia was insisting on giving Dom a forty-fifth birthday dinner party and he didn't want to go. The next day was the annual swimathon and barbecue at Valentine's in aid of SIDS and tonight he would have much preferred a pizza at home with the kids. And leaving the two of them alone was something he dreaded. They were having a few friends over to celebrate the end of their exams and Dom was not happy — despite Erin's reassurance that they could and should be trusted.

By the time he got home, she was ready — dressed in a lemon-coloured summer dress with navy espadrilles, her hair loose around her shoulders. 'You can't be late for your own party,' she sighed.

'What are we taking?' he asked as he peeled his work clothes off and headed into the shower.

'Under control' she yelled in. 'Hurry up, Dom! Jude! Someone at the door?'

He was ready in less than five minutes. She smiled. 'You look nice,' she said, kissing him lightly, leaving a faint trace of frosted pink gloss. 'Do your thing, will you?' she said, and he grinned as he licked his lips. 'Kids? Here now!' he yelled.

Jude was at the door to their bedroom in seconds. 'Yup?' His sixteen-year-old frame filled the doorway. He swept a long foppish fringe from his eyes and looked intently at them. Dom would swear he was already looking guilty about something and they hadn't even left the house yet. 'Behave,' he told him. 'No smoking. No drinking. No — '

'Dad, I got it. Okay.'

Rachel appeared, lurking behind him in his shadow. 'What?' she asked. 'And must you yell at us as 'Kids'? We're sixteen and we were christened, I believe.' She held a hand out to Dominic and then Erin. 'I'm Rachel Marianne Carter and this is my brother, Jude Dominic Carter.'

Despite himself, Dom, smiled. 'Jude, Rachel. No smoking. No drinking. No more than eight people here in total, that's a maximum of six guests. No loud music, no — '

'Right. Dad. Okay,' Jude sighed, looked at his father with the disdain that teenagers reserved for their parents alone.

'You right?' he asked Erin, who was watching proceedings from the edge of their bed.

'Yes.'

'You look lovely.'

'Thank you.'

'Where's the grub we're taking?'

'In a bag on the kitchen counter.'

Downstairs, Dom nodded at the bodies that were already accumulating around the fridge.

'Soft drinks only,' he repeated to the horde as he passed, grabbing the only bag in sight. As he made his way back to Erin, he rattled it. 'What are we taking?'

She took it from him. 'Lydia said it's fine just to bring wine. She has loads of food. What?' She blushed and waved both her hands about. 'I've had a busy day!'

★ ★ ★

By the time they got to eat the meringue that Hannah had brought, Dom was a bottle of Merlot in, thought the world looked like a wonderful place and that forty-five was a magnificent age to be. 'To this lady!' He held Erin's hand up in the air. 'To this lady, who I love.'

'*Whom* I love,' Nigel mock-tutted. 'Standards.'

'Yep. That,' Dom said, and they raised their glasses. 'Ever since I saw her dancing like a tree at another party you gave, dear sister!'

He felt Lydia's arms hug him from behind. 'Happy birthday, little brother,' she whispered before heading to her kitchen to get the cheese.

Dom stood and followed her. 'Can I help?' he asked from the kitchen door.

'It's all unwrapped,' she said, 'just got to put it on the board.'

'Thanks for tonight, you didn't have to do it.'

'I wanted to. And,' she turned around towards a top cupboard and opened it. 'I got you something.'

'Lydia, we don't do presents.'

317

'It's not really a present.'

He opened the envelope she handed to him in front of her, unfolded an A4 sheet of paper and lay it flat on the countertop to straighten out the creases. 'What is it?' he asked.

'A made-up, typed by me, sort of 'school report'.'

Dom read aloud:

Grasp of the English language	A
Ability to argue with the English language	A*
Positive strides forward	B
Understanding of Nigel	B (Could do better.)

Dom laughed and hugged her.

'Finish reading,' she urged.

Understanding the past	A
Letting it go	B+ (Room for improvement)
New appreciation for the world	A
Gratitude to and for family	A*

'I'm going to keep this,' he waved it at her. 'I'd like another one when they're all A*.' He put both arms around her and whispered. 'I'm proud of you, Lydia *but*,' he pulled back, 'I'm going to have to miss this lovely course and make a move. Everyone but you is swimming tomorrow!' He patted his stomach and backed out of the room towards the dining room.

'I think I should take you home,' Erin stood when she saw him. 'Before you sit down again and think about another glass or some cheese.'

Hannah looked at her watch. 'It's 10.42. At

least one of Jude or Rachel will be shagging by now.'

Dom frowned.

Nigel laughed. 'I'd put my money on Jude.'

'Er, thank you, folks, it's been a lovely evening but duty calls. See you all at the lido tomorrow. Erin?'

They left to the sound of their friends taking bets over what they'd find when they got home.

In the car, he sneezed and rooted in the glovebox for tissues.

'You're not coming down with something, are you?' Erin asked him.

'Only acute parenthood,' Dom mused. 'I'm trying to feel grateful for whatever we find when we get home, bearing in mind we just left Nigel and Lydia's child-free home and Hannah who's trying to share her lovely little boy with a man who's no longer interested.'

'We should be grateful. We are, aren't we?'

'We are.' Dom reminded himself, thinking of Lydia's report in his pocket. He reminded himself of his wife's beautiful body, free of any scares or scars for the last three years. He was nodding his gratitude as they turned into the street and could see their house lit up like a lighthouse beacon. A low drum and base thud could be heard pulsing in the night.

Erin sighed, a puffed elongated sound.

'I will kill them both,' Dom muttered.

Erin reached for his arm as she pulled into the parking space. 'We will do this calmly, Dom, please.'

The distinctive scent of weed met them on the

pathway going in. In the hallway, draped over their beautiful stairway, a couple of kids were making out. Dom switched the lights on and off. 'Jude Dominic Carter! Rachel Marianne Carter! Get your butts down here now!' He noticed his wife flinch at the sound of his voice. Bodies were already scarpering out the front door. Jude appeared first followed shortly after by his sister. 'You're early!' his son said.

'Everyone out. Now,' Dom spoke through gritted teeth. He put a hand on a boy coming down the stairs. 'Not you, you stay,' he said.

Less than ten minutes later, the house had been cleared of people and Rachel and the boy sat on a sofa in the living room. Jude was finding all the ashtrays which were in fact saucers. Dom stared at Rachel and then pointed towards the boy with his head and jerked it towards the door. 'You,' he barked, 'out. And don't come back again until you're invited by me.'

Rachel folded her arms, threw her head back on the sofa. Erin took a seat next to her. 'In here now, Jude, and you can bring your collection of saucers with you.'

Jude sat on the arm of an armchair next to the sofa with Rachel and Erin. Dom stood next to the fireplace. 'That bloke,' he addressed Rachel but looked towards the front door. 'I've never seen him before, who is he?'

'His name is Kevin,' Rachel said, staring at her painted fingernails.

'So, is he the one responsible for the fact that you're wearing different clothes to the ones you were wearing when your mother and I left?'

He and Erin would laugh later at how their daughter at least had the grace to blush.

'I hope I don't need to remind you that you're only sixteen.'

'Perfectly legal,' she retorted.

'Or to remind you that, if you're having sex, it had better be safe sex.'

Rachel scratched the back of her neck. 'I am not stupid, Father.'

'Good to know.' Dom sat down on the armchair that Jude was perched on. 'What about you, Jude?' He looked up at him. 'Are you stupid?'

His son shook his head.

'What do you think, Erin? Do you think either of our children is stupid?'

'Stupid enough to get caught tonight.' Erin looked around her. 'Stupid enough to get grounded for at least a week and stupid enough to lose a few hours tomorrow morning cleaning this place.'

Dom reached forward and poked through the fag ends and joints on the saucers. 'Stupid enough to smoke weed here . . . '

'We weren't smoking weed.' Jude, looking worried, glanced at his sister. 'Were we?'

Rachel shook her head.

'Well, your guests were and not just six of them like you were allowed to have here.'

'Someone put it on Facebook, it just got out of hand,' Jude grumbled.

'It sure did,' Dom agreed. 'Now bed, both of you. You're up at eight to start the clean-up and I swear you will even be moving furniture, making sure every crevice in this house is spotless. You'll have it all done by the time we leave for the lido at eleven. Understood?'

Jude muttered something under his breath.

'You have something to say, Jude?' Dom asked, catching the glare from Rachel.

'Nothing,' he muttered as he stood and walked away.

'You forgotten something?' Dom called after them.

'We're sorry, Mum and Dad. Sorry,' Rachel said. 'Sorry we got caught,' she added and marched up the stairs.

'She's your daughter.' Dom shook his head in her wake.

Erin laughed softly. 'Hmmm, she is, but then again, sex at sixteen and bold enough to do it here? You know anyone else like that?'

Dom pinched his nose and rubbed his eyes. 'Nothing more sobering than arriving home to this,' he said. 'Happy birthday, Dominic.'

He felt Erin's arms slide around his neck from behind. 'I don't know, the night's still young.' She pointed to the saucers. 'How long has it been? It's a 'pot' — luck supper night and it's a shame to waste it.'

Dom laughed. 'You're incorrigible,' he said as she grabbed a couple of joints and led him out the back door.

They lay side by side on the sun loungers in the garden, Dom looking at the night sky and Erin looking at him.

'You're staring,' he said.

'Not.' She sat up. 'I think you handled our

teenagers very well.' She took a drag on the joint. 'Christ, I'd forgotten how relaxing this stuff is . . . '

Dom would have preferred a pint of beer but didn't want to spoil the moment.

'We are so on the naughty step if they see us,' Erin giggled.

'They won't see us,' Dom said. 'They're already asleep, wired into their bloody awful shouty music.'

'Getting some rest before the cleanathon, and the swimathon.'

He smiled, leaned across and kissed his wife, was just about to slide his hand up her skirt when he heard a sound behind him.

'So, this is where you are. The word hypocrite comes to mind.'

Dom jumped backwards at the sound of Jude's voice and fell from the lounger to the grass. He stood up, rubbed his thigh.

Erin giggled louder, her fingers resting on her lips. 'Oh dear,' she said.

'You two are so not fucking funny!' Jude strode back to the house.

'Naughty step, definitely,' Erin said as Dom stared after their son.

'Fuck,' Dom whispered. 'I hate when he's mad at me.'

'Pull up a chair again,' Erin sighed. 'He'll get over it.'

Dom lay back down again, looked up at Jude's window in darkness. He imagined his sullen frame lurking behind the curtains staring at his errant parents. Still he re-lit the joint, sucked on it, before passing it to her. 'He will,' he nodded sagely.

'He will,' she repeated, her eyes fixed on the heavens. 'So, you think we're alone in the universe, Mister 'I'm a forty-five-year-old heathen and believe in nothing?''

'I object to that. I believe in love.'

'You think the sky could be filled with love-making aliens? Other-world beings who can fall in love?'

'I think you've had enough of the wacky-baccy, Mrs Carter.' Dom yawned, stretched a hand to her. 'We should go in.'

'Five more minutes.'

'Okay, I'm counting to three hundred.'

'Do it quietly,' she said, closing her eyes and lying back as she handed the joint back to him.

Dom began to count and by the time he'd reached a hundred, Erin was asleep.

He sat up, slung his legs over the side of the lounger and planted his feet on the ground. For a while, a lot longer than three hundred seconds, he simply stared at her as he took the last few defiant tokes. Then, gazing skyward again, he convinced himself that his son might be smiling by now and that the night-sky *was* definitely filled with love-making aliens.

39. Erin

From *The Book of Love*:
'Dom, it's all very well saying that love is all
there is but sometimes it's hard.'

— Original Message —
From: Erinthebrave101@btinternet.com
Sent: 20 June 2017 9:04
To: Lydia@TheBeanPod.co.uk
Re: Everything

Lydia,
I'm sorry about yesterday. I did go to meet you
but couldn't get out of the car. I did hear you at
the door but . . . it's better this way.

That said, there *are* things that need saying:

1. You have my resignation. There isn't a way
   we could ever have worked together again.
2. I'm seeing two estate agents today to give me
   valuations on Valentine's Way. We'll take the
   average of both prices and buy Valentine's
   back from Gerard. As you know already, he's
   moving into Sunshine Homes at the weekend
   and the proceeds of the sale will make sure he
   can remain there for as long as he needs.

Lydia, this is what needs to be done. It's what

Gerard wants and what Dom wants.

You have power of attorney for Gerard, so rather than extend this timewise where he has to be sent documents in the post, please instruct someone at Burley's solicitors to handle his side too so they can talk internally and get this done, as soon as possible.

If you need me, please email. No more banging on my door. Please.

Erin

— Original Message —
From: Lydia@TheBeanPod.co.uk
Sent: 20 June 2017 13:30
To: Erinthebrave101@btinternet.com
Re: Everything

I'm so sorry I turned up at the house like that. I was upset.

Of course I'll do as you ask. I will respect your decision to leave work though I think it's a mistake. A solicitor has been instructed in Burleys re Valentine's and says as it's an easy transfer that contracts can be raised to sign within a couple of days.

In the meantime, let me just say this. I'm worried about you. Hannah's worried about you. At least allow me/us that?

I'm here. That's all I can say. I'm here if you need me.

Lydia

40. Dominic

Dom was looking for a bottle of Pinot Grigio when he first heard him. Instinct made him immediately look away; made his grip on the handle of the wire basket he carried tighten. He lowered his head, walked in the opposite direction. The voice he recognised was talking to a woman, both discussing different Riojas. Theirs was a comfortable sound; the dialogue of a couple who had been together a long time. Dom tried not to look but just at the end of the wine aisle he stopped and glanced back.

Isaac looked exactly the same as the last time he'd seen him over eight years ago. Though he was ten metres away, Dom could see him clearly for the few seconds he looked. Same height, same buzz-cut hair, same flat stomach. The only thing different was the glasses he wore to read a label that the woman, probably his wife, was showing him. He was in uniform. Still a paramedic, Dom thought, before heading to the exit and discarding his empty basket en route. He'd pick up a bottle of wine somewhere else. Some people, just like some things or events, were best left firmly lodged in the past.

At home, Erin seemed amused. 'You left the wine?' she asked when he told her.

327

Dom waved a bag. 'I got it, just got it somewhere else.'

'You should have said hello,' she teased.

'I thought he'd moved up north, Manchester, wasn't it?'

'He's probably visiting family.' Erin stopped wiping the worktop and shook her head gently, a small smile forming. 'I can't believe after all this time you'd run away from Isaac.'

Dom slipped his arms around her waist from behind. 'I didn't run away from Isaac, Mrs Carter. To be fair, I've never once run away from Isaac.' He kissed her neck. 'I just thought it best to avoid any awkward moments, not to poke old worries.'

Erin turned around to face him. ' "Old worries?" '

'He did feature a bit during the time I thought I'd lost you.'

'You knew you hadn't lost me. You told me often enough that you were just waiting it out.'

His eyes fixed on hers. 'Have you ever noticed that whenever something bothers you or me, we separate? If it's something small, you head to the bath and me to my study, ending up chatting about it in the book. *That* was something big. You headed to another man and I . . . I stayed far enough away to give you space and near enough to hope that you could see I wasn't leaving.'

Her eyes never left his and he could almost hear the cogs and wheels in her head clicking.

'I've never asked you . . . ' she began.

No, she hadn't. Dom had often wondered why

not, but she had never asked him, and he had never told her.

'And I don't need to now,' she added, not sounding particularly convincing.

'You can ask me anything.'

'I don't need to know.'

'There was no one,' he said. 'Not a sinner, not a soul. No one. I never touched another woman in all that time.'

Dom watched her throat swallow hard, her top teeth steady her lower lip.

'No one?' she said wrapping her long arms around him, lowering her head into his neck.

'Believe me, Tree Girl, I'd remember.'

★　★　★

Dom tapped in the alarm code and closed the front door behind them.

'It still feels really odd,' Erin said looking up at the house towards Rachel's bedroom.

'She's happy, love,' he said. It was his stock reply when Erin would start to talk about missing Rachel. He missed her. He missed her awful, flying, two-tone dreadlocks. He missed her cheeky laugh. He missed her rushing around the house plugged into whatever awful shit she listened to. He missed the noise that went with his daughter and missing her made him think of Maisie in a way he hadn't done for years.

'I'm going to start that photography course, the evening one.' Erin filled the silence as they walked towards his father's house for their fortnightly takeaway with him.

'You should! Your photos have always been good.' He felt grateful for the change of subject.

''Good?'' she said. 'You have to qualify for this course and the tutor said I show 'remarkable talent'.'

'That too! I'm sorry, you know I think you should do it. I think you can do anything you want to, and you've wanted to take better photos for ages.'

'What's up with you, Dom?'

He had increased his pace. 'Nothing, why?'

'You're antsy.'

'I've never understood what that word actually means.' He took her hand in his as he walked.

'Ants in your pants, agitated, a little restless. Dare I say it, even a little anxious?'

'There's nothing wrong,' he said, then felt her hand fall from his as she stopped walking.

'This isn't about Isaac this morning, is it?'

Dom laughed. 'No, Erin, this isn't about Isaac.'

'Then what. Spill before we get to your dad's because everyone will be there, including Jude who has surfaced after spending the night, and day, at Tigger's.'

He hesitated.

'Did you lie? Dominic Carter, was that another of your whiter shade of pale lies when you told me earlier that there had never been anyone else? This your guilt clouding your craggy face?' She was smiling as she spoke and there under the yellow light from the street lamp he believed she had never looked lovelier. She touched his bracelet. 'Atone,' she

330

whispered. 'Immediately.'

'I didn't lie.' He pulled her to him. 'Why in hell would I ever want another woman?'

'Because you were lonely back then and I was busy hating you.'

'You never hated me.' He kissed her gently on the lips. Strawberry lipbalm.

'I was busy disliking you so much that it really felt like hate. What's up? You're not yourself.'

'Ignore me. It's just a mood. And what's a craggy face? Isn't craggy a word used for rocks? Is it code for old?'

As always, when she smiled and laughed he stored it; kept the image and the easy sound alive in some vault in his head for when he might need them. 'Rugged, then,' she offered. 'Odd and irregular in a handsome sort of way.'

'You're a proper walking thesaurus tonight. Come on,' he pulled her by the hand. 'We need to get a move on.'

'I don't think you're old, by the way.'

'Yeah, you do.'

'Older, not old. And I love it. I love that we're older together.'

They crossed the cobbled high street and Erin stopped outside an estate agents. 'We will own Valentine's again, won't we?' she asked suddenly.

He frowned. 'You know the plan is to buy it back from Dad in January after year end. But you only have to look in that window to guess how much it's gone up and we'll be buying it back at the peak of the market.'

Erin pressed her nose up against the glass. 'We'd have done it by now if it wasn't for Miss

331

Masterchef in Wales.'

Rachel's course fees and accommodation over two years *had* put a dent in their plans.

'It'll happen,' he told her, before nudging his head urgently in the direction of his father's.

They walked the remaining five minutes in silence, her arm linked in his. He wondered what she was thinking. Maybe the house, maybe not. He wondered if Valentine's Way could feel any more their home when they owned it one more time. Possibly. Probably. He wondered if she'd thought of Isaac since this morning or if she ever thought of him. He didn't think so. He wondered if she believed him when he said he hadn't — because it was the truth. Isaac was in their past. And just before they reached Gerard's home, just before he rang the bell, when she raised his hand to her lips and kissed it, he thought only of their future.

41. Erin

NOW — 20th June 2017

From *The Book of Love*:
'With you, I'm strong.'

In town, there's a girl who reminds me of Rachel busking in the central square. She has long dark hair, untouched by dreads and her hands weave magic on the harp she grips between her knees, but something about her makes me stop and think of my daughter. Maybe the way her head lowers and rises as she feels the music — it makes me think of how Rachel used to pretend to conduct an orchestra when she had playmates over as a child. I watch the way this stranger's fingers seem to fan the expanse of her instrument, so completely lost, yet so completely in control.

A small crowd has gathered and opposite me the girl sings lyrics I don't know, though I do recognise the tune, something about having someone to watch over her. When she reaches the chorus I nod at her, smile, and before I make my way home, I throw all the coins in my pocket into the flat cap on the ground.

Passing the bakery, I drop in and buy a large tiger bloomer cut into thick slices by the in-house machine. I take my purse from my pocket and tap the debit machine with my card before putting it back in my purse with the other four things I carry there. Not cash. I never seem to have cash nowadays because that tapping thing is worryingly easy. There are two photos — the one of Dom and me and Maisie that I found in his old wallet that awful day, and a more recent photo of Dom and me and the twins, all making faces at the camera. A folded sheet of paper separates them, just a few handwritten lines that Dom wrote for me when we renewed our vows in Tenerife a few years ago. Every time I open my purse I think maybe I should paste it into the Book of Love but then I remember Dom being horrified at that idea, telling me it wasn't a scrapbook . . .

Erin,

I loved you when we first took vows . . .

I shove the loaf into the woven bag I'm carrying next to the magazines I bought earlier and begin to walk home.

And I love you still.

My face is raised slightly towards the sun as I walk, and I slide my sunglasses from the top of my head down over my eyes.

And I will love you every tomorrow.

They cover the tears and the warm sun dries any salty trace on my face instantly.

Every tomorrow . . .

I quicken my pace towards Valentine's Way, one hand gripping my woven bag of purchases, the other still closed around my purse.

And all the while as I walk, my footfall matches my heartbeat. Behind the sunglasses, my eyes blink like shutters blotting out the image of that fifth thing I keep in the purse. It is merely a three-inch newspaper cutting from last October. That's all it is.

I keep it, yes I do.

But it will never be pasted in our Book of Love because it's no scrapbook.

42. Dominic

'The cat has the shits . . . '

'Oh, for fuck's sake. What do you want to do?' Dom looked at his wife. She was tired, her eyes circled by bruise-like dark shadows.

'Want? I *want* to go on holiday and put the cat in the cattery for the week where she's supposed to be, but instead I've had to take her to the vets for something to help and now I have to put the cat in the car for a six-hour drive to Cornwall.' She lowered her voice although there was no one around to hear. 'I *want* to not have a throbbing headache. I *want* to not worry about our children not being with us on holiday. I *want* to be able to accept that they're responsible human beings who don't even live at home anymore and I *want* to not miss them like I do.'

Her voice broke and he reached for her.

'Don't, don't touch me, okay? Please, just put the cat in the bloody carrier and put it in the passenger foot-well.'

'I'll put her in the back,' he suggested.

'She comes in the front with me. Did I mention that I also *want* my daughter to come and take her bloody cat back?'

Dom said nothing. Rachel had got the cat before her latest boyfriend, who was apparently allergic to it. Erin offered to take the cat,

336

thinking the boyfriend wouldn't last, and that had been two months ago. If Dom had his way, the cat would have been deposited back at Rachel's flat as a means of keeping said latest boyfriend away. He hadn't even met him yet but had heard he was 'a lot' older than his daughter.

He didn't want to argue with Erin, not today, so he shoved the cat into the footwell as requested, promising himself that on their return Rachel could take her shit-fest-of-a-cat back and Paul, or whatever his name is, would just have to man up and fucking sneeze.

⋆ ⋆ ⋆

'Shall we stop for lunch?'

Erin rubbed her temples with bunched fingers. 'I'd rather get there quicker.'

'I'll pull in somewhere and grab a couple of sandwiches.'

Dom listened to her sigh.

'I'm sorry. I *want* to not be a bitch to you.'

'If you cheer up,' he said, 'I'll tease you with the fact that I'm taking you to something special in May, something you'll love.'

'What is it?'

'It's a surprise.'

'You're hilarious,' she said, a half-smile forming on her mouth.

He took her hand. 'I am.'

'Sometimes. Where are you taking me in May?'

'Can't tell you. It's a thing, not a place.'

'Are we glamping in Glastonbury?' Erin asked,

her face barely concealing how much she'd hate that.

'Glastonbury's in June but if you fancy it?'

'No, ta, but I'll eat a sandwich if you tell me where we *are* going.'

'Eat the sandwich first and then I'll tell you.' Dom was already pulling into the garage shop. 'You fill up and I'll grab some food.' He picked his wallet up from the central console. 'Anything you'd like, or shall I surprise you?'

'Stop. I'm pissing myself. A chicken wrap, please,' she said as she rummaged in her bag for her ringing phone. 'Hannah,' she mouthed to him as he closed the door.

★   ★   ★

They'd gotten there late, after an accident stopped the traffic on the A303. By the time they'd unloaded the bags into the tiny cottage that backed onto the sea, and greeted Nigel and Lydia, everyone agreed that they weren't hungry, and they were all tired. Nigel excused himself saying he needed sleep and Erin, seeing that Dom wanted to spend some time with Lydia, did the same.

His sister was curled up on an armchair, a large picture window behind her, the sea thumping its way to land below. Dom stood next to her, looked out toward the rolling waves. 'Some spot,' he said, 'well done for finding it.'

Lydia barely nodded. She was beat, he could see that, exhaustion oozed from her.

'Turn up the thermostat behind you, will you,

it's just on the wall to your left.'

Dom did as he was told, watched her cough then sip a hot whisky Nigel had made for her. He could smell the cloves in it from three feet away.

'Anything wrong?' she asked. 'You're hovering.'

'I'm worried about you.'

Lydia shook her head, small tight head shakes. 'Please don't be . . . '

'When you moved into Dad's, you know I didn't agree with it.'

'Dom, I've a stinking cold and we've been over this a hundred times this year. Not again, eh? We're here to relax not bicker.'

'Just over the course of the next few days, when you're away from it and other people are looking after him, just think about it, please. We all agree he needs full-time care. None of us have ever agreed it should be you giving it. Especially not him. Dad *wants* to go into a care home. He's already asked me to check one he picked out and it's — '

She pulled the blanket back and stood. 'That's crap. We'd have to sell the house to finance that and I want to look after Dad. Please? Let's not do this, again.'

Dom ran a hand through his hair, felt her lips brush his shoulder as she passed.

'Stop being such a big brother all the time. I'm fine.'

She blew him another kiss, which he made a point of catching before nodding in her direction.

A home measure of whisky later, Dom began

to do what he'd known all along he would do this weekend. In the narrow hallway, just under the old creaking stairwell, he pulled the red travel bag out and unzipped the side pocket. Removing a pen, a block of Post-its and their book, he took up the space Lydia had left in the armchair. Without thinking about it. In the same manner that he always had, he allowed his thoughts to spill freely:

★ ★ ★

22nd October 2016

My darling Erin,

I could go upstairs right now. I could nudge you from sleep, hold you in my arms and tell you what I have to tell you. We talk now, like never before, so why am I not doing that? Probably because I reckon you'd throw something at me for the first time, because you'd scream and shout and yes, I'm telling you this now, over this weekend, because the latent coward in me is hoping you'll temper your response while we're away with Lydia and Nigel for half-term.

Who am I kidding? You're probably going to fucking lose your shit anyway and I know it.

But when considering what I've written here, I'm asking you to please, please, understand that I really believe it's for the best. There are some things that I've felt truly frustrated by this last year and yes, we've talked about them, but they've always ended up being things we felt we couldn't change, so we went around and around in circles. These things, primarily, my father and his care for however many years he has left, Lydia's decision to move in and look after him, and our ownership of Valentine's are the main things that stop me sleeping or wake me up in the night.

Erin, I tried to raise the solution with you at the end of last year and you were having none of it. I listened. I didn't agree, but at that time I listened. And then, the same 'solution' arose again last month and timing to talk to you about it was all wrong, so I just did it.

I sold the company to Tim.

It's done and dusted. Signed, no going back. And this is where you'd throw something at me if I was telling you this face to face. But, hear me out.

Dad is bedridden now but, as he says, still has all his marbles. There are two things he has never wanted since recurring kidney problems have affected him. One, he refused to entertain the idea of us mortgaging to buy back Valentine's when 'if we're a little patient, it will be ours anyway', and two, he did not want Lydia to take on the challenge of his care. I can't say this any other way, Erin than, I owe him. He has rescued me so many times and it's my turn to help him now. We have, for the first time, in our lives a small fortune in the bank. And money means choices. We can buy Valentine's own it again, something I feel I owe you. The money Dad gets, he will move into a care home with, one he has already chosen. I know, Lydia will take some convincing but that's where Dad will come in. With cash in the bank, he's more than capable of making his own argument. Sure, Lydia will live at Dad's — the house is hers in all but name anyway, but what he doesn't want is her taking on responsibility for him. His old friend Trevor is already at the same care home. I think he'd like his company and the company of other 'oldies' as he calls them.

In selling the firm, the three things that have kept me awake for the last year have been sorted or are, at least, on the way to being sorted.

I didn't tell you because just as a potential sale was mooted by Tim again, you, (just under a year from your five-year-clear anniversary), had to have another of those skin-fuckers removed, this time from the back of your neck. The timing wasn't good.

I didn't tell you because when we spoke about it as an option last year, all you kept saying was 'No! You love your job! You set that place up!'

But the truth is, Erin, that though the Cairns View project and subsequent big contracts have now made us rich, I've not had much fun. It's been hard. Working twenty-four seven for the last three years has meant no time with you and the kids. And for quite a long while now, I've not enjoyed the actual work as it's gone more building-centric than pure architecture. Your first question will probably be, 'What will you do?' Followed by a rapid, 'You're forty-seven — you can't retire! Of course, I can't, but I can become a consultant university lecturer and talk endlessly about the beauty of creating exciting buildings, to young people who have a passion like I used to.

And the truth is that we have to face that though we're constantly told not to worry, I *wanted there to be money there should you ever need the option of private health care.*

There you have it.

I'm making sure I'm going to be out first thing tomorrow, when you read this, so line up the things you want to throw for when I get back. I'll duck where I can.

Love you always,

Looking forward to taking some holidays, spending some real time together, because you're still the one I want to grow old with.

Mightily,

Dom xx

★ ★ ★

Dom climbed the narrow steps. At the top just to the left of a tiny landing was the room Erin slept in. He pushed the door ajar, listened for her breathing, prodded a small tear of peeling wallpaper back into the door frame. Asleep . . . definitely. He crossed to her bedside table and placed the Book of Love there next to a glass of water, tapping the leather cover twice as if for good luck. The small yellow square with Erin's name on it, he placed on top and then walked around to the free side of the bed. Expecting it to creak, he moved gingerly. Despite the sleeting rain and biting cold from the ocean side of the house, the tiny cottage was warm inside. He undressed and slipped in beside his wife. Not wanting to wake her, he kissed his fingertips and laid them on her cheek. And then he slept, with none of the things that had kept him awake for so many months bothering him.

★ ★ ★

The next morning, he woke to the sound of the front door opening and shutting and then again, the same, five minutes later. Silently, he picked up his clothes and left the room. He rubbed the sleep from his eyes, cricked his neck side to side. Next to the coffee machine downstairs, Nigel had left a note saying he'd gone into town to get some supplies. In true head teacher fashion, he'd timed the note at 08.03, listed the things he'd gone to buy and asked whoever was up next, to call him if he'd missed anything. Dom looked at his watch 08.24, rubbed his head with both hands, felt as if a cleaver had parted his brain. Whisky and he had never been friends.

He drank an instant coffee and, taking his coat from a brass rack on the wall shaped like a sailing cleat, he left the house. A walk; a brisk walk along the pier would clear his head. He ambled down the cobbled lane where other rendered fisherman's cottages backed onto the wild sea, his neck back, his face lifted towards the heavy grey clouds, feeling the rain pelt his face. Dodging an enormous kamikaze gull, he stumbled on a wet mossy cobble and broke his fall with his hands. Just grazed, he shoved them in his pockets and kept walking.

The few people that were about nodded greetings as he marched around the arc of the harbour bay heading to the lighthouse at the end of the pier. It was small, painted white — he wondered if someone lived in it, if it had one of those circular staircases that hugged the wall all the way to the top. Scents of fresh baking beckoned. Windows with saucer-size fruit scones, volcanic meringues. His mouth began to water. They'd come back later. He and Erin would come back and have Cornish tea and scones. He had done the right thing, he told himself. Erin would see that.

He stopped to look out to sea. Though the day was grim, the light was bright, and he narrowed his eyes, gazed at the huge expanse of ocean — nothing for thousands of miles until America. The tide was in. Swirling surf circled a lone rock just beneath him. Boats bobbed about on the full, restless, ocean. Cormorants dipped and dived as Dom filled his lungs with fresh sea-air. He turned right towards the lighthouse and, in the distance, saw someone standing on the pier, a palm raised to their eyes, staring beyond to the other side of the horseshoe-shaped harbour. The neon yellow jacket he recognised as Lydia's. Dom quickened his pace as the rain got heavier.

Something, instinct, called out to her, but left him in no more than a whisper. Where she was standing, his fatherly instinct kicked in.

Be careful. Slippery. Top step. Rain.

Not far now. He stopped himself yelling her name; instead watched her looking inwards across the bay — towards the small cottages and taller dark, granite houses, towards the street they'd both just walked from, and then she raised her face up to the sky as if to also feel the rain on her skin. And as she did, her body toppled forward.

'Lydia!' Dom screamed her name, began to run, tearing at the buttons on his coat, tossing it into the wind. At the steps, he kicked his shoes off and looked once to see if he could spot the neon yellow. Nothing. He dived.

The water was freezing. For a moment, it felt as if his heart had stopped as his body registered the cold and his clothes hampered every movement. Under the water, murky with silt and seaweed, he turned in a full circle once, twice, before coming up for air. 'Lydia!' he called her name, gasped and dived again. As he did, he caught a glance of something floating to his right. It was her. As he swam to her, he could see panic had filled her beautiful face as her arms and legs flailed wildly. Her eyes widened as she saw him and underwater he watched her scream his name. He grabbed hold of her and pulled her towards the surface.

Stop struggling, Lyd, please.

With his lungs tight, his chest about to explode, he pleaded eye to eye for her to still and then pushed her towards the light, towards the nearing silver glinting links of a chain above. From below he could see her hand, a hand, someone's hand . . .

Grab hold of the chain. Lydia, take hold.

Dom felt something hit the back of his head hard. Above him, near the air he so desperately needed, boats bounced like corks in the water. His grip on his sister loosened as the keel of the boat the chain was anchored to rose and fell in

346

the swell. He felt the force again. Pain . . . His mouth opened when every survival instinct told him to keep it closed. He felt his lungs fill. And slowly, too slowly, as he slipped away from the surface, he felt his body convulse and his eyelids close.

Beautiful Erin,

I'm falling. Colours. I see colours, blues, greens; none as green as your eyes . . . Noise; the waves booming to shore. Erin, I'm cold. I don't want to leave you.

Love . . . you . . . mightily.

★   ★   ★

23rd October 2016

Dear Dom,

You're an idiot, but all in all, you're a kind idiot.

Where are you? I've tried calling you.

I have nothing lined up to throw at you. Just let me yell at you once for not telling me and then we'll make some plans. No one is 'losing their shit,' as you put it, except this infernal cat of Rachel's.

WHERE ARE YOU?

Love,

Erin xx

PART FIVE

43.

Tuesday 20th June 2017

Struggling with the lock, I push the front door, throw my purse on the hall table and drop the bag of shopping. Marching down the hall to the back of the house I open the back doors and slump onto the swing seat just outside. I'm shivering, despite the heat in the sun and despite all my techniques over the years, all the deep breathing, all the learning to handle and work with my fear — I'm pulled right back there. I'm yanked back to that 'New York Minute' in Cornwall.

★ ★ ★

My phone starts to ring upstairs. It's plugged in on the nightstand and when I reach it, answer it, all I hear is Nigel screaming, 'Get down here, Erin!'

'What? Where are you?' Something in his voice scares me, makes me force my feet into shoes immediately. There's no one home when there should be and that four-word order from him ices my soul.

'The pier, get here, there's been an accident. Lydia, Dom . . . '

The phone still held up to my ear, I start to run. The pier. It's quicker to leave the car. I run down the street, yell at them that I'm coming. From the bottom, where the road branches into a left-hand side access for cars and a right-hand walkway along the bay, I can already see across the small, horseshoe bay. There's a crowd gathered at the end of the jetty, an ambulance, it's blue-and-white lights flashing. No. No. No.

I run. Faster than I've ever run until my lungs hurt. I stub my toe on the cobbles and fall, grab some air and run again. And when I get there, when I push my way through the crowd I see someone being loaded into the ambulance on a stretcher. I see Nigel standing next to it sobbing. I clutch my chest, bend forward a little, try to refill my lungs as I spot something on the ground near him. A heap of coats, stranger's coats.

I move towards Nigel and a gasp catches in my throat because I see the broken look in his eyes the same time as I see feet — feet poking out from the end of that long pile of coats. One with a sock, one without. And I know those feet. I've rubbed those feet; kissed those feet and smacked them away when they played footsie with me under the dinner table. Those feet have walked miles for me, have helped him stand when he felt like falling, have helped him hold me up. I shake my head slowly at Nigel before I fall by the coats, start pulling them off one by one to get to him and then the sounds come. I start to thump his chest, remember seeing it on a television advert; remember old colleagues in the ambulance service saying it. Pump the chest to the rhythm of 'Stayin' Alive'.

'Dom? Come on, baby,' I'm screeching, like

352

the banshees in the tales Fitz used to tell me as a child.

'Dom, can you hear me? You have to live.' I hold his hand, rub it between both of mine to warm it.

I lift his head onto my lap and there's green stuff on it and when I try to rub it off him, my fingers tangle in his beautiful hair. His face is covered in slimy stuff and I pull a tissue from under my sleeve and wipe it away. I blow into his briny mouth; his beautiful pink lips are blue.

'Come on, wake up, baby.' Dom isn't moving. His eyelids haven't flickered. I cling to him, can hear myself crying, and convince myself it's someone else.

'Erin?'

I feel someone's arms try to pull me away from him.

'No, no, no.' I try to hang on to his arm but my grip slips because of the water on his clothes.

'Erin, listen to me.'

Nigel. Nigel's voice. Nigel's arms.

'Lydia's in the ambulance. I need to be with her. Come with me. He's gone, Erin, he's gone.'

No. No, he's not. I feel myself dragged away by him.

From him.

★   ★   ★

I'm winding the dog tag I now wear on my wrist around and around until it almost stops the flow of blood.

'Don't do that.'

353

I blink slowly, look at him, just inside the house, sloped up against the wall in our kitchen as if none of it had happened. And the elephant in the room parks itself right next to him, its trunk almost curving upwards into a smile.

'You're not here,' I tell him, shaking my head. 'Are you here?'

'I sure as hell hope so,' he laughs. 'This is funny. You and I having an existential conversation.'

'See, the thing is . . . ' I'd swear I can hear him breathing, 'that you died . . . ' There; the words are out. 'You died, Dom, and Hannah and Lydia,' I continue, 'they all think I'm a teensy bit insane — that you're a part of my grieving process. Not really here, but my imagination willing you into being. You heard your sister howling through the letterbox. Though she'd love to believe you're here, really she thinks I've conjured you up because I can't let you go.'

'Oh, right.' He nods sagely as he approaches me.

'And I haven't been able to bear the thought of asking you if you're real.'

'Why not, Erin?' He bends down to my level.

'Because I don't want you to confirm it either way.'

Dom tugs me towards him and kisses me and I feel him — really sense his full lips on mine, gentle, reassuring. 'What do you think, love?' he asks. 'What do you believe?'

I hold his hand, feel the life force in it, and tell myself again that it's possible, that anything's possible; that love has made it happen. 'I think

354

you're here,' I tell him. 'If that makes me crazy, I don't care because I never believed that death is the end. You, on the other hand . . . I think I can show you in our book exactly what you thought about this.' I wave my hands about us. 'About the likelihood of this being real.'

'Pay no attention to that. Another time I wrote in there and gave you instructions, remember?'

I've no idea what he's talking about.

'I told you we'd die when we were old and wrinkled and tied to one another's Zimmer frames or something along those lines. I told you I'd be eighty-five and you'd be eighty-two.'

I remember. 'Sorry, my love,' I say, stroking the face of the only man I've ever loved. 'As usual, life had other plans.'

★ ★ ★

20th June 2017

Darling Dom,

You're dead but you're not. You're alive but you're dead.

You're here. That's all I care about.

I love you because you didn't leave me.

Erin x

44.

Wednesday 21st June 2017

'Holy shit!' I look out the upstairs window and, within seconds, Dom is by my side. The kids. Both of them — arriving at the same time — Jude with a bottle of wine under his arm, Rachel with flowers.

We strain to see them as they disappear out of eyeline. I grip the windowsill and the doorbell rings.

'An intervention,' I whisper.

'Don't worry,' he says. 'I'm right behind you.'

I take the stairs two at a time, barefoot, open the door just as Jude's about to use his key.

'I'm here, I'm here.' I tap my chest rapidly. 'Gosh, both of you. Together. How brilliant. Have you eaten? I haven't got much in, maybe some crisps.' I look back towards the kitchen to where Dom is already seated at the table. 'And you've just missed Fitz! He's down at the house with an agent meeting someone who wants to buy . . . '

'Mum, we came to see you, not Fitz and not to have dinner. You sound like you have a cold.' Jude kisses my cheek and Rachel follows and I close the door behind them. It makes a 'swish' sound as it shuts, as if it's sealing all the air inside. My heart hammers as Jude makes his way to the back and sits at the table too.

'I was telling Rachel you're leaving work,' he says, handing her the wine. From his tone I already regret telling him this morning on the phone. Rachel hands him the flowers which he lies on the table and she heads to the kitchen to get glasses. 'Yes, I'm not sure I believe it!' she says. 'You never said anything, Mum!'

I squirm, try not to take it as an accusation but tension pulses through my veins. 'I only really decided on it this week . . . '

'She's going to do a photography course,' Dom says from his seat and I'm reminded of the last time we sat at the dining table together — Jude's announcement.

'I'm going to do a photography course,' I echo.

'I think it's a great idea,' Rachel says, handing me an overfilled glass. I have to almost slurp the top of it to stop it from spilling. 'Home measure,' she says. 'They'd fire me at work if I ever thought that was a measure of wine.' She puts hers down and reclaims the flowers.

'They're lovely,' I tell her.

'I figured Lydia's had died by now so thought you deserved more.'

Lydia's flowers — the ones she sent me on my return from the States, the ones I binned the next day because every time I looked at them I resented her presence in my home.

'I do?' I ask Rachel.

'You do,' she says hunting for a vase in the cupboard under the sink.

'Try at the back,' Dom shouts to her, 'behind all the dishcloths on the left-hand side.'

Dom is grinning at Rachel's search and I look to Jude, who's staring at a photograph of his father on the shelf next to him.

'So, why are you both here?' I stay standing.

'See?' Rachel laughs behind me. 'I told you she'd think we have an agenda.'

'Of course, you have . . . ' I reply.

'Of course, you have . . . ' Dom says.

'Well, actually we do,' Jude confirms, and I hear Rachel's tut of disgust. True to form with my twins, already this isn't going the way they'd obviously agreed beforehand.

'You think you can see Dad?' Jude stares at me. 'You really think you're seeing Dad?'

Dom is smirking and shaking his head less than three feet from our son.

'What are you talking about?' My voice trembles.

'Lydia called me, ranting about things Hannah had told her. She's worried about you, says you're convinced Dad is . . . still here.'

Rachel sits on a small tub chair I have sitting next to the doors onto the garden. She smiles at me, lets her brother do the talking.

'He didn't believe in any of that crap,' Jude says. 'When you're gone, you're gone — that was what he used to say to me.'

'Yes, he said the same to me.'

'So, what's going on, Mum?'

I have no idea how to answer him, so I curl my hair behind my ears and tell a white lie. 'Nothing. At least nothing to worry about. Everything's good.'

Dom is sitting back on the dining chair, his

legs crossed, arms folded. He blows me a kiss and I'm momentarily distracted.

Jude follows my eyes. 'Do you see him now?'

To hell with it. 'He's sitting on the chair at the far end of the dining table.'

Jude's head whips around, and then slowly turns back to me. 'And you really think he's there.'

'I do.'

My son stretches his eyebrows into tall arcs and looks first to Rachel for help and then to the space where Dom sits.

Rachel raises her shoulders up and down. 'Maybe he is,' she says. 'I hope he is,' she adds before looking towards Dom's chair too. 'Dad, if you're there, anywhere here, I miss you. I miss you every day. I wish I could see you. I wish you could meet Paul. I miss coming here for your roast dinners.' She stops to draw breath. 'I miss calling you on the phone, hearing your voice. Most of all, I miss your hugs and your laugh.'

Dom moves to her, kneels on the floor just in front of her.

Rachel raises her knees up and hugs herself. 'I call here all the time, Dad. Just to hear your voice on the answer machine. As soon as I hear that daft bit of you butting in on top of Mum, I hang up.'

'He's right opposite you,' I whisper, and Rachel leans forward, closes her eyes while I try not to think of how, in my head, I'd blamed Lydia for all those hang-ups.

If Jude could yell the word 'Traitor' at Rachel, he would. 'Mum, I know it's still early days,' he

359

says, 'but I think it's a really bad idea leaving work. You need routine. Dad's *not* here. He's just not.'

'Maybe not, Jude.' I feel a bit defensive. 'I mean, I know why you might *think* I've lost it.'

Dom scrunches his nose and looks at me through only one open eye.

'Because I was the one who tried to beat life into his still heart . . . I tried to blow air into his water-filled lungs.' I shake my head. 'I know it makes no sense. And I'm well aware that seeing my dead husband is probably some form of coping mechanism. But right now, my biggest regret is sharing it with Hannah, who felt the need to tell Lydia,' I nudge my head to Jude, 'who felt the need to tell you. And no doubt each whisper has an added layer of Erin's lunacy.'

'Mum.' Rachel has stood, comes behind me and hugs my neck.

'Answer me honestly,' I address them both. 'It's been eight months. Do you really think I'd be doing this well if I didn't at least *believe* he was still around?' I gulp back the lump crawling up my throat and Jude joins Rachel and me and pulls both of us into a tight hug.

'I miss him too,' he says, 'so very much. I could cry when I think of him. I do cry when I think of him.'

My children don't know but their father has his long arms around all of us and I lean into the squeeze. 'Don't you think he misses you too?' I whisper.

Jude is first to move away and he downs half a glass of wine before sitting down again. 'I

360

googled this,' he says and both Rachel and I glance at one another, smile, because Jude googles everything. 'What? I knew you'd both be saying the same thing so . . . anyway, apparently — ' He thumbs a query into his phone and pulls up a page to read from. 'Apparently,' he continues, 'and I'm not saying I agree, but let's just assume here that there is such a thing as a soul.'

I notice as he speaks that Dom is leaving the room. It's as if he doesn't want to hear this bit.

'He has unfinished business with you,' Jude puts his phone down and shrugs. 'Wants to tell you something. There's a whole piece on there but that's what it's saying. Not with you and me, Rach, because we can't see him. Just you, Mum.'

My tears come fast and steady and I can see the kids are wishing they'd never come. Jude is sitting with his hands on his head, looking like my nineteen-year-old distraught son who's lost his father. He no longer looks like someone's confident young groom. Rachel is tapping my hand rhythmically and I think it's helping her more than me. And Dom? Dom seems to have vanished . . .

*   *   *

'Thanks a bunch,' I tell him later when he sits beside me on the sofa as I'm trying to lose myself in some television series. Dom says nothing. Fitz has texted to say he's staying overnight in the house and will be back in the morning.

361

'Right, you're obviously in a quiet mood, which suits me.' I get up and walk out to the hall table, come back carrying The Book of Love. 'I need you to listen.' I read yesterday's brief words to him and when I've finished, I look up. Dom is staring at me sadly.

'And there's more,' I say before reading the one I wrote after the kids left. Don't look up once, I tell myself. Read it in one go. No glances.

★ ★ ★

21st June 2017

My darling Dom,

Once upon a time you told me you felt trapped. I remember it, as if it was yesterday. We were walking to the river with the twins, just babies, in a double pushchair — both of us overcome with responsibility when we needed to remember how to have some fun. We got over it — we came back to each other. I'm not sure how, but we did.

But I feel it again.

I feel it for you and for me.

I'm trapped because I don't want to let you go. I'm trapped because I can't bear the thought of life without you and this isn't how it was supposed to be. I'm forty-five years old. We were supposed to check out together as octogenarians. Not now and not like this. I'm trapped because I don't want to believe how you died. It's one thing to have to come to terms with you being gone; it's another thing completely to accept that you lost your life saving another. And where I should think the saving of a life is laudable, I'm angry at you. Because sad as it would have been, I'd have been able to bear the loss of Lydia easier than losing you.

You're trapped because if this is real, if any of it is real, you should be gone from my life, yet you're not. Is this some sort of limbo for you? Why do I only see you in Valentine's or nearby? Do you have to stay here? Is that the real reason you couldn't come with me to the States? Whatever's going on I really only see you here, so all that talk of travelling together gets shelved. Is this where your limbo is — our happy place? Is Jude right, do you have something you need to say to me, something that was unfinished or left unsaid? Do you need to be here? Are you being pulled to join your mum and Maisie?

How do either of us move on?

So many questions . . .

I want you here with me forever. If I could have that, I'd lock the door and swallow the key.

But I can't have that, can I? Because we'd both be trapped. You stuck in whatever halfway house this is, and me, hiding away from the other people I love so I can be with you.

And here's the part where I tell you that I know you have to leave me. I know it — can feel it in my bones and all I want to do is to beg you to stay a while. I'm not ready to say goodbye again — not yet.

Please . . .

I love you forever, my darling Dom.

Erin xx

★   ★   ★

When I look up, my face is stained with tears and he's standing behind me. I have to deep breathe to allow myself to catch air. He leans down and kisses my hair and I reach up to touch his hand, to feel him.

'I didn't read the letters,' he admits, 'but it doesn't matter. I hear your thoughts as you write them. So, I knew.'

I turn and look up, frame his face with my hands. 'If I imagined you, like made you up, I made you quite clever then.'

'It would appear so.' He looks at the clock on the wall and back to me. 'Bed?' he says, and I drop the book and take his hand.

45.

Thursday 22nd June 2017

Fitz is back. He has a small box under his arm which he places on the table, all the while frowning at me. 'You look awful,' he says.

Having woken with the feeling that my throat has been shredded by blades, my response is to sniff into an already damp tissue. 'Summer cold,' I whisper.

'Hot toddy,' he says, already filling the kettle, and I'm reminded of Lydia sipping the same concoction that night we arrived in Cornwall.

'Have you cloves?' He's nosing around the cupboard that will have cloves and I try to tell him I really don't want his cure-all-colds drink.

'Would you, just for once,' he peers at me from behind the open door, 'do as you're told?'

The kettle bubbles to the boil. He pours water on brown sugar and cloves, stirs it and then adds whisky. I grimace as he hands it to me.

'Drink.'

It's an order but all I can do for now is hold the glass, feel the heat warm my hands.

Fitz sits opposite me. 'I've accepted an offer on the house.'

I nod slowly, sip the drink, rather than speak, feel it coat my sore throat. It's vile yet somehow makes swallowing easier.

'A young couple with a child on the way.

They're nice . . . it feels like the house will have a new lease of life.'

My eyes lock on his and I'm not sure what he wants me to say. 'That's good,' is what comes out, and he seems okay with that.

'I brought some things back for you.' He pulls the box towards us both. 'Things I thought you might like but everything else is being packed up in three weeks, so maybe you and I could go down there, and you could see — '

'I don't want anything.' My voice is raspy.

He taps the lid of the brown box. 'It's just a few of your mum's favourite books, and that scarf she used to wear all the time, remember the one?'

Oranges, reds, purples, multiple geometric shapes — I remember it. I imagine her wearing it now sitting next to Fitz at the table.

'Do you see her, Dad?'

He turns to face me. 'Sometimes, though less now . . . '

'You talk to her?'

I watch his Adam's apple move slowly. 'All the time. More now.' He laughs. 'She doesn't always approve.'

My smile is slight, and he reaches for my hand. 'But I think she was the one who reminded me what you're going through. I woke one morning feeling that she and I had been talking in my sleep and I — ' He pauses. 'I felt like you needed me here.'

I put the glass down and hug myself. 'Dom's here all the time.'

Dad looks around the room as if he might

catch a glimpse. He squeezes my fingers. 'If it helps you.'

I say nothing.

' 'Goodbyes are only for those who love with their eyes. Because for those who love with heart and soul there is no such thing as separation.' '

My lower lip trembles.

'Rumi. Penny introduced me to him. A thirteenth-century Persian poet.'

'Lovely words,' I manage.

He lets go of my hand, taps it. 'How did it go yesterday with Lydia?' he changes the subject.

I could admit I never made it, but I just widen my smile. 'Fine,' I say. 'She's agreed to sell Valentine's back, knows it's what Gerard and Dom want.'

And it's instant — that tell-tale crevice between my father's eyes. My use of the present tense with Dom. His poetic words just spoken to humour me. His nod is hesitant and then he decides to leave me marinating in my belief that my husband is here.

'But I'm not going back to work for her,' I add. 'And she knows that now.' What was it she'd said?

I respect your decision.

I can see him decide not to comment. 'I'm going to pop out and get you some soup,' he says instead, already standing in the doorway jangling his keys.

It's thirty degrees outside. I don't want soup. Or hot whisky.

'Maybe some sparkling water,' I suggest.

367

'Okay. Text me if there's anything you feel like eating.'

When he leaves I grab my wide-brimmed hat and walk outside to the patio, sit in the swing seat, and curl myself up under the shade of the Japonicus. My eyes rest on the area where we buried the time capsule and, not for the first time, I wonder.

I feel a gentle push and the seat moves.

'You always knew I buried it,' Dom's voice comes from behind before he takes a seat opposite me, steeples his hands.

'I think I did.' I agree. The missing letter has, I've often sensed, been merely metres from the house.

'You want to dig it up?' he asks.

I shake my head. 'I'd rather you tell me what it says.'

'I never lied about it, Erin. It only ever opened up a possible dialogue that happened years later anyway.'

'Why did you keep it for so long?'

Dom's staring at the exact spot that I'd have pointed the spade. 'To remind me what an idiot I'd been.'

'So, why bury it when you did?'

'To forgive myself. I figured when you managed that, maybe I should try.' He looks skyward before turning to me. 'You sound rough.'

'I feel rough. Fitz is out getting soup.'

Dom laughs. 'You should eat something, maybe not soup, but something, Erin.'

I look down at my body, at my clothes hanging

368

loosely around my body.

'Not a diet I'd recommend,' I tell him before launching into a coughing fit.

'I still would,' he grins. 'If I could. You're still my beautiful Tree Girl.'

We hold hands, sit quietly until I hear the front door open and close.

'Soup,' Dom whispers.

I close my eyes and when I open them Dom has gone, and Fitz is hovering above me. 'Chicken or minestrone?'

★ ★ ★

Thursday 22nd June 2017

Darling Dom,

I keep wondering about what Jude said and whether you have unfinished business with me and it's made me focus on all that's happened since you left and since you've been around again.

Valentine's is coming back to me. Your father's care is being looked after. I have life insurance money to 'give me choices.'

All of that has been set in motion.

Which just leaves Lydia.

And that's at least better than it was.

And here's where one more time in these pages I tell you I'm afraid. I'm to fix it like you want me to because then I think you'll have to go.

I'm right, aren't I?

I love you. Please don't leave me.

Erin xx

46.

The journey is silent but for the noise in my head urging me to turn around. As we near the house, Fitz asks about the care home Gerard will move into. I assure him that it's lovely — a newly built state-of-the-art facility — that it's what Gerard wants and that there's room for Fitz there too. He laughs — that deep-throated rumble that I miss. I'm doing this for him, I remind myself. For him. For Dad. He's travelled to be here with me and this is for him.

I pull into the driveway. The building that Dom grew up in would have scared me away from him, had I seen it before I met him. Even Fitz is a little intimidated and I can't believe he's never been here before.

'You could fit my place in a few times over,' he says, taking in all four floors of the semi-detached Victorian house from the outside. I climb the stone steps, lift the knocker but Lydia has the door open before it sounds. 'Fitz,' she says, throwing her arms around his neck, 'it's good to see you here.' She smiles at me over his shoulder, mouths a 'hello' in my direction and I notice she's wearing the same lemon-coloured Bermuda shorts as me.

'Ahh, you too. You look well, love.' He holds out both of her hands and looks her up and down. 'How's your dad doing?' He loops an arm through hers and leads her down the hallway. I follow, listen to my feet tapping in my summer flip-flops. I think of Dom's feet treading these tiles for years. I think of Dom's feet . . .

Lydia looks over her shoulder at me, looks as if she's going to say something and then thinks twice. Dad, without knowing it, had led us to the back of the house, to the kitchen I remember Sophie cooking lots of Christmas dinners in. It's weird, I think, it feels like she's still here and then I remember, coming from my head, that it's not weird at all.

'Can I get you guys something?' Lydia asks. 'Maybe a cold drink, a soft drink or a beer?'

'No thanks,' I answer for both of us. The last thing I want is Dad lingering over a beer. 'We're only here because Dad wants to see Gerard.'

'You're not very well,' she says.

'Hurts to talk,' I tell her, hoping she won't try and make me.

She nods then leads the way out of the kitchen, down a set of stone steps to the lower ground floor where Gerard has been living for the last ten months. He's sitting in a wing-back chair with a book on his lap and the television muted on a game of rugby. When he sees us, he opens his arms wide and I bend into his hug.

'Erin, how are you, my dear?' Both his hands frame my face, and his rheumy eyes look into mine. It feels like there's no need for me to reply as he kisses my cheek.

'Fitz!' Gerard pulls himself up to standing.

'How are you, old boy? I hear you've got a younger woman!'

I slink back towards the door, wanting to leave them to it but Lydia's there, hovering in the shadows of the hallway.

'Did you instruct the solicitor?' I croak.

'Yes. I emailed you — she'll have contracts ready in a few days. We could probably exchange and complete in one go.' She keeps her voice low.

'You were happy with the valuation?'

Lydia nods, squeezing her pale, veiny, hands as if she's trying to get blood flowing through them. Suddenly, she reaches her hand to briefly touch my arm and I flinch. Fitz is only metres away in the next room talking to Gerard about the many framed photos surrounding him.

'It's good to actually see you,' Lydia says cautiously.

Gerard's telling Fitz that there's a Dom shelf and a Lydia shelf, all arranged chronologically, from baby to wedding day. Dom's shelf has pictures of Rachel and Jude, even one of Maisie, and I just want to run screaming from the building.

'Erin,' she reaches for my arm harder. 'Are you alright?'

'Did you fall?' The words are out. Through the doorway I see Fitz turn to glare at me. 'Or did you jump?'

Lydia jerks back and steadies herself against the wall. 'I *fell*,' she says, dropping my arm as if I've scalded her. Quiet tears slide down her cheeks as she backs down the hallway and I follow.

'I fell,' she repeats, shaking her head.

'Your being so near water?' When I think of all of the charity swims over the years where she baulked at the thought of ever learning to swim, of ever taking part. 'It never made sense.'

'I'd just stopped to look at the view. It was wild . . . I was just — '

'You'd lie anyway, Lydia, so I'll never know.'

'Erin.' Her face is twisted with horror.

'You were exhausted, had moved in here, volunteered yourself to look after Gerard's needs.'

Fitz closes over the door, shuts us in the hallway.

'Your life wasn't what you'd imagined it would be — ' I continue.

Lydia whips around. 'I slipped, fell in the water. Dom saved my life and I can't spend the rest of my life apologising for that. And you know that's not what he'd want either.'

She has no idea what Dom would want, what Dom wants.

'I should go,' I say, trying to edge past her.

'I fell,' she repeats as I climb the stairs. 'But I still wish I'd died that day instead of him.' Her voice gets louder, pursues me, as I move away from her. 'Every day,' she yells. 'Every single day since, I wish he was still here instead.'

★   ★   ★

Fitz takes his time coming out and, when he does, says nothing until I switch the ignition on.

'That's one gorgeous house.' He looks up at it

373

while biting a thumbnail at the same time.

'It is.' I put the car into gear and reverse out.

'And that's one fucked-up lady, seriously Erin.' He holds a flat palm in the air. 'That's one fucked-up lady.'

'At least she's here,' I tell him as I drive away.

I stare straight ahead while he watches me.

'Didn't you hear her tell you that she wishes she wasn't?'

'Makes two of us.'

'You're angry. You've a right to be pissed off at the world but you need to get a grip, girl.'

'Dad.' I pull into the end of someone's driveway and stop the car. 'What the hell is this? Lydia's begging for forgiveness lately after months of being unable to look me in the eye. You come from America *now*, indefinitely, to 'sell the house', but when Dom died you barely managed to stay for forty-eight hours after the funeral.'

'Maybe she's sensed that you always thought what you blurted out today. Maybe she *did* jump — if she did — imagine what she has to live with now?' Fitz draws a deep breath before continuing. 'I think she fell, for what it's worth. And maybe I had to see you in the States a few weeks ago before I realised how much you need me here. My bad . . . '

I do not need you here. I have Dom. And stop talking like a teenager. Get lost, all of you.

'I was wrong,' he adds.

I pull my shirt off, leaving just a white T-shirt on, turn the air-con up. 'You should go back to Penny.'

He ignores me. 'Lydia spoke to me about you not going back to work.'

I smack my lips together.

'What? When you walked out, we talked,' he says.

'I've resigned. I told you that already. I don't need to or want to be involved with the business anymore.'

'Yes, I know but it seems to me like you might need routine and a job you used to love more than ever.'

'I have money.'

'So?'

I shrug, roll the window down. 'Money gives me choices.' One of Dom's favourite lines.

Fitz nods sagely. 'And what choices are you making?'

'The money from the sale of the company will buy back Valentine's.'

More nodding.

'And the other money . . . ' The life insurance settlement — our adventure money, according to Dom.

'The other money?' Fitz prompts me.

'The insurance money, I don't know yet, but it'll provide an income — '

Fitz hoots with laughter. 'You're forty-five years old. No amount of life insurance is going to give you an income for another forty years. You should stay in work for a while. Keep something familiar in your life and keep a salary coming in.'

'Maybe I'll open my own coffee joint, or a gin joint. Some sort of rival joint.'

I dare not look but I can feel Fitz's despair sizzle from him. 'You wouldn't do that.'

He's right but I like the thought of it. 'Maybe I'll die young like Mum,' I say, starting the car again. 'That takes care of the forty years problem.'

Fitz says nothing. My throat hurts from talking. The rest of the journey is silent but for the sounds from outside through two open windows; horns honking, pedestrian chatter from the pavements, music from other cars, the whirring in my father's head.

'Look,' I say as I stop outside our house by his car, 'I really don't feel like company tonight. Do you mind?'

Fitz takes my hand, folds it into both of his. 'I *do* know what you're going through.' He reaches over and kisses my cheek. 'Call me.'

He waits, staring from his driver's seat, until I've closed the front door behind me. And I wait until he's gone to exhale.

'Dom?' I call out. 'I'm home.'

47.

It's five thirty, all the shops are closing and I'm sitting in a pub just outside the mall waiting for Jude. The crowds and staff from the shops all seem to be heading home to a beautiful evening where, if they can, they'll sit in their gardens till late. The bar's surprisingly quiet. My shopping is by my feet and I'm seated with a bottle of sparkling elderflower water in front of me ten minutes before he's due. Jude is a time pedant — always on time, hates people being late.

While doubt stews in my chest, I swallow a couple of tablets and, just as I'm about to stand up and pretend I never made it, my son is standing in front of me looking at me with Dom's eyes.

'Mum,' he says, air kissing my cheek. 'Were you about to bolt?'

'No, no, I was thinking you'd be here any second and was just going to get you a drink.'

'Sit,' he says, 'I'll get it. You not having anything stronger?'

'Antibiotics,' I say and also mimic my hands on a steering wheel.

Minutes later, he's back with a pint of Guinness. I watch it as it does its brewing thing before our eyes; as the dark liquid seems to form

377

from the bottom up, bubbling to a creamy top line.

'Three times in ten days?' he says. 'A record for us.'

'Yes.' I steady my breathing. 'I wanted to see you alone.'

Jude makes a joke of looking around the empty bar. 'You got me,' he says.

'I have something for you,' I tap the shopping bag.

He looks uncomfortable and then seems to regret it. 'Sorry. I've inherited your love of surprises.'

'When your dad and I got married,' I say, 'Fitz gave us a leather-bound notebook which we called The Book of Love. I've been racking my brains what to give you and Freya as a wedding present and . . . anyway, here it is. This is my gift to you.' I remove the notebook I'd found in the department store — leather, not exactly the same, but similar. I've wrapped it in newspaper and blue ribbon and copied Fitz's words onto a new card for them.

He looks at the package I put between us on the table. 'Shit, Mum, we were hoping for a dishwasher.'

My face must react because he laughs, shakes his head. 'Relax, I'm kidding. Do I open it now?'

'No, wait for Freya, do it together.' For some reason, I feel embarrassed and shift around on the narrow stool.

'Thank you,' he says, 'thanks.'

'I'll get you a dishwasher if you need one,' I add.

'Oh, Mum . . . ' He swallows about a third of the pint in one go.

'I'm serious, if you want a dishwasher, I — '

'We don't need a dishwasher. We don't have room for a dishwasher.'

'Is there anything you *do* need?'

'No.'

'The gift,' I nudge my head towards it. 'When Fitz gave it to us, I thought it was a mad idea until the first time I used it and . . . anyway . . . I hope that you and Freya might find it useful. It helps people communicate differently, maybe if there's something you can't say — '

'There's nothing Freya and I couldn't say to one another.' He says this with a confidence I didn't know he possessed.

'Right. Well, your dad and I, we had lots of times we couldn't, and it really helped. But you know that already . . . '

He colours under the facial hair he's been growing for the last few months. It's as if he stopped shaving the day Dom died.

'We knew you read our book at least once.'

'I'm sorry about that.'

'It's okay. Means I don't really even have to explain how it works.'

The bar is so empty now that all I can hear is the swishing sound of glasses on a wash cycle behind the bar. I find myself studying his hands. He has long tapered fingers like a pianist, nothing like mine or Dom's.

'You speak to Rach today?' he asks.

I nod. Rachel and I speak every day about nothing at all.

'I used to be jealous of that,' he says, turning to face me. 'Your easy relationship with her, and I'd give you a hard time but that's all a long time ago now.'

'What went through your head back then?'

'Mum, this is one of those times you're asking a question, but I think you don't really want an answer.'

'I do.' Lines criss-cross my brow. 'What, is this somehow my 'control freakery' again?'

'No,' he laughs and puts his pint down. 'To be fair, that comment was way out of line, no this . . . this is when the truth might hurt so I don't want to be honest.'

I'm not sure my boy is going to need that book, after all.

'You have to be now — I asked.'

'O-k-ay. Maisie died. Rachel replaced her, which sort of meant I was a spare child.'

I swallow his blunt truth, am mute and still.

'It's not how I feel now. Just for a bit when I was younger, when I hated lots of stuff and people in school and — ' He shrugs. 'You were lumped in there, in the 'stuff'. You and Rach were so easy together and I was envious of that.' Hand up in between us, he stops me interrupting. 'I know what you're going to say, Dad and I were easy too.'

I nod.

'We were, which is why I know it's silly but, hey, like I said, you asked.' He looks at my glass of flavoured water. 'Don't worry about it, Mum. It's all old shit. I'm going to go and get another half, you sure you don't want a glass of wine?'

I could really do with a drink. 'I do. I want a glass of wine. And a bag of nuts.'

Jude leans his six-foot frame down to me and kisses the top of my head. 'Coming up.'

'Jude.'

He looks back.

'I'm sorry.'

'Mum, forget it, okay?'

As he walks away I touch the space he kissed with my fingertips. I think of the hundreds of times that this boy has made me proud; the school reports, the smiling school photos, the joker in the family, the sensitive child with other children, the dedication to sport, his running trophies, the times I've known he's protected his sister, the way he held me when his father died. And I have never been surer that our son, this man-child will, in the long run, be alright.

Soon I'm sipping the slightly tart Chardonnay when he raises his glass to me. 'You and Dad had a great marriage. I hope Freya and I are as lucky.'

I tap the package. 'Make some luck. You'll be given plenty but some you have to create.'

'Rachel going to get one of these when she gets married?'

'She sure is.'

'You think she'll marry Paul?'

'God, no.'

'Me neither.'

'But then again, I never saw you running off to Gretna Green with Freya either. What the hell do I know?'

48.

Sunday 25th June 2017

When I get back from evening mass, I tread on an envelope on the mat before I see it. Then I walk past it. Years of seeing her handwriting on papers at work means I can recognise Lydia's scrawl from a metre away, even under a dusty footprint.

'You should read that,' Dom says immediately.

'*You* read it.'

'It's addressed to you.'

I grab it from the floor and head upstairs. 'I'm running a bath,' I tell him, yet again avoiding the discussion that's been hovering around both of us for days, the one that would begin, 'So . . . Lydia?' In the bathroom, I place the stopper in the plughole, run both taps, stand back and watch the roll-top bathtub fill, dropping my clothes on the floor. I toss some salts in, wait for them to disperse, test the water with my elbow the way I used to when I had babies. Stepping in, I lower myself, let the water caress me. It takes only minutes for me to reach for the envelope sitting by the sink and tear it open with wet hands.

I cannot not read it.

Dear Erin,
Both of us, have for different reasons,

over the years, come to believe that writing things down works. I could have emailed you but I thought you'd just delete it like others I've sent. Hopefully, this letter will be harder to ignore.

I only have a few things to say:

I miss you. You've been my 'sister' for a very long time and I miss you in my life.

My life — yes, a life I very stupidly tried to end once when I struggled so hard with the reality of not having children. Erin. I hope because you've had your own anxieties over the years that you'll understand and hear this. Someone who comes back from that despair intact, NEVER wants to go there again. I know that anytime I feel remotely close to anything that destructive, I have people ready and willing to listen and to help.

I fell clear and simple. Awful, and ending in the most horrific tragedy but my part in that was an accident. Dom's part was deliberate, heroic. He saved my life, Erin, and I'm grateful. But I also feel overwhelming guilt and I feel his absence so strongly that it's nowadays, not back then, that I need professionals to listen and help me. That is mine to deal with and I am. I'm dealing with it.

You've been left without the love of your life. And there are no words. Really, I've really thought about this, whether there's anything I can possibly say to make you realise that I know this, and I feel for you *and I want to (probably need to) help you. And you're screaming at the page at the moment, telling me to take my pity and stick it up my ass.*

Your job is here waiting for you if ever you want it. If ever you need it.

I'm here waiting for you if you ever want me or need me.

Whether you and I can ever get back to being friends again. I don't know, but I hope so. It will take forgiveness. I'm learning to forgive myself for being there that day but for us to move forward you have to forgive me too. Dom was a huge believer in hope. He knew how fear could restrict us (you know that too) but he believed in hope, told me once it was the only thing that could set us free.

They're the words I'll end with.

I love you. I'm sorry. I hope you can forgive me.

Lydia

I drop the single page into the water, feel my resolve weaken as I watch the paper slowly soak, the ink run off the page. Then I scrunch it up into a tight ball and fling it across the room. Sinking my head under the water, I feel the briny bath salts line my nostrils. My hair fans out in rusty waves almost blocking out the light in the room. I close my eyes, listen to Dom chattering in my head as I hold my breath. My hair parts and I see a hand hover above me before I jump upwards, gasping.

★　★　★

Just as the daylight breaks, I hear myself whimper. I'm flat on my back, my right arm lying straight by my side, my left at a right angle. Dom is still asleep beside me and his left hand rests over mine, shadowing it, minding it. It's so much bigger than my hand and the feel of his fingers spread out over mine relaxes me and I close my eyes again. One, two, three, four, five — our fingers lace. Sleep is instant.

★　★　★

Erin, my love,

I'm hoping you can hear me . . .

Ours was the best marriage. Let's at least give ourselves that.

Sure, like many, there have been white lies throughout. There have been some wounding lies. But above all, Erin, I still believe it was built on love, survived on love and will last for eternity on love.

Please, be able to hear this . . . I have our hands just touching; each finger mirroring. There's me and you and Maisie and Jude and Rachel. One, two, three, four, five.

Jude was right and yet he's wrong. Yes, I'm here, with things to say to you but not just because there was unfinished business exactly, more because I couldn't bear to let you go either. I wasn't ready. I'm still not ready. And I felt your pain. I've never been able to bear seeing you in pain, whether it be childbirth or your old

385

anxieties, or when I may have hurt you. I've always wanted to iron out your sadness. So, no, I couldn't leave you — not when all I could feel was your aching loss. You thought the threat of skin cancer was your biggest fear until you realised it was life without me. You miss me. You want the life we planned. I'm so sorry.

And I'm here to reassure you.

You're going to live a fine life. And now it's your job to live that life. Take some time off for yourself. You might go back to work — you might not. Do that photography course. Have some adventures that I've somehow hoped we could still have together but I feel myself fading around you.

One, two, three, four, five. I've just pressed your fingertips with mine and you moaned a little in your sleep. Good, you're hearing me.

It's you now, Erin. It's you who will be the parent to our children, and you and I both know how much we need our parents even when we're 'grown up', probably more than — when they become a friend. Don't doubt yourself. They love you. They need you and you need them. You'll need each other until you all get to the point where you can sit around and talk about me without tears.

It will happen. Believe that and yes, I'll be there.

They're wonderful people, our kids.

Love each other. Never forget what love can heal.

And be brave enough to love another man, Erin. What you and I had will forever be what you and I still have.

And never forget.
I love you mightily.

★ ★ ★

I wake to the sound of children laughing as they kick a can along the street outside. Thoughts of Dom and our history are whirring around my head as I yawn. Turning over, I move my hand over the space that he'd lain in. Cold. Sitting up, hands rubbing each other, I call out to him. My hands stop moving, left on right, fingers laced together, and the truth seems caught in between.

I know.

As sure as I know that Dom died on another weekend last October, I know he's left me again on this one.

49.

Wednesday 28th June 2017

The underground is hot, sticky and uncomfortable — the backs of my knees almost clinging to the seat. Up top, the summer showers that poured since early morning have cooled the air and as I climb the steps from the station, it's such a relief to peel my shirt from my skin. Immediately, bakery scents hit in a wave; croissants, biscuits, small pastries with oozing savoury insides remind me I'm hungry — a sensation I can't remember feeling for a while. The croissant is overpriced but delicious and when I arrive at the solicitor's office, I'm covered in tiny flakes of buttery pastry.

Lydia's already there. She stands when I come in and makes small talk about me sounding much better. It's as if our last conversation at her house never happened, as if that letter had never been sent. A young guy approaches, asks if we'd like a tea or coffee. Lydia refuses the offer, and I tell him yes. Caffeine is needed. Ten minutes later, in the room I now know that all of Dom's legal transactions were handled by the man sitting opposite Lydia and me, I picture Dom being here too. I see him sitting opposite the skinny wisp of a man who goes by the name of William Burley, probably in the same seat I'm in now. He looks like he's come straight from

388

central casting for nineteenth-century solicitors. He sits behind an enormous wooden desk, surrounded by stacks of papers that I imagine no one can touch apart from him. His hair is wire wool. His steel-coloured caterpillar eyebrows meet in the middle and his voice roars with such unexpected authority that I look around to see where it actually came from and I don't dare ask any questions.

When Lydia and I both sign the contracts, she as seller and power of attorney for Gerard and me as the buyer of Valentine's, Burley assures us that because of the simple transaction, contracts will be exchanged and completed this week. Before we know it, both of us are standing outside his office and the reason we're here is already done.

'Lunch?' she asks casually.

'I ate something on the way in.' As if to prove the point, I flick a final crispy flake from my shirt.

'Do you mind if I travel back with you?' she asks.

I'd rather be alone, but I shake my head and together we walk side by side to the tube.

At Waterloo, she doesn't need to check the flashing timetable above us for the departure time of our next train. 'It's twenty past from platform ten,' she tells me. 'We have time. You want to get a drink?'

It's hot. The station is heaving with people. 'Okay.'

I follow her through the throng to the escalator and upstairs we find two seats at the edge of a bar overlooking the concourse. Without asking what I want, she heads to order drinks.

'French, rosé,' she says, minutes later, and hands me the drink I would have asked her to get as she sits with a lemon-heavy G&T.

I mutter my thanks, look at my wrist.

'I just checked the screen,' she says. 'The twenty past has been cancelled. Looks like we're stuck with each other for an hour.'

I feel my heart hammer in my chest.

'Will you please consider staying on at work?' she spits out.

'Right now, because you're asking me right now, my answer is no.' I hesitate. Rachel is the only one who agrees with my decision about giving up work. And I've convinced myself that Rachel is the voice of reason in my life, so she must know what's best for me. But both Fitz and Jude think I need the routine that the Bean Pod brings. 'But if you asked me next week, I don't know. My head's all over the place at the moment.'

'What does Dom think you should do?'

I glance across at her face, convinced I'd see some shades of her indulging me but her expression is sincere. She's asking a genuine question.

'Dom and I were maybe going to have an adventure,' I swallow some wine and look down at the hundreds of people I don't know. 'But then we sort of knew that might not be possible. He thinks I should do a photography course.'

'That's a good idea.'

'But Dom's gone now,' I tell her. 'So . . . '

'I'm sorry.'

I can't look at her but know she's genuine. She's sorry. She's sorry that Dom saved her and she's sorry that Dom's gone. Again.

Rubbing my arms, I just nod.

'He loved you so very much, Erin.'

'I know.'

'And he loved me.'

'He did. And you owe it to him to live a big life, Lydia.'

She sits back on the chair, wipes her eye with her hand. 'To do that, I need you to be a part of it, to be in my life. To forgive me for being there that morning.'

And in that moment, I find myself remembering my husband's capacity to forgive. It was as if he was made of the stuff and the memories start to melt my resistance.

Before I have a chance to reply, I notice something happening down below me and I find myself looking over the balustrade, staring. There's a guy in the middle of a crowded space and he's just started to dance. People around him are moving away and just as Lydia looks over the balcony too, music sounds in the station.

The guy moves beautifully; his arms swaying and legs flick-kicking to a 'Thriller' track that booms from the tannoy. I feel a smile sneak across my lips and when others join in, I see it's stage-managed and I hear Lydia scramble in her bag.

'A flash mob,' she removes her phone and starts to film it. Soon, hundreds of people are dancing to a medley of music that has both of us standing by our seats. I'm moving side to side, taking still photographs. Just underneath me, two uniformed police officers stand, their arms folded, smiling and tapping their feet. The guy who started the routine beckons to people to join in and at the edges of the choreographed mass, commuters and tourists alike are bopping side to side.

Lydia has the iPhone in the air still filming but she's looking at me. I move closer to her, lean my head on her shoulder.

I sing along. 'Dom would love this,' I tell her.

She keeps filming. 'He would but he'd tell you to stop singing.'

I laugh. She's right. That's exactly what he'd say if he were here.

If he were here.

When the music changes to a Queen track and all the dancers drop to the floor to air guitar, I catch her eye and we're both nineteen again working in that boutique where we met. We're in the stock room and we're crazy dancing to whatever comes on the radio. She drops her phone in her bag and I take her offered hand, and we dance together, head banging and strumming our imaginary guitars.

And when the music stops, and everyone slinks off at the end, as if the moment had never happened, Lydia and I both know it did. She looks at me, tears in her eyes and tells me she loves me.

I nod, my father's twenty-year-old words echoing in my head:

'*I am Love, and if real, I will never fade . . .* '

Epilogue

From *The Book of Love*:
'I love you because it works for us,
this love thing.'

My Tree Girl isn't dancing.

No, the only slight movement is the blanket rising and falling with each breath; a mechanical sounding 'whoosh' both in and out. The 'in' lasts for a fraction less than the raspy 'out'. Her long arms that first reminded him of a tree's branches lie alongside her skinny body. If she were a tree now, she would bend in the wind, her weak limbs unable to take any strain. The hippy sway of oh so long ago would break her . . .

She lies in a bed, one that angles however she pleases with a voice instruction, but her voice is weak. It neither speaks to the bed or her loved ones these last few days. Beside the mattress is a pull-down diagnostic touch screen and underneath that, a small table protrudes from the wall with a jug of water and a glass on it. Some things will always remain the same, he thinks. She is, as he knew she would be, surrounded by people. Only one remains from their original gang. He rests a hand on Hannah's shoulder as he passes, and she flinches a little, looks up and reaches her bony hand to the spot he'd just touched.

Rachel sits opposite, her head back, eyes closed. It's the woman by her side that holds Erin's hand, that tightens her grip as Erin moans a little. When Dom hears her voice, it's still the same to him. Even a tiny groan jolts a memory of her deep and throaty timbre and he laughs as he remembers her first words to him. 'I'm Erin.'

★   ★   ★

Darling Dom,

I've not felt you around for such a very long time and now I think you're here. I'm sure I saw you skulking in the corner of this room the other day when I tried to open my eyes, It was you, wasn't it? Is it you, my love. Have you come for me?

I wrote in The Book of Love every year on our anniversary you know, until last year when my eyes finally gave in — thirty-six updates. I hated not being able to do it then; hate not being able to write this one now but I remember you saying that you hear me as I think the words. I hope you still can.

Thirty-six years. That's a long time to wait for someone, Dom. I never loved another, by the way, despite your last request but I'm quite sure you know that already. I did try — there were a few candidates — a few men I tried to love but that feeling never came, that feeling of tenderness and warmth and safety that I felt with you. And by the time you'd been gone for ten years, I came to the conclusion that love, for me, was definitely a once in a lifetime thing. We had the good fortune to find that rare thing, a love that lasts forever.

I've asked Rachel and her husband Rav to make sure our book goes in the box with me and that it's burned with me. I can't bear to leave it.

I've had a good life, Dom. You told me I would. The best half with you but I think you somehow had a hand in making sure the second half was blessed too. I managed to completely dodge the cancer bullet again but six months ago my heart decided that it's weary. But look around me — it's amazing how even my emaciated heart can still love so very much.

We have only one grandchild, Leila. She's the woman holding my hand right now. Can you see? She looks just like Rav and she has Rachel's nature. And Leila has two boys, beautiful, beautiful, twin boys. What a joy they are!

Jude was here earlier. We were right, by the way, many of those thirty-six updates would have been about Jude in some way — his many highs and lows. No written thoughts saved him and Freya, they were just too young But he did marry again, in his late thirties; a lovely lady, Julia, four years older than him, and he has three gorgeous step-children. He's head teacher now at the school. How weird the circles turn . . .

Are they with you? Is there a group of people I've loved with you? Fitz, Rob and Maisie. Sophie and Gerard. Nigel and Lydia and you. Or are you alone, my love?

Will you come and lay by me when the moment's here? Or will you grasp my hand and whisper in my ear. I have to confess I'm scared — not of dying, not of being with you again, just of saying goodbye. I love them all so very much.

I've had so many more years than you of touching them and feeling them and I can't bear to let go.

That sound is my breathing. It's awful isn't it? That death rasp rattle in my lungs. Still I made it to eighty-two, Dom. You told me I would . . .

★   ★   ★

Darling Erin,

I was with you all the way, girl. Not just listening to the thirty-six entries but whenever you needed me and many times when you didn't think you did. That time when you were driving just that bit too fast on a German autobahn a few years after I died. I slowed you down that day. The time when Freya left Jude and he came home to live in Valentine's and you were at your wit's end. But you loved him through it. You propped him up and I held you up.

It's almost time, love. And I'm here like I said I would be.

Don't be afraid. I'll wait until you're sure. I'm right here, lying beside you and when you're ready, just take my hand. That's all you have to do, my love, one small reach, Erin the Brave. Take my hand, clasp my fingers.

One, two, three, four, five.

I'm here and I love you mightily.

Acknowledgements

A huge, and I mean *massive* thanks to HarperCollins UK and Ireland — to everyone across editorial, cover design, sales, marketing and PR. Special heartfelt thanks and hugs to Kim Young and Charlotte Ledger for all their hard work and patience. Thanks too to Mary Byrne, Tony Purdue, Liz Dawson, Jaime Frost and Laura Gerard. To my agent, Maddy, thank you for keeping the faith and always being there. Thanks too to her incredible team Milburn, especially Alice who helps get my words translated all over the world. Publisher and agent, I really am blessed to work with the very best in the business.

Thanks to my sister Annie, who read quite a few early versions of this book — LYM, girl, and to Brian, my brother, for *that* line! And the rest of my siblings, the mad clan and in-laws, it's been a tough few years but hey, we're all still standing . . . Thank you to Sally Metcalf for that Christmas 'top-box' tale! To Claire Allan, greatest writer pal and the most patient beta reader ever, thanks for pushing me each step of the way. And to my late great friend, Vanessa Lafaye, a beautiful writer and person, who also beta read and encouraged me, telling me 'This is the one' just before she died. I hope I never have to be as brave as her, but if I do, she showed me how. Her loss was one of a few this last year which somehow makes this act of thanking those I'm grateful to more important than ever.

A big shout out to all of the wonderful book-bloggers, reviewers and book-sellers, who I'm enormously grateful to — thank you for your continued support. To everyone I know on Twitter and Facebook, thanks for the procrastination moments and so much more. Thanks too to the amazing online book-clubs especially The Rick O'Shea Book Club, Tracy Fenton's The Book Club, The Good Housekeeping Book Room, Woman&Home Reading Room and The Book Tribe — all wonderful spaces for readers. And the Prime Writers, you know who you are — your support and friendship in this mad world of writing means so much. Here's to many more scones! To my friends, especially Mary and Steph, the book club gang (Ta for the 'I love you because . . . ' brainstorm) and also the extended Camberley crew, the GK exes, all the FB school group and everyone else whom I call a friend.

As always, thanks to my man, our daughters, their men and our gorgeous Esme who just makes us hoot with her chat. That one has been here before . . . I hope you all feel as loved as you make me feel every single day. As Dom once said somewhere in these pages — 'It's love that brings meaning to life.'

And finally, to you, the readers, thank you. Every day I get to work at the very best job and make up stories to tell and each one of you makes that possible. Thank you for helping make my dreams come true.

We do hope that you have enjoyed reading this large print book.

Did you know that all of our titles are available for purchase?

We publish a wide range of high quality large print books including:
Romances, Mysteries, Classics
General Fiction
Non Fiction and Westerns

Special interest titles available in large print are:
The Little Oxford Dictionary
Music Book
Song Book
Hymn Book
Service Book

Also available from us courtesy of Oxford University Press:
Young Readers' Dictionary
(large print edition)
Young Readers' Thesaurus
(large print edition)

For further information or a free brochure, please contact us at:
Ulverscroft Large Print Books Ltd.,
The Green, Bradgate Road, Anstey,
Leicester, LE7 7FU, England.
Tel: (00 44) 0116 236 4325
Fax: (00 44) 0116 234 0205

THE DAY I LOST YOU

Fionnuala Kearney

Contentedly sipping a cup of tea at home after a fun-filled afternoon at a Christmas fair, Jess receives the most terrible news a mother can get: her daughter Anna has been reported missing after an avalanche while on a ski trip. Though she's heartbroken, Jess knows she must be strong for Anna's five-year-old daughter Rose, who is now her responsibility. As she waits for more news, Jess starts to uncover details about Anna's other life — unearthing a secret that alters their whole world irrevocably . . .